PRAISE FOR DONNA GRANT'S BEST-SELLING ROMANCE NOVELS

"Grant's ability to quickly convey complicated backstory makes this jam-packed love story accessible even to new or periodic readers." - *Publisher's Weekly*

"Donna Grant has given the paranormal genre a burst of fresh air..." – *San Francisco Book Review*

"The premise is dramatic and heartbreaking; the characters are colorful and engaging; the romance is spirited and seductive." – *The Reading Cafe*

"The central romance, fueled by a hostage drama, plays out in glorious detail against a backdrop of multiple ongoing issues in the "Dark Kings" books. This seemingly penultimate installment creates a nice segue to a climactic end." – *Library Journal*

"...intense romance amid the growing war between the Dragons and the Dark Fae is scorching hot." – *Booklist*

DON'T MISS THESE OTHER NOVELS

BY NYT & USA TODAY BESTSELLING AUTHOR DONNA GRANT

CONTEMPORARY PARANORMAL

DRAGON KINGS® SERIES

Dragon Revealed ~ Dragon Mine ~ Dragon Unbound

Dragon Eternal ~ Dragon Lover ~ Dragon Arisen

REAPER SERIES

Dark Alpha's Claim ~ Dark Alpha's Embrace

Dark Alpha's Demand ~ Dark Alpha's Lover

Dark Alpha's Night ~ Dark Alpha's Hunger

Dark Alpha's Awakening ~ Dark Alpha's Redemption

Dark Alpha's Temptation ~ Dark Alpha's Caress

Dark Alpha's Obsession ~ Dark Alpha's Need

Dark Alpha's Silent Night ~ Dark Alpha's Passion

Dark Alpha's Command ~ Dark Alpha's Fury

SKYE DRUIDS SERIES

Iron Ember ~ Shoulder the Skye ~ Heart of Glass

DARK KINGS SERIES

Dark Heat ~ Darkest Flame ~ Fire Rising ~ Burning Desire

Hot Blooded ~ Night's Blaze ~ Soul Scorched ~ Dragon King

Passion Ignites ~ Smoldering Hunger ~ Smoke and Fire

Dragon Fever ~ Firestorm ~ Blaze ~ Dragon Burn

Constantine: A History, Parts 1-3 ~ Heat ~ Torched

Dragon Night ~ Dragonfire ~ Dragon Claimed

Ignite ~ Fever ~ Dragon Lost ~ Flame ~ Inferno

A Dragon's Tale (Whisky and Wishes: *A Holiday Novella*,

Heart of Gold: *A Valentine's Novella*, & Of Fire and Flame)

My Fiery Valentine ~ The Dragon King Coloring Book

Dragon King Special Edition Character Coloring Book: Rhi

DARK WARRIORS SERIES

Midnight's Master ~ Midnight's Lover

Midnight's Seduction ~ Midnight's Warrior

Midnight's Kiss ~ Midnight's Captive

Midnight's Temptation ~ Midnight's Promise

Midnight's Surrender ~ A Warrior for Christmas

CHIASSON SERIES

Wild Fever ~ Wild Dream ~ Wild Need

Wild Flame ~ Wild Rapture

LARUE SERIES

Moon Kissed ~ Moon Thrall ~ Moon Struck ~ Moon Bound

WICKED TREASURES

Seized by Passion ~ Enticed by Ecstasy ~ Captured by Desire

Books 1-3: Wicked Treasures Box Set

HISTORICAL PARANORMAL

THE KINDRED SERIES

Everkin ~ Eversong ~ Everwylde ~ Everbound

Evernight ~ Everspell

KINDRED: THE FATED SERIES

Rage ~ Ruin ~ Reign

DARK SWORD SERIES

Dangerous Highlander ~ Forbidden Highlander

Wicked Highlander ~ Untamed Highlander

Shadow Highlander ~ Darkest Highlander

ROGUES OF SCOTLAND SERIES

The Craving ~ The Hunger ~ The Tempted ~ The Seduced

Books 1-4: Rogues of Scotland Box Set

THE SHIELDS SERIES

A Dark Guardian ~ A Kind of Magic ~ A Dark Seduction

A Forbidden Temptation ~ A Warrior's Heart

Mystic Trinity (a series connecting novel)

DRUIDS GLEN SERIES

Highland Mist ~ Highland Nights ~ Highland Dawn

Highland Fires ~ Highland Magic

Mystic Trinity (a series connecting novel)

THE SHIELDS SERIES

A Dark Guardian ~ A Kind of Magic ~ A Dark Seduction

A Forbidden Temptation ~ A Warrior's Heart

Mystic Trinity (a series connecting novel)

DRUIDS GLEN SERIES

Highland Mist ~ Highland Nights ~ Highland Dawn

Highland Fires ~ Highland Magic

Mystic Trinity (a series connecting novel)

SISTERS OF MAGIC TRILOGY

Shadow Magic ~ Echoes of Magic ~ Dangerous Magic

Books 1-3: Sisters of Magic Box Set

THE ROYAL CHRONICLES NOVELLA SERIES

Prince of Desire ~ Prince of Seduction

Prince of Love ~ Prince of Passion

Books 1-4: The Royal Chronicles Box Set

Mystic Trinity (a series connecting novel)

DARK BEGINNINGS: A FIRST IN SERIES BOXSET

Chiasson Series, Book 1: Wild Fever

LaRue Series, Book 1: Moon Kissed

The Royal Chronicles Series, Book 1: Prince of Desire

MILITARY ROMANCE / ROMANTIC SUSPENSE

SONS OF TEXAS SERIES

The Hero ~ The Protector ~ The Legend

The Defender ~ The Guardian

COWBOY / CONTEMPORARY

HEART OF TEXAS SERIES

The Christmas Cowboy Hero ~ Cowboy, Cross My Heart

My Favorite Cowboy ~ A Cowboy Like You

Looking for a Cowboy ~ A Cowboy Kind of Love

STAND ALONE BOOKS

That Cowboy of Mine

Home for a Cowboy Christmas

Mutual Desire

Forever Mine

Savage Moon

Check out Donna Grant's Online Store at
www.DonnaGrant.com/shop
for autographed books, character
themed goodies, and more!

LARUE SERIES

Excerpt from: **WILD FEVER**

Sneak Peek from: **EVERSONG**

www.DonnaGrant.com
www.MotherofDragonsBooks.com

READING ORDER
THE CHIASSON AND LARUE SERIES STORIES ARE INTERTWINED.

A generations old family of hunters fight the many evils that abound in the bayous of southwest Louisiana and New Orleans.

Chiasson & LaRue intertwined series reading order:

Wild Fever, Chiasson Series

Wild Dream, Chiasson Series

Wild Need, Chiasson Series

Moon Kissed, LaRue Series

Moon Thrall, LaRue Series

Wild Flame, Chiasson Series

Moon Struck, LaRue Series

Wild Rapture, Chiasson Series

Moon Bound, LaRue Series

PRONUNCIATIONS

Arcineaux (are-cen-o)

Chiasson (ch-ay-son)

Davena (dav-E-na)

Delia (d-ee-l-ee-uh)

Delphine (d-eh-l-FEEN)

Dumas (dOO-mah-s)

Lafayette (lah-fai-EHt)

LaRue (l-er-OO)

GLOSSARY:

Andouille (ahn-doo-ee) & **Boudin** (boo-dan)

Two types of Cajun sausage. Andouille is made with pork while boudin with pork and rice.

Bayou (by-you)

A sluggish stream bigger than a creek and smaller than a river

Beignet (bin-yay)

A fritter or doughnut without a hole, sprinkled with powdered sugar

Cajun ('ka-jun)

A person of French-Canadian descent born or living along southern Louisiana.

Etoufee (ay-two-fay)

Tangy tomato-based sauce dish usually made with crawfish or shrimp and rice

Gumbo (gum-bo)

Thick, savory soup with chicken, seafood, sausage, or wild game

Hoodoo (hu-du)

Also known as "conjure" or witchcraft. Thought of as "folk magic" and "superstition". Some say it is the main force against the use of Voodoo.

Jambalaya (jom-bah-LIE-yah)
Highly seasoned mixture of sausage, chicken, or seafood and vegetables, simmered with rice until liquid is absorbed

Maman (muh-mahn)
Term used for grandmother

Parish
A Louisiana state district; equivalent to the word county

Sha (a as in cat)
Term of affection meaning darling, dear, or sweetheart.

Voodoo (vu-du) – New Orleans
Spiritual folkways originating in the Caribbean. New Orleans Voodoo is separate from other forms (Haitian Vodou and southern Hoodoo). New Orleans Voodoo puts emphasis on Voodoo Queens and Voodoo dolls.

Zydeco (zy-dey-coh)
Accordion-based music originating in Louisiana combined with guitar and violin while combing traditional French melodies with Caribbean and blues influences

GLOSSARY

Andouille (ahn-doo-ee) & **Boudin** (boo-dan)

Two types of Cajun sausage. Andouille is made with pork while boudin with pork and rice.

Bayou (by-you)

A sluggish stream bigger than a creek and smaller than a river

Beignet (bin-yay)

A fritter or doughnut without a hole, sprinkled with powdered sugar

Cajun ('ka-jun)

A person of French-Canadian descent born or living along southern Louisiana.

Etoufee (ay-two-fay)

Tangy tomato-based sauce dish usually made with crawfish or shrimp and rice

Gumbo (gum-bo)

Thick, savory soup with chicken, seafood, sausage, or wild game

Hoodoo (hu-du)

Also known as "conjure" or witchcraft. Thought of as "folk magic" and "superstition". Some say it is the main force against the use of Voodoo.

Jambalaya (jom-bah-LIE-yah)

Highly seasoned mixture of sausage, chicken, or seafood and vegetables, simmered with rice until liquid is absorbed

Maman (muh-mahn)

Term used for grandmother

Parish

A Louisiana state district; equivalent to the word county

Sha (a as in cat)

Term of affection meaning darling, dear, or sweetheart.

Voodoo (vu-du) – New Orleans

Spiritual folkways originating in the Caribbean. New Orleans Voodoo is separate from other forms (Haitian Vodou and southern Hoodoo). New Orleans Voodoo puts emphasis on Voodoo Queens and Voodoo dolls.

Zydeco (zy-dey-coh)

Accordion-based music originating in Louisiana combined with guitar and violin while combing traditional French melodies with Caribbean and blues influences

LARUE SERIES

BOOKS 1-4

DONNA GRANT

A LARUE NOVEL

MOON
KISSED

NEW YORK TIMES BESTSELLING AUTHOR
DONNA GRANT

BROUGHT TOGETHER BY CHANCE...
BOUND TOGETHER BY CIRCUMSTANCE.

CHAPTER
ONE

Gator Bait Bar

New Orleans, Louisiana

MYLES LOOKED through the receipts from the night before from his seat at the end of the bar. While he tallied their profits and balanced the books, his younger brother, Kane, was going through their liquor supply to place another order.

A shout from the pool tables interrupted Myles as he was inputting numbers in his laptop. He turned his head to the side and glared at his other two brothers—Solomon and Court—who were enjoying their daily pool game.

The game began when Court was barely tall enough to play properly. Solomon was the one to teach Court the game, beating him soundly every time. It was a LaRue trait that once they set their minds to something, they didn't relent until they had whatever it was they wanted. For Court, that had been beating Solomon. When it had finally happened, Solomon had been unprepared, thinking he still had years of winning.

From that day onward, there had been few things that disrupted their daily games, and that included hurricanes.

"You'd think they would've ended the rivalry," Kane said, without looking up from his clipboard as he wrote down numbers.

Myles watched his brother closely. After the fiasco with the daughter of the Devil himself, Delphine, and their cousins in Lyons Point, Kane hadn't been the same.

Then again, who would be unchanged after being cursed by a Voodoo priestess out to annihilate your family?

"They'll be using walkers and still playing pool," Myles said. He closed his laptop. "You know you'll have to talk about what happened one day."

Kane was in the process of replacing a bottle of Ciroc vodka on the shelf when he froze. There was just the slightest tightening of his shoulders before he turned his head and glowered at Myles with his bright blue eyes—eyes that every LaRue had.

"I've done all the talking I'm going to," Kane stated in a hard voice.

Myles didn't respond as Kane turned back around. Everything about Kane was perfectly tailored, from his golden blond hair, to his shirt tucked into his jeans, down to the laces of his shoes exactly the same length when tied. This was not the Kane of old. That Kane would roll out of bed with his messy hair, throw on a tee shirt and jeans, wearing a smile that stopped women in their tracks.

This new Kane was too uptight, too...controlled.

"It's not your fault."

Kane whirled around, his eyes blazing with fury, but there was no shouting from this new Kane. His nostrils flared, his hands fisted. "It's my fault I caught Delphine's attention. Wasn't it bad enough that one of our ancestors screwed with a Voodoo priestess that caused us to be werewolves? Apparently not for me. I thought I could do whatever I wanted. Delphine wanted to teach me a lesson." Kane snorted derisively. "She wanted Ava killed, and who better to do it than the cousins of the Chiassons who were protecting her?"

"You didn't kill her," Myles pointed out.

Kane rolled his eyes. "It's a good thing too, or Lincoln would've killed me. And I would've welcomed it. We know what we are when we shift, but if I had killed Ava, all of my memories would've been wiped. I'd have been a monster we hunt."

"It's why we called our cousins, remember? We couldn't

come after you because we captured Delphine." Myles always wanted to scrub himself in acid after he thought of that vile bitch. It had taken almost every trick they knew to confine Delphine, and then it nearly backfired on them.

Kane braced his hands on the bar and let out a deep breath. "I was reckless, Myles. I didn't just put our family at risk, I put our cousins' as well. If Ava hadn't been with them..." he trailed off, unable to answer.

It was a feeling each of them experienced. Kane was dealing with nearly losing himself to the wolf within, but he had no idea how the events had changed the rest of them. And Myles wasn't about to tell him.

It hadn't been just the curse from Delphine, or even capturing her, it was Court with his fangs around Delphine's throat, ready to clamp down. It was Solomon ready to kill every last one of her followers. It was Myles sprinkling the goofer dust around them so none of Delphine's people could get to her.

That night, all three of the brothers had been prepared—and willing—to do anything and everything to save Kane.

"It'd been too long since we saw our cousins. Each side of the family has been so busy fighting the supernatural that we forgot family." Myles shrugged with a grin, hoping to take both of their minds off Delphine. "You changed all that."

Kane shot him a look and tossed a towel at him. The

softening of Kane's mouth was as close to a smile as they would get, but it was enough for Myles.

Since it wasn't yet ten in the morning, all four LaRue's were surprised when the door to the bar opened and in walked a woman with hair so brown it was almost black. She shoved the long hair over her shoulder as the door shut behind her and she looked around the room with bright blue eyes.

Myles slid off the stool as he realized he was looking at his only female cousin, Riley Chiasson. He stopped in front of her and smiled. "The last time I saw you, you were in pigtails and running roughshod over your brothers."

Riley's smile was slow, showing a dimple in her left cheek. "I wondered if you'd know who I was."

"With eyes like that?" Solomon asked as he set down his cue stick and walked to her. "There's no denying our family. What brings you to our neck of the woods?"

Riley swallowed and looked at each of them until she met Myles's gaze. "Since you so graciously pointed out that I was a little girl the last time we saw each other, names put to faces would be great."

Myles pointed to Solomon. "That's the jackass who thinks just because he's the eldest that he can make decisions for us."

"Solomon," Riley said with a nod at him.

"Next up in the order is me," Myles said, waiting to see if she would know.

Riley raised a dark brow. "Then you're Myles."

"Very good," he said. "The scowling one behind the bar is next."

Riley's smile slipped as she shifted her gaze. "Kane." They stared at each other for a heartbeat before Riley turned her head to the pool table. "Which leaves the youngest, Court."

Solomon crossed his arms over his chest. "Now that that's settled, why not tell us why you're visiting."

When she hesitated, Myles wrapped an arm around her and walked her to the bar where Kane filled a glass with ice and then water. She sat on one of the stools and closed her fingers around the glass.

Myles exchanged a look with Solomon. By the way Riley was acting, it was obvious she hadn't told her brothers where she was.

"Do you know I was sent away?" she asked, her gaze on the bar. "Vin said he didn't want me to be a part of the family business."

"You're his only sister. I'd have done the same," Court said as he joined them.

Riley shrugged. "I'd have liked to have some say in it. All of my brothers agreed with Vin, even Beau. The day after I graduated high school, Vincent drove me to Austin. For years I've lived in Texas, going to college. I wanted to go home."

"Did you tell Vin that?" Solomon asked.

Riley shook her head. "I thought since Vin was marrying

Olivia, and Lincoln and Ava were together, that it would be okay to go home."

"You just showed up, didn't you?" Kane asked softly.

Riley looked up at him. "Olivia and Ava knew what I planned. They told me how Beau had met Davena. There were three women at the house now. Surely that meant Vin wouldn't keep me away."

"But you didn't know about what all happened," Myles guessed.

Riley snorted and said, "The Chiasson and LaRue's have been fighting the supernatural since before I was born. My mother had five children and still fought beside her husband. I should be able to go home."

"Your brothers just want what's best." Solomon took the stool on her left. "Surely you understand that."

"I do, but I've not seen my home in over four years. They always had some crises around my breaks that prevented me from returning."

Myles saw the desolation and unhappiness in her gaze, a look he recognized all too well in Kane's eyes of late. "What happened?"

"There was no big family reunion as I'd hoped," she said with a laugh, her lips in a tight smile. "Vin was furious. He and Olivia got in a huge fight because she tried to convince him to let me stay. It didn't take long for all of them to begin arguing. That's when Vin told me to go back to Texas. I told him to kiss my ass, and I stormed out to my car. Then I started driving. Before I knew it, I was here."

Court leaned his forearms on the end of the bar. "I spoke to Christian yesterday. He filled me in on Delphine's appearance in Lyons Point. These are dangerous times, Riley."

"They're always dangerous. She's a Chiasson. She knows how to fight," Kane said to Court. He then turned his gaze to Riley. "What's your plan?"

She tucked her hair behind her ear. "I'd like to stay here a couple of days to figure out what I'll do next."

"Next?" Solomon repeated. "You're not going back to Austin?"

Her smile was sad. "I graduated in June. My brothers didn't even know it. All the times I called home, they didn't have time to talk because of something they were hunting. I had no family in attendance. I even remained for a few months thinking they might realize their mistake, but there's always something to keep them from remembering me."

Kane covered her hand with his. "They remember. Trust me. You had the chance at a normal life, Riley. They didn't, and neither did we."

"Of course," she said too quickly.

Myles wasn't fooled. Riley was hurting and she needed someplace to lick her wounds. "You're welcome here for as long as you need."

His brothers were nodding in agreement before he finished talking.

"Thank you, but I can only accept on one condition," Riley said.

Court shrugged, not understanding. "Name it."

"None of you tell any of my brothers' or their women."

Riley might be beautiful, but she had a sharp mind. Myles realized the trap she led them into at that moment. If they didn't allow her to stay, they couldn't keep an eye on her, and as hunters and her family, that was their duty. By agreeing to her terms, she ensured that she wouldn't have her brothers descending upon her to get her back to Texas.

"I never saw that coming," Kane said, one side of his lips lifted in a grin.

Myles caught Solomon's and Court's gazes. Perhaps Riley was just what Kane needed to remember to smile and laugh again. Kane could look out for her, which would help him heal.

"You do know the full moon will be here in a few days?" Solomon asked her.

Riley looked at him as if he were a simpleton. "I'm a Chiasson. Of course I know. So don't bother trying to lecture me. I know the divides in New Orleans where vampires, witches, demons, werewolves, and djinns are housed. I also know enough to stay away from Delphine and anything to do with Voodoo."

"She's a Chiasson all right," Myles said with a grin.

Riley was a breath of fresh air that seemed to be just what the LaRues needed. Vincent might lament having a sister and the worry it took to keep her safe, but Myles wondered how different their lives would've been had they had a sister among them.

"I'll get her settled," Kane said as he came around the bar.

Myles, Solomon, and Court watched the two of them walk from the building with Riley talking and Kane nodding his head.

"I don't know if this is a good idea," Solomon said.

Court ran his hand through his chin-length butterscotch-blond hair. "It's done now. She knew we couldn't let her leave."

"She got Kane to smile. That's a vast improvement over the last few weeks," Myles pointed out. "He needs something to do, and Riley just gave him the opportunity."

Solomon slid off the stool. "Let's hope you're right, because when Vin discovers Riley is here, we may well have the entire Chiasson clan here."

"Think how we could clear out New Orleans with all of us," Court said. "No more pacts with the five houses. New Orleans could be clear once more."

Myles knew Court had been joking, but it made sense. "We can't bring Delphine and her followers down by ourselves. With four more, we'd stand a really good chance."

"Especially with Beau's woman being a witch," Court pointed out.

Solomon pinned Myles with a look. "First, we make sure nothing happens to Riley, because Chiasson or not, she's not been hunting as we have. If anything happens to her—"

"You don't even need to say it," Myles said.

Maybe it wasn't such a good idea that Riley was there.

CHAPTER

TWO

Addison Moore sat in her parked car along the street and stared unseeing out of the windshield. In her hands was a letter that changed her life in a second.

Something dropped onto the paper. Addison looked down and saw the bead of wetness that soaked into the letter. It took her a moment to realize it was from the sweat running down her face from being in the car in hundred-degree heat with the engine turned off.

She folded up the letter neatly and tucked it into her purse. Then she opened the door to the car and stepped out into the sunshine.

Addison shut the door and leaned back against the car, staring at all the tourists. They were laughing and smiling, not a care in the world. It was so at odds with what she was going through that it almost felt like she wasn't in her body, that she was on the outside looking in.

"Miss, are you all right?"

Addison shook herself and saw the police officer standing beside her. He was middle aged with gray at the temples of his black hair and concern in his eyes.

"Are you lost?" he asked.

She forced a smile. "Just daydreaming, officer. I'm fine."

"You need to get out of the heat and get some water soon," he warned before moving on.

Knowing he was right, Addison pushed away from the car. She hadn't taken two steps before her cell phone buzzed with a text. She reached in her purse for it, and then groaned when she saw it was her roommate, Wendy.

"I haven't been gone that long," she mumbled as she hastily wrote that she'd have Wendy's car back within the hour.

How she hated not having money for her own vehicle. After only one semester at Tulane, Addison had no choice but to sell her clunker of a car to make ends meet. It had been her only choice, but it also put a heavy strain on her.

Addison put away the phone and strolled along the street. Since the first time she saw New Orleans at the age of ten, she had been fascinated. The history of the city was mesmerizing. The food and vibrancy of the streets and buildings drew a constant crowd, no matter the time of year.

Yet there was no denying the dark, dangerous edge of the city either.

Addison walked the streets of the Quarter, watching others stand for pictures or stare in wide-eyed wonder at the cemeteries. By getting a glimpse in someone else's life, she was able to forget hers for a short while.

A glance at her watch proved that her time was done. Reluctantly, she started back to the car. She wasn't ready to return to the university, not when it was the end. There was no one to go home to. In fact, there was no home to go back to.

"Stop pitying yourself," she said aloud. "Stand tall. Stand proud. You're a Moore."

Those were the last words her father said before he was deployed. He was a career Navy man, never happier than when he was at sea. That never bothered her, because he always came home. Until he hadn't.

Addison didn't want to think about her father, or the lonely years after. At twenty-three, she was ready to get on with her life, except that she couldn't do that until she finished her degree.

Which was going to be impossible now that the last of her scholarship had run out. Already she'd racked up a considerable amount of student loans that were reaching cosmic proportions. If she were lucky, she might pay them off before she died.

She was almost to the car when a scream rent the air and

someone came rushing toward her, knocking her to the ground. Addison looked up in time to see a young kid with a navy hoodie duck into an alley.

Suddenly people began to crowd around. Someone helped her to her feet as sirens blared. Addison looked down to see that both knees were scraped and bleeding, and her shirt was ripped.

"Excuse me. Pardon me," she said as she slowly made her way through the throng of people to the car.

She reached the car and glanced around to see someone pointing her out to a policeman. Addison stilled and waited for the officer to reach her. It was the same one from earlier.

"Did you see what happened?" he asked.

She threw up her hands. "I've no idea what happened. I heard a scream, then someone bumped into me, knocking me down."

"Did you see anyone?"

"I saw what looked like a teenager with a hoodie duck into an alley."

The policeman's face was grim. "I'm going to need a formal statement from you."

"Because the guy bumped into me?" she asked in disbelief.

"Because he mugged an elderly woman. When he took her purse, she fell, hitting her head. She's dead."

Addison briefly squeezed her eyes closed. "Oh, my God. I had no idea."

were a sore subject, even after so many years. Myles turned back to Addison. "Our parents are dead."

"I'm sorry."

She said it without the embarrassment of discovering death, but with the sincerity of someone well acquainted with it. The more Myles spoke to her, the more he wanted to know.

"Thank you," he mumbled. "It was a long time ago."

"Those wounds never go away."

Now he knew someone close to her died, and he would bet it was her parents. "No, they don't."

"You're lucky to have siblings to turn to."

The conversation needed some levity. "When I'm not wanting to knock their heads off. Do you have any siblings?"

"It's just me," she replied with a too bright smile. "So, how long has this place been in business?"

"Ten years or so. Are you sure you want to work here? The tips are good for the girls, but things can get rowdy on occasion."

Addison shrugged. "I need the job."

Kane did the hiring, and Myles knew there was nothing about Addison that would prevent his brother from bringing her on. "Give me a moment, and I'll take you to the office."

"Take your time. I don't have anywhere to be," she said with a smile before turning back to the pool game.

Court stopped beside him and said over the music,

"You're looking at her as if you want to devour her. I say make your move."

Every time Myles thought about having a relationship, all he had to do was look at Solomon. "We know how those things end."

"If our cousins can do it, so can we."

"The Chiassons don't have our...affliction," Myles reminded him.

Court glanced at Addison again. "You want her. There's no reason you can't have her, even if it's only for a little while."

"As long as she works here, all I'll ever do is look."

TWO EXCRUCIATING DAYS LATER, Myles was still looking. Just as he expected, Kane had hired Addison the night she applied. She started working the next day, and each time she came in wearing the tight black shirt and denim shorts, Myles couldn't think of anything but her.

He tried staying in his office, but that didn't work. He tried remaining in the kitchen so he could catch glimpses of her, but it wasn't enough. He then tried working behind the bar, which proved too much anytime a patron so much as gave her an admiring look.

Nickleback played through the speakers, and Addison swayed with the music as she set up the tables.

"She's pretty," Riley said as she put away glasses, readying for the evening crowd.

Myles glanced at his cousin, knowing none of her brothers would likely approve of her working there. "I suppose."

Riley snorted loudly. "You're a terrible liar, Myles. You've been staring at her for days, and when you aren't looking, she's staring at you."

That was exactly what he didn't want to hear. It made him want to pursue whatever was between them, but it wasn't something any of the LaRues would ever attempt again.

Riley set the glass down and positioned herself so that he had to look at her. "What is it? Are you telling me you won't go after her? Why? My brothers manage it."

"We're not exactly like your brothers."

She rolled her blue eyes and smoothed her hands over her hair pulled back into a sleek ponytail. "Your father and grandfather didn't see an issue. Nor did any of your other ancestors." She frowned suddenly. "Something happened, didn't it? Something to make all of you shy away from relationships."

Myles glanced through the arched doorway to the kitchen where Solomon was. "Leave it, Riley. Please."

"Do my brothers know?"

"No, and we want it to stay that way," he warned her.

She put her hand on his arm. "It must have been pretty bad."

"You can't begin to fathom it."

Riley dropped her hand and swallowed. "Ava said her father is here. I've not seen him."

"Jack does his own thing. He comes and goes often. There is a lot of hunting to be done around here."

"Hunting?" Addison said as she walked up and placed dirty glasses on the bar. "What do you hunt?"

Myles had been so lost in the past that he hadn't realized Addison was near or he would've never spoken. "Anything really."

"You know these Cajun boys," Riley said as she turned to face Addison. "They do enjoy their hunting."

Addison looked from Riley to him, and then back to Riley, a slight frown marring her forehead. "Right."

Myles didn't let out his breath until Addison disappeared into the kitchen. "Speaking of hunting, I think I'm going to go tonight."

"I'm coming with you," Riley said.

Myles jerked away from her. "The hell you are. It's one thing to have you here and not tell your brothers. It's another entirely to take you hunting."

"Do you forget I'm a Chiasson? I've known what's out there since I was old enough to hold a weapon. My parents made sure all of us knew how to hunt—and kill—those things."

"Yes, but when was the last time you hunted?"

"Two weeks ago."

Myles ran a hand down his face, suddenly very happy he didn't have a sister. "Are you kidding?"

"Really?" she asked angrily. "You think I went to Austin and pretended evil didn't exist?"

"Do your brothers know what you were doing?"

She put her hands on her hips. "They might have had they bothered to visit."

"You're going to drive me to drink, Riley," Myles said and sighed. "I know that stubborn streak within you, because we all have it. If we don't take you, you'll go hunting yourself. You can come with me tonight. I heard about a wraith being spotted."

She gave him a wink. "Thanks, cuz."

RILEY LEFT Myles still a bit stricken, and made her way to the kitchen. It didn't take her long to find Addison in the back peeling shrimp. "I thought you worked the front."

Addison glanced at her and shrugged. "I do, but everything is ready, and I hate being idle. So I asked Solomon what I could do to help."

"Did I hear Kane right earlier? Do you have another job as well?"

Addison rubbed her chin on her shoulder. "I've got three

altogether, but if I can bring home as much money as I did last night on a regular basis, I think I can drop one."

"Are you Super Woman?" Riley asked with a laugh. "Three jobs and you're still going for your degree? I'm impressed."

"I'm taking the semester off."

Riley was instantly on alert as she heard the break in Addison's voice. "Sometimes we need that break. The classes will still be there in the spring. I was tempted to quit midway through my third year."

"Where did you get your degree?"

"UT. My brothers sent me to Austin as soon as I got my high school diploma."

Addison shifted her weight from one foot to the other as she leaned her hip against the stainless-steel table. "So, you're from New Orleans?"

"I was raised a few hours from here." Riley hid a smile as she realized that Addison was trying to see if she was interested in any of the guys. Riley then decided to ease her mind. "I wanted to spend some time with my cousins. The LaRue boys can be a lot of fun."

Addison's head snapped to her. "Cousins?"

"Cousins," Riley repeated and gave in to the smile. "I'll warn you that they're as obstinate as mules. Sometimes we women have to show them what it is they want."

"I don't know," Addison hedged.

Riley leaned close. "Trust me. Go after what you want. Or

should I say *who* you want." When Addison simply stared at her like a deer in headlights, Riley bumped her shoulder against Addison's. "You never know what tomorrow will bring."

Addison looked through the doorway into the bar at Myles. "That's so true."

CHAPTER

FOUR

Addison yawned as she walked from the coffee shop after splurging on a java chip Frappuccino. Every day she thought of Riley's words, but she had yet to make any sort of move on Myles.

She had an hour until she had to be at Gator Bait. It had been only a week, but she managed to bring in twice as much money as her other two jobs combined. Holding three jobs was taking its toll on her, which was why she opted to quit her cleaning job. She kept her job at the attorney's office because of the hours and their willingness to work around her college courses.

Of course, that wasn't an issue this semester.

Addison walked to a bench across the street and sat. Not even the wonders of the French Quarter could pull her from the funk she fell in every time she thought about her finishing college.

If she saved everything she made, she might have enough to cover another semester, but what about the one after that? Thanks to the tips from Gator Bait, she was able to pay Wendy for two months past due rent as well as the current month.

Getting behind on bills sucked a big one. Addison felt as if she were forever getting caught up. It was one of the reasons she wanted a degree, to get a good job so she could make enough money to support herself.

Ever since her father's death, she felt as if she were fighting for handouts. There hadn't been much family to even consider taking her in, but she felt fortunate that she had that and not had to go into a foster home.

Looking back, Addison knew her first few years with her grandmother might have been strict and regulated. After her grandmother died, she briefly lived with her mother's brother and his wife until he was diagnosed with cystic fibrosis. Then she went to the only other family to take her in, her father's brother and his wife. They didn't have any children of their own, and they struggled with money, but at least she had a home.

Addison had gotten her first job two months shy of her sixteenth birthday just so she wouldn't have to ask them for lunch money. And then to learn... She couldn't even think about it. Every time she did, she grew so infuriated that she thought she might explode from the anger it was so fierce.

As she sat drinking her Frappuccino, Addison's thoughts turned to Myles. At first she believed the sexual tension between them was her imagination. Over the past week, she found him watching her often. His gaze was direct and... needy. The one thing she wasn't was a take-charge kind of girl. She liked the guy to make the first move, but she was seriously considering going outside of her comfort zone when it came to Myles.

He was...dependable, steady, and so damn handsome she wanted to lick his entire body. It was sinful for a man to look so good. Not to mention the havoc it played on her hormones.

Still, Myles was the type of guy to go after a woman he wanted. He had yet to make any perceived moves on her, which meant...he wasn't interested.

"Well, this day just gets better and better," she mumbled to herself as she came to the conclusion.

Addison people watched—one of her favorite pastimes —as she continued to wrestle with her thoughts on Myles. If he rejected her, Addison would never be able to step foot inside the bar again she'd be so mortified.

A breeze ruffled her hair, pulling the strands into her eye. She wiped them away, tucking them behind her ear. That's when she spotted a woman with rich, dark hair blatantly staring at her from across the street near a row of artists and fortunetellers.

Addison raised a brow in question. To her shock, the woman started walking toward her. In a city known for its crazies, Addison sat up straighter, prepared to defend herself if need be.

The woman was tall, slender. She wore a gauzy cream shirt that was cinched at the waist with a brown belt. It was paired with a long, full skirt of red with small beige flowers. Around her head was a scarf of cream with dark-brown beads hanging against her forehead.

The woman stopped before Addison, her brown eyes large and tilted slightly at the corners. She had rich russet-brown skin that hinted at mixed ancestry. "Your life is in danger."

How did one react to such a statement? Addison frowned as she cocked her head. "By you?"

"Of course not," the woman said impatiently and sat down while covertly looking around. "I know you may not believe me, but I saw you in danger last night."

Addison was beginning to wonder if the woman had escaped a mental institute. "Saw me? I doubt that. I was working all night, and the only thing I'm in danger of there is having beer spilled on me."

The woman let out a long-suffering sigh. "When I say I saw you, I meant that I had a vision. I was doing a reading last night when your face flashed in my mind and I saw it all. A wolf was chasing you."

"Whoa," Addison said and scooted away on the bench. "Hold up a minute. Did you just say a reading? Are you a fortuneteller?"

The woman rolled her eyes and motioned with her hands to her outfit. "Bingo. Now, can you get past that so you can hear what else I'm saying?"

"I heard you. Danger. Wolf."

She stared at Addison for a moment before she stuck out her hand. "Let's start over. I'm Minka Verdin. I'm from a long line of fortunetellers descended from gypsies that came here from Romania."

"Addison Moore," she said as she shook Minka's hand. "You're serious."

"As a heart attack. Listen, most of the time I bullshit my way through reading someone's palm. I've had visions since I was six years old, but they were stupid like an image of a live oak outside of town or an old rusty car sitting in a yard. There have been three instances in my life where I saw someone's face. Last night, it was yours."

Addison didn't want to believe her, but the truth shining in her eyes couldn't be ignored. "Just say I believe you. How did you know I'd be here?"

"My stand is over there," Minka said and pointed across the street in the square. "I've had that same space for five years. I didn't just see the wolf chasing you. I saw you sitting here in that same navy shirt and white shorts. So, I kept a lookout."

Addison lived all her life in New Orleans. She knew the things said about the city, and she even witnessed some things that made her want to hide under the covers.

"There are no wolves in New Orleans."

Minka turned her gaze away. "Look around. Tell me what you see."

Addison did as she requested. She turned her head from one side to the other. "I see people returning to their homes after work. I see tourists. I see artists painting. I see musicians. Regular everyday people."

"Do you know what I see?"

She shifted her eyes to Minka, curious. "What?"

Minka pointed to where her stand was behind the artists. "I see witches." She jerked her chin in the direction behind her. "I see demons." Next, she nodded her head to the left. "I see vampires. Farther down the street...werewolves. And to the right are djinn."

"Right," Addison said with a laugh, thinking Minka was teasing her. Then Addison saw her face and the seriousness in which Minka's dark eyes stared. "You want me to believe I'm surrounded by those things? Besides, everyone knows vampires can't come out in the day."

"Yes, they can. They prefer night, but they can move in

the daylight. And yes, I want you to believe the supernatural surrounds you, because it does. It always has. New Orleans is a mecca for such creatures."

"Just New Orleans?"

"No," Minka said sadly. "There are other places the supernatural are drawn to, and there are people who hunt them."

Hunters. Addison remembered what she had overheard between Myles and Riley a few days earlier. "If these… beings…know they're being hunted, why do they remain?"

"Because, in New Orleans, they have a sort of truce so that all five factions can remain. And they're being watched. If they step out of line, they are eliminated instantly. It keeps the factions in line for the most part. There are too many of the supernatural gathered here for the hunters to wipe out by themselves."

"You know these hunters?"

Minka hesitated for a second before she nodded. "I do. I'm part of the supernatural world because I have gifts, but I'm not a threat like vampires, demons, or other things."

"You left out werewolves. Aren't they dangerous?" Addison asked curiously.

Minka bit her bottom lip a moment. "They can be, but they are also loyal to a fault."

"You said one was chasing me. I'm gathering it isn't loyal to me."

"That's just it," Minka said, her forehead furrowing. "He shouldn't have been chasing you."

That got Addison's attention. "He? You know who it is? Tell me so I can keep my distance."

"That might be difficult."

There was something in Minka's tone that set warning bells off in Addison's head. "Who is he?"

"He's not your enemy. If anything, you're safer near him."

"Safer?" she cried, standing up. "You said he was chasing me."

Minka rose to her feet and very calmly said, "That's what I saw, but that doesn't mean that's what happens."

Addison had about had enough. She crossed her arms over her chest. "Did you, or did you not just come over here and tell me I'm in danger?"

"Yes," Minka answered.

"Did you, or did you not tell me a werewolf was chasing me in this vision you saw?"

Minka's lips flattened for a moment. "Yes."

"Then why are you backtracking all of a sudden?"

"Did you not hear what else I said?" Minka asked testily. "I said he shouldn't have been chasing you."

Addison dropped her hands and adjusted the strap of her crossbody purse. "Why?"

"I recognized the wolf."

"And?" Addison urged tightly, her patience at an end.

Minka plopped back down on the bench. "Because he's one of the good guys."

"A werewolf that's good? Isn't that a contradiction?"

"If you knew him, you'd understand," Minka said. "They're known throughout the Quarter, throughout all of New Orleans. They help keep the factions in line. They would never hurt a human."

"But other werewolves would?"

Minka looked up and nodded. "Some."

"You keep saying 'they'."

She shook her head and shoved a stray strand of dark hair out of her face. "Have you met any new people recently?"

"I work at a bar. I meet new people every day."

That got Minka's attention. "What bar?"

"Gator Bait."

Minka took a step back. "Watch yourself, Addison. You're in danger, but I don't know from who."

Addison's jaw dropped when Minka turned and began to walk off. "So that's it? You're going to dump that foretelling in my lap, and then just walk away?"

Minka's steps halted and she looked at Addison over her shoulder. "I've never told a stranger any of this before. I couldn't help you anyway."

"And if you have another vision that tells you more? Don't you want a way to contact me?" By her hesitation,

Addison knew the answer was a resounding no, but whatever drew Minka to proclaim her vision kept her still.

Finally, Minka nodded. "Yes."

"I live in an apartment off of Rue Parc Fontaine. If I'm not there, you can find me at Gator Bait most nights."

Minka nodded. "Be safe, Addison."

CHAPTER

FIVE

MYLES KNEW something was wrong with Addison by the way she jumped at every sound. Ever since she walked into the bar that afternoon, she had been skittish and hyper-alert. Almost as if she were waiting for someone to attack her.

As if he would allow that to happen. Not in their bar, and most especially not to her.

"Trouble?" Solomon asked.

Myles shrugged from his place at the doorway of the kitchen. "I don't know. Something has her spooked."

"She's in New Orleans. She'd be stupid not to be spooked."

"According to Riley, Addison has lived here her entire life. She's lived this long without an incident. Need I remind you until this semester she was enrolled at Tulane? You know what happens there."

Solomon grunted and let his gaze wander the patrons. "There's no one here that should cause such a reaction."

Myles raised a brow and looked at his brother. "The full moon is upon us. The entire city goes apeshit during this time."

"That could be what's bothering her."

Myles hoped to hell it wasn't. "I've made excuses for you and Court. It'd be hell if Addison saw you after the nice lie I told."

"Point taken. And you and Kane? When will y'all get out?"

"Soon," Myles said and looked back at Addison.

Solomon let out a sigh. "Just because of the...past... doesn't mean you shouldn't take what you so obviously want. Namely, Addison."

Myles turned and put his back to the wall. "You went through the hell, but we were right there with you. We weren't the ones in love with her, but we loved her. You're more of a moron that I could've ever thought if you don't think that affected each of us."

"I know it did." Solomon ran a hand down his face lined with fatigue, his blue eyes troubled. "When I was in Lyons Point, I saw Vincent and Linc with their women. I hated them for being able to hold onto them. If they only knew how easy they had it."

Myles clasped his brother's shoulder and squeezed.

"Take your anger out on the fuckers stupid enough to cross the line tonight."

Solomon's eyes flashed with an unholy light from the wolf within. "I'll see you out there."

Myles watched Solomon walk out the back door before he checked on the cooks. There were an inordinate amount of humans in the bar that night, but that's always how it was on a full moon. Humans were temptation to the supernaturals that lived in the darkness.

He walked out of the back and gave a nod to Kane, who slipped out without anyone noticing. Myles walked behind the bar where Riley was busying pouring drinks.

"What are you doing here still?" she asked as she glanced at her watch. "The sun just set. You should be out there."

"I'm going. Are you sure you have everything?"

She laughed and popped the lids off two beers with an opener before setting the bottles in front of the customers. "Of course."

Myles leaned close when she turned to run the credit card. "One of us will be close. We never leave the bar completely unattended."

"It'll be fine," she assured him. "Didn't I prove in the last two nights that I knew exactly what I was doing? I took down that wraith and just last night two vampires all by myself. Remember?"

"I remember." He shook his head, unable to hold back

the grin. "It's the only reason we aren't locking you in the walk-in fridge in the back."

Riley cut him a dry look. "Very funny. Now get going while Addison is busy."

Myles glanced in Addison's direction to see her taking down an order. Something nagged at him to stay, but he had a job to do. He walked to the kitchen and out the back door to the alley.

He did a quick look to make sure no one was around before he ran two steps, jumped on a stack of crates, and then launched himself over the wooden fence to the roof of the next building.

The moon beckoned, summoned. And the wolf within answered.

ADDISON DELIVERED THE FRIED ALLIGATOR, dubbed "gator bites," along with a pitcher of beer to the table of three college guys who eyed her appreciatively. A week ago, she'd have blushed at their blatant looks, but it hadn't taken her long to get used to such things. If she were honest with herself, she would admit that the only one who could make her blush now was Myles.

She turned from the table and looked around for him. At least one of four LaRue brothers were always at the bar. As far as she could tell, none of them were there now.

Addison decided not to read too much into it. Everyone needed a night off. Hers was supposed to be tomorrow night, but she picked up a shift from another waitress who wanted the time off.

She couldn't believe she hadn't thought to get a job at a bar before. The money was so much more than she made in her other two combined. It had been so freeing to quit her cleaning job. Walking in the office buildings at night when no one was there to clean had been boring, freaky, and just plain disgusting at times.

Whoever said professionals were neat freaks who always picked up after themselves never had to clean their offices after they had eaten two meals and didn't bother to throw anything away.

Just thinking about it had her shuddering. Although the food was gross, finding it half in the garbage and half on the floor was bad, it wasn't near as bad as finding spent condoms.

Addison walked into the kitchen to get a breather. One of the three cooks looked up, his smile wide as he spotted her.

"What's up, Addy-girl?"

Marcus was so fun-loving and cheery that she didn't mind his nickname for her. His skin was deep black, his head shaved, and his face in a perpetual smile. As far as she could tell, nothing got Marcus down.

"What is it with tonight?" she asked as she put a hand on

her lower back to stretch it. "It's like the crazies have come out."

Marcus laughed as the other two cooks joined in. Marcus plated a dish of blackened catfish and winked at her. "It's a full moon, girl. Didn't you know?"

"I didn't." She knew animals reacted weird during full moons. There were more dead animals littering the roads during a full moon than any other time of the month.

Marcus motioned her over, his smile dropping. Once she was near, he leaned in and said, "Let one of us walk you home, Addy-girl. It's not a night to be out by yourself."

She looked into his black eyes and saw that he wasn't teasing her. He was truly worried. And it made her nervous, especially after Minka's announcement that afternoon. "All right," she agreed.

With his smile once more in place, Marcus nodded. "Good, good."

She watched as he turned and effortlessly sliced a chicken breast into pieces before putting them in a bowl of pasta and tossing them. Addison pivoted and walked back into the bar. That's when she saw Riley by herself looking ragged and dead on her feet. Addison quickly went to help.

"Thank you," Riley said with a grateful look.

For the next two hours Addison went from one person to another, filling drinks and getting the waitresses their drink orders. It was after one in the morning before she was able to take a breather and survey the place. Many of the patrons were gone, but there were still a few tables occupied.

"Think you can handle them?" Riley asked. "If so, I'll send two of the waitresses home."

"I've got them covered," Addison said as she walked from behind the bar to check on the tables.

She was clearing dishes from a table of two couples, when one of the women gasped and dropped her glass. Addison looked up to see the customer had gone white, her gaze beyond Addison.

Addison spun to the door to see a woman dressed in all white standing just inside the bar. Her dark skin was in direct contrast to her attire, and brought all the attention of the bar to her. The woman's gaze scanned the bar until she spotted Addison.

A shiver went through Addison when the woman smiled and then walked to a table. It was only belatedly that Addison realized the woman wasn't alone. A tall man, dressed in white pants and a white shirt, followed close behind, and only sitting once the woman had chosen a chair.

It was one of those rare times when Addison would have gladly turned the table over to someone else, but she had told Riley she could handle things alone.

Her legs were wooden as she walked to the kitchen. She put the dirty plates in the sink and hurried back out to the front to clean up the broken glass, but Riley was already taking care of it. Which left Addison nothing else to do but go to her new table.

With her best smile, she stopped at the table. "Welcome to Gator Bait. What can I get for y'all this evening?"

The woman watched her with a half smile, the kind that gave the impression that she knew something Addison didn't. Her black hair was done in dozens of tiny braids that fell to her waist. With her flawless dark skin and high cheekbones, the woman was spectacularly beautiful.

"Things have improved for you since coming to work here, Addison," the woman said in a rich voice that seemed to fill every inch of the bar.

Addison swallowed as she gripped her pencil tightly. "Do I know you?"

"Not as of yet, but I know you."

"How?"

The woman's smile grew a fraction. "Where are the LaRue brothers?"

"I don't know. It's not my business to keep up with them," Addison replied stiffly. Her arms began to shake from keeping them locked in place as she waited to take down the order. "Now. What can I get you to eat or drink?"

"I didn't come for the food," the woman said and crossed one leg over the other, her long skirt moving fluidly. "And I can get drinks anywhere."

Addison lowered her arms to her sides. She knew the woman was goading her into asking the question, and even though she knew it would be better to walk away, she asked, "Then why are you here?"

"For you."

Addison was so shocked, she took a step back. Who was the woman, and why had she come for her? Addison knew enough to comprehend the dress as that of the Voodoo culture. It was a religion she knew nothing about, other than it could be dangerous in the wrong hands, and she didn't want—or need—to know any more than that.

"Is there a problem?" Riley asked as she walked up beside Addison.

The woman's smile grew slowly as she took in Riley. "I didn't expect to see a Chiasson here in New Orleans. I don't think my day could get any better."

"Who are you?" Addison asked.

The woman bowed her head as she slid her gaze from Riley to Addison. "I'm Delphine." She narrowed her eyes on Riley. "Didn't your brothers mention me?"

Addison glanced over at Riley to see her shaking with anger. Her lips were pinched tight and her hands were fisted at her sides.

Delphine threw back her head and laughed. "Ah. I see that they have. I wonder, do your brothers know you're here? I can't imagine after our encounter that they wouldn't do everything in their power to keep you out of New Orleans. Hmm. Is there discord in the tight Chiasson clan?"

"Get out," Riley said between clenched teeth. "Now."

Delphine rose to her feet. Her smile was gone, but a look of utter delight shone in her black eyes. "You should know more about your employers, Addison. Just being associated with such...people...could get you in all sorts of trouble."

With that, Delphine turned on her heel and walked out of the bar.

Everyone breathed easier once Delphine was gone. Everyone but Addison, that is.

"Don't listen to her," Riley said as she stared at the closed door. "She has a grudge against my family that started with the LaRues and has since expanded to encompass the Chiassons."

Addison swallowed and rubbed her hands over her arms. "Why did she seek me out?"

"To frighten you." Riley faced her and flashed a quick grin. "Delphine is a Voodoo priestess. Watch yourself around her."

They turned to find Marcus behind them, his face a thunderous expression of fury and hate. "Riley is right, Addy-girl. Delphine is bad business."

Addison didn't need either of them to tell her that. She sensed it the moment she saw Delphine, but that still didn't stop the priestess's words from running through her head over and over again.

CHAPTER

SIX

ADDISON COULDN'T WAIT to call it a night. She was exhausted both physically and mentally. Delphine's visit had only agitated things, mostly because she was more than curious where Myles and his brothers were.

When she asked Riley about it, Riley shrugged it off and said the boys needed a night off. Which didn't sound off except for what Delphine said.

Addison walked out the back with a bag of trash. She opened the dumpster and threw it in. After she dusted off her hands, she looked up at the sky, but she couldn't see the moon from where she was.

She turned to go back inside when a man stepped out of the shadows. Addison took a look at the door, but the narrow alley prevented her from having enough room to go around him and reach the door. No one inside would hear her scream with the music blaring.

Addison glanced over her shoulder to the wooden fence that locked her in. She didn't think she could climb it fast enough or open the locked gate quick enough to get away.

She took in the man, who was on the short side and thin-framed, but there was something about him that made her wary, that made her think he was much stronger than he looked.

"Here's the morsel I've been looking for," he said with a smile.

His skin looked pale in the light flooding the alley. His eyes were in shadow, but she knew they were trained on her as he began to move toward her. Addison backed up, her heart pounding in fear.

The man smoothed his hand over his slicked-back dark-brown hair. "You're all that's being talked about." He licked his lips. "I'm famished."

"I can get you some food," she hurried to say.

Apparently he thought that was funny, because he laughed. "Take a look at my clothes, sweetheart. Do I look as if I can't afford whatever it is I want?"

"You said you were hungry."

"Oh, I am." He peeled back his lips and his eyeteeth lengthened.

Addison had the second shock of the night, and it

brought her up short, halting her retreat. Surely it was some trick of the light.

Minka said there were vampires.

Oh, God. She was going to die from a vampire. The terror that consumed her locked her limbs so she couldn't move for a moment. Addison stumbled backwards against the fence, a scream welling in her throat.

Then a flash of dark fur leapt from over her head. She yelped as something large and furry landed in front of her, a low, menacing growl emanating from it. The vampire took a step back and hissed. Addison wanted to think it was a dog, but there was no denying she was looking at a wolf—a very large, very scary wolf.

Its body was low to the ground as it snapped its jaws at the vampire and issued another growl. For a second, Addison thought the vampire would leave, and then she realized the wolf had no intentions of letting it go anywhere.

She plastered herself against the fence, praying the wolf didn't see her. Addison's hand shook as she tried to open the gate to her right. The jiggle of the metal caused the vampire's gaze to shift to her.

Her breath locked in her chest. Then the wolf turned its head to her and she saw into its yellow eyes that seemed to glow from within. She was taken aback at the fierce beauty of the wolf. The next second, the wolf surprised both her and the vampire as it launched itself at the man and locked its powerful jaws around the vamp's neck. The yells from the vampire were drowned out by the growling of the wolf.

Addison screamed and focused on getting the gate open, because she knew she was getting a firsthand look at a werewolf. It took her a moment to realize it was as quiet as death around her except for the thump of the music from within the bar.

She closed her eyes, both of her hands on the gate latch that refused to open. Addison slowly turned her head and looked over her shoulder.

The wolf was off to the side, standing over the dead body of the vampire that was turning gray and crumbling before her eyes. She lifted her gaze to the wolf and took a good look at its fur of chocolate brown. It wasn't just more muscular than a normal wolf, but taller as well.

No longer was it growling. It simply stared at her as if it were waiting on something.

"Thank you," she whispered.

From its position, it leaped over the fence with nary a sound. Addison gulped back a yelp of surprise, and then hurried around the dust of the vampire as fast as she could and then rushed into the kitchen.

All Addison wanted to do was to get the night over with so she could try and sleep. Perhaps then she could forget all that she witnessed.

When she walked back into the front of the bar to finish cleaning off the tables, Riley stopped her by grabbing both of her hands. "You're shaking," Riley said. "What happened?"

Addison wasn't sure if she could tell Riley about what had happened. She didn't want anyone thinking she belonged in a loony bin.

"Addison, please," Riley urged.

"There was a man out back."

Riley frowned and glanced at the kitchen. She released Addison and strode to the back. Addison followed her outside. With one look, Riley walked to the last bit of ashes. She knelt down and touched something on the ground.

Her gaze lifted and locked on Addison. "By the paleness of your face, I'm gathering you saw this?"

Addison nodded.

Riley sighed and got to her feet. "What happened?"

The acceptance on her face sent Addison's head spinning. She wrapped her arms around her middle. "You accept this as if you've known. You're not shocked there is a pile of ash there, and you know what it is."

"I could've lied to you, pretended I didn't see anything, and waited until you left to get a better look. But I didn't. I do know about vampires, demons, witches—"

"Werewolves?" Addison asked.

Riley hesitated for a heartbeat. "Yes."

"That's what got the vampire."

Riley jerked her thumb over her shoulder to the fence. "I saw the fresh claw marks."

Addison dropped her head into her hands. "I can't believe I'm standing out here talking about werewolves and vampires. I've lived in New Orleans all my life. All of those rumors were just to keep the tourists coming."

"How I wish it were true." Riley came to stand beside her. "You're freaked out, but not nearly as much as I would've expected."

Addison dropped her hands and looked up. "This has been a really weird day. I was approached earlier by a fortuneteller who said she saw a vision of me being chased by a werewolf."

"What?" Riley exploded. "Did she say werewolf?"

"She said wolf, but she said she was confused because she knew the wolves around the Quarter protected people." As Addison learned firsthand that evening. "But she warned I was in danger."

Riley grunted and crossed her arms over her chest as her frown deepened. "That's obvious by Delphine's visit tonight. Someone is taking an interest in you, Addison, and it's cause for concern."

"Really?" she asked sarcastically.

Riley's face broke into a smile. "I think this calls for a drink. Only Marcus is left. Come inside and tell me in detail what happened out here."

MYLES WATCHED Addison and Riley walk back into the kitchen through a slat in the fence. By the way Riley glanced over her shoulder, she guessed he was still out there.

He was glad he listened to his instincts and remained behind. Not even killing the vamp cooled the fury that raced through him. The vampire should never have gotten that close to the bar, and he wouldn't have had Myles not been led on a merry chase through the Quarter after another group of vamps.

It wasn't unusual for the Quarter to be a hotbed of activity on a full moon, but he realized now he'd been led away on purpose. The vamp had been after Addison.

But why? And what did the vampire mean that everyone was talking about Addison?

More disturbing was the mention of Delphine's name, despite Riley whispering it. In wolf form, he could hear everything—even the frantic beating of Addison's heart.

Knowing Riley would keep Addison safe inside, Myles made another round of the area. He and his brothers certainly had their hands full tonight, and the longer it took for him to return to Addison, the more frustrated he became.

It wasn't until the first rays of sun lightened the sky that he was able to follow Addison and Riley's scent, though Addison's was stronger for him. He loped along the streets, staying hidden, until he came to Rue Parc Fontaine. He peered down the street and saw Riley sitting on the hood of a bright green Jeep.

She spotted him and slid off the car with a grin. "Am I glad to see you," she said when he trotted up. "You saved her, didn't you?"

Myles stopped beside her and looked up to the second floor where he could smell Addison.

"She's safe," Riley said as she patted his back.

That could only comfort him so much, especially knowing that she was in danger. The fact a witch from the Quarter told her she had a vision of Addison being chased by a wolf disturbed him.

"I figured you'd come," Riley continued as she reached for a bag on the ground, and straightened with something in her hand. "So I grabbed some clothes. You can't be seen like that, cuz."

Myles took the jeans in his mouth and moved off to a secluded spot. He dropped the jeans, and let the transformation back into his human body begin. It was always easier to revert back into human form than to shift into a wolf. He gritted his teeth as bones, tendons, and muscles returned to their true form.

Myles was panting, sweat covering his body, when he pushed up on his hands and looked around to make sure no one saw him. Then he stood and pulled on the jeans before walking barefoot back to Riley.

She smiled brightly, holding out a red shirt and a pair of brown leather flip-flops. "We can't have you walking barefoot. You don't know what you could step on. And the shirt is a necessity. If women caught sight of you, you'd never make it back to the bar."

He chuckled and put on the shirt. As he slid his feet in the shoes, he cut his eyes to her. "Let's get back to the bar."

"I suppose you have questions?"

Myles waited for her to get the bag before he started walking. "Yep. I won't be the only one."

"I knew you were out there," Riley grumbled.

"Was Delphine really there?"

Riley nodded. "I heard about her from Ava, but I wasn't expecting to feel the evil of Delphine so strongly. It was like she was the center of it all."

Myles put his arm around Riley and pulled her against him. "You shouldn't have had to face her alone the first time. Shit. Your brothers are going to have my head."

"She knew who I was without even knowing my name," Riley said and rested her head on his shoulders.

They walked the rest of the way to the bar in silence. Riley was tough. She had to be, as a Chiasson, but she had been doing things herself for so long that she desperately wanted someone to take some of the load off her shoulders. She just didn't comprehend that yet.

Myles walked them through the back of the building. As soon as they entered the kitchen, she pulled away, pushed her shoulders back, and lifted her chin. Whether she knew it or not, she acted as if she were going into battle, and in some ways she was—the battle for herself.

He stopped when he entered the front of the bar and he spotted Court, Solomon, and Kane sitting with Marcus. Marcus was the only other person at the bar who knew what they truly were, and only because it had been Solomon who saved his life ten years earlier when a demon tried to possess Marcus as a teenager.

Marcus ran a hand over his bald head and met Myles's gaze. "Delphine was here for Addison."

CHAPTER
SEVEN

HOURS LATER, Myles lay in his bed with his arm behind his head staring at the ceiling. He was supposed to be sleeping, but his mind kept going over everything Marcus and Riley had told him about Delphine's visit and the fortuneteller who spoke to Addison.

What was it about Addison that was drawing the eye of every faction of supernatural in the city? As far as Myles knew, she was a normal, everyday southern girl. Obviously he was wrong.

He rose and took a quick shower, not bothering to shave. He threw on a fresh pair of jeans, a black shirt, and boots before he made his way out of his apartment.

That was something the LaRues did differently than the Chiassons. Solomon still lived in the LaRue house on the outskirts of New Orleans on the bayou. It was a grand place that was too big for one man. Myles, Court, and Kane opted to reside in New Orleans, each of them taking a section close to each other, but still able to keep an eye on the factions.

His place was an old warehouse he bought six years ago and converted into large studio apartments. He owned a car, but rarely drove it since he lived close enough to Gator Bait to walk.

He pulled his keys out as he reached the bar. Just as he was about to slide them into the opening, he heard something within. Myles opened the door and stepped inside to find Solomon pulling chairs off the tables.

"Couldn't sleep?" Solomon asked.

Myles shook his head. "You either?"

Solomon grunted. "You know I don't sleep."

It was true, and something they rarely spoke about. "I can't figure out why Addison is so important to the factions."

"Did you ever stop to think it was because she came to work here?"

Myles walked behind the bar and poured himself a cup of strong, black coffee. "How many people have we had work for us through the years? Not a one of them have been singled out."

"True," Solomon conceded as he set the last chair in place getting ready for the midday rush. He walked to the bar and sat on a stool. "Something in her past, maybe?"

Myles shrugged. "Could be. I don't want to interrogate her about it."

"It's either that, or we call in a favor at NOPD."

He scratched his cheek and drank more of the coffee, hoping the caffeine would kick in soon. "I'll be surprised if she returns. After everything, she's probably too freaked out to come back."

"Making it harder for us to protect her." Solomon raised his brows and looked pointedly at Myles.

"Since when was I voted the one to watch over her?"

"Since you can't take your eyes off her."

Myles couldn't deny that. He thought he'd been covert about it.

"We're wiser now," Solomon said as he rested his forearms on the bar and laced his fingers together. His dark blond hair was disheveled, as if he'd been running his hands through it. "We made mistakes with M.... We made mistakes."

Myles looked away when Solomon couldn't say the name of the woman he had loved. Six years hadn't dulled the pain of losing her—or the way she died. "I hear there are two new females that arrived at the were camp in Slidell. Go take a look."

Solomon's gaze went hard. "We're talking about you, not me. The point is, Addison is going to need to be watched, regardless if she comes back to work or not. A vampire was here to kill her. Delphine purposefully walked into our bar on the night she knew we wouldn't be here to talk to

Addison. Last but not least, someone from the witch faction had a vision about her being chased by a wolf."

"I know all of it. You don't have to repeat it," Myles said testily.

"Apparently I do, to beat it into that thick skull of yours."

Myles finished off his coffee and set the mug down hard. "You think I don't know you're shoving me at her in the hopes that I'll give in?"

Solomon held his gaze for several long moments. "I think you're fighting every natural instinct to take her. I think you're going out of your way to ensure you won't give in to the desire. I think you want her more than anything else. Ever."

"I can't," Myles whispered.

"Because you're afraid of falling in love? Or afraid of losing her?"

Myles didn't think he was strong enough to endure what Solomon had. To have found love, then to have lost it in such a heinous way, was too much. Now, knowing so many were interested in Addison only brought the possibility home.

"Both," Myles admitted.

Solomon put his hands on the bar and stood. "It still doesn't change the fact that she's in danger. I'll put Kane to watch her first. We three can divvy up the time. You don't have to be involved."

Myles clenched his hand into fists at the thought of his brothers watching Addison's every move as he stayed behind. It was for the best. At least, that's what he told himself as Solomon started toward the kitchen.

"No," Myles said, before Solomon could go through the doorway. "I'll talk to her. And stop smiling, you jackass. I can see you."

Solomon laughed as he disappeared into the kitchen. Myles sighed and decided to go over yesterday's numbers to take his mind off things.

Except he learned an hour later that nothing could pull his mind from Addison. He finally gave up and left the bar. With no destination in mind, he wandered the streets until he came to Jackson Square.

Myles ambled through the many artists displaying their wares. As he walked, he studied the witches set up as fortunetellers. There were more than ever before. Some were frauds, but some were the genuine article.

He spotted a young witch who was more interested in watching someone than pulling in clients who walked right past her. Myles followed her gaze until he saw none other than Addison.

Myles walked to the witch and sat. She jumped, her head swinging to him. Her eyes widened, indicating she knew exactly who he was.

"Minka, right? You told Addison she was in danger," he said.

The witch had long deep-brown hair that curled. A bright pink piece of fabric wrapped around her head with tiny beads in various shades of pink hanging across her forehead. Her eyes were pale brown, ringed in black, giving her a dramatic look.

She leaned back, her black blouse hanging off one shoulder. One dark brow rose as she returned his stare. Then she crossed one leg over another, her pink skirt hiking up enough to show black beaded sandals. "Because she is."

It took her long enough, but at least the witch was talking. "From a wolf?"

Minka looked away briefly. "As I told Addison, that's where it gets complicated."

"How?"

"I sense danger involving her, and I know that she's chased by a wolf, but I don't think it's the wolf."

Myles glanced to where Addison shopped across the square. "What color is the wolf?"

"Brown."

"Then you've got it wrong, witch. I would never hurt her."

Minka's head tilted as she studied him. "No, you wouldn't. Does she know how badly you yearn for her?"

"That's none of your concern."

"So, that's a no," Minka said with a twist of her lips. "Why are men so stupid?"

Myles snapped his fingers at her. "Focus. I need to know who is after Addison. A vampire tried to get her last night, and Delphine paid her a visit."

The witch paled at the mention of the priestess. "Delphine? She went to Addison's apartment?"

"No. She came to the bar."

Minka whistled low. "After you and your brothers captured her and tortured her? Are you sure she's after Addison and not one of you?"

"We're not stupid. We know we'll always be in Delphine's crosshairs. I don't like her attention on Addison. How did she even learn of Addison?"

Minka sat forward and lowered her voice. "There have been whispers for a few weeks about someone who has enough power to put Delphine in her place."

"I know who she is, but she's not in New Orleans," Myles said.

Minka shook her head, her brow furrowed. "I know about Davena. I was leading up to the fact that it isn't just Davena that's being talked about."

When she didn't continue, Myles gave her a flat look. "You can't come that far, witch, and not finish."

"Fine," she stated angrily. "But understand I put my own life in danger by telling you this."

"Just spit it out."

Minka looked around and suddenly became nervous. "Not here," she whispered.

Myles sat back and held out his hand. "You're a fortuneteller, right? What better way to cover up what we're talking about than reading my palm?"

"You're nuts," she grumbled, but cupped his hand in both of hers. She ran a finger along his palm, her gaze focused on his hand. "They're still watching."

"Who?"

"My people. They don't want to be involved."

Myles looked at the table a few feet away to find the woman watching them. As soon as their eyes met, she hastily looked away. "Why?" he asked Minka.

"They say it isn't our fight." Her fingernail lightly scraped down his palm. "I haven't told them what I saw, but they know something is up."

He leaned his head down as if intently watching what she was doing to his palm. "Ignoring it won't make the situation go away."

"No kidding?" she replied, her words dripping with sarcasm. "I also can't make myself see anything."

"Tell me what you know," he urged softly.

She met his gaze and then sighed. "The word is that Delphine is worried. She needs to make a sacrifice of someone pure in spirit as well as a witch to boost her power."

"Addison isn't a witch," Myles said, his other hand gripping the side of the table. "She must be the one pure in spirit."

"That's the conclusion I came to yesterday. I don't know why I saw you chasing her though."

He shrugged. "One thing at a time. If the other factions

know Delphine's plan, then that could be why the vampire tried to kill Addison last night."

"Addison is a good soul, but pure in spirit? There aren't a whole lot of those around, especially in the city. No one wants Delphine to gain more power. She has too much as it is," Minka said, looking up at him with a smile so she appeared to be delivering good news to anyone watching.

Myles smiled in return. "We couldn't kill her when we had her. You know that, don't you?"

"We know what she did to Kane, but if you thwart her in this, I have a feeling she'll come gunning for you."

"Better me than Addison."

Minka jerked, her eyes going milky as she stared at him, unblinking. Her nails dug into his hand, causing blood to well from the half-moon shapes.

Myles surreptitiously looked around before he leaned forward. "Minka? Hey, witch? Talk to me."

Her lids closed and Minka took in a deep breath. When she opened her eyes they were once more the pale brown. She began to shake, and it was Myles who took her hands in his.

"Talk to me, witch. What just happened?"

"I saw your death."

CHAPTER
EIGHT

MYLES RELEASED Minka's hands and sat back. "Death is part of being a hunter. It finds us sooner or later."

"This is sooner," Minka whispered fervently. "Why aren't you freaking out? I would be."

"You think anyone in my family has lived to a ripe old age? We've too many enemies."

Minka raised a brow. "Such a macho man. Why can't you say that you don't want to die?"

"Does anyone *want* to die, witch?"

All the heat went out of her words. "Some do."

Myles immediately thought of Solomon. Six years ago, Solomon had begged for death. He sighed and focused on the present. "What can you tell me about your vision?"

"You were injured badly when the vision started," Minka said.

"I need details, Minka. Where was I? Who was I fighting? What were the injuries?" he pressed.

She slid her hands into her hair near her temples and closed her eyes. "There were trees and grass around you. I couldn't see the wounds, just blood. So much blood."

Myles leaned forward and lowered his voice. "Could you see who I fought?"

"No," she said with a shake of her head. Her eyes flew open as she dropped her hands. "You were in wolf form."

"Good. That will help. Did you get a look at what killed me?"

"A silver blade."

Damn. That really would end him for good. Myles stood and fished out two twenties from his pocket as he tossed them on the table to make their exchange look legit. "Thank you. The LaRues owe you. If you ever need anything, you come find us, witch."

He walked away with the new information rolling around in his mind. If he was going to die soon, it put things into a new perspective. Since Delphine was involved, there was a chance that his life could end that very day.

Myles stopped at the edge of the sidewalk, his gaze searching for Addison. He found her looking through a stack of paintings. If he was going to die, he was going to die knowing the taste of Addison's kiss.

Addison tried to tell herself she returned to Jackson Square to fill the time, but the truth was that she hoped Minka had more information. Although Addison hadn't worked up the courage to go to Minka herself. But she was working on it.

She paused in her flipping through the paintings as she came to one of the Quarter at night, a large, full moon rising. It was a big piece, one that would look amazing over her bed.

Addison knew she shouldn't spend any of her money on something that wasn't a necessity, and yet she wanted the painting. She glanced at the price and cringed. It was much more than she wanted to pay, but every time she tried to put it down and walk away, she couldn't.

"Find something you like?" asked a deep voice behind her.

A shiver went through her as she recognized Myles's voice. She turned her head to him. "Just browsing."

His crooked smile told her he knew she was lying. "I know the painter. He's good. I like his view of the city."

"Yes." Addison made herself set the painting down.

"I hear the bar was packed last night. Riley should've called one of us in."

It might be Addison's imagination, but she had the feeling Myles knew everything that had happened the night before. "We handled it."

"So I hear. I also heard there was a dangerous visitor to the bar."

Addison wasn't sure if he was talking about the vampire, the wolf, or Delphine. "Uh, huh."

"So, Delphine didn't frighten you?" he asked with a narrowed gaze.

She shrugged and started walking. Myles fell into step beside her. "She was definitely freaky. The way she looked at me made me feel as if someone walked over my grave."

"Delphine isn't someone you need to mess with. At all."

"I'd love to take your advice, and I wish I'd have known that before she came into the bar."

"Yeah," he said tightly. "She knew we weren't there and waited until then to pay you a visit."

Addison glanced sideways at him. "It's all right. Riley and Marcus got her to leave. I'd still love to know how she knew my name."

"What do you know of Voodoo?"

"I know it can do very bad things."

Myles caught her gaze as they walked. "There are many rumors spoken in our city, but the ones about Delphine are true. She cursed Kane not that long ago, and she's not fond of our cousins."

"I kinda got that by the way she spoke to Riley."

He smiled and stopped to put his hand on her lower back and move her out of the way as a group of tourists walked past. "Delphine has killed many people," Myles leaned down and whispered in her ear.

Addison's body heated at his touch, and her heart skipped a beat when his warm breath fanned her neck.

"It's not good if she's put her focus on you." He fingered a strand of her hair.

She looked up at him, caught in his mesmerizing blue gaze. "She isn't the only evil in the city."

"No, but she's one of the most dangerous. She's unpredictable and power-hungry."

Addison licked her lips. Her stomach flip-flopped when his gaze lowered to her mouth. She held her breath when he leaned forward slightly.

God, yes. Please kiss me.

As if realizing where they were, Myles looked around. "You need to be careful and vigilant. Delphine could be watching now."

Addison was still trying to bring her body under control, and he expected her to think? And if he could do that to her with a near kiss, what would he do to her if they ever did share a kiss?

Myles's gaze looked over her head, his face becoming hard. He then took her hand and hastily led her away. "It looks like my words are coming true. You're being followed."

Addison looked behind her as Myles pushed his way through the crowd. She spotted two men in all white hurrying after them. She gripped Myles's hand and had to jog to keep up with his long strides. Not once did he stop or slow. Addison had no idea where they were going, and she didn't care as long as she got away from the two men.

To her surprise, Myles pulled her beneath an iron arch of one of the city's famous cemeteries. If she thought he would halt then, she was wrong.

They meandered through the tombs until he suddenly stopped and pushed her against a crypt. He put his fingers to his lips. Addison nodded, gulping in air, as she wiped the sweat from her face.

Something felt odd at her feet. She looked down to see her sandal had broken. How it remained on her foot during their flight she had no idea. Her gaze lifted to discover Myles gone. Addison rolled her eyes and sank down on the stones to try and see if she could repair the shoe enough to get her to a store before her shift.

The crunch of stone made her head jerk up and she spotted one of the men who had been following her. Sweat ran down his skin, a smile curving his lips when he saw her. He let out a whistle, and a moment later, the second man joined him.

Addison opened her mouth to scream. Before a sound could escape, Myles came out of nowhere moving with lethal speed as he punched the men with his fists and elbows. In a matter of seconds, both men lay unconscious at her feet.

Myles held out his hand, barely breathing hard. "I'm thirsty. How about you?"

She blinked up at him. "How did you do that?"

"Years of training and living in the Quarter."

Addison took his hand and let him pull her up. She hadn't taken two steps before her sandal fell off. With a curse, she picked it up and began to walk with one foot bare.

One minute she was standing, and the next she was in Myles's arms. She locked her arm around his neck, her broken shoe forgotten.

"What are you doing?" she asked.

He gave her a droll look. "What does it look like?"

"You can't carry me all the way to the bar."

"Wanna bet?"

She had seen his muscles through his clothing, but there was nothing like feeling the hard sinew under her hands. There was no doubt he could carry her. It wasn't that she minded being there, but it was embarrassing. Or it should be.

Her body heated from more than just the August sun.

"See?" he asked with a wink. "It isn't so bad."

She licked her lips, pulling her mind away from his close proximity. "How did you know I was followed?"

His mood darkened as a frown formed. "I didn't. At least not until I began to realize how easily they could snatch you off the street."

"I've never felt unsafe before. I don't like this." When he didn't respond, she asked, "How do you know about Delphine?"

"Everyone knows of her."

"Including the vampires?"

His gaze jerked to hers, but there was no shock or surprise reflected at her words. "Everyone."

"I didn't."

Myles looked away. "You do now."

"What aren't you telling me? Why didn't you freak at my mention of vampires?"

A muscle in his jaw jumped. She was so close to his face that she wanted to touch his cheek and feel the scrape of his shadow beard beneath her fingers. Addison gave in to the urge to touch him and smoothed her fingers along his blond hair at his temples. The strands were warm from the sun, and soft.

"Riley knew of them, which means you do to. You also know what happened to me last night. Were you looking for me today?"

He sighed loudly and stopped. "Yes, I was looking for you, but not only because of last night." He released her legs and slowly lowered her until her feet touched concrete. "I know of the vampires. I know a lot of things you're better off not knowing."

She stared into his bright blue eyes. Despite everything he said, she focused on the one thing that made her heart pound. "Why else were you looking for me?"

"For this," he said as he slid a hand around her neck and pulled her against him as his mouth descended upon hers.

Addison rose up on her tiptoes and wrapped her arms around him. The fire, the uncontrollable need in his kiss sent her spiraling into an abyss of desire so deep she knew she never wanted to climb out.

His moan, so full of yearning, made her knees weak. He then tilted her head to the side as his tongue slipped past her lips. The world melted away, vanished. She was unprepared for the intensity of the kiss, the force of the passion that flared between them.

He deepened the kiss and she tightened her arms. She had to be closer to him, to feel his skin. Once she found the hem of his shirt, she skimmed her hand beneath and connected to his rock-hard abs.

Myles pulled back, ending the kiss to stare down at her with eyes blazing with desire. "I've wanted to do that for awhile."

"What took you so long?" she teased.

Except he didn't smile in return. In fact, he looked sad.

Myles threaded his fingers with hers and turned her around. Addison saw then they were at the bar. Had she been so wrapped up in him that she hadn't realized where she was? He led her inside, the dim light inside taking her a minute to adjust to after the bright sunlight.

"What the hell happened?" Riley asked as she hurried around the bar.

"Delphine sent some men," Myles answered.

Addison shifted her gaze to a table where the other three

LaRue brothers sat. Solomon looked at their joined hands before lifting his eyes to her. She waited to see what he would do, and when Solomon sent her a small smile, she was able to breathe again. Because, somehow, she knew her best chance to survive was with the brothers.

CHAPTER
NINE

M YLES DIDN'T WANT to release Addison, even to Riley. He watched the pair disappear into the back where Riley had some shoes for Addison.

"Tell us what you're leaving out," Solomon bade.

Myles swiveled his head to his brothers. He walked to the small round table and pulled out a chair, turning it backwards before he sat between Kane and Solomon. "I went to see the witch who told Addison she was in danger."

Court whistled. "You're a brave man. You wouldn't catch me dead talking to them."

Myles tried to smile at Court's jest, but he couldn't manage it. "It took some doing, but I learned why Delphine wants Addison."

"The fact the bitch wants her is enough to kill Delphine in my book," Kane said through clenched teeth.

Solomon glanced at Kane before he looked at Myles. "Well?"

"Delphine wants to increase her power. To do that she needs two things—a witch, and a mortal pure of spirit."

Court grunted and looped one arm on the back of his chair. "I don't have to guess which category Addison falls in."

"Exactly." Myles ran a hand down his face, deciding what the witch foretold about his death he would keep to himself. No need to worry his brothers.

Solomon studied him carefully. "What are you leaving out?"

"Nothing," Myles lied. "The witch said the other factions know of Delphine's plan and don't want her to get more power, so they decided to eliminate Addison."

Kane drummed his fingers on the table. "So, others will be coming after Addison?"

"Possibly. If Delphine doesn't get to her first."

Court made a face. "She sent a clear message by going after Addison in the middle of the day. My guess is she heard about the vampire last night. Delphine isn't going to want to take another chance."

"It's not like Addison is the only one pure in spirit," Solomon said.

Myles shrugged. "According to the witch, she is in New Orleans."

"How many of Delphine's men were after Addison?" Kane asked.

"Three. Only two attacked. The other watched from a distance."

"You should've gone after him," Court said as he leaned one forearm on the table.

"And leave Addison alone for a fourth I might not have seen?" Myles pointed out.

Solomon held up a hand when Court started to argue. "Myles did the right thing. If Delphine wants Addison bad enough that she's willing to snatch her in the middle of the day, then it could have been a trap."

"Y'all could've killed Delphine," Kane said as he stared at the table, both of his fists clenched tightly atop the table. "Had I not messed around and gotten cursed, you could've killed her. You should have anyway."

Myles reached over and placed his hand on Kane's shoulder. "If we'd done that, you would've remained in wolf form forever."

"Only until one of our cousins killed me," Kane said as he looked at Myles. "Each of you would be free of Delphine now, and Addison wouldn't be in danger."

Solomon rested one of his fists atop Kane's. "Then we wouldn't have you. We made the right call."

"We sure as shit did," Court stated loudly.

Myles dropped his hand when Addison and Riley returned. He couldn't stop staring at Addison's mouth. The kiss had been everything he knew it would be and so much more. He forgot everything, including where he was, when she was in his arms. Why did she have to be so damn alluring? Why did he crave her as if she were life itself?

He didn't care that there were no answers. He didn't need them. All he needed was Addison. What a fool he had been to push her away, to keep his distance. Now, he feared he wouldn't have even a day with her.

A blush stained her cheeks, causing him to smile, because he knew she was thinking of their kiss, just as he was. He loved the way her hazel eyes looked at him, as if she wanted to devour him.

"I don't think it's a good idea for Addison to work today," Riley said.

Myles wanted to hug his cousin for her quick thinking. His smile grew, even as Addison began to argue that she needed to work.

"Riley is right. We can't watch everyone Addison comes into contact with if she's working," Myles said. "She needs to be somewhere safe."

Like his place.

Addison glanced away. "I have to work. Not only do I need the money, but I took a shift."

"That I can easily take over," Riley said. She nudged Addison. "I'm sorry, but I think it's for the best. Delphine can't get her hands on you."

Solomon got to his feet. "Then it's settled. Myles, I gather you'll take Addison to your place?"

"It's warded," Myles said and stood, his cock already swelling with the idea of being alone with Addison.

Kane pulled out his cell phone. "As much as I appreciate the warding, I think it might be prudent to bring in reinforcements."

Myles looked from Kane to Court to Solomon and shrugged. "Your call," he told Solomon.

For long seconds Solomon mulled over Kane's proposal. He inhaled deeply and gave a rueful shake of his head. "I'm going to regret this, but all right."

As Kane made the call to the Moonstone pack, Myles waited for Addison to walk to him. Once she was beside him, it was everything he could do not to pull her in his arms and kiss her again.

She had no idea how tempting her dark pink lips were, how irresistible her taste. Or perhaps she did. Maybe she knew the way she tantalized and seduced him with her soft touch and big eyes.

"Your place?" she asked, a hint of siren in her voice.

Myles could feel the eyes of his brothers and Riley on him, and he didn't care if they could see the hunger, the yearning for Addison in his gaze. "My place," he whispered and held out his hand.

There was a smile on his face as she laced her fingers with his. They walked from Gator Bait together, no words spoken. None needed.

Myles was alert and wary as they strolled down the

sidewalk. He was wound tight by the time they reached his building. After quickly punching the code to open the door, Myles ushered her inside and up the four flights of stairs, bypassing the elevator.

He unlocked the steel door and slid it open. "Make yourself at home," he said as he waved her inside.

"I love the space," she said, looking around.

Myles shut the door and watched her. He looked around the large room with the fifteen-foot ceilings. He left the brick walls and the air vent piping exposed, instead using them as part of his décor.

His bed was against the far back wall with burgundy bed curtains that he could pull closed to shut out the light from the many windows. The kitchen was small, but adequate. He had no cabinets, instead storing what little he needed on shelves.

There was a small table in the kitchen where he ate if he didn't take the food to his brown leather couch that separated the bedroom from the living room with the TV hanging on the wall.

"It's amazing," Addison said with a smile as she looked over her shoulder at him.

"It's simple."

She stopped and turned to face him. "It suits you perfectly."

Myles pushed off the door. "I've got movies. There's an

Xbox if you prefer. I can also make you something to eat if you're hungry."

"I'm not hungry, I don't play video games, and I don't want to watch a movie." She pulled her purse strap over her head and dropped the purse on the couch.

Myles held his ground, afraid to move or utter a single sound and break the spell. Addison removed the too-big flip-flops while holding his gaze. He'd seen those amazing eyes up close. There were flecks of gold in her hazel eyes, and when she was scared, there was more green than blue.

"What do you want to do?" he asked.

She smiled a little shyly and glanced down. "This," she said and closed the distance between them before she kissed him.

Myles locked his arms around her and gave himself up to the fiery, fierce kiss. This time he didn't have to worry about an attack. This time he didn't have to end it.

He backed her across the space to the bed and lifted her up. A laugh escaped her as she broke the kiss and looked down at him. Myles carefully tossed her on the bed and quickly placed a knee on the mattress as he crawled over her.

"That look makes me feel as if I have butterflies," she whispered.

Myles paused. "What look?"

"This one," she said and placed her hands on his face tracing his nose, brows, jaw, and lips.

He turned his head to place a kiss on the inside of one of

her arms. "Ah. You mean the one that says I crave you more than anything."

"Yes," she said breathlessly. "No one has ever looked at me like that before."

"Stupid fools. Then again, they saved you for me."

He lowered his weight atop her as they kissed again. She began to tug at his shirt. Myles stopped kissing her long enough to yank off his shirt. The way her body nestled his caused his blood to pound relentlessly with need. He wanted to take his time, to love her accordingly, but he'd spent too long fantasizing about making her his.

He rolled onto his back, bringing her with him. As he did, he pulled off her shirt and tossed it aside. Her skin was warm, soft. Her lips were enticing, tempting.

It took little more to remove her denim shorts, leaving her in nothing more than her plain white cotton bra and panties. With a flick of his wrist, he unhooked her bra and slid the straps down her arms. It was Addison who pulled it from between their bodies and flung it. He returned her to her back and leaned over her.

"My God," he murmured as he looked down at her pert breasts and pink tipped nipples. He skimmed his hand along her flat belly to cup one breast. "You're gorgeous."

Her blush stained her cheeks, her chest, and even her breasts. How one compliment could embarrass her only made him want more time with her. He watched her face as he flicked his thumb across her nipple. She inhaled sharply at first. As he circled the taut bud, her hips began to move.

She was a lovely sight, a mixture of innocence and seduction that was slowly driving him mad with lust. His hand moved to her other breast and teased the nipple until both were hard peaks. Only then did he bend down and fasten his lips around them, suckling first one, then the other. He used his tongue, and his teeth, to arouse.

Small cries of pleasure filled the area. With a nipple still in his mouth, he caressed down her stomach to her panties and then between her legs. His cock jumped when he felt the wet spot from her arousal.

It sent him over the edge. Myles turned his head away and closed his eyes as he struggled to get control.

"What is it?" Addison asked softly.

"I want you," he ground out.

"Then take me."

Her words, simply spoken, surprised him. He looked down at her and frowned. "I want to go slow, for you to savor every moment, but I want you too desperately. I can't do slow."

"Then don't."

CHAPTER

TEN

ADDISON WAS ON FIRE. Every place Myles touched made her ache, long for more.

His confession only made the flames of need grow higher.

With a moan—or was it a growl?—Myles jumped off the bed and jerked off his pants. Addison rose up on her elbows and stared open-mouthed at the magnificent specimen before her.

Myles was sculpted to perfection. Every muscle defined, every inch of sinew rock-hard. She rose up on her knees and reached for him. His hands were clenched at his side, his jaw locked as she ran her hands over his chest and shoulders. There were a few scars—more than he should have—on various places of his body. But she wasn't interested in the scars.

She was interested in him. In the skin so hot it scorched her, in the thick arousal that jutted between them. Addison looked at the muscles bulging in his arms and shoulders as she trailed her hand over his washboard stomach to his narrow waist. A quick glance showed his legs were as muscular as the rest of him.

Just as she began to close her hand around his cock, she found herself on her back. Excitement raced through her when he ripped her panties off and spread her legs. She trembled when he stared at her sex for long moments. Then he bent and licked her. She sighed, warmth spreading through her body. His fingers found her clit and rolled the nub between his fingers.

Addison moaned and clutched the covers. The pleasure was too much, the need too great. She felt as if her skin were too tight, as if her body couldn't hold in the ecstasy that threatened to shatter her.

"Open your eyes," Myles demanded in a gravelly voice. "Look at me."

She forced her lids open and met his gaze. He stood holding one of her legs in each hand. His rod jumped, brushing against her sex as he knelt on the bed. He released one of her legs so he could take himself in hand and guide his cock to her entrance. She swallowed loudly, her legs trembling with the need to wrap around his waist.

Addison bit her lip as he pushed inside her, stretching her. He shifted his hips twice, sinking farther each time. The third time, he plunged inside her, filling her fully. She cried out, her back arching at the pleasure that rocked through her. He fell over her, locking his arms around her. The next instant she was gathered in his arms as he began to drive hard and fast. She wrapped her arms and legs around him, meeting him thrust for thrust.

He was relentless, ruthless, as he pounded her body. She closed her eyes, desire tightening inside her and pushing her ever closer to the pinnacle of pleasure. She was reaching for it when it struck suddenly, sucking her breath with the force of the climax. Her body clamped around Myles's rod and convulsed repeatedly.

He rose up on his hands, his hips jerking faster. His bright blue eyes shifted to her. She was drowning in her climax and his eyes when they flashed yellow right before he threw back his head and shouted her name.

Her body was still pulsing with the orgasm when he pulled out of her. Seeing his cock wet with her pleasure and his seed made her realize they hadn't used any protection.

Myles fell to his back and reached for her. He tucked her against his body, their skin damp from the exertion. "I've not lost control like that in...well, ever."

"Ditto," she said with a smile. But it soon slipped. "Myles, we didn't use protection."

He was silent for a moment before his arm tightened around her. "I was so caught up in you, I didn't even think about it."

"Ditto," she said again.

"I'm sorry."

Addison turned her head to look at him. "It's just as much my fault. The blame doesn't rest on your shoulders alone."

He ran a hand down her hair. "You're one in a million, Addison Moore. I don't know what brought you into the bar, but I'm glad it did."

She looked down at his chest as she thought of that day that changed her life. "At the time, I thought it was the worst day of my life."

"Worst?" he asked with a frown. "Why?"

"I had just received a letter telling me I could no longer get financial aid for the fall semester."

"Get a student loan."

"I have several, all extremely large amounts, but they don't cover everything." She licked her lips and looked into his handsome face. "My mother died when I was four. I don't remember her at all except for pictures Dad kept for me."

"And your father?"

"A Navy pilot. He died when I was twelve in a training accident out in the Gulf. You know, I've never told anyone that," she said, wondering what made Myles so different.

He touched her face gently. "I'm sorry. I know what it's like."

"You had your brothers. I didn't have anyone."

"There was no family to take you in?" he asked, surprise

flickering in his blue eyes.

Addison shifted on her elbow, her hand bracing her head, so she could play with his ash-blond locks. "I was with my grandmother for two years before she died. My mother's brother took me in, but then he grew ill. They had three other children, and I knew I was a burden. I went to live with my dad's only surviving sister. I thought I was so lucky to remain near everyone."

"Did they mistreat you?"

"They never laid a hand on me. They were...cordial, but I never felt like I was a part of the family. They were very poor, but I didn't care. I had a house, food, and clothing. We scraped for every penny. I got a job as soon as I could just so I could have lunch money."

"My God."

She shrugged. "We weren't the only poor people, and compared to some, we were doing well."

"How long did you stay with them?"

"Until I graduated. Unbeknownst to them, I opened a bank account and was putting my money there. I had enough to cover an apartment, but not near enough for a semester of college. I then took a little over a year saving every penny I could. Once I had enough money, I registered at Tulane and found a roommate."

Myles put his other arm under his head. "This sounds like the start of a happy ending."

"It should've been." It was supposed to have been.

Addison swallowed and dropped her hand from his hair to rest on his chest. "I was able to get grants as well as student loans, but even all of that didn't cover everything. It took me working two jobs, which cut into how many hours I was able to take."

"Which extended when you should've gotten your degree," Myles guessed.

Addison flashed a grin. "Bingo! I applied for another grant over the summer for the fall semester. The day I came into Gator Bait for the first time was the day I got a letter stating that I wouldn't be receiving the grant since my family made too much money."

"What?" he asked, his brow furrowed deeply. "You just said—"

"I know," she interrupted him. "That was my thought as well, but the letter went on to explain that the government learned my aunt and uncle were actually part of a money laundering ring." She laughed lightly. "To think they could've paid for some of my college, that I didn't have to have two or three jobs to make ends meet, that I didn't have to sell my car, infuriates me."

"It should."

She fell onto her back and looked at the ceiling. "I didn't expect a lot from them, but if they had that kind of money, I would have only asked for a little bit of it."

"What now?" Myles asked as he rolled up on his elbow to look at her.

"I'm working and saving money so that I can hopefully return to Tulane for the spring semester. I only have a year left."

"You never said. What are you getting a degree in?"

"Accounting." At his smile, a burst of laughter left her. "I forgot you're an accountant."

He shrugged, grinning.

"Did you get your degree from Tulane?" she asked.

Myles leaned over and gave her a quick kiss. "We missed lunch, and I'm starving. How about you?"

"Yep," she answered as she watched him jump from the bed and pad naked into the kitchen area. She wondered why he hadn't wanted to answer her question about his degree.

She forgot about his non-answer as she looked her fill at his splendid body. If she thought he was going to cook, she was sadly mistaken. He got his phone and sent off a text.

"No cooking?" she asked when he turned back to her.

Myles laughed. "I burn everything I attempt to cook. I'm a disaster in the kitchen. It's so bad, Solomon has banned me from even thinking of cooking at the bar."

Addison laughed so hard her cheeks began to hurt.

"What?" he asked with a big grin. "You find that funny? Didn't you know there are those of us who can burn water?"

Unable to form words because of the laughter, she held up a hand, begging him to stop.

He was suddenly on top of her, his eyes twinkling with joy. "You have an amazing laugh."

"I've not laughed like that in a long time," she said when she was able.

"You should do it more."

Addison was about to agree if it meant Myles was there, but the idea of hoping whatever was between them would be long term was too soon. "You just like to see me laughing so hard I can't even talk."

"I like to see you laughing," he said suddenly turning serious. "I like to see you moaning. I like to see you climaxing."

Desire, only banked, flamed once again. With just words, he had her melting, aching for his touch. His head lowered, and she parted her lips for his kiss.

Just before their mouths met, something buzzed loudly throughout the room. Myles groaned in frustration and once more climbed off the bed.

He walked to an armoire that looked antique and opened the doors. He pulled on a pair of jeans. "Our food is here. I'm more than happy to see you naked, but if you want something to put on besides your clothes, feel free to dig in here. There are some old sweats."

Addison remained on the bed until the door slid closed behind him. Then she rose and made a beeline for the armoire. She found the old sweatpants, but opted for a pair of cut off sweats that she had to roll several times at the waist so they would remain on.

Beneath the cut offs was an old sweatshirt that had the

sleeves and neck removed. It wasn't until she pulled it on that she realized the bottom of the sweatshirt had been cut as well. The steel door opened and she was only able to glance down at herself before she heard an appreciative whistle.

"Now I know why I saved those," Myles said.

Addison smiled and faced him. "These look older than you. I'm thinking I shouldn't be wearing them."

"I told you to help yourself." He set the bag of food on the table. "Those were my father's. When he died, I couldn't fit into them, so I cut them until I could."

She knew she shouldn't have put them on. Addison started to remove them when Myles's hand wrapped around her wrist. How had he gotten to her so quickly across the large expanse?

"It's all right," he said softly. "They look good on you. Besides, they were just collecting dust."

Addison lowered her gaze to his chest and saw what looked like four scars cutting across his left side. The scars were old, and whoever stitched it had done a good job. "What happened?"

"You know how crazy Mardi Gras can get. Come on. Let's eat," he said and tugged her after him.

Addison was beginning to think there was much more to Myles than he was telling her. Then she recalled how his eyes flashed yellow.

The same yellow the wolf who saved her had.

CHAPTER

ELEVEN

MYLES WASN'T surprised when they finished eating the crawfish etouffee that Addison fell asleep midway through the movie she had chosen. He carefully lifted her in his arms and brought her to the bed. Myles laid her down and covered her with a sheet. Unable to turn away, he stared at her for several seconds.

Her short champagne-blonde hair fell against her cheek when she turned her head to the side. Myles gently moved the strands away. Somehow he'd known making love to Addison would eclipse anyone from his past. And it had.

She was sweet, tender, brave, courageous, beautiful, giving, and trusting. He didn't want to lie to her, but also wasn't ready to tell her who he was. It wasn't because he feared she wouldn't accept it. It was because he was terrified she would then want nothing to do with him.

Myles ran a hand through his hair and turned on his heel to clean up what was left of their meal. He didn't take the bar receipts from the previous night out of the bag as he should, but instead sat on the couch with his laptop.

Addison had told him some of her past, but he wanted to know more details. As difficult as it had been for her to share what she had, he was loathe to ask more. So, instead, he went to the internet.

It didn't take him long to find her father, Colonel James Moore, and the malfunction of his jet during a training exercise. There hadn't even been a body to recover. His search took a bit longer for Addison's mother since he didn't know her first name, but eventually he found where she died from ovarian cancer.

Addison's aunt and uncle took no time to learn about. The article he read explained how the couple had been under investigation by the FBI for years, and had been unable to get any proof until five years ago—when Addison left.

Fury burned within him. The idiots lived in poverty because they didn't want to share any of their stolen money with Addison. She worked herself to death just to make a better life when her family had the means to make it easier for her.

It was a good thing they were already in the custody of the FBI, because Myles seriously contemplated paying them a visit—in wolf form.

He wasn't rich, but he and his brothers were

comfortable, thanks to the money left them by their parents. The four of them had invested that money and recouped enough to buy the bar, leaving a little bit for each of them. Myles had invested his money once more and returned a much larger profit, which netted him the building. With his tenants, he was bringing in enough that he lived very comfortably.

Myles could give some money to Addison, but he knew she wouldn't take it. She had done everything herself so far, and she wouldn't stop now. He closed the laptop and set it aside. Then he rose and walked from window to window looking out to see if the wolves from the Moonstone pack had answered Kane's call.

A guy with dark hair reaching his jaw looked up from his post on the corner across the street and met Myles's gaze. Kane had the interaction with the pack outside of New Orleans, but Myles recognized another werewolf.

He nodded to the guy who quickly moved into the shadows. Myles found three more wolves stationed around the building. Normally, the LaRues handled whatever cropped up in the city themselves, but they learned the hard way that when it came to Delphine, they couldn't do it alone.

Ever since Delphine had taken over as priestess thirty years earlier, the Quarter had gone to shit. The tentative peace Myles's parents had instituted after five long years between the factions was destroyed in a single night.

The peace hadn't been the only thing wrecked. His family had been as well.

A sigh passed through his lips when he felt Addison's small hands wrap around him from behind. She rested her head on his back and held him tightly.

"You looked as if the weight of the world rested on your shoulders."

He covered one of her hands with his. "It feels that way at times."

"Want to talk about it?"

It was never spoken about, and maybe that was the problem. Maybe keeping it inside, letting it fester and rot only made things worse. "You never asked why we hate Delphine so much."

"There was mention of her cursing Kane." She shrugged. "I figured that was it."

Myles turned around in her arms and rested his hands on her small waist. "There are many reasons my brothers and I detest her. The fact she tortured one of our friends, Jack, for years, and then cursed Kane to try and kill Jack's daughter ranks pretty high. She also has an affinity for killing for the fun of it and keeping our city in constant terror."

"Why don't the police do anything?"

"She controls most of them."

Addison nodded slowly, a frown forming. "You want to kill her."

It wasn't a question. "More than anything."

"Why?" she whispered.

"Because she killed my parents."

ADDISON HADN'T BEEN PREPARED for such a statement. She stared up at Myles, trying to find the right words.

"My parents worked tirelessly to bring about an accord between the vampires, demons, witches, wolves, djinns, and those involved in Voodoo. It worked. After three months of peace, my parents left us behind and went out to celebrate."

She didn't want to hear any more, and yet she couldn't tell him to stop.

"The restaurant was one known as neutral ground for all the factions. Delphine blew it up."

"Oh God," Addison mumbled, feeling sick to her stomach.

"My parents were far enough from the blast they weren't killed, but badly injured. My father had a shard of steel in his leg, but he still carried my mother through the rubble outside."

Addison closed her eyes, but the picture Myles painted was clearly visible.

"Delphine and her people were waiting for anyone who tried to get away. My parents were killed by a knife to the heart." He snorted, a rueful smile playing upon his lips. "I was watching TV with Solomon when we heard, and felt, the explosion. We got Kane and Court up and went to see what happened. That's when we found my parents. They were facing each other, their hands linked. They looked so peaceful that at first I didn't believe they were dead."

Addison covered her mouth as tears seeped between her lids and fell upon her cheek. The horror that Myles and his brothers endured was beyond imagining.

"You can conceive the chaos such an event would cause, and yet Delphine, clad in her white clothes, stood with her people watching with a smile upon her face. I tried to kill her then, but Solomon held me back. He'd seen what I hadn't."

She blinked open her eyes and sniffed. "What?"

"Delphine sent men to kill us."

Addison shook her head, unable to fathom such a thing. "What? Why?"

"My parents weren't just powerful, they had a lot of influence in the city, and especially the Quarter."

The way he spoke, the conviction in his voice, spoke volumes. If his parents were so active with the supernatural factions, then that must mean they were somehow a part of it. Suddenly, Addison knew to the depths of her soul that Myles was a werewolf.

She licked her lips and wiped at the tears. "Y'all obviously got away from Delphine."

"Not without some help," he said, his eyes looking over her head and going distant, as if he were lost in the memories. "Our parents had a lot of friends. Some human, some not. Together, they got the four of us out of the Quarter. An old witch who was close to my mother did a cloaking spell that kept Delphine from finding us."

"Where did you go?"

Myles looked down at her. "We moved around constantly, just in case. It wasn't until all four of us were strong enough to take care of ourselves that we came back to the Quarter."

"Were your parents' friends still around to help?"

His lips thinned slightly. "A few. Most were killed by Delphine."

Addison backed up, leading him to the couch. She gave him a little push so that he sat, a small smile playing about his lips. It did her heart good to see even a hint of his smile. It meant the memories hadn't kept their stranglehold over him.

His arms snaked out and wrapped around her. He pulled her back, toppling her into his lap. They looked at each other, sharing a grin. Myles tucked a strand of hair behind her ear before tracing her ear with the pad of his finger.

"You've not asked," he said.

"Asked what?"

"What my parents were. What I am."

His voice was low, as if he hated saying the words. "Are you embarrassed by what you are?"

"No," he said forcefully. "Never."

"Good. I've not asked because it's easy to deduce that you're some faction of the supernatural."

His bright blue eyes narrowed on her. "Which one?"

She trailed her thumb over his lip and recalled the flash of yellow. "Wolf."

Surprise flickered in his eyes before the frown marred his face. "How did you know?"

"When we made love...your eyes flickered yellow."

Myles's jaw went slack. "What?"

"Didn't you know they did that?"

"No. They've never done that before."

Addison raised her brows. "And you're always looking in a mirror when you orgasm?"

"No," he said gruffly. "But it's something a woman would remark upon, right?"

She had to concede with him. "Right. What do you think it means?"

"I'm not sure. I've never heard of it happening before."

With a sigh, she rested her head on his shoulder. "You know why Delphine wants me, don't you?"

"I do," he replied softly.

"Tell me."

His arms came around her. "Remember when I told you she went after Jack's daughter?"

"Yeah. That's when she cursed Kane."

"Exactly. That daughter, Ava, is engaged to Riley's brother, Lincoln. They live in Lyons Point, near Lafayette, which has always been a hotbed of paranormal activity. It recently drew a witch who had been running from Delphine for years after watching Delphine kill her mother."

Addison clicked her tongue. "Delphine really needs to go and step on a Lego."

Myles burst out laughing, his chest shaking as it went on for a moment. He was finally able to take a deep breath. "Do you have even one mean bone in that body?"

"Yes."

"I doubt it," he said, still chuckling. "The witch, Davena, ended up being more powerful than Delphine expected."

"She wanted to kill Davena, too?"

"That's what we all thought, but it turns out Delphine wanted to recruit her. Davena told her to kiss off in no uncertain terms, while demonstrating just how strong her magic was."

Addison lifted her head, trying to connect all the dots. "I gather Delphine wasn't happy."

"Until now, there hasn't been anyone to challenge her. Davena fell in love with another of Riley's brothers, Beau, so has no interest in coming to New Orleans now. But she will."

"And Delphine is nervous," Addison surmised. "How does taking me help her? I don't have magic."

He rubbed his hand up and down her arm. "You are pure of spirit."

"What? Not possible. Trust me on this, Myles. I've done bad things."

"Name one," he dared.

She opened her mouth, searching her memories. "Oh! I once left without paying for my coffee."

He looked at her as if she were ludicrous. "That's the best you can come up with?"

"I've said mean things."

"Like the Lego statement?" he questioned. "That's not mean."

Addison pushed away from his chest and stood. "I'm not a good person. I've missed church, I've not left tips because I didn't have the money, I've said hateful things behind my aunt and uncle's backs. Oh! And I even cheated on an exam. Well, only two questions of it, but it was still cheating."

"You're adorable," he said with a sexy grin.

She plunked down on the wooden chest that served as a coffee table. "Why does she need someone pure in spirit?"

"Because with you and a witch, she can combine magic with purity and give a boost to her own power," he explained, his face gone serious.

Addison lifted her chin. "Fine. How do we stop her?"

CHAPTER

TWELVE

FOR HOURS, Myles walked the roof of his building. Addison had been like a dog with a bone. Once she learned the details, she wasn't content until she began to research. He gave up his computer and watched as she jotted page after page of notes from her findings. For his part, he was on the phone, calling friends to see if they could give him any more information than what the witch had already given him.

All he was able to discern was that Delphine was making waves with all the factions. No wonder the vampire came after Addison. The factions were worried, scared even. If Delphine gained more power, she would be unstoppable.

Myles braced his hands on the side of the roof and leaned over the side. The Moonstone wolves were still on guard, though they were doing a good job of remaining hidden.

They wouldn't be able to remain for long, however, since night approached, and it was still in the faze of a full moon.

He couldn't believe Addison guessed what he was. After everything he divulged about his past, he assumed she would piece it together that he was part of a faction. But she had been so sure of her answer.

With a shake of his head, Myles chuckled. He knew his eyes had never flashed yellow before. Did she know it was him that killed the vampire? Was that why she wasn't afraid?

His mobile rang. Myles withdrew it from his pocket and saw it was Solomon. "Hey."

"Hey yourself. How are things?" Solomon asked.

"They're quiet. Too quiet."

"I know. I feel it too." Solomon released a breath. "The Moonstone pack will have to leave soon. I don't like the idea of you being there alone if Delphine shows up."

Myles continued to walk the perimeter of the roof. "This entire block is warded, especially against her. She can't get in here. As long as Addison stays inside, she's safe."

"And you?" Solomon asked. "What about you?"

"We're werewolves, brother. We protect the city and keep the factions in line. We have few allies and many enemies. It's a fact that no one in the LaRue or Chiasson line lives long."

Solomon was quiet for a moment, the sounds of the kitchen at Gator Bait coming through the phone. A moment later the squeak of the back door sounded, and then silence.

If Solomon walked outside, then Myles wasn't going to like whatever he had to say.

"Spit it out," Myles said.

"I think Kane, Court, and myself should come help you."

Myles was flabbergasted. "And leave the Quarter unmonitored during a full moon? Have you lost your mind?"

"You've been looking at Addison for weeks, and today that wistful look changed to one of possession. Wolves mate for life, Myles."

"No shit," he said icily.

"There's a very real chance that no matter what we do, Addison could die. Today, tomorrow, next week. She's not going to stay holed up in your place for long. Delphine will kill her. Trust me, Myles, you don't want to go through that."

Myles sat on the edge of the roof. "You want me to walk away from her?"

"I wan—"

Solomon's words were suddenly cut off. Myles stood, apprehension flooding him. "Solomon?" he yelled.

The sound of boards breaking came through the phone, and then the growl of a wolf.

"Shit!" Myles turned around in a circle, unsure of what to do. He didn't want to leave Addison, but if Solomon turned in the middle of the day it was because he was ganged up on. And if Court and Kane were inside the bar, they would never know.

Myles slammed his hands down on the concrete of the

roof edge, cracking it from his supernatural strength. He drew in a breath and opened his eyes to see the dark-headed wolf staring up at him.

He pointed to the entrance to the building, telling the wolf to watch it, and then he turned and jumped from roof to roof, making his way to the bar. Myles landed at the back of the bar breathing heavily. One look showed that a fight had taken place. All but one side of the fence had been obliterated. There were bits of white fur and blood about.

He leaned his head back and sniffed. Yet, he couldn't pick up Solomon's scent outside of the bar. Myles strode to the back door and threw it open. As he entered, he turned his head to the right and found Solomon leaning over the sink, bare chested, washing blood off his arm.

ADDISON WINCED as she stretched her back. All of her research proved how dangerous a Voodoo priestess could be. Nothing she discovered gave her any hope that Delphine could be stopped with anything other than magic.

She rose from the table and walked around the space, stretching her neck from side to side. Myles had gone to the roof to have a look around. He was trying to make her think it was all going to be all right, but there was no denying things were on high alert.

Addison wished she had Minka's number. She'd give the

fortuneteller a call and see if there might be something she could do.

Her stomach rumbled loudly. A glance at the clock showed it was six in the evening. The sun wouldn't set for another two and a half hours, meaning there was plenty of light outside still. But it was dwindling quickly.

It was silly to think that evil only came at night, but darkness seemed to hide evil so well. She hadn't been scared in the daylight, but with each tick of the clock's hand, she was becoming more and more frightened.

Her cell phone rang, startling her so that she let out a small scream. When she reached for it in her purse, her hand was shaking.

"Hello?" she answered.

"Addison?"

She closed her eyes with joy at recognizing Myles's voice. "How do things look from the roof?"

"Normal. I called the bar for some food about ten minutes ago. It should arrive any moment. I want to make one more round before I come in."

"No problem. I'll get the food."

She disconnected the phone and set it by the laptop. She didn't bother with Riley's flip-flops as she opened the door and hurried down the three flights of stairs. Addison tried to look out the glass window of the entrance door, but she couldn't see anything. She then opened it a crack and poked her head outside.

Movement from her side had her turning her head toward it when something froze her muscles in place. She tried to scream, but her airway was closed off.

"What are you doing here?" Solomon demanded angrily when he spotted Myles.

Myles gaped at him. "We have the threat of Delphine, and you're attacked while on the phone with me, and you want to know what I'm doing here? You're such a prick."

Solomon wiped off his arms with a towel before he tossed it aside. "I'm fine. It wasn't anything I couldn't handle."

"Who was it?"

"Two demons."

Court and Kane walked into the kitchen and hurried to them. "What the hell?" Kane asked.

Solomon turned to the row of lockers behind him and opened one to pull out a shirt. "As I told Myles, it was just two demons."

"In the middle of the day?" Court asked incredulously.

Kane swung his head to Myles. "Did you leave Addison alone?"

"I don't plan on being here long," Myles said. "I'm returning now. And for the record, as I told Solomon, she'll be fine as long as she doesn't leave the building."

Solomon threw him a hard look. "You told Addison that, right?"

Myles started to say yes when he paused. Had he? He wasn't sure.

"Oh, fuck," Court mumbled.

Myles turned and ran out the back. He didn't bother going to the rooftops. He could get there just as fast on the sidewalks. His legs pumped hard as he went around throngs of people. He heard footfalls behind him and knew at least one of his brothers was with him. Myles didn't slow until he reached his building.

A glance across the street showed the werewolf was gone. "Damn," Myles muttered and quickly punched in the code to open the door.

He threw it open and raced up the stairs, Kane on his heels.

"Addison!" Myles shouted as he slid open the metal door.

Kane pushed passed him to the table. "Her phone is here."

"As is her purse, shoes, and clothes." Those were the only trace of Addison. "She's gone."

"The wolves might have saw something."

Myles wanted to hit something. "I left one watching the door, and he was gone."

"Griffin?"

"I don't know who the fuck he is!"

Kane came to stand in front of him and poked Myles in the chest. "You should. They're wolves, just like us."

"He's gone."

Kane made a sound at the back of his throat and walked out. Myles followed, shutting and locking the door behind him. The both of them walked outside.

Myles stopped at the door when he caught a strand of champagne-blonde hair mixed in the handle. Kane marched across the street. Myles looked up as he held the strand of Addison's hair in his fingers and saw Kane talking to two wolves. A moment later and Kane waved him over.

With a sigh, Myles walked to his brother and the Moonstone wolves. His mother had been a part of the pack, but after her death, the wolves scattered. Myles had never forgiven them for that. He hadn't been happy when five years ago they began to return to New Orleans.

"Tell him what you told me," Kane ordered them.

The youngest, a tow-headed teenager with eerie eyes so pale a blue they were almost white said, "We saw the woman taken by two men dressed in all white. Delphine was there as well. Griffin followed them so he could come back and let you know where she was."

"Did they hurt her?" Myles asked.

Another of the wolves with brown hair and deep-brown eyes nodded grimly. "Delphine did something to prevent her from moving, but your woman fought them."

His woman. Myles briefly closed his eyes as urgency pushed him. "I'm going to kill every last one of them."

"And I'll be there with you," Kane said.

The tow-headed wolf said, "We all will."

Myles frowned at the teenager. "Why? You don't know me or Addison."

It was the third wolf with a shaved head and tattoos peeking up from the neck of his shirt that shrugged. "Of course we do. Why do you think Griffin brought us back after our parents ran off? We shouldn't have left, and we're here to make up for the past."

"Just help me find Addison." Myles was in turns terrified and furious.

The emotions swirled through him with the force of a hurricane until he couldn't decipher one from the other. Like a fool, he'd kept away from Addison, and he refused to believe he was only meant to have one day with her.

Addison was his woman. Wolves did mate for life, and though she wasn't a wolf, his heart, his soul, his life was hers.

Myles nodded to the wolves. "Spread the word. Full moon or not, the Quarter is going to be invaded with us."

"Delphine still needs a witch," Kane said.

Solomon walked up with Court. "Which she already has."

"It's all over the Quarter," Court said miserably. "The

witch was reading palms and went to get something to drink and never returned."

Myles lifted his head when he heard a wolf's cry pierce the night.

"Griffin is calling," said the tow-headed wolf.

The wolf within Myles wanted free, to wreak havoc on those who would threaten what was his. "Then let's find him."

CHAPTER

THIRTEEN

MYLES ROUNDED the corner of a building a half mile from his place and spotted a shape move away from the shadows. The dark-headed wolf he'd seen earlier walked toward him.

Griffin looked to his men and gave a nod. "I wondered if you would believe my men or not."

"I told you we would," Kane said.

Griffin stared at Myles with his green eyes. "I followed Delphine. They've taken your women to a cemetery."

"Which one?" Myles demanded.

"St. Louis number one."

Solomon snorted. "Of course. It's where the Voodoo Queen, Marie Laveau, is buried."

"She's going to channel Marie," Kane murmured with a curse.

Myles didn't take his gaze from Griffin. "Delphine and

her people likely heard your call. They'll be on the lookout for any wolf."

"Not if some of my men lead them away." Griffin pointed to the black-headed werewolf. "Jaxon and a small group will cause a distraction for us."

"And me," replied the tow-headed teenager. Myles figured he was just sixteen since he hadn't filled out as weres did in their late teens.

"Colt," Griffin said with a warning look. "I need you to return to the pack and get as many wolves as will come." Griffin's gaze swung to Myles. "I'm guessing the LaRues want to make an impact."

Solomon moved forward so that he stood beside Myles. "Without a doubt."

"This is going to cause a shit storm for sure," Court said.

Kane shrugged. "Everyone can kiss my sweet ass for all I care."

Myles turned his head to look at Kane. He missed his reckless brother that had been more concerned with women and drink than their family legacy. What Delphine had done to him with her curse had changed Kane. He was still reckless, but there was a carelessness about him, one that said it didn't matter if he lived or died. One that screamed retribution and vengeance.

Myles was glad he wasn't on the receiving end of Kane's fury, because Kane was a man with a mission, and nothing and no one would be able to stop him.

Why hadn't they realized it before? They should've recognized the lethal gleam in his eyes, or perhaps Kane had just gotten good at hiding it.

"The distraction needs to be big enough to cause Delphine to worry," Myles warned.

Griffin smiled menacingly. "I think setting her temple on fire might do it."

"Uh, yeah that'd do it," Court said with a grin.

Myles wished now he had gone out to the Moonstone camp and seen the weres. "How many do you think you can get?"

"All of them," Colt stated with conviction.

Griffin nodded in agreement. "They've been waiting for just such an event."

"What are you thinking?" Solomon asked Myles.

Myles looked at his brothers and grinned. "I'm thinking one of Dad's strategies. Surround and conquer."

"Simple, but efficient." Solomon gave a nod of approval. "It's worked before."

Myles looked back at Griffin. "Timing is everything. Delphine expects me and my brothers. I want your pack to hold back and wait for our signal."

"What will the signal be?" Griffin asked.

Kane slapped him on the back. "Trust me, you'll know."

With a look, Griffin sent Colt and Jaxon on their missions. The third wolf remained, moving to stand just behind Griffin.

"Give my wolves some time to get into place," Griffin said.

Myles looked at the sky and the growing darkness. "That might not be an option."

"Delphine won't start the spell until midnight."

Court crossed his arms over his chest. "And just how do you know that?"

"I know a lot about Delphine." Griffin looked over his shoulder at the other were. "We know a lot." He turned back to the LaRues. "This is my brother, Gage. Delphine didn't just turn our parents into mindless wolves that we had to kill ourselves, but she has our sister."

Myles drew in a deep breath. "No wonder you were so eager to help us with Delphine."

"Our parents made a mistake in running away the night Delphine went on a killing spree. Worse, they shouldn't have left the four of you behind."

Solomon was stony-faced as he said, "We turned out all right."

Myles couldn't stand around talking any more. He had to see Addison for himself, to know she hadn't been harmed yet. "I'm going to the cemetery."

"Not now," Kane said with a hand on his arm.

Myles looked from his hand to Kane's blue eyes. "Try and stop me."

"He's right," Griffin stated. "If you arrive now, it could ruin your plan."

Solomon turned on his heel. "I think there's another faction we need to talk to before we confront Delphine."

Myles hesitated while Court, Griffin, and Gage followed Solomon. After a moment, Kane released him and also followed. Myles blew out a frustrated breath and fell into step with the rest.

ADDISON WOKE to the pounding of her head. She tried to grab her head, but her arms were jerked to a stop at her side. A look down confirmed that she was tied with thick, coarse rope that already cut into her skin, rubbing it raw.

She laid her head back and looked up at the clear sky after glancing from one direction to the other at the huge stone monuments. The cemetery. Great. She wondered what she was laying on, then thought it was better if she didn't know.

Addison tried to yank against the ropes, which only made her wrists bleed.

"Don't bother. You won't get anywhere," said a recognizable voice.

She looked around but didn't see Minka. "Where are you?"

"Behind you. For now."

That sounded ominous. "How are you here?"

"Funny thing, that," she said sarcastically. "I heard

rumors about Delphine's plan, and even shared those with Myles. I didn't know I was the one she would take for my magic."

Fear snaked through Addison, turning her blood to ice. "Surely you can get us out of here, right? You have magic."

"I have visions."

"Obviously you have more than that," Addison argued. "Why else would you be taken?"

"How very astute of you, Addison," Delphine said, her voice seemingly all around them.

Addison turned her head to the left and saw Delphine's white dress seconds before her face came into view.

Delphine smiled and came to stand beside her. "It won't be long now, girls. Soon you'll be free of this world. You'll be doing something for the good of the Quarter."

Minka snorted loudly. "Just shut up with your crap. You're a murderer any way you look at it."

"That's right, Minka," Delphine said sharply. "Because every leader must sacrifice individuals for the good of the cause."

"Do people actually believe that drivel?"

Addison tried to turn her head when Delphine walked behind her, but Addison could only catch a glimpse of white.

"I can make your death easy, or I can make it hard," Delphine said in a hard voice to Minka. "You choose, witch."

"I'm not a witch!" Minka shouted.

Delphine chuckled, the sound getting louder as it went

on. "Oh, how your family has lied to you. Do you think you were chosen on a whim? You have untapped potential they've been keeping from you."

"Don't believe her," Addison said to Minka.

Delphine's laugh was as hollow as her soul. "She better listen to me. There are many witches to choose from, but it was you I wanted. Imagine my surprise as I plotted to kidnap you, and one of your elders came to me."

If Addison was shocked, she could only imagine what Minka was feeling.

"It seems," Delphine continued, "that she was afraid of you taking over. She offered you in exchange for me leaving your coven alone for the next twenty years."

There was a squeak of rope before Minka said, "Liar."

But there was no heat in her words, as if she knew what Delphine said was true. Addison knew that feeling of betrayal, of having family turn their backs.

"And you, Addison." Delphine tsked and returned to stand beside her. "I didn't think a phone call pretending to be Myles would work with you. How easily you were captured. Did Myles tell you his entire building was warded against me?"

Addison felt sick to her stomach. She should've known not to go outside. Myles would never have sent her down for food. What an idiot she was. And now, she was smack in the middle of something she didn't want a part of.

"To think of the lengths he went to in order to keep me

from you." Delphine shook her head, her long black hair falling around her. "Tonight's ceremony is going to be one remembered for ages."

Addison glared up at the priestess. "Myles will come for me. He'll find me."

"Are you sure? A werewolf can't be trusted. I know, because it was one of my ancestors who cursed the LaRues into werewolves hundreds of years ago."

"He'll come." At least Addison hoped he would. They had shared their bodies only once. That didn't constitute a commitment, and yet she felt sure Myles would at least look for her.

Delphine turned and walked away, her laughter fading with her.

"Don't listen to a word that bitch says," Minka said.

Addison pulled on the ropes again. "Like you didn't listen to her?"

"Because I know what she said is the truth."

Addison stilled, her eyes widening. "You know who betrayed you?"

"There are five elders of our coven. That narrows things down significantly. I didn't want to be a witch," Minka said softly. "I was unable to do the simplest of spells, but I had visions."

Addison was quiet for a minute. "You spoke to Myles?"

"I knew he wouldn't tell you," Minka said with a loud sigh. "Men can be so...stupid sometimes."

She took exception to that. Myles wasn't stupid. "He told me about Delphine's plan. He just didn't tell me how he heard of it. When did he talk to you?"

"This morning. Just in case you don't know it, that man has it bad for you."

That brought a smile to Addison's face. "The feeling is mutual."

"Yeah, I figured. Do you know who he really is?"

"He's a werewolf."

"Well aren't you the smart one of the bunch."

Addison heard the smile in Minka's voice. "He'll come for me."

"Everything you've heard about wolves is true, Addison. Nothing will stop him from getting to you. Nothing."

"Delphine will kill him."

"Remember what I told you about the hunters? The ones who guard the city? The LaRues are those hunters. If there is anyone who can find a way, it's them."

Addison tried to swallow, but her mouth was bone dry. "I hope you're right."

"I am," Minka whispered. "I have to be."

FOURTEEN

It had taken two excruciating hours to talk three of the five witch covens and the Blood Mark pack into joining them. The witches hadn't been thrilled with the idea of joining two wolf packs, but the thought of Delphine gaining more power eventually swayed them.

"Stop pacing," Court said. "You're giving me a headache."

Myles threw him a dark look.

Kane gave a dismissive shake of his head. "It's the growling that's getting on my nerves."

"Leave it," Solomon said to Court and Kane.

Myles leaned against the building as his gaze stared at the entrance to the cemetery. Was this how Solomon had felt when his woman was taken from him? His heart clutched, because Myles knew he wouldn't survive if Addison was killed. How did Solomon bear the crushing weight?

"Just a little longer," Griffin said from beside Myles.

Myles looked at the leader of the Moonstone wolves. "Do you have a mate?"

"No," Griffin said with a laugh. "My father told us kids that we'd know when we found ours. I'm still searching."

"I didn't want one. Hell, I don't even know if she wants to be mine." Myles ran both hands down his face.

Solomon glanced at him from his position at the corner of the building. "She wants you. Trust me on that."

"Yep," Court said, nodding.

Kane stretched his neck from side to side. "We've seen it with our own eyes. She's yours, Myles."

"It's time," Griffin said and pushed away from the wall.

Myles felt his own wolf push against him. He began to remove his clothes, his breaths coming quicker and quicker. Griffin threw back his head as bones began to break and reform into that of a wolf.

The pain of the shift was indescribable. It battered them from all sides, taking their breath and ripping them from the inside out. Myles's wolf rose up quickly. Urgency pushing him, driving him.

He fell to his hands and knees. For the first time he didn't feel any pain. His thoughts were centered on Addison. And killing Delphine.

When he opened his eyes he watched his brothers finish their transition. He saw the solid white fur of Solomon. Next to him was a wolf of inky black—Kane. On the other side of Solomon was Court with his tawny fur.

Another wolf trotted up. Myles eyed the mottled gray fur of Griffin. Griffin stared at Myles for a moment before swinging his gaze toward the cemetery.

Out of the corner of his eye, Myles saw Solomon's ears flick. Myles lifted his head and listened. Only one other time in the history of the city had wolves descended upon it en masse as they were now. Tonight, the wolves weren't there to claim dominance, but to free two innocents and stop a priestess.

It felt like an eternity before he smelled the first flames. Soon, sirens from the fire department and the police rang out through the city.

Myles and his brothers hid behind the building, the shadows deep enough to conceal them thoroughly. He peered around the corner and spotted one of Delphine's men, dressed in all white, come to the entrance of the cemetery to see what was going on.

Beside Myles, Kane growled, the sound rumbling through his chest. Solomon nudged Kane with his head to silence him.

The man ran back inside the cemetery, and just seconds later he and three others ran out and got into a car to drive off. That lessened who they had to fight by four, but Myles wasn't concerned with Delphine's followers. He was apprehensive about her.

One wrong move would seal all their fates.

He hadn't forgotten Minka's prediction of his death. If it happened that night, Myles wanted it to be after Addison was freed. He had to be smart, cunning, and ruthless. Those were the only traits that would save his woman.

Myles looked at his brothers. They lined up side-by-side and walked out of the shadows, through the parking lot, and across the street. They each had their destinations. Once they passed through the tall iron gate, they split up, slinking quiet as death around the tombs. Delphine's evil stench was suffocating, but it made her easy to track.

Myles went all the way to the back of the cemetery, and then made his way toward Delphine, hoping he'd be the one to find Addison. His steps slowed when he heard Delphine's voice chanting. He shifted to his right and moved stealthily toward her. Myles leapt atop a tomb and crawled on his belly to the edge.

Delphine was without the white turban. Her hair was loose and hanging around her deep umber skin. Where normally she was covered almost head to foot in white, this night she wore a white tank top that was thin enough to see her nipples. Her skirt was long, but sheer.

Myles had to force himself to remain still when he heard Addison's voice. A second later she came into view with a man on either side of her, holding her. Minka was also held by two men as she was brought after Addison.

Delphine slowly raised her hands above her head. Flames

surged, encircling the seven of them. Minka kicked one of the men, who backhanded her so hard she fell to the side, narrowly missing the flames.

"Minka!" Addison yelled.

The men hauled Minka back up, blood running from her lip. Delphine began to sway, her eyes closed and the words coming faster. One by one, her followers appeared seemingly out of nowhere to form a large circle. They clapped slowly and hummed. Delphine's eyes suddenly opened, shining with an unholy red light. She pointed first one hand at Addison and the other at Minka.

Myles growled in fury when Addison's entire body jerked and her lids fell closed. Minka mimicked her a second later. The men stepped back and out of the flaming circle, since both girls were now controlled by Delphine.

Delphine's voice grew louder, her words indecipherable. Myles could only watch as both Addison and Minka fell straight back. But they never hit the ground. They were stiff when their legs lifted, tilting their bodies horizontally.

"Our temple is on fire!" shouted a male voice.

Delphine stopped chanting and slowly looked around. "Our home must be saved."

There was commotion as half of the men and a few women rushed out of the cemetery to help put out the fire. By the way Delphine studied every shadow, she suspected the fire had been a diversion.

Myles hoped to catch her unawares, but that was no

longer an option. She would be on guard now, prepared for whatever came at her.

She focused on Addison and Minka again and walked to stand between them. Delphine touched Minka's forehead and skimmed her hand down her body to her toes. Then Delphine repeated the movement with Addison, unfamiliar words spilling from her lips all the while.

He snarled, his lips lifting. The hate was unbearable. It consumed him, devoured him. It kept him going for years, but if he let it take him completely now, there would be no room for any other emotion like...love.

Delphine held her hands out in front of her, palms up. Out of nowhere a curved blade made of bone appeared in her palms. Holding it in one hand, her other traced it as if it were an object to be worshiped.

When she held the bone blade high, her remaining flock sent up a cheer and continued clapping in a rhythm. Delphine turned to Addison first and gripped the bone in both hands above her head, preparing to plunge it in Addison's chest.

Myles leapt from atop the tomb between the worshippers and the fire, growling fiercely. Kane, Solomon, and Court each walked from their hiding places, their growls mixing with his. Delphine's people quickly moved to make paths for his brothers until they also stood at the fire facing the priestess.

"I knew you would come," Delphine said as she looked at each of them. "Which one of you is Myles?"

It was Court who snapped his jaws at her in response.

Delphine laughed. "Oh, this is just too simple. How silly of you LaRue boys to think the four of you could stop me. I'll kill these girls, and then I'll make sure to end the LaRue line once and for all."

Myles looked at Solomon from across the fire and nodded. Myles, Court, and Kane turned and charged Delphine's followers. Their screams filled the air. Though they never sank their teeth into a single one of them, their screams said otherwise.

With their signal shouting from the rooftops, Myles turned back to Delphine who stood glaring at Solomon. Just as Myles expected, the bitch was taking the bait. Because in her mind, only he would be the one to stand guard watching over Addison.

And Myles was, just not in the way she expected.

The screams of her followers intensified as Griffin's pack filled the cemetery, with the witches right behind them. Myles threw his head back and let loose a howl.

Delphine turned in a circle staring in confusion and anger at the witches and wolves closing in on her people, standing atop tombs and filling the spaces.

"Enough!" Delphine shouted.

One young witch with dark red hair standing atop the tomb Myles had been on spread her fingers as she held her arms out at her sides. "You don't rule us. You'll never rule us."

The other witches spread their arms wide until they made one huge circle. Their eyes were locked on Delphine while they focused their magic. Delphine had no choice but to fight them.

It was time for the wolves. Myles was the first to launch himself over the flames and tackle Delphine to the ground. Right before he turned to go to Addison, he felt something sharp sink into his shoulder. Myles turned and snapped, but Solomon, Court, and Kane were already atop Delphine. Griffin soon joined in the fray.

Myles limped to Addison. He watched in surprise as both the girls dropped to the ground. Delphine had to conserve her power for herself, which freed Addison and Minka. He saw the blood on Addison's wrists and licked them to help spur the healing. When he lifted his head, her hazel eyes were open and looking at him.

"You came." She smiled and ran her hand over his head, sinking her hands in his fur. "I knew you'd come."

Myles nuzzled her until she had both hands around his neck. Then he stepped back and helped her into a sitting position.

"Nice trick there, wolf," Minka said with a groan. "Who the hell is going to help me?"

Addison reached over and helped Minka. Myles took the

hem of Addison's shorts in his mouth and tugged, trying to tell her they needed to go.

"I think that means we've got to go," Minka said.

Addison glanced at the wolves attacking Delphine. "Yeah. The sooner the better."

Solomon bumped against Minka and loped away. Minka quickly followed him. Myles ignored the pain of his wound and waited for Addison. As he ran behind her, he ensured there wouldn't be any other surprises from Delphine that night.

While Solomon ran them through the city down quiet streets until they were out of the city and into the bayou, Myles saw Griffin and his wolves with them. The girls would never make it to the Moonstone camp, and Myles didn't want Addison there anyway. He let out a sound that brought Solomon to a halt.

Minka and Addison stumbled to a stop, their hands on their knees as they bent over sucking in air. Myles circled them trying to think of a place to take them, because he wasn't sure how much longer he could keep going. His wound was weakening him significantly. Something that would only happen if silver were used.

Myles looked at Addison. At least she was out of Delphine's grasp now. There was no sense in telling his brothers of his wound. Nothing could help him now. He was dying, slowly, but surely.

Griffin and his wolves spread out, checking the bayou

while Solomon remained on point, too concerned about an attack to realize anything was wrong.

After a moment, Minka lifted her head and looked at Addison. "I know a place we can go."

"Where?" Addison asked breathlessly.

Minka straightened, a sad look coming over her. "The old Gilbeaux plantation. Or what's left of it."

Solomon let out a low growl and shook his head. Myles had to agree. That place wasn't fit for animals, much less the girls.

"It's where I'm going," Minka stated determinedly. "There's no other place for me. I can't go back to the Quarter."

Addison looked up then and shoved her short champagne locks out of her face. "No. There's no going back to those who betrayed you. What about one of the other covens?"

Minka was shaking her head before Addison finished. "Not possible."

"All right then." Addison slid her gaze to him. "We need to go to the Gilbeaux plantation."

Myles sighed and turned west, their course set.

CHAPTER
FIFTEEN

NOW THAT THEY had escaped the Quarter, Addison's feet were throbbing. She was afraid to look down and see the damage done. They had been walking for another hour, and she was weary to her bones.

Myles suddenly bumped against her, halting her. Was it her imagination, or was he limping? Addison looked up from the ground and heard the roar of an engine. Suddenly, wolves closed in tight around her and Minka. She tried to hold onto Myles, but he slipped away, going to stand in front of the pack with a white wolf and a gray one.

A 4x4 truck drove through the pasture they were crossing and came to a sliding stop. The headlights blinded her, but Addison was able to shield her eyes enough to see the door of the truck open.

"Which of my asshole cousins thought it would be a good idea to leave me out of things?"

"Riley?" Addison said with a smile. "Is that you?"

"Addison? Are you all right?" Riley asked and jumped from the truck. She raced to her, the wolves instantly moving out of the way. Riley wrapped her arms around her and held tight.

"Yes, thanks to Myles and all the other wolves."

Riley stepped away. Her smile dropped as she glared at Myles and the white wolf. "That was shit. If I hadn't saw the group of witches walking down the street talking about all the wolves, I'd never have known. Then I found these two jerks," she said with a thumb over her finger.

Just then a black wolf and one with tawny fur loped up.

"But that's family business," Riley said taking notice of all the other wolves. "Y'all must be from the Moonstone pack Kane talks about. Thanks for helping." Riley then shifted her eyes back to Addison. "Where are y'all headed?"

"The old Gilbeaux plantation," Minka said.

"Y'all look like death warmed over. Get in the truck. I'll drive while you give directions. There's some bottled water inside."

Minka didn't have to be told twice. She hurried to the 4x4 and climbed in the passenger side back door. Addison took a step and winced at something sticking in her foot.

"You don't have shoes?" Riley asked in consternation.

Addison shrugged. "I was taken without them."

Riley linked Addison's arm around her shoulder and helped her limp to the truck. Addison got in and saw Myles standing by her door.

"Want to ride?" He took a step back, causing her to laugh. "I'm fine. Let's just get to the plantation."

Once Myles trotted off and all the wolves disappeared into the trees, Addison closed her door and let out a sigh. She shut her eyes while Minka directed Riley through backwoods roads to the plantation. Addison didn't need to look. She knew Myles was near.

The certainty of that, of knowing that he would be there for her, was as calming as it was wonderful. She'd never been able to say that about anyone before, and she was hesitant to even think it with him.

It wasn't because he was a werewolf and changed with the moon. It was because of who he was, what he did. He fought for the innocents of the Quarter, which meant putting his life in danger every day.

Her father had done the same, and look how he ended up. As much as that bothered her, Addison knew she couldn't walk away from Myles.

He was everything she hadn't even known she wanted or needed. His gentleness with her, coupled with his unwavering loyalty and defense of her against someone as evil as Delphine was staggering.

She didn't know where their relationship might lead, but she certainly wanted to find out.

"How does it feel to be the woman of a wolf?" Riley asked.

Addison opened her eyes and smiled. Minka shoved a bottle of water at her that she opened and drank deeply from. "It feels...right. Is that how it's supposed to feel?"

"I don't know," Riley said. "I think that could be the right answer for any couple."

"I just don't want to read too much into things. I suppose Myles was just doing his duty as a hunter."

Minka gave a snort of laughter. "Girl, I'm seriously about to knock you in the head. Didn't we have this conversation in the cemetery?"

"Yeah," Addison said. "It's just, everyone I've ever wanted in my life has left me. I don't want to lose him."

Riley shot her a smile. "The only way you would lose Myles is if you told him you didn't love him, and even then, it would take months of him attempting to get you back and you refusing before he thought about giving up. Once a wolf chooses who is his, there's no going back."

"Really?" Addison asked as she sank further in the seat.

Minka leaned up between the two front seats. "Really."

Addison let that knowledge settle into her mind—and her heart. It was almost too much to hope for to think that she found someone who wouldn't leave her.

"Chiasson blood runs through his veins just as much as LaRue," Riley said as she continued to drive. "It was a Chiasson who left France and settled in Nova Scotia for a while, bringing his sister and two brothers with him. They eventually made their way down to Louisiana. He settled in Lyons Point while his brothers decided to go different directions to see what the country held."

Addison was transfixed listening to the history of the Chiasson and LaRue families.

Riley smiled as she glanced at Addison and then at Minka. "His sister came to New Orleans with him on a trip and fell in love with a LaRue. She married and taught her husband how to hunt the paranormal."

"I wondered how the LaRues came to be hunters," Minka said as she sat back.

The truck bounced over some deep holes on the dirt road as Riley shrugged. "Being in New Orleans has its perks, but also its drawbacks. Namely, all the beings with some form of supernatural abilities."

"I take exception to that," Minka said, but there was no heat in her words.

Addison turned in her seat and said, "Yeah, but you're not trying to kill people. I think Riley is talking about them."

"I am," Riley said. "We have witches in Lyons Point. Hell, Beau is dating one. But I think it's the mix of all the beings in New Orleans that is so different. You see, one of the LaRue children did something to incur the wrath of a Voodoo priestess."

"Oh my God," Minka said with a sigh. "What is it with the LaRues and the priestesses?"

Riley shook her head. "I wish I knew. I don't know what happened to cause the Voodoo priestess to become so angry, but in response, she placed a curse on all LaRues to become werewolves."

Addison turned the water bottle in her hand. "How long will the curse be in place?"

"Forever," Riley and Minka replied in unison.

Addison was outraged. "Are you kidding? That's a little extreme, don't you think?"

"Damn straight," Minka mumbled.

Riley twisted her lips. "My cousins have managed to use it to their advantage. They've befriended witches who have used spells to help them be able to shift whenever they choose instead of only on a full moon. It comes in handy while they hunt in the Quarter."

Minka leaned up again and pointed out the windshield. "There's a live oak with its branches growing on the ground. Take a left there."

Addison peered through the darkness to where the headlights penetrated the night and spotted the gnarly limbs of the large tree having grown so heavy that they did indeed touch the ground.

Riley slowed the truck and turned to the left just as Minka instructed. They rode in silence along the narrow road with thick brush growing up on either side as Myles and the white wolf ran ahead of the truck.

"Damn, girl," Riley said to Minka. "Just how far back in

the bayou are we going? This isn't a road. It's a path that hasn't been used in years."

There was silence as Minka remained leaning forward between the two front seats. "It was my great-aunt's. She never joined the coven. She didn't trust them or agree with their methods. So she moved off to St. Louis for many years before she returned. She did it without any of the others knowing she was here, and she kept to herself."

"Do the witches get mad if others don't join the coven?" Addison asked.

Minka nodded. "Especially when the coven is made up of family."

Riley and Addison exchanged a quick look.

"My aunt lived out her days on this land in peace," Minka explained. "She left it to me when she died four years ago. I pay someone to keep the place up."

At that moment the brush cleared and what was left of a white plantation house came into view.

"Please tell me you're not staying there," Addison said when she spotted the second-floor porch caving in.

Minka chuckled. "Nope."

"There's nothing else but land and water," Riley said as ash slowed the truck to a stop.

Addison looked outside to find Myles watching them. She started to smile, but it slipped when she saw something wet on at his shoulder. Her heart missed a beat. "Please tell me that's water and not blood."

"What?" Riley asked as she looked from Addison to outside. There was a short pause before she said, "It's blood."

"He should've healed already," Minka said. "Unless…"

She trailed off, which made Addison jerk around. "Unless what? What aren't you telling me?"

"Unless silver was used," Riley whispered.

Addison slowly turned back around, but Myles no longer stood in the headlights. "I just found him. I can't lose him."

"Once silver is in their bloodstream, there's no way to stop it. I'm sorry."

"I told him to be careful," Minka said.

Addison squeezed her eyes closed. "You saw his death, didn't you?"

"Yes. I didn't know when it would happen though," Minka added.

Addison opened her eyes. "I'm not going to give up so easily. I just found him. I can't lose him."

She opened the door, ending the conversation. As soon as she did, Myles and the white wolf stood there.

Minka wasted no time in getting out of the truck and walking to Myles. "Idiot. This needs to be seen to."

The white wolf gave a low growl as he noticed the wound. Myles ignored both as he stared at Addison. Addison slid from the truck. She limped to Myles and touched him while Minka stood and walked to the water.

Riley shut off the engine. "I really hope she's not wanting to go across the bayou."

"Let's find out." Addison shut the door and winced as she shifted her weight.

The driver's side door shut and Riley came around the front, her body cutting in front of headlights that hadn't shut off yet. She looked down at Addison's feet and frowned. "You're not going anywhere."

"I'm not staying here either."

Riley smiled and turned to open the back passenger door of the truck. "It's a good thing I always carry extra stuff with me." She dug in the back of the truck for a moment and straightened with another pair of flip-flops. "They're not optimal for trekking in the bayou, but it's better than bare feet."

"Do you always travel with your closet?" Addison asked with a grin.

"I grew up hunting, and I hate to walk around in wet shoes, so I keep extra in my purse."

Addison took a moment to use the light from inside the truck's cabin to clean off her feet and pull out some stickers and a piece of glass. Even with the shoes on, her feet hurt, but at least now they were protected.

"They're going to need seen to when we get back to the Quarter," Riley said.

As if to agree, Myles nudged her arm with his cold, wet nose. She smiled and sank her hand into the fur at his neck. She'd seen a wolf at the zoo once, and she knew the werewolves were more than twice their size.

"You should've told me you were hurt," she admonished Myles.

"Oh. Time to go," Riley stated and walked away.

Addison looked to see Minka turn to the left and walk away from the plantation. The white wolf walked beside Minka, and Addison saw two other wolves dart out of the brush and follow.

She couldn't wait to learn who was who. If she had to guess, Solomon was the white wolf. She knew which one was Myles, and that's all that mattered.

Addison walked as fast as she could with her injured feet to follow Minka and Riley. She was grateful for the shoes when the trail took her through some woods. Myles, limping as well, remained beside her.

All around her were wolves. They made no sounds, but she caught glimpses of them from time to time. With her hand on Myles, she felt safe and comforted. Who knew that could happen with a werewolf?

Addison stepped out of the forest and came to a stop when she saw the old house built on stilts over the bayou, the water gently lapping at the wooden pillars while the moon cast everything in a pale-blue glow.

Myles nudged her. She startled, and began walking again. Addison eyed the water and the dark shapes she saw.

God, please let this house be in better condition than the plantation. It would be so wrong to be saved from Delphine to die by alligator.

CHAPTER
SIXTEEN

MYLES WAS at the porch looking out over the water a half hour after dawn. He and the other wolves had gone into the forest to shift back. He hated leaving Addison, but he wasn't sure she was ready to see all of that quite yet. Not to mention, he wanted a look at his wound first.

Addison slept like the dead after Minka put some salve on her feet and added some herb to her sweet tea, otherwise he knew she'd have been right there with him. Myles had remained near, patrolling the porch that went all the way around the small house even as his wound festered.

The wound itself was ugly, black lines branching out as the silver continued to poison him. He had no idea how much longer he had. Every breath was a struggle, but he fought because he wasn't ready to leave Addison.

"Where did you get the clothes?" Minka asked as she

came out onto the porch. She sat in one of the wooden chairs and drew her knees up to her chest.

"The truck Riley drove was Kane's. We always keep clothes for such occasions."

"Lucky for you." Minka's smile was soft, sad. "How are you feeling?"

"Like shit," he said. He sighed loudly. "I never saw the blade. I knew Delphine had a bone knife in her hand, but there wasn't a silver one."

Minka dropped her feet to the ground and leaned forward in the chair. "Let me look at it. I might be able to do something."

"You know as well as I that nothing can be done."

"Let her look."

Myles felt his heart plummet to his feet as he heard Addison's voice. He'd remained to see her, but now that she was awake, he knew it would've been better had he went off to die alone.

"Please," Addison said. "Let her try if she can."

Myles couldn't form any words. When Addison came to stand beside him, her arms wrapped around one of his, there wasn't anything she could ask for that he would deny her.

"Am I yours?" she asked.

Myles turned his head to look down into her hazel eyes. "For now and always."

"Then I'll fight for you, just as you fought for me."

He shifted so that he faced her, careful to keep his wound

on his left shoulder as hidden as he could. "I don't want to give you false hope."

"It's better than giving up," she replied softly. "Myles, against everything, we found each other. I can't explain the attraction or the..." she paused and swallowed loudly. "The love I have for you. I don't want it to end."

As if he would die now without fighting. Myles touched her cheek. "My sweet, Addison. You stole my heart the day you walked into the bar. I desired you, longed for you with such hunger. Then I got a taste of you. I didn't want you in my heart, but you found your way there anyway. Wolves mate for life."

Her eyes were shining with unshed tears. "So I've been told."

"You're mine," he said thickly.

"Then don't leave me."

Minka rose suddenly. "Great. So y'all love each other. Let's get down to business. Addison, go into the kitchen and look in the lower cabinet next to the sink. You'll see a wooden box. Bring it. Myles," she said and pointed to the chair she vacated. "Remove your shirt and sit."

Myles stared after Addison as he did as Minka bade. He ground his teeth together while trying to pull off his shirt. Suddenly, someone gripped the neck of the tee and ripped it in half. He turned and saw Kane beside him.

"This looks like shit," his brother said of the wound.

Myles shrugged his good shoulder. "Feels like it, too."

Boot heels sounded on the porch, and a moment later Solomon and Court were standing in front of him. Myles couldn't hold the gazes of his brothers. He couldn't stand to see the sorrow or anger in their eyes.

Then Addison returned with Minka's box, a small smile on her face that made Myles want to yank her against him and kiss her. It went against everything inside him to waste what little time he had on trying to heal the wound instead of kissing the woman he loved.

"This will work," Addison said with a firm nod.

Myles grinned. "You don't even know what Minka will do."

"Doesn't matter. It'll work."

Minka's look of doubt that she kept hidden from Addison told Myles everything he needed to know. Magic or not, it would be a miracle if Minka was able to reverse the silver poisoning him.

Kane remained behind Myles, his hands upon his shoulders. Solomon moved to Myles's right while Court walked to the left. There had been a few occasions when wolves tried to stop the silver, and not a single one of them had been painless.

"You should go," Myles told Addison.

She lifted her chin. "Never. I'll be beside you through it all."

"I don't know what will happen," he said, concern about her welfare filling him. "I don't want you hurt."

"She won't be," Griffin said as he and Gage came to stand on either side of Addison.

Myles saw the quick look of interest exchanged between Minka and Griffin, but it was swiftly forgotten when Minka touched his wound. He pulled back his lips as pain ripped through him.

He gripped the handle of the chair and heard the wood crack beneath his hold. Instantly, he felt the hands of his brothers' holding him in place even as he squeezed his eyes shut. He thought of Addison, of her tempting mouth and soft body. How unfair to find her only to have to let her go so soon.

ADDISON COULDN'T STOP the tears no matter how hard she tried. She watched Myles's body shudder in pain as his brothers held him in place. The wound looked horrible, as if his body were rotting from the inside out. And the dark veins spreading outward over his chest and abdomen, down his arm to his hand, and across his back showed how fast the silver spread through him.

Minka, for her part, was working frantically as she searched through herbs applying one after the other to no effect, her face lined with worry.

"Use your magic," Griffin urged her.

Minka cut him a look. "I don't have any."

"Delphine thought differently. Find it, and use it. Or Myles dies."

Myles was shaking from the pain, the silver moving faster through him as the veins grew darker, thicker with the black. Addison rushed to him, kneeling between his legs. She put her hands atop his.

No one stopped her or tried to push her out of the way. Was it because they knew Myles wasn't going to live? She refused to accept that.

Addison turned her gaze to Minka. "You have magic. Delphine said you did. It's inside you. Please, Minka."

Minka looked from Addison to Myles and then took a deep, shuddering breath. She calmed herself and erased all emotion from her face. Then she placed her hands over Myles's wound and closed her eyes.

Myles jerked, a low growl coming from deep within him. His eyes flew open, glowing yellow as his face contorted with pain. With his teeth beginning to lengthen and his nails growing long and sharp, Griffin tried to drag her away.

"No!" she yelled and pulled out of his grasp. "I'm not leaving him."

"Addison!" Solomon yelled over Myles's growls. "He wouldn't want you hurt."

She stood, Myles's gaze locked on her. "I'm not leaving you," she told him and took his face in her hands. Then she leaned down and kissed him.

Myles stilled instantly. When Addison pulled back, his blue eyes had returned. She smiled at him.

"Addison?" he whispered right before he went slack and his eyes shut.

"Myles!" she yelled and shook him.

This time it was Court who took a hold of her and pulled her away. Court held her tightly so there was no way she could get free. She watched as Solomon and Kane backed away with a grim look on their faces.

Addison looked over the porch to see dozens of people—werewolves—watching Myles in silence. She wiped at the tears and noticed Riley for the first time standing just inside the house with her arms wrapped around herself crying silently, her shoulders shaking.

"No," Addison whispered. "I can't lose him. I've lost everyone else."

Griffin placed a hand on her shoulder. "Shh."

She frowned at him, but saw his gaze was on Minka. Addison swiveled her head to the witch. Minka was hovering a few inches off the porch, a strange light surrounding her. Solomon started toward Minka, but Griffin moved with lightning speed, stopping Solomon with a hand on his arm.

"Leave her," Griffin said in a low, dangerous voice.

Solomon's gaze narrowed, his lips pulled back in a snarl. "Why?"

"Because her magic is being released. Look at your brother's wound if you don't believe me."

Addison gasped when she saw the black veins on Myles begin to shrink in size and length until there was nothing but the ugly, festering wound. And then, even that began to heal.

"Impossible," Court murmured.

Griffin was smiling as he said, "No, just not something any witch can do."

Blood began to run from Minka's ears and her nose as the last bit of Myles's injury vanished, including a drop of silver. Minka went lax, but was caught in Solomon's arms before she could hit the floor.

Solomon stared down at her a moment before he slowly walked her into the house past Riley. Addison shoved Court's hands away and rushed to Myles, but he wasn't moving. Kane and Court quickly lifted him and brought him to the couch inside.

As soon as he was laid down, Addison sat on the floor beside the couch, his hand in hers. She rested her forehead on his side and simply held him, praying that he woke.

It was dark when Myles opened his eyes. He grinned as he saw Addison asleep as she leaned against the couch. Myles was careful as he sat up, expecting pain, and when there was none, he looked at his shoulder to find himself healed. There was a large scar, but no wound.

He gently gathered Addison in his arms and moved her to the couch. As he stood, he saw Minka and Griffin on the porch talking in low voices. The interest in Griffin's eyes was obvious, and Myles suspected Minka might be interested as well.

Myles was about to walk onto the porch when he caught sight of Solomon standing in the corner of the kitchen looking out the window at Minka and Griffin. Suddenly, Solomon's gaze swung to him and he smiled.

"I'll be damned," Solomon whispered.

"Minka's magic worked then?" Myles asked.

Solomon motioned to Myles's shoulder. "Obviously. Addison hasn't left your side, or eaten, all day."

Myles would see that changed as soon as she woke. "Where are Court and Kane?"

"With the Moonstone pack."

There was something in the way Solomon said the words, paired with the glare he shot Griffin, that made Myles wonder what was going on. Then he heard Minka's soft laughter and saw Solomon's brow furrow before he turned away.

"Griffin and his wolves have said they would keep an eye on Minka," Solomon stated.

Myles crossed his arms over his chest. "We owe her a debt. I don't think it should be just the Moonstone pack. I think we owe it to Minka to check on her ourselves."

Solomon shrugged and leaned against the counter of the kitchen. "I agree."

Myles saw Griffin depart and took the opportunity to talk to Minka. He walked outside, softly closing the screen door behind him. There was no air conditioning in the old house, so the windows and doors remained open to let in any breeze available.

"You look much better," Minka said with a smile when she saw him.

He leaned against one of the posts. "Because of you. Thank you, Minka. I owe you a debt I'm not sure I'll ever repay."

"I'm glad it worked."

He watched her profile for a moment as she looked out over the bayou. "Are you sure this is where you want to stay?"

"My great-aunt did it. It'll work as long as my coven thinks I'm dead."

"You still need to eat. You'll have to go into town for supplies."

She faced him and shrugged. "I'll be fine for awhile. There are still those that live on the bayou that my great-aunt trusted."

"We'll come to check on you when we can." He scratched at his cheek, longing for a shave. "However, the Moonstone pack have promised to keep an eye on you."

Minka glanced inside the door to the couch that Addison

slept on. "What about y'all? What happens now, because we both know Delphine won't give up. There are plenty of witches around for her to use."

"No," he replied with a weary sigh. "She won't give up, but I'm hoping the other factions saw us working with the witches. That could go a long way in convincing the others to join us and defeating Delphine."

"Watch out for my coven. They can't be trusted."

"Isn't that said of all witches?" he teased.

There was no smile on her face. "And keep a close eye on Addison."

"You don't have to worry." He looked inside, his gaze locking on his woman. "I wasn't looking to find someone, and then she walked into my life. Now, I can't live without her."

"Then don't. You two have something special, something most crave with every fiber of their being." Minka pushed away from the railing. "Now, get in there and let her know you're all right."

Myles chuckled but took her advice and walked into the house. He sat on the edge of the couch, marveling at his woman. He lifted a lock of champagne-blonde hair and twirled it around his finger.

One eye cracked open and saw him. She sat up and threw her arms around his neck, hugging him tightly. "You're alive. You're really alive."

He held her firmly. "I'm alive."

"I thought I'd lost you."

"For a moment there, I thought I was gone."

She sniffed and buried her head in his neck. "That was the scariest night of my life."

Myles pulled back and cupped her face in his hands. "Addison, I love you with every ounce of my being, but this is my life. I risk it all every night–"

"I know."

"–to help those that need it. If it's too much–"

"It's not."

"–then I understand. There isn't just the hunting, it's also my family being werewolves. And lest we forget, there's Delphine."

"Are you listening to me?" Addison demanded as he pulled his hands away. "I know it's dangerous. I know this is your life. I know you're a werewolf, and that if we ever have children, they will be as well. I know there are Delphine, and vampires, witches, djinn, werewolves, and demons. I know all of it, and I still remain beside you."

He stared at her a full minute.

Addison shook her head as she looked up at him. "You saved my life. You saved Minka's life. How many people have you and your family saved, Myles?"

"I don't know," he said with a shrug.

"You bear a curse not of your doing. That in itself is amazing," she said. "But then you go the extra mile and protect the Quarter, at the peril of your own life. I know what's out there now. I'll never look at the Quarter the same again, but knowing you and your brothers are there to protect as many as you can makes me smile."

He was the luckiest bastard to ever walk the earth. Myles kissed her hard and quick. "I'm never letting you out of my sight again."

"Good," she said with a wicked smile. "It's taken you long enough."

"I can be a little slow at times, but I eventually come around."

"Hm," Addison said as she smoothed her hands down his chest. "I'm thinking I'd like to see more of your place."

"I can make that happen."

Riley made a noise at the back of her throat. "Yes, please do. You're making all of us sick with this love talk."

Myles looked over and saw all three of his brothers standing behind Riley and Minka. Addison blushed and dropped her head on his shoulder as everyone laughed.

Today was a good day. The LaRues learned to grasp each one tightly, because they never knew when the next threat might come around.

EPILOGUE

Two days later…

TWO HOURS BEFORE OPENING, Addison was laughing as her and Myles came out of the kitchen at Gator Bait. She had moved into Myles's place, and though he asked her every day to marry him, she had yet to say yes. She was going to. She just wanted a little more time with him. Everything had happened so fast, and yet she had no doubt she was meant to be his.

"So, you stole the materials out of Tulane and learned to be an accountant that way?" she asked in disbelief.

Myles set the box of rum on the bar and shrugged. "We'd just bought the bar, and each of us had our jobs. I've always liked numbers, just not school. Plus, I didn't want to put a strain on my brothers by going to college."

"How do you know you're not screwing things up?" she asked as she took a bottle of rum from his hand and climbed the stool to stock it on a shelf.

"I hire a CPA every few years to double check me."

She raised a brow. "So, you're that smart?"

"He was asked to join Mensa," Solomon shouted from the kitchen.

Addison gaped at him. "Mensa? Seriously? The International High IQ Society?"

Myles shrugged and handed her another two bottles.

"Tell me again why you haven't gone back and gotten your degree?" she asked.

"Not interested. It'd be repeating things."

"Yes, but you'd actually have your degree."

"That's what you're for."

She paused in setting the last bottle in place. Then she slowly looked at him. "What?"

He grabbed her by the waist and swung her to the ground. Keeping his hands on her, Myles brought her against him. "You've got one year left. Let me help you finish. We can do the accounting together."

It was in her nature to refuse any handouts, and yet this wasn't a handout. This was from the man she loved, the man she would spend the rest of her life with. How could she refuse him?

"Don't answer now," he said when she hesitated. "Think it over."

Addison rose up on her toes and kissed him. "I love you, Myles LaRue."

"And I love you, Addison Moore, that should be Addison LaRue."

She laughed as they kissed again. They were interrupted by a throat clearing.

Addison turned her head to see a man with dark hair and bright blue eyes. She didn't need to be told this was a Chiasson. She could see the resemblance between him and Riley.

"You must be Myles," the man said with a smile.

Myles was smiling, his head cocked to the side. "Well, I'll be damned. If it isn't Beau Chiasson. It's been too damn long."

The two met at the end of the bar and clapped each other on the back in a quick embrace. Addison saw the way Beau looked around and how Myles watched him.

"What brings you to town?" Myles asked.

Beau started to answer when he turned his head toward the kitchen and saw Solomon, Court, and Kane walking out.

Addison walked to Myles and linked her hand with his. In her weeks at Gator Bait she had come to value Riley's friendship. Riley was still finding her way, and Addison didn't intend to let any of her family—including the LaRues—force her to return to Texas.

"Riley," Beau finally answered. "I've come for Riley."

Kane crossed his arms over his chest. "Why do you think she'd come here?"

"Where else would she go?" Beau answered with a crooked smile. "Look, I just want to know she's all right. Vin is losing his mind, and Linc is ready to start scouring Louisiana for her. Christian is in Austin hoping that's where she's at, but I know Riley the best. She was hurt."

"Damn straight I was," Riley said as she came out of the back.

Beau let out a relieved sigh. "Thank God you're all right."

"I'm not going back," Riley stated.

Beau held up his hands. "I'm not here to make you. I intended to, but Davena set my ass straight. We did you wrong, Riley. Vin isn't ready to admit that, but it's the truth. Take whatever time you need before you return to Texas."

Riley rolled her eyes. "I've no need to return there, dumbass. I've already graduated!"

Addison had to turn away to keep from laughing at Beau's dumbfounded expression.

"You really fucked up there, cuz," Court told Beau.

Beau ignored him and walked to Riley. He pulled her into his arms and hugged her. "I'm sorry, sis. Let me make it up to you?"

"How?" she asked.

"I won't tell them I found you. Call tomorrow and let Vin know things are fine."

Riley was shaking her head before he finished. "No, Vin and Linc will look for me."

"You have my word they won't. Olivia is still angry with Vin, and she won't let him force you to do anything. As for Lincoln, he's not about to do anything to upset Ava again."

Riley stared at him a moment before she sniffed and discreetly wiped at her eyes. "Since you're here, you might as well stay and eat. Where is Davena? I wanted to meet her."

"She wasn't ready to come to New Orleans just yet," Beau said as he took a stool at the bar.

Myles glanced at Addison. "She should get ready to do so."

Beau's eyes hardened. "What's happened?"

The rest of the LaRues sat around Beau and began to recount everything. Addison watched it all with interest. If she was going to be a LaRue, it meant the Chiassons were also part of her family.

"What are you smiling at?" Myles whispered in her ear.

"The fact I've gone from an only child to having an entire family."

Myles turned to look at her. "Are you saying what I think you're saying?"

"Yes," she said with a smile.

Myles let out a whoop and gathered Addison in his arms. "We're getting married!" he shouted.

The two were swarmed by Riley, Solomon, Court, Kane,

and Beau congratulating them. Addison couldn't take her eyes from Myles. He was her best friend, her lover, her soon-to-be husband, and her werewolf.

Life couldn't get any better.

A LARUE NOVEL
MOON THRALL
NEW YORK TIMES BESTSELLING AUTHOR
DONNA GRANT
HER QUEST FOR THE TRUTH...
HIS REASON FOR BEING.

CHAPTER
ONE

September

It was the smell of bacon frying that pulled him from sleep. Court threw an arm over his eyes to block out the light coming through the row of windows behind him.

"This is beyond anything I've read in years," his brother Kane said.

There was a thud that Court recognized as Kane firmly setting down his mug of coffee. Court released a breath, hoping to fall back asleep quickly. It wasn't going to be easy when Kane was sitting at the table six feet away.

"What now?" Riley asked.

His cousin from Lyons Point had been sharing Kane's apartment for weeks now, and it looked like she had no intention of leaving anytime soon.

"This...well, there's no other way to put it. It's shit," Kane grumbled.

Court sat up and glared at both of them. It was wasted since Riley was focused on cooking and Kane was absorbed in reading the paper.

"It's too damn early in the morning for this," Court said as he rose from the couch and shuffled into the kitchen. He palmed a mug and poured himself some coffee.

Riley chuckled as she munched on a slice of crispy bacon and eyed him. "It's not early for us."

"Perhaps if you got in at a reasonable hour," Kane said as he set the paper down. "Besides, tell me again why you aren't at your place?"

Court took two sips of coffee and let the caffeine settle in his stomach before he replied. "It's not my fault the women won't leave me alone."

"You might try not sleeping with the nut jobs," Riley stated and pulled out the last of the bacon before she dumped eggs into the pan and began to scramble them.

Court frowned as he looked at the food, feeling a little jealous that he had been missing out on such a delicious start to the day. "Do you cook for Kane every morning?"

Kane sat back in his chair. "Sometimes I cook."

Riley shot Kane a smile. Court hadn't been sure anyone could bring Kane out of his funk. He hadn't been the same since the chaos that happened in Lyons Point when he had been cursed and sent after Lincoln's woman. Riley was doing what no one else could.

Kane still wasn't his easygoing self—yet. But he was getting there. He didn't snap at people as often, and Court even saw his mouth easing into what could almost be considered a smile more and more.

"This," Kane said, pointing to the newspaper, "is stupidity at its finest."

Court leaned back against the counter and scratched his bare chest. Kane read the paper religiously every morning. While everyone else had moved into the modern age and either didn't bother to read the paper at all or read it electronically, Kane was still old school.

Riley dished out eggs onto three plates. She turned to the table with plates in each hand and waited as Kane folded the paper so that the article he'd been reading was on top. She set the plates, bacon, and biscuits on the table and motioned for Court to sit as she gathered utensils and napkins. Court hurried to put on his shirt from the night before.

Riley was the last to take her chair at the round table. Then she looked at Kane and asked, "What did you find?"

"An article on the supernatural in New Orleans."

Court shook his head as he cut open a biscuit and slathered it with butter. "That's nothing new."

"It is when the reporter is going to clubs where the supernatural visit and then writing about it."

Riley choked on her coffee. She wiped her mouth with her napkin, her eyes wide. "Are you serious?"

Court watched Kane nod his head of golden-blond hair. "It's just a piece in the paper. No one is going to read that drivel, and even if they do, no one will believe the reporter."

"It's not the article that has me so upset," Kane stated around a mouthful of eggs. "It's that she points out the factions and describes some of the leaders perfectly."

Court waited until he swallowed his bite before he asked, "Who is described?"

Kane leaned over the paper and read, "Though tattooing has always been appreciated in our fair city, there is a faction who likes to tat their heads. These beings should be steered clear of at all costs."

"At least she recognizes that the Djinn are dangerous," Riley said.

"People are going to be heading out to the Viper's Nest and Boudreaux's looking for these tattooed people now."

Court realized that Kane had a point. "How long is the article?"

"Long enough." Kane stabbed the eggs with his fork and held the utensil at his mouth for a bite. "This is her third article. I don't expect it to be her last."

Riley swallowed the last of her biscuit while she held another piece of bacon in her hand. "Perhaps I should go have a talk with her."

"That would be a bad idea." Court pushed his cleared

plate away and scooted down in his chair as he leaned back. "If we go to her, she'll know that we know something. I don't want to be mentioned in any of her articles."

Kane's lips twisted in revulsion as he chewed. "Her first articles merely mentioned the supernatural part of the city. It seemed harmless enough until this morning. She's visiting these bars, Court. If she's not careful, she's going to die."

"That's what we're for." Riley smiled when they turned to her. "I say 'we' because I have been helping out."

Court stared at his beautiful cousin. Riley had long black hair and the same blue eyes that all the Chiassons and LaRues had. She was tall, lithe, and had a smile that could make the Devil beg her to take over Hell itself.

He understood all too well why his four male cousins in Lyons Point had done everything in their power to keep her away from the monsters they hunted. What Riley's brothers didn't understand, was that she was stubborn and completely immovable when she focused on something she wanted.

There was no way Riley wasn't going to help them, whether it was hunting a rogue vampire or protecting a human getting too close to danger. All the LaRues could do was make sure that Riley never went out alone. One of them was always with her to watch her back.

Because none of them wanted the Chiassons descending on New Orleans if Riley got hurt.

Riley flicked her long hair over her shoulder and held

Court's gaze. "I've more than pulled my weight in the weeks I've been here."

"Without a doubt," Court agreed.

"Don't you dare start treating me like my brothers do."

Kane rose and walked behind Riley on the way to get more coffee, tugging on her hair. "We're protective, cousin. Even you can understand that. We know you can hold your own."

Court met Kane's gaze as he turned and tilted the mug to his lips. Kane's blue eyes were intense with meaning. Don't fuck this up, was read loud and clear.

That's when Court realized that Kane needed Riley as much as Riley needed him. Whether the two of them knew it or not, each was the anchor for the other.

Kane because he couldn't forgive himself for what had happened to get him doubly cursed by the nastiest of Voodoo priestesses, Delphine, and Riley because her brothers kept pushing her away.

"Riley's right. If we're going to do this, she needs to come along," Court said. "The reporter might respond better if it comes from another female."

Kane ran a hand through his golden-blond hair that now came down to his chin. "I'll do some research on her today. Court, you've got fifteen minutes to get to the bar. It's your turn to open."

"Shit," Court said as he jumped out of the chair and

grabbed the shoes he had kicked off when he'd crashed there last night.

He stuffed his feet in his boots, made sure he had his wallet and cell phone, and then he was out the door.

RILEY WAITED until the door shut behind him before she turned in her chair to look at Kane. "He has no idea about the details of your parents' deaths, does he?"

"None." Kane crossed one ankle over the other, his blue gaze still on the door. "There was much he didn't see or know about while we were growing up because he's the youngest. We wanted it that way."

"Trust me when I say that won't turn out well. I'm the youngest, as well as the only girl in my family. Having things kept from me only pisses me off."

Kane's gaze lowered, a wall coming down. "I hear you, but that doesn't make revealing them any easier. Court doesn't carry the troubles that Solomon, Myles, or I do. I like it that way."

"If he keeps moving from woman to woman like he has been, you're going to have a different kind of trouble on your hands," she warned.

"He likes the attention from the females." Kane set down his mug and braced his hands behind him on the counter. "There's nothing wrong with that."

"None at all."

After weeks of living with Kane, Riley could tell he was closing himself off again. It happened frequently. Something would trigger a memory or thought, and he would become detached and reserved.

He opened up to her more and more. Progress was being made, but it wasn't quick enough for Kane's brothers. Solomon had taken her aside the day she'd arrived in New Orleans and asked her to do what she could for Kane.

Most times, Kane was content letting her ramble on as she often did. His gaze would become distant, and she was sure he never heard her. Yet he always had a comment to make after her stories.

She couldn't imagine what Kane was going through. It was bad enough that the LaRues were cursed generations ago to live as werewolves. Then Kane had to go and piss off Delphine.

Riley liked to call her the Bitch Queen. The Voodoo priestess had it out for the LaRues and the Chiassons, mostly because they were the only ones who had the power to keep her in check.

Delphine had put a curse on Kane to seek out Ava Ledet and kill her. Years before, Jack Ledet had killed a vampire who happened to be Delphine's niece. Delphine had never forgiven him for that.

It was all very complicated. Kane had been unable to stop

himself from seeking out Ava, who just happened to be in Lyons Point and near Riley's brothers at the time.

The worst part about it wasn't that the curse sent Kane to kill Ava—which was bad enough—it was that if he did, he would remain in werewolf form forever, forgetting who he was.

Luckily, it was Lincoln who'd found Ava—and fell hard for her. Solomon had then arrived in Lyons Point to help Lincoln keep Ava safe, as well as prevent Kane from completing Delphine's task.

It didn't seem to matter to Kane that he wasn't responsible for going after Ava. In his mind, the blame lay squarely with him. His actions ate at him like acid.

Riley rose and walked to Kane. He was so tortured that she wondered if anyone would ever be able to heal him. Myles said time would heal his brother. Riley wasn't so sure.

Every time she thought Kane was making progress, he would revert. Just like now.

She put her hand on his cheek. "Do you need anything?"

"To forget."

The words were spoken so softly she almost didn't hear them. And they broke her heart.

"Delphine no longer has control over you," Riley reminded him. "You control yourself, Kane."

"What about the next time we have to fight her?" His blue gaze clashed with hers. "And what about us combining forces with the Moonstone wolves and every witch group in the Quarter to free Addison and Minka from her spell to gain ultimate power? Do you think she's going to let that go?"

Riley tried not to think about what Delphine might do. Everyone knew she would retaliate. It was the when that kept them on edge.

"She won't," Kane continued. "She'll come for one of us. She's more powerful than you can possibly imagine. I fought her spell. I fought with everything I had. Only to lose."

"You won."

Kane shoved her hand away and walked off a few steps then whirled around. "No one wins against that bitch. She keeps score, Riley. She marked us, and she marked your brothers. Do you think you can remain in this city without her turning her attention to you? It'll happen, cousin. If it hasn't already."

"It'll happen no matter where I am," she stated.

But there was no denying the fear that began to spread within her.

CHAPTER

TWO

SKYE PARRISH STOOD on the sidewalk and smiled as she read over her article on her iPad. Every time she saw her name in print, she realized she was living a dream.

It had taken all her skills to sell herself, and her idea for the articles, to her editor. Helen was a tough bird, but Skye eventually wore her down. Now that her column was gaining more readers each week, Skye couldn't wait to tell everyone what was truly out in the world.

People had a right to know what was living next door to them and who was truly dangerous. Or maybe she should say *what*. She didn't exactly think the supernatural beings were human. How could they be if they were immortal and had magic?

Skye looked over the so-called fortune tellers in Jackson Square. They were, in fact, witches. The witch faction in New

183

Orleans was huge. It could easily rule the city, except that it was made up mostly of people who bickered constantly.

The witches were grouped by families, with four of the largest holding the most power among the faction. There was one group descended from the gypsies of Romania. Another group came from a long line of witches from France, one from Ireland, and another from the United Kingdom.

The smaller witch families were a mishmash of heritage, but that didn't make them any less dangerous.

Though Skye was curious about the witch faction, she was more focused on all the other beings that called New Orleans home. She also wanted to know what it was about the city that drew them.

Her next article was due in three days. Since she'd discovered so much about the Djinn by visiting the Viper's Nest, she thought it would be smart to return.

She pulled her phone from her purse and sent a text to Matthew to make sure he was free that night. He replied that he was.

"Fill up before I get there," she said aloud as she typed the words.

Matthew was a vampire, and she had no interest in being his meal. She still couldn't believe she had a vampire as a source. Even she rolled her eyes at the thought. What Skye wasn't sure about, was why Matthew wanted to help her. Exposing the supernatural also exposed him.

The one thing Skye did know was that she didn't trust

him. Matthew had been helpful so far, especially by keeping others away from her at the bar. Still, he scared her.

However, a story was a story. And she had a whopper of one. If that meant she had to sit next to a vampire some nights while in the middle of a club full of other supernatural beings, she could do it.

Besides, she wore a silver necklace at all times. A thick silver chain.

She might be weaker than most, but she knew how to stop a vampire. It was something she'd learned while in college. A lesson that had sunk deep.

"WHAT?" Solomon shouted.

Court winced at his eldest brother's tone. "I'm just thankful Kane still reads the damn newspaper."

Solomon ran a hand down his face and sighed. Myles hadn't said a word from his chair behind his desk. Court stood by the door as Solomon paced Myles's office.

"Does this woman have a death wish?" Solomon asked.

Myles threw down his pencil. "Apparently."

"It's times like these that make me want to sit back and let the idiots that get themselves into these messes get whatever is coming." Solomon's big hands fisted at his sides as his anger grew. "How fucking stupid do you have to be to go meddling in the affairs of the supernatural?"

Court couldn't agree more, but he also couldn't stand by and let an innocent get hurt. "It won't be long before one of the factions realize that Ms. Skye Parrish is a reporter for *The Times-Picayune.*"

"A newspaper that thankfully has cut its distribution drastically," Solomon mumbled.

Myles leaned back in his office chair. "It's down to three times a week for print, but it goes out every day online."

"That's good news, right?" Solomon looked from Myles to Court.

Court shook his head. "Afraid not. It looks like subscription service has increased fifteen percent since her first article three weeks ago."

"Goddamn it!"

Myles flattened his lips for a moment. "She has to be stopped."

"We can't just tell her to stop," Court argued. "She'll want to know why. I'm a hundred percent certain none of us want our names in anything she writes."

Solomon rubbed his fingers back and forth over his forehead. "A full moon is coming. If that...woman...isn't brought to heel, there's no telling what she'll find out."

"I'm on it," Court told his brothers. "I'll be tracking her with the help of Kane and Riley."

At the mention of their brother, Myles's and Solomon's eyes snapped to him. Court blew out a breath and pushed away from the wall.

"Kane is doing some research on Skye Parrish for us. Riley will be the connection we need to the reporter. Hopefully, to get her to back down."

Myles sat forward, his face creased in lines of worry. "It may take all of us."

"We're just visiting bars, Myles. The Viper's Nest and Boudreaux's. Besides, you and Solomon can take care of Gator Bait for a few nights."

Solomon had a perturbed look on his face as he turned to Myles. "What do you think?"

"I think they have it well enough in hand," Myles said. "All they'll be doing is tracking Skye for a few nights. If there is a problem, we can get to them fast enough."

There was a long stretch of silence before Solomon nodded as he slid his gaze to Court. "I don't need to tell you what will happen if Riley is hurt."

"She's the sister we never had. I'd never let anything happen to her," Court vowed.

Myles threw a pencil at him and grinned. "Get to it then. But first, it's your turn to accept the delivery out back."

Right at that moment, the bell at the back of the bar rang. Court left Myles's office to make his way to the kitchen to accept their daily delivery.

He glanced at the clock. Just a few more hours before he met with Kane to go over what he'd learned about Skye Parrish.

"THERE ISN'T MUCH," Kane said from his spot at the kitchen table as he pushed the laptop toward Court.

Court made a face. "As if, Kane. There has to be something."

"He's not lying," Riley said from the bathroom.

Court glanced at his cousin to see her hand moving as she brushed out her hair. He returned his attention to Kane. "What did you find out?"

"She wasn't raised anywhere in the US that I can find."

"You had to have found something more," Court stated.

Riley leaned back to peer around the bathroom doorway and grinned. "Oh, we did."

There was a ghost of a smile as Kane pointed to the laptop. "I traced Skye Parrish backwards. She came to New Orleans from LA, where she did a brief stint at the *Los Angeles Times*. Before that, she got her degree in journalism from UCLA."

"Where is she from though?" Court asked.

Kane waited a few seconds before he said, "The Bahamas."

Court was so surprised at the news that he sat back in his chair without anything to say.

"I know, right?" Riley said as she walked out of the bathroom. "I had that exact reaction. Who grows up in the Bahamas?"

Court blinked as he looked at his cousin in her dark jeans and bright pink shirt. The top dipped low enough to show ample cleavage. He didn't think she should be wearing anything like that going to the places they were headed.

"Wipe that look off your face right now, Court LaRue," she told him sternly. "I'm a grown woman who has lived by myself for years."

Court looked to Kane for help, but Kane was busy typing on his laptop again. Court gave up with a shake of his head. "Is that all you found out about Skye?"

"It seems Ms. Parrish came from a family with big connections. Her mother came from money, and her father was the CEO of a plastics corporation. She was born in New York, but the family made their permanent home in Nassau," Kane answered.

Riley walked to the sink and rinsed out a cup to load in the dishwasher. "I'd like to know why she left the cushy life. If her parents had that kind of money, why not use it?"

"They're dead."

Kane's statement had Court frowning. "When and how?"

"Her first year at UCLA." Kane leaned forward, his brow furrowed as his gaze scanned the computer screen. "I can't get to the police report, but the newspaper article states there was a car accident. Mr. Parrish was driving and the car flipped, going into the ocean. Both of Skye's parents were killed."

Riley stood next to Kane. "How tragic."

"It also appears the Parrishs didn't have as much money as they let on. All of their properties, cars, jewels, and most of their belongings had to be sold to cover their debt after their death."

Court couldn't imagine having that kind of money and then losing it. It made him look at Skye Parrish differently.

"That's about it, at least from what I could dig up," Kane said.

Court didn't believe that for a minute. "There's more. There's always more."

"That's what I'm for," Riley said. "I'll suss it out of her quick enough."

Kane looked up from the computer screen. "No doubt you will, Riley, but don't trust her. She's looking for a story. Any story."

"Heard. Loud and clear."

Court stood. "Time's a wastin'. Let's get moving. The sooner we find Skye Parrish, the sooner we can figure out what she's looking for."

Kane closed the laptop and got to his feet. "I think we should let Riley take the lead. You and I will hang back and observe."

"Sure."

The three left Kane's apartment. As soon as they reached the streets, Riley went ahead of them. They were staying in the French Quarter. If Skye wanted to find something, that's the place she would look.

Riley was about fifty steps in front of them. As he kept his eye on her, Court wondered how long it would take for the remaining Chiasson brothers to realize that Beau had found his sister weeks ago and was keeping it from the rest of them.

If Court were in their shoes, he would be furious. Then again, Beau was looking out for his sister. He knew she was safe. That was the only reason he hadn't told his brothers.

What Riley didn't know was that Solomon and Beau talked every week. As long as Beau was getting regular reports on his sister, he would keep his mouth shut about where she was.

All Court could hope for was that Riley never found out what Solomon was doing. If she did, she might leave and then no one would know where she was. Given that she was a Chiasson with a need to fight the supernatural in her blood, she could get herself into all kinds of trouble.

"What's got you all sour?" Kane asked.

Court jerked his chin to Riley. "Her."

"We are some kind of blessed not to have had a sister." Kane blew out a long breath. "I can't imagine growing up with one. Riley is blood, but I didn't have to watch her growing up while keeping her away from the monsters—and men."

Court cut him a look. "Do you think it'll be any better if Myles and Addison ever have a daughter?"

"Oh shit. You just had to make me think of that." Kane

gave a firm shake of his head. "I'm never having kids. Ever. Or a wife. I don't need that kind of constant worry and strain."

Court was nodding in agreement. Life was hard enough as a LaRue. Adding a female into the mix only complicated things further.

Myles had gotten lucky with Addison. Solomon...he hadn't been so fortunate. He knew firsthand the sorrow of being a LaRue in love.

CHAPTER

THREE

SKYE KEPT her clothes simple and plain. She wanted to blend in and observe, not draw attention. She wore a black long-sleeved shirt with a cowlneck and black jeans. Her hair was pulled back in a low ponytail. She wore no jewelry other than her thick silver necklace, and she didn't carry a purse. Her cell phone was in her pocket, along with a few twenties.

"Still nervous?" Matthew asked from beside her.

They stood across the street from the Viper's Nest, a known vampire hangout. She gave Matthew a dark look, but inside, she was a shaking bundle of nerves.

She was petrified, though she would never let Matthew know just how much vampires scared her.

"A brave face," he murmured. "You're going to need it in there."

Skye took a deep breath. Humans went into the Viper's

Nest all the time. Most came out just as they had gone in, but there were others who never came out at all. Some went in knowing exactly what the Viper's Nest was and were ready to willingly give their blood to a vamp.

She gagged at the thought. Why did movies and TV shows make vampires out to be sexy, romantic figures? They were monsters that fed off blood. And killed.

Without a conscience.

After waiting for a car to pass, Skye crossed the street and strode to the door of the Viper's Nest. Matthew reached the door before her and held it open.

She walked inside and was deafened by the music. It was hard rock, the kind where the singers screamed rather than sang. Matthew guided her to the left as she looked to the dance floor where a number of people were gyrating sexually.

Matthew suddenly jerked her to the right. Skye whirled around, ready to tell him not to be so rough, when she realized he'd moved her out of the way of a group of males who surrounded a young woman with blond hair. She was completely naked and letting them touch her. Everywhere.

Skye was shaking by the time she and Matthew reached the bar. She thought it would be a safe place, but there was no safe place in this club.

"We can leave now," Matthew leaned down to say in her ear.

She wanted nothing more than to get to the door as fast

as she could, but she'd promised Helen an article on the vampires. What had she been thinking? Oh, Skye knew exactly what had led her to agree to such a thing. It was seeing her name and picture next to the words she had written.

It was a heady thing, having a dream come true. Though it might very well lead to her death.

Skye shook her head. "I have to stay."

"It's a mistake," Matthew mumbled and ordered her a draft beer.

She knew it was a risk. Her editor knew exactly where she was going though, and there was a file that would automatically be sent to Helen if Skye didn't key in the password by eight a.m.

Journalists who went into the middle of a combat zone knew they might die. Skye was in the middle of a war herself. Only hers had supernatural beings such as vampires, Djinn, and witches. So far, she had steered clear of the Voodoo faction, and as far as she knew, she had yet to see any werewolves.

But both were on her list to get to know.

Skye made sure not to put her beer down. She drank it slowly as she made mental notes of everything about the club and the people in it.

She had no idea how long she'd sat there before she realized that Matthew was gone and her beer was empty. Skye set the glass aside and looked for Matthew, but he was nowhere to be found. She was about to get up and leave when two large men boxed her in. An uneasy feeling overtook her as she looked up into their faces.

They were dangerous looking, rough. She knew without having to be told that they were vampires. And, unfortunately, they had taken an interest in her.

Skye belatedly realized that one of them had been drinking from the neck of a Creole woman earlier. However, there was no sign of that woman now. The vampire's hair was black and thick as it hung to his chin. His eyes were beady, and the gold hoop earring in his left ear was mesmerizing.

"Going somewhere?" he asked.

Skye pointed to her drink. "I've had my limit, and I'm supposed to meet a friend down the street."

She tried to get up again, but they pushed her down, none too gently. Skye's heart pounded in her chest, dread turning her blood to ice.

"You want to be with us," said the second man.

She swiveled her head to him and forgot who or where she was for a moment. He had a look about him that spoke of ancient times, snow-capped mountains, and wealth. His hair was deep mahogany and parted on the side. He smiled crookedly, stroking her cheek.

"You do want to be with us, don't you?"

"Damn," Court said when he saw Skye nod her head at the vampire.

Kane touched his arm and slipped out of the bar. Court managed to reach Riley before she got close to Skye. He turned his cousin to the door and put her in a position that would allow her to leave in a hurry if needed.

Court remained in the bar. For the past two hours, he had been watching Skye Parrish study everyone. She was so intent on catching every detail that she'd missed the most crucial one—the fact that she was drawing attention to herself.

The man who'd stood beside her most of the night had left without a word. Court couldn't wait to get his hands on the bastard. Only the slimiest of assholes left a woman defenseless, especially in a place like the Viper's Nest.

Skye had drawn the attention of two of the most powerful vampires in the bar. Many of the vamps were trying to get near her, but the two with her now had stopped any of the others from getting close.

The wolf within Court yearned to be free, wanted to clamp his jaws down on their throats. The need was so overwhelming that Court found himself about to shift right there.

He shook his head and focused on Skye. The two vamps had her on her feet, flanking her as they walked her to the door. If they got her out of the bar, there was a chance they could spirit her away, and that would be the end of Skye Parrish.

Court waited for them to pass before he set aside his full glass of beer and followed them. He stopped the door before it closed on him and stepped out into the humid night air.

The vampires were so intrigued by their new catch they had no idea Court was following them, or that Kane was on one side of the street while Riley was on the other.

For the next four blocks, Court slowly gained on them until he was only a couple of steps behind. Suddenly, the tall vamp with the gold earring whirled around.

Jacques' eyes blazed for a moment before he recognized Court. "What do you want, wolf?"

"The woman."

The two vampires laughed. Court joined in while Skye stood silently staring straight ahead, completely unaware of what was going on around her.

"I'm not kidding," Court said.

Anton turned to the side and tilted his head. "The Viper's Nest is neutral territory."

"That doesn't mean you can forcefully leave with a human."

"She wants to come with us," Jacques argued.

Court lifted a brow as he looked at Skye. "Right. And you didn't use your mind control to get her to do what you wanted."

Anton wrapped his arm around Skye and turned her so

that she faced Court. "We're not making her do anything. Ask her."

Skye's eyes weren't dilated or unfocused. She met Court's gaze. "I want to go with them."

"What's your name?" he asked her.

Jacques stepped in front of Skye. "Why can't you believe that some humans want to be with us?"

"Because some of them might not want to have all of their blood drained or to become a vampire," Court retorted.

Anton pulled Skye closer to him. "By the rules of the city, if she wants to come with us, you can't interfere."

The two vampires began to turn around, taking Skye with them again. Court didn't know how they had gotten Skye to comply so easily, but he wasn't going to stand by and let the vamps take her.

"Release her. Now," Court demanded.

Jacques turned, his lips peeled back to show his fangs as he hissed. Kane ran from across the street and rammed a shoulder into Jacques, sending both of them crashing into a store window. Glass shattered everywhere.

Anton dropped his arm from around Skye and glared at Court. "You've made a deadly mistake, wolf. Now you'll pay for it with your life."

Court dodged the vampire's fangs and jammed his fist into Anton's stomach. He tried to keep the vampire away from Skye, but Anton kept trying to reach her and throw her over his shoulder.

With no other choice, Court fought near the woman who stood staring blankly at them. Court got off two quick punches to Anton's face as they circled each other. He was ready to land a third when Anton stepped back, right into Skye.

They toppled over with Anton landing heavily upon Skye. As much as Court wanted to kill the vampire, he couldn't. Not without proof that they'd used some kind of magic on Skye.

While he couldn't kill the bloodsucker, he could beat him plenty. He jerked Anton off Skye. With every punch he landed, Court felt better. There was nothing like beating up on a vampire.

Suddenly, both Anton and Jacques were gone. Court wiped the blood from his split lip as he looked at Kane, who was bent over, his hands upon his knees.

Riley walked out of the shadows. "Three vampires paused long enough to see what was going on, but it was one of Delphine's people who was observing from the far corner that worries me."

"Let them watch," Kane said and straightened.

Court walked to Skye and knelt beside her. Her eyes were closed. She lay unmoving. He had the urge to take down her carefully styled black hair. Even more annoying, he had the irresistible urge to hear her voice.

"Is she all right?" Riley asked, concern deepening her voice.

Court gently turned Skye's head from one side to the other to look for blood. Thankfully, there was none. He tapped her cheek to wake her, but she didn't stir.

"What did they do to her?" Kane asked.

Riley made a sound at the back of her throat. "Whatever it is, it isn't good. We can't leave her out here."

"And we can't take her back to any of our places," Court pointed out.

Riley suddenly smiled. "I know where we can take her. Follow me."

Court gathered Skye's petite frame in his arms and stood. He and Kane followed Riley to her car. After they were inside, Kane and Court began to try and figure out what the vamps had used to subdue Skye while Riley drove.

"It was something new," Court said.

Kane nodded grimly. "That's my worry. How many other women are they carting off that we don't know about?"

"Let's not think about that right now," Riley said. "We have Skye. She can tell us what happened and how it made her feel when she wakes up. That should help us figure out what it is. If we don't know, Minka will."

Court looked down at the woman in his arms. Skye had yet to move. She was breathing evenly, her golden skin warm beneath his hands.

"Is going to the witch wise?" Kane asked.

Riley gave him a dour look. "Have a better idea?"

Of course, Kane didn't. Neither did Court. He tried to

look up from Skye's face, but his eyes kept getting drawn back down to her. She appeared asleep, innocent. The fact that she had no idea the shit storm she had created didn't turn him off. In fact, it's what interested him.

Her oval face was flawless. She was a classic beauty with her high cheekbones, gently arching black brows, and thick lashes. Her mouth, however, was a seduction all its own. Deep pink lips that were plump and wide.

Tempting lips, enticing lips.

Court ran the back of his fingers down her cheek. Skye might be delving into a world she should stay out of, but Court couldn't be angry that it had brought her into his life. She intrigued him.

Even if he knew nothing good could come of it.

FOUR

"...DEPENDS ON HOW MUCH."

"It depends on who created it."

Skye heard the voices, but she didn't recognize them. Her head pounded with every beat of her heart, making her a little nauseous. She tried to remain still and take stock of things. Especially since she didn't remember leaving the Viper's Nest.

"She's waking," said a male voice.

"About time," came a throaty female reply.

Skye didn't know how people could wake up and remain perfectly still. She had to move. Perhaps it was a learned trait that spies and military people were taught. Though, at this moment, she would have preferred to remain still and learn more about where she was and who was with her.

She opened her eyes and immediately turned her head

away from the lamplight that blinded her. Covering her eyes with her hand, she blinked and let things come into focus.

"There you are," came a friendly female voice.

Skye looked up to see a woman with long dark hair and bright blue eyes leaning over the back of the couch and smiling down at her.

"You took quite a fall," she continued.

Skye licked her dry lips. She couldn't remember falling. Hell, she couldn't remember much of anything other than sitting in the bar and realizing that Matthew was gone. The bastard.

He'd left her!

Fury spiked through her. She sat up, immediately grabbing her head as the pounding intensified. Her stomach rolled violently.

The couch dipped next to her as the same female said, "Here, this will help."

Skye looked down to see two aspirin in the palm of the woman's hand. Since she couldn't think straight with her head hurting so bad, Skye accepted the pills and tossed them in her mouth.

Next, a tall glass of iced tea was put in front of her. Skye took it and drank deeply, loving the taste of the sweet tea as she swallowed the pills.

"Where am I?" she asked. With her elbow braced on her thigh, she carefully lowered her head into her hand. Her voice sounded hoarse, weak. How she hated that.

"Safe," replied the woman. "I'm Riley, by the way."

Skye turned her head to look at Riley. "What happened?"

Riley hesitated, her gaze dropping to the floor for a moment. "What's the last thing you remember?"

"Being at the bar."

"The Viper's Nest isn't a nice place. You shouldn't have been there."

Skye lifted her head to find the source of the male voice, and found the man sitting at a table in the kitchen looking severe and angry. There was a woman with deep umber skin, dark curly hair, and brown eyes sitting next to him.

These people were strangers. She was in a strange place, with no memory of how she had gotten there. She needed to get out. Now.

"We're friends," Riley said and put her hand atop Skye's. "We rescued you from the men trying to make you leave with them and brought you here."

Skye frowned. There's no way she would have left with men she didn't know. That wasn't like her. Especially from a bar like the Viper's Nest with all those vampires.

Her stomach plummeted to her feet. Vampires. Oh, God. Matthew had left her with all those vampires. Why would he do that? He was getting paid plenty to escort her around such places and ensure she was protected.

"She's remembering," said the man at the table.

Skye ignored him as she closed her eyes. She searched her

mind, trying to fill in the time she was missing between realizing Matthew was gone and waking up here.

"It's as if there's a window blocking those memories," she explained. "Like it's iced over so thick I can't see through it. I know there are people on the other side, but I can't make them out."

"What about voices?"

This came from a second male. She recognized the voice. She had heard it when she was waking. A shiver raced through her at the rich, seductive sound of it. It took her a moment to focus back on her thoughts. "I can hear someone talking, but I can't tell what is being said."

Skye opened her eyes and turned to where the man's voice had come from. He was sitting half in the shadows where the light from the lamp didn't quite reach. Though she couldn't make out his face, she could tell he was staring at her.

She swallowed, entranced by the stranger. He drew not just her gaze but her total concentration. So much so that she forgot they weren't alone in the room.

He sat still as stone, his hands resting on the arms of the chair. He gave off the impression that he was at ease, but she had the sense that he could be up and ready to face whatever came through the door in an instant.

Their gazes locked and held for several quiet moments. Skye couldn't look away, no matter how many times she tried. There was something so...beguiling about him. The thread of danger, of something dark and primal, couldn't be ignored.

She jerked when she saw his eyes flash yellow. Skye blinked and rubbed her eyes. She was mistaken. She had to be. A man's eyes, hidden in shadow, couldn't flash yellow. It was absurd.

You hit your head, remember?

Yes. Her head. She had hit her head. That's why she was seeing things that weren't there. The explanation was enough to calm her racing heart.

"I'd like to leave," she told the room at large and lifted her head.

Riley looked at the man in the shadowed corner before she turned her head to the table.

"Not going to happen," said the man at the table.

The woman next to him glared at him, one brow raised. "She's not staying here, Kane."

Riley got to her feet when Kane opened his mouth to argue. "Skye, the one glaring is my cousin, Kane. This is Minka," she said pointing to the woman. "And you're in her house." There was a short pause before Riley looked to the other man. "The silent one in the corner is Kane's brother, Court."

Skye hated how badly she wanted to see Court's face. She told herself it was because she wanted a good look at the people who'd helped her, but she knew it was more primal than that.

Then she frowned at Riley as she stood, her knees beginning to shake. "You know my name." How was that possible? Skye didn't have any identification on her. Nothing that would tell someone who she was.

"I think we should ease her into it," Riley told Kane.

Kane made a face like Riley had asked him to pluck a cloud from the sky. "Ease her into it? She already jumped."

"*She* would like to know what the hell is going on," Skye said, looking at each of them in turn. "How do you know my name?"

Court leaned forward in the chair so that his forearms rested on his knees. She caught a glimpse of chin-length butterscotch-blond hair. "Of course, we know who you are. By what happened tonight, others know you're the one writing the articles about them, as well."

It was everything Skye could do to remain standing. "You think someone attacked me tonight?"

"That's one way of putting it," Kane mumbled.

Riley rolled her eyes and faced Skye. "We think the articles might have upset some."

Skye took a step back from Riley. "Why do you care about the articles?"

"Look at what happened tonight. You should be worried," Minka said as she rose gracefully from the chair. She wore jeans and a willowy white shirt that complemented her rich skin. She walked past Skye to a door that led out onto a porch. "You stepped into something you had no business digging around in. Now you've put a target on yourself."

The only kinds of people that would be upset about what she wrote were the ones who actually believed. Or the ones who were part of the supernatural.

Skye turned her head to watch Minka and saw the glint of moonlight off water filtered through trees. The bayou. They had brought her out of the city.

"We're not going to hurt you," Riley said in a soft voice, as if reading Skye's thoughts. "We had to get you out of the city in case they came back for you."

Skye rubbed her temple, hoping that would help stop some of the pain. "Tell me what happened. Please."

"You went into the Viper's Nest," Kane said, his voice dripping with derision. "You knew it would be filled with vampires, and yet you willingly went in there alone."

She took exception to that. "I'm not stupid. I wasn't alone. I had someone with me."

"He left you," Court said.

Skye handed Riley the rest of her sweet tea and started out the door Minka had exited. It didn't matter how far she was from the city. She wasn't staying there any longer.

She reached the porch and was turning to tell them just that when Court stood in front of her. The moon hit him square in the face, showing her the hard line of his jaw, the firm contours of his cheekbones, and blue eyes so vivid they were almost electric. He was so tall she had to tilt her head back to look at him. There was space between them, but there was no denying the pure power she saw displayed by the tee that clung to his wide shoulders and thick arms and chest.

He held up his hands, palms out. "Easy, Skye. We brought you here because the vampires were intent on leaving with you. We stopped them, but I know Jacques and Anton well enough to know that they'll come looking for you again. They've singled you out."

Out of the corner of her eye, she saw Riley and Kane standing in the doorway to her right. To her left and behind her, Minka stood at the railing of the porch looking out over the bayou.

Court sighed and dropped his hands. "We need to know how the vamps got you to leave with them. Tell us that and I'll drive you back to the city myself."

"I don't remember anything," she said, frustration growing with every second. She cocked her head to the side. "Why do you have interest in the vampires? Most people don't believe they're real."

At that moment, a howl sounded. A howl that was very wolf-like. Skye glanced around her. There were no wolves in the parish, which meant it was a werewolf. She looked at Court with new eyes. Were he and Kane werewolves?

"You live in New Orleans long enough, you see everything," Court answered.

It was the biggest line of shit Skye had heard all week.

She didn't call him out on it though. Not yet. She wanted to know more about him.

Kane crossed his arms over his chest. "You don't remember anything, my ass. Lady, you've got some nerve. We save your scrawny hide, and you want to give us the runaround."

"I'm not," she said defensively as she looked at him. "I'm trying to figure things out. You're the ones who took me out of the city. Maybe it's you I should be afraid of."

"You're right. It was us that took you," Court said, a hard edge to his voice. "But we didn't lead you out of the club. That was the vampires."

Skye shook her head. "I wouldn't have left with them. I drank my beer and I was getting up to leave. Then I woke up here."

"Someone could've spiked her beer," Riley suggested.

Skye was shaking her head before she finished. "I never set my drink down. I know better."

"The witches wouldn't be involved," Minka said. "So don't even think of blaming them, Kane."

Kane shot her a dark look. "I put blame where blame goes."

With a loud sigh, Minka turned to them. "The witches aligned with the werewolves to take down..." She paused and glanced at Skye. "To do that thing. That was the exception to the rule. The witches never align with anyone."

"She's right," Court said. "The witches wouldn't help the vampires."

Minka lifted her chin, a small smile about her lips. "Then there is that."

Skye felt as if she were in a dream where everyone talked around her, excluding her on purpose.

"That leaves the Djinn and weres," Kane said.

Riley chuckled. "We can cross out the weres."

"Magic was used," Minka said. "That's the only explanation."

Skye's mind was in a whirl. "Wait. I thought vampires could use some kind of mind control on their victims."

"They can," Court said. "But it isn't allowed."

She couldn't help but laugh. "Allowed? These are vampires we're talking about."

"Who are strictly controlled within the city," Riley said.

Kane looked away from her with distaste. "Something you forgot to mention in your articles."

"I didn't mention it because I didn't know. I'm still learning."

Court said, "Which is what almost got you killed tonight."

"I had Matthew," she said. "I pay him to accompany me to places like the Viper's Nest and keep others away."

Minka tucked a long, dark curl behind her ear. "Why would you take Matthew? Who is he?"

"I took him because he's..." Even though there had been

talk of all the factions, Skye was embarrassed to state what Matthew was.

Kane yawned. "Spit it out."

"He's a vampire," Skye said and made a face at Kane.

She was reduced to acting childish with a grown man who despised her. When was the nightmare going to end?

Court's phone vibrated. He pulled it out of his pocket and read the text.

Skye shifted her feet. "Look. I've answered your questions, and I'm obviously no help. I need to get back to the city and look for Matthew. He's never left me before, and I'm going to demand my money back."

"Don't bother," Court said as he lowered his phone and looked at her with his gorgeous eyes. "Matthew is dead. The police found him three blocks from the club with all his blood drained."

Skye blinked, not understanding. "Since when do vampires drink the blood of another vampire?"

"They don't," Minka said.

Kane dropped his arms, his nostrils flaring as he blew out a breath. "Matthew was human."

CHAPTER
FIVE

It was clear to Court that Skye was shocked at the news that Matthew wasn't a vampire. He took a half-step toward her when her eyes went wide.

"That's not possible," she mumbled.

That got Minka's attention. "Why not?"

As if Skye realized she had spoken out loud, she shook her head. "I need to get back to the city."

"Hold on," Riley said. "What made you think Matthew was a vampire?"

Court watched Skye closely. He was mesmerized by the curve of her jaw and her amazing mouth. Her smooth skin glowed in the moonlight, making him want to stroke her face again.

Her throat moved as she swallowed, and she glanced at the bayou again. "I've done research."

But Court knew it was more than that. By the way Skye refused to look at anyone, he suspected she'd had a run-in with a vamp before.

"What research?" Kane asked with a sneer. "Movies? Watching them in their club?"

Court shot his brother a dark look. He understood why Kane had become a hard, easily angered person, but Skye didn't. Court caught Skye's gaze. "I'll drive you home."

"I know you all think I'm crazy, but I have to write these articles," Skye said. "People need to know what's out there."

Minka turned her back to the porch railing and crossed her arms over her chest. "You really think that? How do you think the city would be if everyone knew about vampires and witches? Do you think we would still be a mecca for tourism? Do you think everyone would just continue on as they are?"

"There would be chaos," Kane added.

Riley nodded. "Riots, too. Not to mention murders. Everyone would fear their neighbor, worry they might be a monster."

Skye's spine was straight as she listened to them. She didn't cower, didn't agree. Which made Court think that something had happened to her. If he could find out what that was, it would help him understand her and her need to report on the supernatural.

Kane said, "You need to stop the articles."

When Skye didn't bother to respond, Court held out his

hand to Riley for the keys. She sent a troubled looked to Skye as she handed them over.

Court gave a nod of thanks to Minka and turned to walk around the porch and down the stairs. He would be back to pick up Riley and Kane, unless Kane took to the woods with the Moonstone wolves.

Once Skye was buckled in the seat of the truck, she crossed her arms over her chest and stared out the windshield. Court started the engine and backed up the vehicle before driving through the grass between the trees.

"How are you feeling?" he asked.

"The aspirin has dulled most of the pain."

He recalled how hard she had hit the pavement. "You're likely to have quite the bump."

"I already do."

Court inhaled deeply and swerved to miss a skunk and her three babies, causing him to drive around a group of live oaks.

"Thank you," Skye said. "I didn't say that back there. I know that makes me look ungrateful."

"You were on the defensive. I understand."

Her head turned to him. "Do you? Why? Why did you help me? Why were you even at the Viper's Nest?"

With as smart of a journalist as Skye was, Court knew he had to answer her or take his chances that she'd find out on her own. Perhaps if he made his case well enough, she might back off. It was a long shot, but one he had to take.

"I was there because of you." He glanced at her, the truck rocking as they drove through a muddy section. There was just enough ambient light for him to see her brow rise.

"For me?" she repeated, shaking her head. She returned her gaze forward. "Let me guess. The articles?" she asked, her voice dripping with sarcasm.

Court grinned despite the situation. Skye's annoyed tone sounded so similar to Riley's. "We're not the only ones who are noticing you. As you know, New Orleans is a dangerous city."

"Why are you interested in my articles? The truth, if you please."

"We told you back at the house. You're bringing attention to yourself that is going to get you killed."

"I've thought of that. There are contingencies in place for the police to track down my killer—no matter what or who it is."

Court pulled the truck onto the dirt road. "Seriously? That's your answer? You're a piece of work. We're trying to help you."

"No. You're stifling the people's right to know."

Court slammed on the brakes, and Skye's head snapped toward him. He jerked his head to her, tired of playing it nice. It was time she had the hard truth. "If you paid a little more attention to things, you might realize the supernatural extends far past a few sections of the city. They're inside political offices and every law enforcement agency of the city. So no, Skye, no one would look for your killer. You'd be another statistic in a long line of unsolved murders."

She blinked at him.

Court faced forward, his hands gripping the steering wheel. "You're up to your ass in a bad situation. Had we not been there tonight, the vamps would've taken you. Whether they wanted to feed off you or turn you, I don't know. Either way, you would no longer be the person you are now."

"It happened in college," she said softly.

Court swiveled his head toward Skye to find her looking down at her hands. He was silent, waiting for her to continue.

"I knew my roommate, Jo, was a bit different. I just thought she was goth. I didn't find out until we had lived in the dorms for almost a year that she was a witch."

Skye laughed, the sound forced as she rubbed her hands up and down her arms. "Jo didn't hide it exactly, but she didn't announce it either. I kept to myself most times, so I didn't pay attention to her much. We ran in different social circles too, but she was nice, and we got along."

"Until," Court urged when she stopped talking.

Skye looked at him. "It was during Christmas break. I had nowhere to go, and she chose to take an extra course during that time. It was late. She was up studying, and I had just gotten back from a date. That's when it walked into our dorm room."

"A vampire," Court guessed.

Skye nodded and glanced down. "I was so terrified I couldn't move. Since I was closer, he came at me first. Jo knew what he was, even if I didn't. She used a spell, along with silver, to keep him from me. But he was determined to have one of us."

Court reached over and placed his hand on hers, giving Skye what little comfort he could. It may have happened years ago, but it obviously still affected her.

"Jo was so brave," Skye said with a smile. "I could only sit there and watch as she battled him. I never thought he would leave, but eventually she won. For the next two weeks, she told me everything she knew about the supernatural. I made notes, bought as much silver jewelry as I could, and soaked up everything she told me."

Skye paused and shifted in her seat. "One night, I came back to our room with an armload of books on the occult from the library only to find the room empty except for her silver necklace lying broken in the middle of the room. The police found her body three days later completely drained of blood."

"The vamp got her," Court said. "As powerful a witch as Jo was, she was overtaken by a vampire. That should tell you something."

Skye wiped at her eyes and sniffed. "I've been focused on the supernatural ever since. I had no idea vampires were real until that day. So many books and movies romanticize them, when in fact, they're monsters."

"They're beings who were once human. They were turned, whether willingly or by force," he told her. "Not all vampires are monsters. They do need blood to survive, but there are those in New Orleans who don't kill. Those vamps get their food supply from humans who willingly give their blood to the vampires. In return, the vamps pay them well and give them protection."

Skye made a sound. "Who would they need protection from? The worst monster is now their friend."

"There's the Djinn, witches, werewolves, and more importantly, there is Delphine."

"I've heard that name," Skye said with a small frown. "She's a Voodoo priestess, right?"

Court nodded as he pressed the accelerator and began driving again. "Stay far away from her, Skye. Trust me when I say you don't want to be on her radar. She's lethal and has no compunction about killing you on a crowded street."

"Noted."

"So you came to New Orleans to expose the supernatural." He shook his head, still unable to believe it. "That takes some balls."

She smiled and faced forward. "I told you my story. You still haven't told me why you're so concerned about what I put in my articles."

"Off the record?" he asked, glancing at her. She would find out all about his family with a little digging anyway.

"Off the record," Skye confirmed.

He rested one hand atop the steering wheel and put the other on the gearshift. "We keep the peace in the city."

"We?"

"Me and my three brothers."

She smoothed a hand over her slicked backed ponytail. "You're a supernatural being, aren't you?"

"Yep." He spared her another quick look to gauge her reaction. She didn't seem the least bit surprised. "Figure out what kind yet?"

Riley shrugged. "A matter of deduction, really. You're not a vampire or a Djinn. You don't look the type to practice Voodoo, nor are you a witch. That leaves...werewolf."

He was impressed. "Are you scared?"

"Should I be?"

Court laughed. "With that attitude, you just might make it out of New Orleans alive."

"Who said anything about leaving?"

He drove onto the highway. "You really want to risk your life to report on the craziness of the city?"

"I'd be dead if it hadn't been for Jo," she argued.

"You'd be dead tonight if it hadn't been for me." Court flattened his lips. "No matter how much you know about the supernatural, you're still not prepared to defend yourself."

CHAPTER
SIX

As DAWN CAME and the sky turned a brilliant pink and gold, all Skye could think about was what Court had said to her. As much as she hated to admit it, he was right.

She'd assumed because Jo had taught her a few things that she was more than capable of doing research on the supernatural. What the previous night had taught her was that she only knew a thimbleful of what was out there.

Coffee in hand, Skye stood at the windows of her townhouse and looked out over the streets of the city. Vampires had almost kidnapped her. If not for Court and the others, Skye wouldn't be standing there now.

It galled her that she hadn't been able to take care of herself. She hadn't looked the vamps in the eye for more than a second, so she knew they hadn't used mind control on her. No one had spiked her drink. The vampires had touched her, that was the only thing that happened.

Skye jerked so hard the coffee spilled over the rim of the mug and burned her hand. She hissed and rushed barefoot into the kitchen to set the coffee down and wipe her hand.

Then she ran to her desk and tapped the keyboard to wake up her laptop. She might not know Court's last name, but she had enough skill to find him.

Thirty minutes later, she sat back with a smile on her face. "Court LaRue. Looks like I'm going to be paying you a visit at Gator Bait."

Skye got up from her chair and was headed into the bathroom to take a shower when her cell phone rang. She glanced at the phone to see it was her editor, Helen.

"Sorry, Helen. I can't talk right now," she said as she declined the call.

Turning on her music through her phone, Skye started the shower. She was taking off her sleep shirt when her phone dinged with a text. Skye tossed her sleep shirt on the bed and hurried into the bathroom where her phone rested on the counter.

She read the message, frowning as she did. Helen never demanded she come into the office when she was writing a story. What was going on?

Skye quickly texted back that she was in the middle of research and would try to get there later that day.

"Before lunch," Skye read Helen's reply aloud.

What the hell was going on?

Skye showered and got ready. Forty minutes later, she was walking out the door and headed to the newspaper. A short fifteen-minute stroll and she was at the office.

No sooner had Skye entered Helen's office than her editor rose and closed the door behind her. "What's going on?" Skye asked as she took one of the two chairs.

Helen sat down behind her desk and shoved her reading glasses on her head. She let out a long sigh. "Where were you last night?"

"Observing the supernatural." Skye didn't feel the need to lie to Helen. Yet, anyway.

Her editor leaned back in her chair and smoothed down her navy and white striped blouse. "Were you alone?"

Shit, shit, shit. In all the turmoil, Skye had completely forgotten about Matthew. She kept her expression blank. "Matthew went with me to a club, but he left me there."

"When did you arrive at the club?"

"About ten-ish."

Helen nodded. "And when did Matthew leave you?"

Skye shrugged, not liking the questions. "It was about midnight, I think. He always stays in the background. He could've left much earlier than I noticed. Why?" she added, since she didn't want to admit what a failure she was in spotting supernatural beings.

"What did you do when you discovered that Matthew was gone?"

Skye scooted to the end of the chair. "Why does this feel like an interrogation?"

"Please answer me, Skye."

"I stayed until it became uncomfortable and then I left."

"Alone?"

There was something about the way Helen said it that made Skye aware her boss knew something. Once again, she decided on the truth. Mostly. "I tried to leave on my own, but two vampires attempted to get me to go with them. Two guys and a girl helped me out. They walked me home, and here I am."

"Good. Those are good answers. You'll do fine, Skye," Helen said as she leaned forward and rested her arms on the desk.

"Do fine?" Skye repeated. "What's that mean?"

Helen's face pinched in worry. "I hate to be the one to tell you this, but Matthew was found dead this morning."

Even though Skye knew he was dead, hearing it again was like a punch to the gut. She looked down, feeling sick. "How?" she croaked out.

"The police are calling it a homicide. They think it was an attempted robbery, and assume Matthew tried to resist. His attacker used a knife."

Skye could only stare at Helen. The police were covering it up. Aside from saving her, Court had given her no reason to trust him, but what he'd said about the supernatural in law enforcement made sense.

"They're going to want to talk to you," Helen was saying.

Skye mentally shook herself. "How do they even know my connection to Matthew?"

"Someone at the club said they saw the two of you enter together."

Just freaking wonderful. Skye wished she had remained in the bayou with Court instead of insisting that she return to the city.

"I see."

"I wanted to let you know so you wouldn't be surprised."

Skye ran her hands through her hair. "Should I go to the police?"

"There's no need yet," Helen said. "They'll find you if they want to talk to you."

Skye stood then. "I need to finish some research for the article."

"Stay in touch," Helen said.

Skye walked out of the office on shaky legs. Not even the fresh air calmed her. She spotted a patrol car driving slowly down the street, and she remained where she was, waiting for them to come for her.

It drove past.

She released a relieved breath and turned to the left. It was time to visit Court. Even in late September, the streets were crowded with tourists. October was a truly crazy month for New Orleans since everyone equated the city at Halloween with the supernatural.

It was all the innocents walking around that had prompted her to write the articles. The college kids just looking to get lucky, the high schoolers looking to score some alcohol, the families just wanting to make lasting memories, and the business professionals wanting to have some fun.

Those were the people the supernatural hunted.

Or so she'd thought, before last night. Court had said some of the vampires didn't kill. The thought boggled her mind. A vampire that didn't kill? How was that even possible? And who made the laws?

Court mentioned that his family enforced the laws, but how could four brothers control an entire city of supernaturals when a thousand policemen couldn't govern the humans?

Skye spotted the LaRue's bar situated at the corner of the street. The wooden sign hung above the sidewalk with a bite taken out of the side, as if by an alligator. The lettering was done in a deep green with a gator below the name, its mouth wide open.

It was after noon, and already the bar was busy. The sound of music thumping could be heard even from outside. It wasn't until customers walked from the bar that she recognized Godsmack playing.

Skye glanced at her reflection in the window before she stepped inside Gator Bait. As soon as she entered, she stopped and looked around.

The place was welcoming with its wood floors and

highly polished bar. Hundreds of pictures of celebrities who had visited lined the walls. There were also alligator jaws of various sizes hung here and there.

All in all, it looked like Court.

"Court said you would come!" Riley said as she walked up with a smile.

Skye returned her grin, intrigued that Court would know her well enough to announce what she would do. "Did he?"

"He's insufferably right most of the time," Riley said with a wink.

Skye laughed at the remark. Whatever she might think of the LaRues, they were obviously a close-knit family.

"You hungry?" Riley asked as she motioned Skye to follow her. "We've got the best gator in town."

"Sure." Skye's stomach rumbled, reminding her the banana she'd had for breakfast was long gone.

Skye took a seat at the bar and watched two men playing pool. Riley wasn't the only waitress at the bar. There were three others, and all were busy.

A man with ash-blond hair walked out from the kitchen with papers in hand and a pencil in his mouth. His blue eyes, as well as the shape of his face, reminded Skye so much of Court that she knew this had to be another LaRue brother.

He walked to a woman with jaw-length champagne-blonde hair and took the pencil out of his mouth to whisper something in her ear. She laughed and gave him a quick kiss.

"That's Addison."

Skye jumped at the sound of Riley's voice. She turned and found a glass of beer in front of her.

"Addison and Myles are engaged," Riley continued.

Skye tasted the beer and nodded in approval. "Does she know everything?"

"Yep." Riley grinned. "It's a long story. Suffice it to say, Addison had a crash course in it."

"Ah. I'm surprised it's not kept more secret."

Riley tucked her hair behind her ear. "If people want to know the truth, they're going to go looking for it, whether we want them to or not."

"Are you...?" Skye asked, not quite able to spit it out.

Riley chuckled and pulled at her black shirt with the Gator Bait logo. "Nope. That's contained to the LaRues. I'm just a normal girl who keeps the supernatural in line. My brothers live a couple hours away."

"But they know?"

"Of course." Riley walked around the bar and came to sit beside Skye. "I'm going to just put it out there because you obviously want to know. The Chiassons, my immediate family, came to Louisiana from France with a stop in Nova Scotia. They were hunters of the supernatural. The ones that kill innocents anyway."

Skye was listening raptly.

"There were two brothers and one sister. The sister came to New Orleans and married a LaRue. One brother chose to go west, and the other settled in Lyons Point, outside of

Lafayette, which is a hotbed of supernatural activity. All of us, both the Chiassons and LaRues, are raised to protect the innocent and kill the monsters."

"But the LaRues are werewolves."

Riley lifted one shoulder in a shrug. "That they are. If you want that story, you'll have to ask Court. The point is, the LaRues have always kept the peace in New Orleans. Before they were cursed, and after. That's never changed."

"Nor will it," said a voice behind Skye.

She turned and found Court. If she'd thought him handsome by the light of the moon, he took her breath away in the daytime. He was startlingly good-looking. The kind of gorgeous that left a woman speechless.

His chin-length hair was parted down the middle, the butterscotch-blond strands having a slight wave as they framed his face. His brilliant blue eyes were just as powerful as before.

Skye glanced down and saw that he was wearing a pair of jeans, slung low on his narrow hips, and a cream Henley shirt with a big bronze fleur-de-lis on the upper right side by his shoulder.

"I told you she'd come, Riley," Court said without taking his gaze from Skye.

Riley slid off the barstool and paused beside Skye long enough to say, "He's conceited. Feel free to bring him down a notch or two."

Skye couldn't help but smile. Court was self-assured. It

showed in the way he held himself and how he greeted the world. Conceited? Skye didn't know him well enough to say, but she could see it was a possibility.

"Why did you think I'd come?"

Court took her beer in one hand and grabbed her hand with the other, pulling her off the stool. He led her through the doorway into the back, but it wasn't the kitchens he brought her to. It was an office.

"You're curious," he said. "I knew you would want to know more."

He wasn't wrong. Apparently, she was easy to figure out. Skye frowned. That wasn't a good thing, was it?

Her thoughts stopped when she was shown a chair and given her beer. Court took the seat next to her the same time Myles walked in reading over some papers with the pencil once more in his mouth.

He didn't look up at them even as he sat behind the desk and keyed something in the computer. A few minutes later, Kane and another man entered the office.

So, these were the four LaRue brothers.

Court hadn't lied. She was up to her neck in werewolves now.

CHAPTER

SEVEN

COURT WATCHED SKYE CAREFULLY. Her entire body tightened when Kane and Solomon entered the room. Solomon ran a hand through his dark blond hair as he leaned against the corner of Myles's desk.

"I'm sure you've done some checking on us, but I'm Solomon," he said. He motioned with his thumb over his shoulder. "The one buried in the computer doing the accounting for this place is Myles. You've already met Kane and Court."

Skye held Solomon's gaze. "I have done my checking. I know that you're the eldest, followed by Myles, Kane, and then Court. You four have owned Gator Bait for years now and are upstanding citizens in all ways. And you have a very big secret."

"Everyone has secrets," Kane said, eyeing her. "Everyone."

Skye crossed one leg over the other. "I do have a secret. I shared it with Court last night."

"He told us," Myles said as he set aside his pencil. "That's one hell of a story."

Court's balls tightened when Skye glanced at him. Damn but she was a beautiful woman. It wasn't just her beauty that drew him, it was her courage and nerve—even if she had been foolish to go into the Viper's Nest.

"It is." Skye licked her lips and let her gaze land on each one of them. "I told Court last night, but I want to say it here. Thank you for helping me. I thought I knew enough to handle myself. I was wrong."

Court didn't know who was more surprised by her words, him or Kane. He merely smiled at Skye because the woman was good. The fact that she could admit she was wrong, right after thanking them, meant there was no way any of them was going to get on her case now.

"My editor called me into the office this morning," Skye said. "She says the police are calling Matthew's death a homicide and saying that he was killed with a knife."

Solomon rubbed his chin as he considered Skye. "I saw Matthew's body myself. There was no denying the holes in his neck, or the fact that all his blood was gone."

"We're not the ones lying here," Court said.

Skye's dark brown gaze turned to him. "I know. It's just a lot to take in. I assumed every human was innocent."

Kane snorted but didn't make a comment.

Court could only imagine how she felt with her world turned upside down. "The witches are human, and not all of them are innocent."

"Minka is," Myles said.

Court nodded in agreement, even as he saw Solomon's jaw tighten at the mention of the witch. Court really hoped his eldest brother could get over whatever was eating at him when it came to Minka. Having a witch as an ally was something Court didn't want ruined.

"This is my job," Skye said. "I'm paid to write these articles, and the only way to do that is by gaining information."

Myles made a face. "Not if it means your death."

"We're trying to keep you alive," Court said. "You have to choose what to do. If you go back to the Viper's Nest, we may not be there next time."

She squared her shoulders. "I understand. I also came here because I think I remember something about what happened last night."

Court sat forward. "What?"

"I told you I guard my drink well. I also know never to look a vampire in the eye in case they use their mind control." She paused for a moment. "What I do remember is one of the vampires touching me. After that, my memory is blank until I woke up at Minka's."

Court got to his feet and paced. "They touched her. No way a vamp can use their mind control that way."

"They have to make eye contact," Myles added.

Solomon's hands tightened on the desk. "Someone has to be helping the vampires."

"Just what we need," Kane mumbled.

Court stopped beside Skye's chair and squatted. "What did the vampires say to you exactly?"

"I don't remember," she said with a shrug. "I've been thinking about it since I woke up."

Solomon straightened. "It doesn't matter. We have what we need. We must find who is helping the vampires. It's never a good thing when two factions align."

"You knew it would come to this," Kane said.

Court stood and put a hand on Kane's shoulder. "We had to get the witches to help us."

"Addison's life was at stake," Myles said sharply. "I would've welcomed anyone's help. We're lucky the witches agreed to join forces with us."

By the way Skye looked between them, Court knew she was going to ask about it later.

"What can I do to help?" Skye asked.

Court was as taken aback by her offer as the rest of them. "I don't know if that would be a good idea."

She raised a brow and speared him with a look. "You

said yourself they're after me. If they see me again, they'll come for me. Let them. It's your best bet to finding out who is helping the vampires and discovering what is being done."

"No," Court stated.

The same time Solomon said, "That could work."

Court looked askance at his eldest brother. "Have you lost your mind?"

"He knows it's the best way," Skye said.

Court looked at Myles for help, but Myles was looking at Skye as if she could be the answer for them. Court turned to Kane.

Kane threw up his hands. "Don't look at me. I don't think she should be out there either, but Solomon has the bit between his teeth now."

Court turned back to Skye. "Don't do this."

"I have to." She smiled up at him. "If I don't, they'll use whatever they're doing on an innocent. That blood will be on my hands because I could've stopped this and didn't."

"They would've used whatever this is regardless. You didn't start it," he argued.

"How do you know that?"

Court opened his mouth to dispute her question when he realized he had no ground to stand on. "You barely escaped last night with your life."

"I'll be fine if you're there."

Court looked into her eyes. Since the first moment he

saw Skye, he felt the attraction. Strong. Undeniable. So far, he had been able to hold it at bay.

But with the way she was looking at him now, as if he alone could keep her alive, Court knew his ironclad control would shatter the first moment they were alone.

"What do you say?" Skye asked. "Will you help me?"

Court found himself nodding, even though he knew it was the worst idea they'd had in a long history of bad ideas. If Skye were taken...

He couldn't even finish the thought. She wasn't going to be taken.

Court slowly released a deep breath. "All right. But only with the condition that you do as I ask," he hurried to say when she smiled.

"Agreed," Skye said.

Myles lifted the phone receiver on his desk. "I'm going to call the NOPD. Perhaps our contact there can help turn the attention away from Skye in Matthew's murder."

"Good idea." Solomon slapped Court on the shoulder as he passed by. "Let's roll on this tonight. As soon as you have a plan, Court, we'll call another meeting."

Kane nodded to Skye and turned on his heel to follow Solomon out of the office. Court fidgeted. He looked at Myles to see his brother giving him a grin that said he knew exactly what Court was thinking—and feeling.

"What do I need to do?" Skye got to her feet and squared her shoulders. "I want to help, Court."

His gaze lowered to her lips. Full, dark pink lips. It was a mouth he pictured wrapping around his cock. He barely bit back a groan at the image that flashed in his head.

Those tempting lips parted slightly. Court jerked his eyes back up to her face, his blood heating when he saw the blatant interest reflected in her gaze.

Damn, he was in trouble.

"What happens when this is done?" he asked her.

A small frown appeared on her forehead. "What happens?"

"Yeah. Are you going to keep on exposing the supernatural? Are you going to expose me and my family?"

Her head nodded in understanding, but a furrow formed between her brows. "Oh. You think I would do that?"

"I think what my brother wants to know," Myles said, "is if your need to find answers will be satisfied."

Skye's dark gaze held Court's. "My roommate was killed by a vampire. I thought I knew how to protect myself. It's a truly horrific feeling to realize that I'm as unprepared and naïve as I was back in college." She paused to swallow. "I want a family one day. I want to be able to focus my worries on normal things, like who my kids are texting and what they're watching on TV. I want to have my concern focused on their grades and teaching them the right things."

Court wasn't sure how he felt about the warmth that spread through him when she spoke of children. He could easily imagine her as a mother. She would look even more beautiful with her stomach swollen with child.

He halted his thoughts right there. What the hell was wrong with him? Pregnant women weren't sexy.

No, but Skye sure as hell would be.

"You know what's out there. There's no going back from that." Court fisted his hands so he wouldn't reach out and touch her. "There are things you can do to protect yourself, your family, and your home. We can teach you that."

"After all I've done, you would do that?"

"Yes."

God, he would do so much more if she only asked.

Screwed. That's what he was. Royally, totally screwed.

Myles cleared his throat and got to his feet. "It might be better if you stayed here, Skye. Between the police and the vampires, no one will look for you here."

"Thank you," she said with a smile directed at Myles.

Court could have punched his brother. Her sweet and sexy smiles should only be directed at him. Certainly not at Myles, who was engaged to Addison.

Myles chuckled. Court shifted his gaze from Skye to his brother to see Myles looking at him. Court flipped him off. He didn't need anyone else noticing that he was becoming tangled in all that was Skye Parrish.

Addison poked her head around the door of Myles's office, her jaw-length blonde hair drawing his brother's gaze.

"Hey," she said with a smile full of love, happiness, and desire, all of it directed at Myles.

"Hey," Myles replied as he came around his desk. He held out his hand for her. "Come meet Skye."

Addison walked to Myles's side and wrapped an arm around him. She gave a welcoming smile to Skye as Myles did the introductions.

"Damn," Riley said when she came in. "You beat me to it, cuz," she said with a wink to Myles.

Myles laughed and pulled Addison close. "Skye, I think you'll find you fit in quite well here. Riley already thinks she runs things."

"Because I do," Riley interjected.

Addison rose up and kissed Myles. "Riley and I thought we'd take Skye off your hands for a bit. We can show her around."

"Show her around?" Court knew exactly what his cousin and soon-to-be sister-in-law were going to do. Talk. "The bar isn't that big."

Riley rammed her hip into his. Her sly smile said she also recognized his attraction to Skye. "Worried?"

"No," he mumbled. It was a lie, and they all knew it.

Skye grabbed her purse. "Show me the way, girls. Looks like I'll be here all day."

Court watched Skye walk out with Addison on one side of her and Riley on the other. He was glad Skye was making friends. Both the women would watch over her through the day. But he could do a better job.

"You got it bad, bro," Myles said as he walked up beside him.

"How screwed am I?"

Myles rubbed his chin. "One hundred percent. Don't bother fighting it. Just go for it."

CHAPTER

EIGHT

JUST GO FOR IT.

Those words reverberated in Court's head for the next four hours.

It was nice to look up from the bar to see Skye. She had put on one of the Gator Bait shirts and was waiting tables with Riley and Addison. Skye had said she couldn't stand to sit around, so she began to help the others out.

The more Court was around Skye, the more he found he liked. She might have originally caught his attention by the article in the paper. Her beauty might have kept his interest. But it was the warm, intelligent, friendly woman who drew him in deeper.

The lunch hour was busy, keeping him moving and filling drink orders. All the while, he kept running over scenarios in his head of how they could trap the vampires without using Skye. What irritated him was that they were going to have to use her. She might appear strong, but he saw the thread of fear she couldn't quite mask in those pretty eyes of hers.

That fear would help to keep her from doing something rash and reckless. At least he hoped it would. She had already done something careless by going to the Viper's Nest.

"A beer, please," came a deep voice behind him.

Court nodded as he finished making a martini. "Be right with you, bud." He put the garnish on the drink and turned around to find an NOPD detective sitting on a barstool.

It had been years since Scott Theriot was inside Gator Bait. Before Scott joined the police, he had been a regular at the bar. Such a regular that he and Court had become tight friends.

That friendship was strained when Scott had seen Court shift one night to save a woman and her child from a vampire. Scott wanted to know all about the LaRue curse after that.

Unfortunately, once Scott had learned everything, he stopped coming around. There were a few phone calls when Scott would want to know if a homicide he was investigating were supernaturally related or not. Other than that, nothing.

"Court," Scott said with a nod as he leaned his arms on the bar.

Court looked over his old friend's long and shaggy black

hair and scruffy jaw in need of a shave. Scott's hazel gaze was cynical, distrustful.

"Detective," Court replied.

Scott looked around the bar. "You act surprised to see me. Myles left a message for me to come by. Said it had something to do with the murder last night."

Court looked down at the sink and the basin of water where he had been washing glasses. "Did he now?"

"Should I talk to Myles?"

"Up to you." Court poured Scott's beer and set it in front of him.

Scott blew out a breath. "Tell me what's going on."

"The murder last night wasn't done with a knife as it's being reported."

Scott lowered his gaze to the mug of beer. "I know. I didn't draw the case, but I had a look. Two small wounds on the victim's neck and all the blood gone. I know what that means."

"The woman your colleagues are looking for to question isn't involved. The victim accompanied her to a club but left without her. Kane and I had to save her from two vamps."

Scott shook his head, mumbling a string of curses. Then he looked back at Court. "Vamps means the Viper's Nest."

"Yep. They're after her. She's under our protection until we can get them off her trail. I don't trust anyone with her. She's found herself with a lot of enemies in a short time, and we know how well connected the supes are in town."

"You want me to keep the cops away from her?"

Court leaned his hands on the bar. "What we would appreciate is a heads up if NOPD decides to take a look here or any of our places. I don't know if the vamps want to kill her or turn her, but either way, they got her to leave the Viper's Nest without using their mind control."

That made Scott frown. "What?"

"They used some form of magic. We need to find out what it is, as well as who is teaming up with the vamps."

"I suppose you have a plan?"

Court nodded. "It'll involve returning to the Viper's Nest. We have to learn who is helping the vamps."

Scott turned his glass in a circle. "I saw what happened in the cemetery a few weeks back."

Court straightened. Why would Scott have been there? And why hadn't he shown himself?

"Y'all handled getting Myles's woman free well. None of the tourists, and most of the residents, didn't even know what was going on. Delphine almost got one over on you though."

"She won't ever stop." Court ran a hand down his face. "You should've let us know you were there."

Scott sat up and sighed loudly. He ran a hand through his hair and adjusted his faded red tee. "With all those weres and witches? I think not. The witch that was taken with Addison hasn't been seen since."

"She's fine," Court was quick to say. "Her coven turned

on her so she decided to put some distance between them and her."

"Smart girl. Pretty, too."

Court shrugged. Minka was attractive, but she didn't compare to Skye.

Scott slid off the stool. "I can't promise anything, but I'll do my best."

He watched Scott walk out of the bar and into the bright sunlight. Court turned and found Riley beside him.

"He's cute," she said, watching until the door closed. Then she turned her gaze to Court. "Who was that?"

"Detective Scott Theriot."

"Really? How do you know him?"

"We used to be friends. Until he found out what I was."

Riley's face shifted into a frown. "What a jerk. None of us need friends like that."

"It scared him, Riley."

"I don't give a shit. He knew you, Court. He should've realized you never would have sharpened your teeth on his bones. Has he come here to make amends?"

Court grinned at his cousin, thankful for her words. "Myles called him about Skye. Scott said he would try to keep us informed if the cops turn this way."

"Right," Riley said with a roll of her eyes.

IT HAD BEEN years since Skye had waited tables, but it was something to occupy her time. Besides, she enjoyed Addison and Riley. The bar was much different than a restaurant, as well. It could be the music that made it such a good atmosphere to work in. It could be the place itself, or even the great food.

But she had a suspicion it had to do with a hunky blond werewolf with piercing blue eyes working behind the bar. Several times, Skye had looked up to find Court watching her.

It had been so long since she'd flirted with a guy that she was pretty rusty at it. Still, she wasn't going to let such an opportunity pass.

Court wasn't just breathtakingly gorgeous. He was focused on his family. She could see the man he was just by watching him with Riley, Addison, and his brothers. Court was a good guy. Even if there was a primal, dangerous vibe about him that made her heart race with excitement and a bit of fear.

Skye put on a brave face about returning to the vampire club. In truth, she wanted to be as far from it as she could get. The simple fact was, no matter how far she ran, the vampires would still be there.

She had created some enemies, and she never liked looking over her shoulder anyway. The only way she could get through the night was knowing that Court was there.

It still boggled her mind that she was surrounded by

werewolves. Riley told her there was a pack that lived out in the swamps, as well. The Moonstone pack was once powerful in New Orleans, but they'd disappeared years ago. It was only recently that they had returned.

The only faction she hadn't met someone from was the Voodoo sect. Based on the story Addison had told her about Delphine, the Voodoo priestess who had taken it upon herself to rid the world of all Chiassons and LaRues, Skye had no interest in meeting her.

The stories hadn't stopped there. Riley had told Skye how Delphine had ventured to Lyons Point to terrorize her family on multiple occasions. Luckily, Riley's brothers and their women had come through it, each time defeating Delphine.

There was one story that was the hardest to hear, and that was Kane's. Myles had been the one to tell her about the laughing, friendly Kane, who rolled out of bed with messy hair and came to work.

But that was before Delphine had cursed him to kill the daughter of her enemy. When Delphine had sent Kane after Ava, she happened to be in Lyons Point. The curse prevented Kane from doing anything but hunting her. It became his singular purpose. Riley's brothers had protected Ava and stopped Kane.

But Kane hadn't been the same since. He was reserved, focused. He rarely smiled. His hair was always combed and his clothes were always neat and orderly.

That story explained so much about Kane that Skye

forgave him immediately for all his harsh words. She immediately dispelled her nasty thoughts toward him.

"You've had a busy day."

Skye smiled as she recognized Court's voice. She set the dirty dishes down in the kitchen and turned to face him. "I have. It's been fun."

"Really?" he asked with a raised brow.

She shrugged. "Really. I'm not sure I'd want to do it all the time, but it kept my mind off things."

"I hear you've been told some of the recent happenings with our family."

"I have." She licked her lips. "Why haven't you killed Delphine?"

Court's chest expanded as he took a deep breath. "She's not easy to kill. We had the chance once."

"Why wouldn't you take it?" she asked, flabbergasted.

"We used the advantage to get her to remove the curse she put on Kane. If he would have killed anyone, whether it was Ava or not, he would've remained in wolf form for the rest of his life without knowing who he really was."

Skye was too shocked to speak for a moment. "I'd have done the same thing as you."

"I think it's time you took a break. Follow me."

He turned and walked from the kitchen. Skye hesitated, letting her gaze linger on his butt before she followed him. The guy could fill out a pair of jeans nicely. It didn't help that his shirt was tight enough to see every bulge and valley of his muscles. He must work out every day to have a body like that.

Skye found herself back in Myles's office again. Except this time, it was just her and Court. She looked around worriedly before she took one of the chairs.

Court sank into the one next to her. "I wanted to talk the plan over with you. If you're uncomfortable with any of it, we can change it."

"I should think the plan is fairly simple. You and I go to the club. You blend in, and I wait to be approached again. When I am, you rush in and take care of the nasties."

"Nasties?" he repeated with a choked laugh.

Skye lifted one shoulder in a shrug. "That's what my mother used to call monsters."

"It fits. Essentially, that is the plan. That's the basic version anyway. Riley and Addison will be there but outside the club. You're right. I'll be inside. We're known around town, so if more than one LaRue shows up, it'll make everyone wary."

She wasn't sure that was smart. Things could happen. Court could be outnumbered, and they could attack him.

"They won't mess with me," Court said, as if reading her mind. "It's not uncommon for one of us to visit the clubs to make sure everyone is obeying the rules."

Skye clasped her hands in her lap. "All right."

"Myles and Kane will be with the girls. Solomon will be hiding right outside the club, as well. If, for some reason, the vamps get you out before I can stop them, Solomon will be there."

She nodded. "Understood."

"You don't have to do this, you know."

She looked into his blue, blue eyes. "I do have to do this. For Jo, for myself, and for all the innocents out in the world. Besides, I need to set this right and get whatever enemies I've amassed off my butt."

"You can back out anytime," he urged.

"I'm doing this."

"Then you'll need to be prepared." Court handed her a silver knife.

CHAPTER

NINE

It was wrong. Court knew it the moment he walked into the Viper's Nest. Now he wished he had waited to leave the bar after seeing Skye one more time. He sent off a text to his brothers so they would stop Skye from entering the club. No sooner had he hit send then the door opened and she walked in.

Court let out a string of curses. He glanced around, noting how a current went through the club. Everyone was looking at Skye. Some because they knew who she was. No doubt they also knew she had escaped from Jacques and Anton the previous night.

But many were eyeing her because of what she was wearing.

Court licked his lips. Her long hair was down, the curtain

of black silk falling midway down her back. It was parted on the side, with one section tucked behind her ear.

She was once more in all black. The black pants emphasized her long legs while the black shirt dipped low to show off a wealth of creamy skin and cleavage.

Skye stood inside the club at the door for several seconds before she slowly walked to the bar in her black booties. The heels weren't nearly as tall as the previous night, but they were tall enough to cause him worry if she had to run.

Hell. Who was he kidding? Just thinking of her near a vamp was enough to cause him anxiety of the worst kind.

He watched as she placed a drink order and turned to watch the dance floor. The couples on the floor were half-naked, their bodies grinding against one another.

Her head turned slightly to the left where a vamp was drinking from a woman's neck as she stroked his cock. Skye quickly turned her head away.

Court's phone vibrated with a text. He looked down to see a reply from Myles asking if he was going to escort Skye out of the club. Court wanted nothing more, but he had a feeling Skye wouldn't leave easily.

He didn't want to make a scene of any kind. There were already too many vamps eyeing Skye as it was. Court waved on a scantily clad blond who was walking his way. She frowned but found a vampire soon enough.

Court spotted Anton making his way to him and sent off

a text to his brothers with just one number—11. That was their signal that things were going to shit in a hurry.

"Well, well, well," Anton said loudly over the music as he stopped next to Court. "I didn't expect this."

Court swiveled his head as he felt someone on his other side and saw Jacques.

"Or that," Jacques said as he jerked his thumb over his shoulder toward Skye.

Court leaned back against the wall as casually as he could. It was one of the most difficult things he had ever done, especially when he wanted to kill both vampires right there. "You two broke the rules. Did you actually think we wouldn't check in on you?"

"Did you bring Skye as a gift?" Jacques asked.

"Touch her and you die." The words were out of Court's mouth before he could stop them.

Anton smiled deviously. "Has the youngest LaRue found himself a woman? Don't get too attached, wolf. I doubt she'll live long."

"Is that a threat?"

Anton glanced at Skye. "Fact."

"Do you know what she's doing?" Jacques asked. "She's writing articles about all of us. We vamps don't mind. The more, the merrier. But some...well, some don't like being pointed out so blatantly."

The Djinn. Court should've realized that sooner. The Djinn liked to keep themselves secret. They only showed themselves to their victims. Unless you were in the supernatural world, no one even knew the Djinn were real. And they certainly weren't like *I Dream of Jeannie*.

They were pure evil, wicked to the extreme. They were malicious and cruel beyond words. They also loved to mess with humans to drive them mad and then torment them endlessly.

Skye had written an article on the Djinn recently. She described them to perfection, which meant she had seen one. That Djinn would want revenge.

But the Djinn hated vampires. They would never lower themselves to align with them.

Court realized he hadn't answered Jacques. "Yes, I know what Skye does for a living. Tourists come to this city to see the supernatural."

"Ah, but she's putting out the truth," Anton said. "We can't let that keep happening."

"So you want to kill her?"

Jacques laughed. "We never said we wanted to kill her."

Court felt sick to his stomach. It was just as he'd imagined. They wanted to turn her, to make her one of them.

"If she's one of us, she won't be writing any more articles," Anton stated.

Court saw two vampires slowly closing in on Skye from opposite ends of the bar. He tried to go to her, but Jacques put his hand on Court's shoulder.

"It'll be done quickly," the vampire said.

Court jerked away from Jacques. "What you two are doing here gives me the right to kill you on the spot."

"You have no proof," Anton said.

Jacques rubbed his hands together. "But there was no way we wouldn't show up once we learned she was returning."

Court's vision turned red with rage. He shoved Jacques against the wall. "You're dead, vampire."

"Good luck with that," Jacques said and jerked his chin toward the bar.

Court's head swiveled toward Skye to see the two vampires nearly upon her. He could kill Jacques and Anton and hope that his brothers helped Skye, or he could go after Skye and find the vamps later.

He chose the latter option.

Court released Jacques and ran to Skye. Vampires came out of nowhere to block his path, shoving him and hitting him. His head was slammed into a table, and Court looked up through the blood dripping down his forehead and into his eyes.

Skye was looking at him wide-eyed with terror. Then she pulled the dagger out of her pocket and slashed at the vampire nearest her.

Court smiled when he heard the vampire scream in pain over the music. He fought against his attackers, his gaze constantly seeking Skye. One moment she was there, and the next she was fighting the vampires amid toppled tables and chairs.

He was glad he had given Skye the weapon. It wouldn't do much damage, but it was enough to keep the vampires at bay until he got to her.

Court could no longer hold back his wolf. He shifted, shredding his clothes on a loud growl. With jaws snapping, he took bites out of several vampires, including Jacques, before he broke free.

Court leapt atop a table and launched himself through the air to land on a vampire who had lunged at Skye. He latched onto the vampire's neck and clamped down hard, his teeth going through skin and muscle.

The vamp screamed and spun around, trying to dislodge Court. It wasn't until the door to the club was thrown open and his brothers walked in that Court released the vampire and landed beside Skye.

SKYE WAS STARTLED beyond words when she saw Court change into a werewolf. First his eyes glowed an inhuman yellow, then a ferocious growl sounded from him. His bones popped out of joint and fur sprouted along his skin as his clothes were ripped and fell to the floor.

It all happened in a matter of seconds, but it was burned into her memory for all eternity. She was so absorbed with watching Court that she forgot about her two attackers.

They got too close. One tried to knock the knife from her hand, but she refused to be that weak.

She fought against them, ducking and spinning to stay out of their reach. They were fast though, super fast. Many times they guessed what she would do and were there before she twisted away.

Adrenaline kept her going, but she knew she wouldn't last long at this rate. And then Court was there, his teeth around the neck of a vampire.

Blood poured down the front of the vamp as Court clamped down harder. Skye slashed the vampire on her left and ducked when he tried to grab her.

The next thing she knew, Court was standing beside her. Her fingers itched to touch his tawny fur. He looked up at her with his yellow eyes, silently asking if she was all right.

She nodded, amazed at how huge he was. Court was easily twice the size of a normal wolf. He stood almost as tall as her chest, all danger and fury to anyone who looked her way.

The fighting had stopped in the club, but the music still played. Skye inched closer to Court as she looked up and saw Solomon, Myles, and Kane standing at the door.

By the way their eyes flashed yellow, they too were ready to shift and take on some vampires.

Court put his head under her hand and took a step. Skye understood. She walked with him to the door as his lips peeled back to show his sharp teeth and he issued a low, rumbling growl to the vampires.

As soon as Skye was out of the club, Solomon wrapped an arm around her. "You're all right now."

"They knew I would be there," she said.

Solomon didn't stop walking. He hurried her away from the Viper's Nest with Myles on her other side. Kane was behind them, and Court loped ahead.

"They didn't get you," Myles said. "Focus on that."

Skye looked down at her hand that still held the knife. It was because of Court. He had been there, but the vampires prevented him from getting to her. If she hadn't had the knife, they would have gotten her.

By the time Gator Bait came into view, Court veered off to the left with Kane following him. Solomon and Myles ushered her around the back of the bar and through the kitchen to Myles's office. Addison and Riley were already there.

"She's in shock," Addison told Myles.

Riley put a glass in Skye's hand. "Drink this. All of it. Now."

Skye didn't look at what was inside. She tossed back the contents and swallowed. Then she spent the next few moments coughing as the bourbon burned its way down her throat.

"Now look at me," Riley said as she leaned over to look into Skye's face. "How do you feel?"

Images of the hissing vampires hitting Court with their fangs out flashed in her mind.

"Skye?"

She blinked as she recognized Court's voice. He was kneeling in front of her. As she looked into his face, she'd never felt so relieved in her life. She threw her arms around his neck and held him.

His arms enfolded her in a fierce hug. "It's all right. You did good."

"They knew I would be there," she repeated.

Court leaned back and cupped his hands around her face. "I know."

"I'll clean the blade," Kane said and tried to take the knife from her.

Skye pulled her hand away, daring him to reach for it again.

Kane smiled. "I'll return it to you."

The night had gotten to her in ways she hadn't known were possible. She knew a few basic moves to fend off an attacker that she'd learned through a website, but she had never been tested like she was tonight.

She breathed through her mouth as she grew nauseous. Skye handed the knife to Kane.

"She's losing color," Riley said.

Skye was soon wrapped in a blanket. She didn't understand why until she started to shiver. That's when she recognized that Riley was right. She was in shock. She knew because she'd experienced it one other time in her life.

Court adjusted the blanket and gave her a comforting smile.

How could he do that after what had happened? How could he pretend that someone hadn't betrayed him?

"Who else knew we would be there?" she asked.

Court sighed. "An old friend."

CHAPTER
TEN

COURT WAS LIVID. The anger was boiling over, souring his stomach like acid. Of all the people who might betray him, he'd never counted Scott as one of them.

Now he knew the truth.

Skye's dark gaze watched him with confusion and worry. He hated that she was more anxious than when she'd left the bar earlier. Tonight was supposed to make her safe from the vamps once and for all. At least, that's what he had hoped for.

"Scott," Myles said with clenched teeth.

Court rubbed Skye's arms through the blanket. He didn't want to talk about it in front of her. She was still in shock. And he was still getting over seeing her surrounded by vampires.

He didn't like the helpless feeling he'd had when the vampires had prevented him from getting to Skye. In all the times he'd shifted, not once had he felt so...savage.

Skye lowered her gaze. Was she scared of him now? Was the shock wearing off as she remembered what she had seen him do? Court dropped his arms and stood, staring at the top of her dark head.

He prayed she wasn't afraid of him. Skye was brave and courageous. If she feared him...

Court refused to finish the thought. He raised his gaze to find his brothers, Addison, and Riley staring at him. It suddenly felt as if he were a lab rat being studied.

"What happened in there?" Riley asked. "As soon as you sent the text, Addison and I came back here."

Court ran a hand through his hair. He was wired after shifting and battling the vampires. It didn't help that he craved the feel of Skye's body like his wolf yearned to run.

He leaned back against Myles's desk. "Jacques and Anton came up on either side of me. I assumed they wanted to give me shit about the previous night, but they were too interested in Skye. I knew every vamp in there was focused on her, but I didn't realize how much until it was too late."

Court closed his eyes as he recalled the fear that had spiked through him when he saw the vampires closing in on Skye. He took a deep breath and opened his eyes. "I saw them moving towards Skye, and I tried to get to her."

"But they stopped him," Skye said with a little tremor in her voice.

Court shifted his gaze to her. She was no longer hunched over, but rather sitting straight in the chair. Beautiful and brave.

Her eyes lifted to look at the others. "They were beating him, kicking him. I had no time to get out with the vampires blocking my way. Then they were on me."

"I shifted," Court said, picking up where Skye left off. "And began attacking. Skye fended off the vampires with the knife until I could get to her. That's when y'all came in."

Kane snorted. "This could've gone very badly."

"Operative word is could've," Solomon said. "It didn't."

Myles grabbed Addison's hand. "How desperately do they want Skye, Court?"

"They'll continue to come after her."

Myles's lips thinned. "That's what I thought. Skye, you realize you can't go home, right?"

"I do," Skye said and lifted her chin.

Solomon crossed his arms over his chest. "Court's place is out. It's the second stop they'll make after Skye's since he was with her inside the club. That leaves Kane's apartment or my house."

"The LaRue house." Riley shrugged when Kane looked at her. "I'm thinking how tiny your apartment is. There is plenty of room at Solomon's. Besides, it's outside the city so we can keep the battle from overflowing into the streets."

Myles winked at her. "I agree with Riley."

"Then we need to get to my place," Solomon said.

Court glanced at the clock on the wall. "They'll be watching the bar. Getting Skye out is going to be difficult."

"Not too difficult," Kane said as he pulled out his phone and dialed a number.

Skye looked from Kane to Court. "Who is he calling?"

"More weres." He watched her carefully to see how she would react to that news.

"Oh," she mumbled.

Other than that one word, she didn't so much as twitch a muscle. Perhaps she wasn't as afraid as he thought. Then again, she had never seen him shift before. For those unaccustomed to such things, it could be very frightening.

A moment later, Kane ended the call and nodded. "Griffin and the Moonstone pack will be here shortly."

"Marcus can lock up the bar," Myles said.

Kane looked at Riley. "You stay beside me. If the vampires can't get Skye, they'll take anyone they can get."

"That goes for you, too," Myles said to Addison.

Skye shifted nervously in her chair, drawing Court's attention. Getting her out of the city and to the house he grew up in was going to be dangerous. But so was staying at the bar.

The LaRues were generally left alone, but the vampires wanted Skye because of her articles. It was time to remind the vampires—and all the factions—who the LaRues were.

Court pushed away from the desk and walked out of the office. He wanted to confront Scott, but it would only end with his jaws around the detective's throat. He wouldn't be able to control his anger. The last thing the LaRues needed was the police at their door because one of their own was dead.

He slammed his hand into the back door in the kitchen and stepped out into the night air. The humidity was thick, the threat of rain hanging heavy in the air. September was prime time for hurricanes. That's all they needed on top of the chaos.

"Talk to me, Court," Solomon said from behind him.

Court clenched his hands into fists. He wanted to be alone. He didn't want or need any of his brothers worrying about him. Ever since their parents were murdered by Delphine and her people, Solomon and Myles had tried to protect him and Kane.

"I'm an adult, Solomon. I can handle this."

"The great thing about family, kid, is that you don't have to. We're here to help. Let us. Scott might have been your friend, but Myles is the one who called him."

Court hung his head, keeping his back to his eldest brother. "She could've been taken. God, you have no idea how close they came."

"I saw the bloody mess you made in the Viper's Nest. With us, words aren't always needed. You got to her, Court. She's safe."

"For now."

Solomon sighed audibly. "I know you like her. I'll do everything I can to ensure you don't have to endure what I did."

Court squeezed his eyes closed. Perhaps there would come a time when Solomon no longer felt the pain of loss from the murder of his woman. It had been years, but the violent death had shaken the brothers as nothing since their parents' murder had.

"She was your fiancée, Solomon. That's a bit different than me desiring Skye."

There was a pregnant pause. "The sooner we get to the house the better. Griffin and his pack will be here soon. I need you ready."

"I am," Court bit out.

"No, you're angry. You need to push that aside. The only way Skye is going to get through this is if you have your head on straight. We'll deal with Scott and his betrayal afterward."

Court lifted his head and faced his brother. "Apparently, the vamps need to be reminded who is keeping the peace around here."

"Agreed." Solomon's eyes flashed yellow. "I'm more than ready to pay the Viper's Nest a visit and deliver some justice. But not until we know for certain who is working with the vampires."

"I've never felt so...powerless. It's a new emotion, and frankly, I fucking hate it."

Solomon's gaze lowered to the ground. "You prepared Skye with a weapon. That's more than I did for my woman. We're werewolves, Court, not superheroes."

"Almost the same damn thing. The vampires used a coordinated attack, Solomon. It worked, sort of. They'll use it again."

Solomon's blue gaze lifted to meet Court's. "I'm counting on it."

Court watched his brother walk back inside the bar. Each of them had dated, but nothing lasted longer than six months. Solomon was the one who hadn't shied away from love. He shouldered the most out of all of them, and it wasn't fair that he'd had his happiness ripped from his arms.

With a glance at the sky, Court returned to the bar. He paused, nodding to Marcus and the other cook as they worked the tickets.

Marcus knew what the LaRues were. He'd known ever since Solomon had saved him years ago. If anyone could keep the bar safe while they were out, it was Marcus.

Court walked through the kitchen. He glanced out into the bar and spotted Gage, Griffin's brother, sitting with another Moonstone were, Jaxon.

It was time.

Court made his way to the office. He stopped in the

doorway when he saw Skye talking to Riley. Skye turned to him, her dark eyes meeting his.

"Ready?" he asked.

"No."

He could understand that. But if they were going to have any sort of chance, Skye had to be on board all the way. Court walked to her and squatted beside her chair.

"I never intended for you to see me shift—"

"I know," she said quickly, looking down at her hands.

Court sighed. She was afraid of him.

"Riley will stay beside you," Court said, glancing at his cousin.

Skye's forehead puckered in a frown as her gaze snapped back to his face. "Where will you be?"

"I'll be near."

Riley rose from the chair. "I think you should be the one with Skye. I've been ordered to stay next to Kane anyway."

"Whatever works," Skye said.

Court would feel better if he was beside her, but he didn't want her any more afraid of him than she already was. "Is there anything you need?"

"My knife."

Kane walked in, followed by Griffin. "It's here, Skye." He handed her the weapon, and she tucked it back in her pocket.

Court stood and motioned to Griffin. "Skye, this is Griffin, head of the Moonstone clan. He's a friend."

She gifted Griffin with a half-smile as she climbed to her feet.

Court watched Griffin's green eyes look Skye over appreciatively. When Griffin turned his gaze to him, Court was using all of his control not to bash the wolf's face in.

Griffin merely smiled before nodding his head of dark brown hair to Skye. "Nice to meet you, ma'am. Kane told me you're in a spot of trouble. My people and I will be happy to help."

"Thank you," Skye said and moved closer to Court.

It helped to tamp down some of his anger, but the more Griffin looked at her, the worse it became.

Griffin laughed and slapped Court on the shoulder. "No need to worry."

"Let's get moving," Myles said as he strode into the office. He grabbed Addison's hand and walked back out.

Kane motioned Riley out with Griffin following them.

Court looked down at Skye. She squared her shoulders and walked out of the office. He waited a moment, watching her before he followed. Behind him was Solomon.

"What's the plan?" Skye asked over her shoulder.

Court put his hand on her back and ushered her through the kitchen and out the back door. "We leave as one. Griffin will stay with us while his wolves set up a wider circle."

"You have a vehicle that will fit all of us?"

Solomon chuckled as he let the bar door close behind him. "We're walking."

Skye's eyes widened. "Isn't that going to give them ample opportunity to attack?"

Court nodded as Griffin walked out of the small fenced-in area at the back of the bar. "Probably."

CHAPTER

ELEVEN

PROBABLY? Had he just said probably? Skye wasn't so sure she was up for this. Matter of fact, she was certain of it.

She was unceremoniously—but gently—pushed through the gate by Court. His large hand was warm through her clothes, steady. He thought she had courage, which was the only thing that kept her legs moving. If he knew the truth —that she was the biggest scaredy cat around—his opinion would change drastically.

But she wasn't going to tell him. She wanted him to think she was courageous and bold for as long as she could. Eventually, he would learn the truth.

Her legs felt wooden, and her stomach still rolled from the adrenaline dump earlier. The bourbon Riley had kept feeding her was helping. Otherwise, she would still be sitting in the office with the blanket as a shield.

"Oh, God," she muttered beneath her breath as they walked farther from the bar.

Every shadow, every sound was a potential attack. Skye was completely reevaluating her love of horror movies. If she survived the night, she was never eagerly watching Freddy Kruger again.

She glanced at Court. He was stoic, solid. Tough. He didn't appear fazed by the night at all.

Except for when he'd shifted and tore through the vampires.

Skye shivered as she recalled those few seconds that had felt like months. Afterward, she'd made a complete fool of herself and threw her arms around him, just thankful that he was alive.

"Are you afraid of me now?" Court asked in a low voice as they walked.

Skye frowned. Afraid of him? Where did he get that idea? "Why would you think that?"

"You won't look at me."

She turned her head to him and gaped. Court grabbed her and moved her out of the way of an oncoming group of people. On her other side, Griffin chuckled.

"No, I'm not afraid of you," she answered and looked forward.

She could feel him watching her. He was a force unto himself, and she didn't even think he realized it. It was obvious as they walked down the sidewalk with Griffin a little ahead of her. Anytime someone got too near her, Court pulled her toward him.

Most took one look at his stern face and gave them a wide berth.

"I never intended to shift in front of you," he finally said.

Skye shook her head in confusion. "Why? It's part of who you are."

"You're freaked enough already with the vampires. Why would I want to scare you more?"

"I like to know what I'm dealing with."

He made a sound at the back of his throat. "Are you telling me that you're not a little uneasy about the fact that so many weres are around?"

"What makes me nervous is the fact there are vampires after me," she said tightly.

Griffin glanced over his shoulder at her and gave her a nod of approval. Strangely, that made her feel better.

They grew quiet as they continued through the city until they reached the outskirts and the sidewalks ended. All around her were huge live oaks with their branches stretching outward, some so heavy they rested on the ground.

Skye thought the city was scary, but it was nothing compared to the woods. Just the thought of it made her shake. Her eyes were wide, her heart pounding in her ears. Vampires were fast. Really fast.

But so was Court. She hadn't expected that of a werewolf. Or the sheer size of him.

He laced his fingers with her cold ones. Skye looked at him, thankful he was beside her.

"How much farther?" she asked.

Court's face was half hidden in the night, but she could still see his anxiety. "Too damn far."

The cicadas were loud, their music surrounding them like a symphony. Above them, the occasional bat in its frenzied flight to catch mosquitos appeared. Skye was busy keeping the nasty insects from biting. How she hated when they buzzed near her ear.

She slapped at her arm, killing a mosquito. An owl hooted twice. The cicadas gave a crescendo of noise before the sound died to nothing for a few seconds.

Griffin slowed until he came even with Skye. He looked over her head to Court and said in a low voice, "I expected something by now."

"We all did," Court whispered.

Skye was just happy that nothing had happened so far.

They moved off the road through the woods. Every moment became scarier than the last. Skye saw multiple opportunities for a vampire to attack or a place for them to hide. She really didn't know how much more stress she could handle before her heart just gave out.

Court never loosened his hold on her hand. Being flanked

by two werewolves was comforting. It was a thought she'd never imagined herself having.

For so long, she thought the only good people in the supernatural world were the witches. Not because she'd had a bad experience with demons, werewolves, or Djinn, but because she assumed they were all evil.

She was learning she had been wrong about a great many things. The one thing that hadn't changed was the knowledge that vampires were nasty, vile creatures.

The group seemed to walk forever on a trail that apparently only the werewolves could see. What little light the moon shed was barely enough to keep Skye from stepping on anything. What she wouldn't give for a flashlight. Or a car.

Practical shoes.

Mosquito spray.

The LaRue house.

Court halted, jerking her against him before spinning her away and shoving her at Griffin. Skye's heart leapt into her throat as she waited to see a vampire, but nothing jumped out into the night. She looked over to find Court bending before grabbing something from the ground. Her mouth fell open when she realized he had a snake by its tail before snapping it like a whip, breaking its neck instantly.

"That was a cottonmouth," Griffin whispered. "One of the only snakes that won't run from humans. They're aggressive."

Court held out his hand after he tossed the snake away, and Skye eagerly went to him. Now she wasn't just scared of vampires. There were snakes out there that were hostile, too.

This night just kept getting better and better.

It felt like an eternity before she saw a structure through the trees. It didn't take her long to realize it was a house.

They came out of the trees to a grand area of nothing but grass. In the middle sat a stately home. Its tall columns and wrap-around porch were indicative of plantation homes in the south.

Court made her stay back as Solomon and several of Griffin's men walked in and around the house to make sure it was safe. As soon as Solomon waved them in, Court ran, pulling her with him.

Skye let out a relieved breath as soon as she was inside. She bent over, her hands on her knees as she drug in deep breaths.

She straightened while the others set up in different rooms with a clear view out the windows. Skye glanced through the narrow pane of glass next to the door and saw many of the Moonstone pack setting up a patrol around the perimeter of the house.

Court placed his hand on her back and turned her away from the door. "Are you hungry? Thirsty? Do you need anything?"

She could only shake her head, her eyes darting in each room as he hurried her past them. She had no time to notice anything about the house other than the very wide foyer she was walking through.

Then she was at the stairs. Court led her up them, turning her left, and not stopping until he reached the second door. He opened it and walked inside.

Skye paused a moment before she followed him in. Court clicked on a light, flooding the room. It was a good-sized bedroom with a black wrought iron bed against the far wall. There was an old, dark wood desk with many dings and scratches on the wall closest to Skye.

She looked up at Court, watching as he looked around the room as if remembering. That's when she knew. "This is your bedroom."

"It was." His chest constricted as he drew in a breath. "The house is warded against any enemy we might have. Nothing will get through the doors."

"Wow." She didn't know what else to say. She hadn't even known those kinds of wards were possible.

Court ran a hand down his face. "It's been a long night. You should try to rest."

Right. As if that were going to happen.

Skye walked deeper into the room and sat on the bed. "Why didn't the vampires attack?"

"I don't know, but it worries me."

"Do they know they can't get to us here?"

Court nodded slowly. "They do. Which makes it even more troublesome."

"Maybe they've given up trying to get to me," she said hopefully.

One side of his mouth kicked up in a grin. "I sincerely hope so, but in my experience with vamps, they don't give up easily."

She glanced down at her hands. "You know, I meant it earlier. I'm not afraid of you."

"I saw your face, Skye."

"I wasn't prepared to see a werewolf, but whatever fear I might have had vanished because you were protecting me. That kinda changes a girl's view."

Court's bright blue eyes watched her for long, silent moments. "You're one of a kind."

"Hardly," she said with a snort. "I'm stubborn, and I don't think things through all the way, which gets me in trouble."

"You're fearless."

"No."

He moved away from the open door across the room and sat beside her. "I've known people who thought they could handle anything. They claimed to be brave, but at the first sign of true and imminent danger, they ran away. You didn't."

"I didn't have a choice," she argued.

"You did." Court turned his head to her and smiled. "You made the choice to go back into the Viper's Nest. You made the choice to stay with us. You made the choice to leave the bar and come here."

He made her sound so...valiant. It warmed her.

She returned his grin. "I wish I could take credit, but I was following your lead."

"Which shows how smart you are," he said with a wink.

Their shoulders were touching, their gazes locked. Skye was drowning in the depths of his blue eyes. Chills raced over her skin from being so close to him.

They had held hands for the past hour, but being so close to him now while they were alone wasn't just comforting. It was heady.

Sexual tension sparked between them as their smiles faded. Her stomach fluttered when his gaze lowered to her mouth. She held her breath when he leaned toward her.

She slowly moved to him, anxious to kiss him. Then they were interrupted by a knock at the door.

TWELVE

COURT JERKED his head to the door, ready to take someone's head off when he saw Solomon. He stood and nodded to his brother. "How's it looking?"

"Quiet. Too quiet." Solomon leaned against the door jam and looked at Skye. "How are you doing?"

Skye smoothed a hand down her hair. "Much better now that I'm here."

"Make yourself at home. I'm not sure how long you'll be staying," Solomon said.

It was something Court had intentionally left out. He'd been afraid if he told Skye she might be at the house for several days, she might not have come. Then again, she wanted to live. She seemed to understand that her best chance to do that was with them.

Skye's eyes widened. She turned her gaze to Court. "How long am I going to have to wait?"

"That's hard to say. We don't know exactly who is working with the vampires, which means it's still not safe for you to go out during the day."

Solomon shrugged. "It's your decision, Skye. You can either stay here and trust us to help you or you can leave."

"If I leave, I won't have your protection. Is that what you're saying?"

Court was about to correct her when Solomon gave him a quick look to silence him.

"That's right," Solomon said. "A lot of people willingly put themselves out there tonight to get you here. You really don't want to waste their efforts, do you?"

Skye slowly let out a long breath. She looked at the floor. "No."

"Good. Get some rest," Solomon said and pulled Court out of the room as he closed the door behind him.

Court opened his mouth, but Solomon turned him around and gave him a shove. Court had no choice but to walk down the hallway and descend the stairs.

When he landed in the foyer, he whirled around. "Why did you lie to her?"

"Do you really need to ask?" Solomon asked as he reached the bottom. "If she leaves, the vamps will find her and turn her. Is that what you want?"

"You know it isn't."

"Then I did what had to be done."

Court briefly squeezed his eyes closed. "Even if she changes her mind and leaves, I'm going to protect her."

"As we all will, but I'm trying to save us that trouble. It's easier to fight here."

Court knew that was the truth, but he still didn't like lying to Skye. She didn't deserve that. The only thing that kept him from running back up the stairs and telling her was the memory of Solomon holding Misty's dead body in his arms.

Solomon walked away, leaving Court standing there trying to come to terms with what was going on. It never entered his mind to fight the attraction he felt for Skye. It had been there from the first time he'd seen her, but the fire had grown the more they were together.

It was a good thing Solomon interrupted them before that kiss because Court wasn't so sure he could've stopped once he'd gotten a taste of her sweet lips.

"She'll be all right," Myles said as he came to stand by him.

Court looked up the stairs. "I sincerely hope so."

Five days. Five very long days.

Skye loved the old house, as well as Riley and Addison's company, but the situation was draining and grating on her nerves. In order to get some time alone, she had closed herself up in her room and wrote the article on her phone.

Typing a text was one thing. Typing an article on her phone was the worst type of torture. Especially with the stupid auto-correct that always changed the wrong words and left misspelled ones.

She didn't tell Court or the others that she was writing it. Skye had a deadline to meet and had promised the article, so she had to write it.

That was three days ago. The article would be up today. She was nervous about it. Mostly, however, she was worried about how the brothers would feel about what she had written.

"It's your turn," Riley said as they sat around the gaming table.

Skye blinked and focused on her hand of cards. They had been playing Spades for the past two hours. She glanced down at the cards that had been played and chose the ten of clubs. She couldn't win the hand, and it was her largest club card.

Minka let out a little whoop and collected the cards, winning the trick. "I'm smoking y'all," she said and tossed down the queen of clubs.

"When are the boys getting back?" Addison asked as she placed a two of clubs.

Riley shrugged, a smirk on her face as she laid the ace of clubs on top of the others. "Any moment."

"Oh, you sneak!" Minka said, laughing.

Skye laughed as she threw down the seven of clubs, giving Riley the win.

Minka rolled her eyes at the look Addison kept giving her. "Stop it. I don't care what Solomon has to say. He can kiss my sweet ass if he doesn't like me here."

"Amen," Riley said with a wink.

Skye took a long drink of her sweet tea. "What is it with Solomon? Why doesn't he like you? You saved Myles from death when he had all that silver in his system."

"I don't know," Minka said with a shrug. "Some people just rub each other wrong. That's us, I suppose. I don't care enough to even worry about it."

But Skye knew that for the lie it was. She hadn't been around very long, but it was obvious from the tightening of Minka's body every time Solomon's name was brought up that she very much cared what the eldest LaRue thought of her.

They played the next round, ribbing each other. Addison thought she was going to win since she had the ace of diamonds, but Skye didn't have any diamonds, so she played a spade, winning the trick.

Skye calmly pulled the cards her way with a smile and a little dance in her chair.

"Oooooh. You got whooped," Riley told Addison.

Minka covered her mouth with her cards, her eyes

playfully wide as she looked at Addison. She lowered the cards. "Looks like we need to watch this one."

Addison lifted her nose and fought to keep the smile from her face as she pretended to be affronted. Then she burst out laughing.

It felt good to be a little normal in such a strange situation. Skye knew Riley, Addison, and even Minka were doing their best to keep her mind off things. However, she wasn't sure how much longer she could stay at the LaRue house.

There was the sound of talking from the front porch. Skye recognized Court's voice. She sat up in her chair, hoping that he'd found something during his patrol of the land around the home.

He was the first one in the house. His tall, muscular form filling the parlor entry. With his windblown blond hair, she knew he had been running. The fact his clothes were spotless told her he had been in wolf form.

"Hey," he said, his gaze going to her.

Her heart leapt and she couldn't help but smile when his blue eyes landed on her. He didn't look at anyone else, and it made her stomach feel as if there were butterflies taking off. "Hey. Good news?"

"No news," he said as he moved over to make room for Myles to walk past as he went to Addison and kissed her.

Skye wished Court would kiss her. It was all she'd

thought about for five days since they'd almost kissed in his room.

"Nothing?" Addison asked.

Solomon stopped next to Court in the doorway. His gaze instantly went to Minka, who sat with her back to him. Minka was looking at her cards as if she didn't have a care in the world.

"What are you doing here?" Solomon asked.

He didn't say Minka's name, nor did he have to. She knew he was talking to her. Skye could've kicked him because the little burst of excitement on Minka's face vanished instantly, her hackles rising.

Minka played her next card and said, her voice dripping with sarcasm, "So good to see you too, Solomon. No, I don't have anything to share, but I'm so glad you asked."

Skye watched as Court elbowed Solomon in the side before motioning his head to Minka.

Solomon rolled his eyes dramatically. "Of course, you're welcome in the house, Minka. We would appreciate anything you can add to help."

He said the words tightly, as if each syllable was painful to get past his lips.

"Of course," Minka replied silkily.

Skye set the rest of her cards face down on the table. "Still nothing? I don't understand."

"We don't either." Court ran a hand through his hair. "There are no tracks out there other than ours."

"This makes no sense," Riley said. "If the vamps want her, and they know she's here, why haven't they attacked? Or at least tried."

Minka lifted her eyes to Skye. "They're waiting on something."

That's when it hit Skye. A small tremor raced down her back. "They're waiting for me to leave."

Minka nodded slowly. "They have all the time in the world. They know you'll eventually think you're safe and return home."

"Not going to happen," Court stated.

Skye glanced at him. Minka was right. She was getting lax. With every day that passed without vampires or other supernatural creatures attacking, she began to think she had imagined it all.

"I can't stay here forever. Nor will the Moonstone clan remain," Skye said.

Court shook his head. "I know what you're thinking. The answer is no. We already put you out there once. Not. Happening."

"I can't live like this, and neither can all of you. I will never be able to repay what any of you have done for me, but we all know we'll have to make a decision soon."

Myles rested his hands on Addison's shoulders as he stood behind her chair. "I hate to agree, but Skye's right."

"The vamps knew we would retreat here," Riley said and flattened her lips. "Man, I hate those assholes."

"It's not just the vampires," Minka pointed out.

That was the kicker. They had no idea which one of the factions was helping the vampires. Magic was being used, but that could be the Djinn, witches, or even Delphine.

"Give me another few days?" Court asked Skye. "Please."

She nodded, unable to tell him no. He turned on his heel and walked out of the house. She tracked him through the window in the parlor until he was out of sight.

"If there's anything to find, Court will find it," Myles said.

Skye slid her gaze to him and forced a smile. "I think you're right."

"You mean a lot to him," Solomon said.

Skye's heart missed a beat. The very idea that that could be true made her extremely happy. She looked at him. "Why do you say that?"

"He's proving it to you every day, Skye," Solomon said as he leaned against the doorway. "He patrols all night, only catching little naps when we make him take a break. He's hardly eaten in days. Like all of us, he knows the attack is coming, and he wants to make sure there are no surprises."

"Which will happen if I leave."

Solomon nodded his head once.

Skye looked at each person in the room. "There has to be something we can do to get this attack over with. If we wait too long, we won't have the other weres for help."

"She's right," Kane said as he walked into the room.

"They're already getting antsy. Griffin is keeping them here for now."

Minka leaned forward and propped her elbows on the table. "I didn't come just to play cards, Skye. I came here because I have an idea. One that I think could get you out of this mess."

"Took you long enough," Solomon mumbled.

Skye watched the two of them, wondering if Solomon disliked Minka as much as he put on. Or if there was something more there. Skye was beginning to think there was something more.

CHAPTER

THIRTEEN

COURT STOOD BACK by a stand of trees and stared at the house he'd grown up in. There were many good memories there, but it was the night their parents were murdered that always came to mind when he looked at it.

He loved coming home, but it was hard. Their family had been shattered in one night because of a vengeful Voodoo priestess who didn't want the five factions to have any type of peace.

Delphine had gotten her wish with his parents' deaths. Now she needed to die. If she wasn't causing problems with the LaRues, she was messing with the Chiassons. So far, neither family had lost another member to Delphine's attempts.

But how long could their luck hold out?

Then there was Skye.

Court blew out a deep breath. The woman was constantly on his mind. He thought about her even in sleep. Her laugh, her lips turning up in a sensual smile, her long black hair, her smoky eyes. Her body.

She drove him mad with desire. He craved her, yearned for her. Burned for her.

Being around her so much over the past days had been the sweetest kind of torture. He would find ways to get as close to her as he dared. Occasionally, he'd let their hands brush. He even sunk so low as to touch her hair when she passed. Each time he returned from a patrol, he fought not to go to her, to pull her into his arms for a kiss as Myles did Addison.

Court grew hard just picturing Skye in his arms, imagined kissing her slowly, seductively, passionately. It was why he chose to patrol all night, because he couldn't be in the same house as her and not go to her.

He wasn't fighting it. He wanted to go to Skye. Court knew making love to her would be amazing. But she was being hunted by the vamps. He had to concentrate on that threat.

There was a slight movement to his left. Court shifted his gaze and saw Kane walk silently around a tree. Kane came to stand beside him, and for long moments, neither brother said a word.

"How many more nights are you going to spend out here watching the house?" Kane asked.

Court took immediate offense. "I patrol."

"In between staring at the house and thinking of Skye."

Court didn't bother to deny it. But he didn't want to talk about it either. "How long do you think Riley will stay?"

"As long as she needs to."

"She's done you good."

Kane lifted one shoulder in a half-shrug. "Riley is a strong woman. She's a Chiasson. But she also needed someone. She's not as happy as she makes out."

That made Court frown. "Is it her brothers?"

"I don't know. I don't ask questions."

"Which is apparently exactly what she needs."

"Yeah," Kane mumbled. After a long stretch of silence, he said, "I don't know if we would've acted any differently than our cousins if we'd had a sister."

Court grunted. "I've thought the same thing. Riley is hurt by their actions, but it's done out of love. They want to protect her."

"I think she believes they think her weak."

"Riley?" Court asked as he swiveled his head to Kane. "Weak? Not possible."

Kane raised a brow as one side of his lips lifted in a sort of smile. "I know. But Vincent, Lincoln, Beau, and Christian might have forgotten her strength while Riley was away at college."

"I'm glad she came here. Even with the danger, it's good to make that connection with our cousins again."

Kane turned so that he faced Court. "There's another connection that needs to be made. Get your ass in the house and kiss Skye like you've been longing to do."

Court blinked, taken aback. "What?"

"I know you, Court. The fact you've kept your distance from Skye tells me how much you like her."

Was it that obvious? Did the others know, as well? Did he care that they knew? No, he realized, he didn't.

"I do like her," he admitted. "I don't want to screw it up."

"Then go see her," Kane said and gave him a little push. "We've got things covered out here."

Once his feet started moving, Court couldn't stop. He walked to the house, up the steps to the porch, and through the front door. He paused long enough to close the door softly behind him, listening for Skye.

Court walked to the kitchen, glancing inside rooms as he went. He found Minka sitting alone at the kitchen table with a glass of untouched bourbon in her hand.

"She's in her room," Minka said with a smile.

Court nodded to the bottle. "Do you not like the brand?"

"I'm just thinking."

"You didn't have to come, but I'm glad you did. I'm sorry Solomon is such an ass."

Minka waved away his words. "I can handle Solomon. I'm more concerned with the plan."

He was too, but Court wasn't going to add more worry to her. "How did you know I was looking for Skye?"

At this, Minka chuckled. "You can't seriously be asking me that question with the way you've been looking at her."

"I guess not," Court said with a smile.

He walked to the fridge and got out two longneck beers. He waved goodnight to Minka and headed up the stairs. When he was outside his old bedroom door, he stopped and knocked.

A moment later, the door opened. Court held up the beers and smiled. "Care for a refreshment?"

"I'd love one," Skye said as she stepped aside and opened the door wider for him.

He walked into his bedroom and looked around at how she had made it hers. There were piles of clothes off in the corner. Her things that he had gotten for her four days earlier from her place.

Court cleared his throat and pulled his gaze away from the laundry and the memory of being inside her house and looking through her belongings.

He turned and set the bottles on the desk, twisting off first one cap and then the other. Then he held one out for her. Their fingers brushed as she took the offered beer.

Their eyes held for a moment before she leaned against the wall. Court remained across from her and propped his shoulder against the opposite wall.

"I'm surprised you aren't on patrol," she said into the silence.

He shrugged. "I wanted to give Myles time with Addison."

"I hate that everyone is doing all of this because of me. I'm a nobody, Court. Why should any of you care if I'm taken?"

He couldn't believe the thought had even entered her head. "Why do you say that?"

"I have no family, no friends, really. There's no one who would even miss me if I died."

"I would."

Her dark gaze locked with his. "You don't know me."

"I do. I know you're funny, brave, stubborn, and relentless. I know you value friendship and responsibility. I know you want to protect the innocent as we do."

"That's not all there is to know about me. I was born into an extremely wealthy family and raised in the Bahamas."

Court didn't interrupt her. He was happy she'd decided to share part of her past.

"My parents loved to spend money," she said with a smile. "They had nice things, but they spent on others, as well. I grew up in a stunningly beautiful place with everything I could ever want. I went off to UCLA for my degree, thinking that nothing would ever change. Then my parents got into a wreck, and they were both killed."

She paused and took a long drink of the beer. "Anyone's life will change with the death of their parents. But it was more. I learned that my parents were all but bankrupt, struggling to keep living as they had been and paying for my college. It was up to me to plan both of their funerals and sell everything they had to pay off the creditors."

Court hated the misery he saw on her face, but it was the glint of tears that about undid him. He could never stand to see a woman cry. It slayed him.

"All those people my parents gave to while they could were nowhere to be found. Not a single one of them helped me," Skye continued. "I had a knack for getting as much money as I could for the artwork and my mother's jewelry. That more than made up for other differences. There was nearly enough left after the bills were paid to pay for the rest of my college."

"Did you use it?"

"Some of it. I worked because I knew I had to change my life. I wouldn't always have money to fall back on. It was a lifestyle shift," she said with a grin.

THE ONLY OTHER person who'd ever heard that story was Jo, because her college roommate had helped her find a job and learn to manage money. Skye wasn't sure why she'd shared it with Court. It left her raw, exposed.

But it also felt as if it healed her.

She watched as he hooked a finger around the longneck

of the bottle and lifted it to his lips to drink. Surely he had to know how incredibly sexy he was.

It was his blond hair and the way it hit his jaw. It had more body than a man's hair had a right to. Even when he ran his fingers through it, it looked amazing.

And his eyes. Damn, the man had eyes that made her feel as if she were drowning in vivid, electric blue.

Then there was his body. With every muscle defined and sculpted to perfection, he made her mouth water.

Despite all of that, or maybe because of it, it was the way he made her feel. She felt special, as if she were the only woman on earth he cared about, and that melted her heart. He made her feel safe, secure. Something that she hadn't felt since her parents.

Skye swallowed as she realized the room had grown quiet as they stared at each other. The sexual tension was back. Truthfully, it had never left. It was only banked when he was away, but it flared to life anew when he was around.

He set his bottle down on the desk and closed the distance between them. He put a hand against the wall near her head and simply stared at her.

Skye's heart was pounding with excitement, her blood warming with need. Her gaze lowered to his mouth for a heartbeat while she struggled to keep oxygen moving through her lungs.

"Are you afraid of me?" he whispered.

"No. Never."

His hands slid to either side of her face as his lips touched hers.

Skye wanted to shout with joy. Her hands immediately rose to touch him, hating that she still held her beer in one hand. His kiss was soft, searching as he lightly kissed her a few times.

Then he groaned softly and slanted his mouth over hers. His tongue slid between her lips. She sagged against him, gripping his shirt with her free hand.

His arms shifted so that they were wrapped around her, holding her tight. The kiss deepened, and desire coiled low in her belly.

Suddenly, the beer was gone from her hand, taken by Court. He ended the kiss and lifted his head enough to look down at her.

"My God, you're beautiful."

Skye closed her eyes and rested her head on his chest as her arms wound around his neck. She had no idea how long they stood there before he set the beer down on the desk and held out his hand.

She knew what he was asking. And she knew there was never any other choice for her. She had known the first time she'd looked into his eyes that they would eventually end up at this moment.

Skye put her hand in his as she lifted her head to meet his gaze. The desire reflected in his gorgeous eyes made her catch her breath. He wanted her. And he wanted her to know it.

No one had ever looked at her so...blatantly before. It was exhilarating, thrilling. But there was another emotion reflected there. Deeper, stronger—fiercer even, an emotion that made her grip him tighter to keep standing.

The sexual tension they had been dancing around for days was no longer being ignored. It took center stage. And it was glorious.

Court's fingers slid into her hair, gently tugging her head back. His mouth was on her exposed neck, kissing a hot trail down to her collarbone while he moved them to the bed.

CHAPTER
FOURTEEN

He was in heaven. Blissful, delightful heaven.

Court couldn't stop touching her, learning her. Skye's skin was as soft as velvet. The more he touched, the more he needed. She was a drug, and after one kiss, he was addicted.

It was everything he could do to keep tight control over the need pounding through him. He wanted to toss her on the bed and cover her body with his, sliding into her until neither knew where one ended and the other began.

But Skye was different.

He wanted their time together to be different.

And God willing, it would serve as a solid foundation for something much more.

Court unbuttoned her shirt while he continued to place small kisses down to her breasts. As soon as the last button gave way, he pushed the shirt open and let his gaze feast upon her royal blue and black bra with leather trim.

It was so sexy, that for a moment, all he could do was stare at the material as his balls tightened.

"Do you like?" she asked, a grin in her voice.

Court nodded without looking up. "Please tell me you have more of these."

"I do."

"Thank goodness," he murmured.

Skye shrugged off the shirt, exposing more of her glorious skin. Court rested his hands on her ribcage and slowly caressed up and around to her back. With a twist of his fingers, he unhooked her bra. The garment sagged as the straps fell from her shoulders.

His gaze met hers then. There was no shyness, no caution. Passion shone brightly in her dark gaze. He loved a woman who knew what she wanted and wasn't embarrassed about it.

It made his own desire burn brighter, hotter. The woman had no idea how she was chipping away at his control. Court had always been able to govern his emotions.

Skye flayed him raw, leaving him bare and unprotected. He should be pushing her away, not pulling her closer. But with her, he wanted her to see all that he was—as well as all that he yearned for.

He refused to allow the walls that he usually erected between him and his lovers to come up. Skye was the kind of woman who would stand beside him, facing whatever the world decided to throw at him.

Those kinds of women were hard to come by, and Court wasn't going to let her slip through his fingers. He was going to do everything in his power to make her fall for him as he had already fallen for her.

Was it love?

If it wasn't, it was damn sure close. He might have cared for other women before, but there had never been one who brought out his protective instincts like Skye.

It wasn't just because she put herself in danger. It was the woman herself. There wasn't a part of her he wasn't completely infatuated with—including her stubbornness.

Court's hands shook when she removed the bra. He dropped his gaze back to her breasts. Unable to resist a moment longer, he cupped the globes, letting the weight of them sink into his memory.

Against his palm, her nipples hardened. The pulse at her neck was erratic, her chest rising and falling rapidly. He massaged her breasts before letting his thumbs circle her nipples until her eyes rolled back in her head.

Court smiled as he watched her. Her obvious pleasure only spiked his own. His cock ached to be free of his jeans.

He wrapped an arm around her waist as he dropped to his knees. Then he clamped his mouth around a turgid nipple and suckled it deep in his mouth.

Her answering moan was just what he needed to hear.

He moved from one breast to the other. Her hands were in his hair, holding him close.

Court unbuttoned her jeans and then lowered the zipper. He slid his hands into the waist at her hips and pushed the denim down. His cock twitched as his hands traveled down one shapely leg and then the other.

When the pants were bunched at her ankles, he lifted each of her legs in turn to step out of them. With one swipe, he shoved them across the floor.

Court kissed first one hip then the other, smiling as he did when he saw the same blue with black leather trim. The woman was going to kill him with her seductive underwear.

But he loved every moment of it.

He looked up at Skye to find her watching him.

She ran her fingers through his hair. "I've dreamt of this moment. I knew it would be amazing, but I didn't realize how much."

"You've not seen anything, yet," Court said as he stood.

He was about to lift her to lay her on the bed when Skye pulled his shirt up. Court raised his arms and helped her remove it.

Somehow, he stood still while her hands roamed over his chest, arms, and stomach. Everywhere she touched burned hotter, his desire increasing at a rapid rate.

SKYE DIDN'T WANT a single moment to pass by that she didn't remember. She touched his skin, amazed at how warm he was. He stood unmoving and let her touch every inch of his upper body. She had no idea how long she stood there before she realized his hands were fisted at his sides and his eyes were closed.

She paused, her gaze fastened to his face.

His eyes snapped open, and that's when she saw how he fought to remain immobile for her. Skye cupped his face with one hand.

Then she sat on the edge of the bed and reached for the waist of his jeans. She unfastened them and pushed them down. The jeans dropped to his ankles, and Court kicked out of them.

His arms were suddenly around her as he laid her back on the bed, kissing her as if there was no tomorrow. Skin to skin, they lay together, their bodies aflame with desire.

Skye was breathless when his mouth left hers and found her breasts again. They swelled once more, her nipples aching for his touch.

She opened her legs when he gave them a nudge with his knee. A gasp tore from her when he shoved aside her underwear and his fingers delved into her sex and found her clit. His touch was light as he teased her swollen nub until she was panting and mindless with need.

He alternated between licking her clit and sinking his

fingers deep inside her for a few thrusts. Skye was on the precipice of an orgasm for the longest time. Then it hit her.

COURT WATCHED HER BACK ARCH, her mouth open on a silent scream as her body jerked with her climax. It was the most beautiful thing he had ever seen. And he wanted to see it every day for the rest of his life.

He rose over her, his cock at her entrance. She was so wet he slid in easily. Her eyes opened to look at him as he pushed deeper.

With his teeth clenched, he thrust deeper into her tight sheath that fit him like a glove. He moved slowly, savoring every minute until he was fully seated within, an overwhelming sense of completeness washing over him.

Then he rolled onto his back, taking Skye with him. She smiled as she straddled him and sat up. A second later, she was rocking her hips.

Court hissed in a breath at the amazing feelings rushing through him. There was a slight clatter hitting the windows and he realized it was raining.

Skye moved faster and faster, pulling Court with her. He rolled her nipples between his fingers as she rode him. It wasn't long before she leaned down, her long curtain of black hair surrounding him.

He gazed into her dark eyes. As they made love, the attraction was strengthening into something much stronger. He could see it reflected in her eyes, and he knew she saw it in his.

Court pulled her down for a kiss and rolled her once more onto her back. Then he rose up on his hands and began to thrust hard and fast.

She gasped and ended the kiss as she clawed the comforter. Her legs wrapped around his waist, urging him faster. He didn't look away from her as he took them both higher and higher.

He wasn't ready for it to end when the orgasm claimed Skye once more. The feel of her body clamping around him was too much. He thrust twice more before his climax swept through him.

Emotion, deep and uncharted, filled Court when Skye wrapped her arms around him and simply held on. They lay with their limbs tangled, listening to the rain.

The night had changed him. Suddenly, he understood why Solomon kept his distance from women, because Court wasn't sure if he could survive losing Skye now.

She was part of his soul, part of his essence.

Part of his heart.

He knew without a doubt that it was love. He had fallen in love and hadn't even known it until that moment. Love had a way of sneaking up on people that way. It couldn't have come at a worse time, but it only spurred Court to think of other ways he could keep Skye safe.

Because he would walk through Hell itself if that's what it took.

Court stared out the window from the bed, watching the water run down the glass. He felt as tall as a giant with the love inside him. But he also felt as helpless as a newborn. It was a frightening situation he found himself in. Not that he would change a minute of it.

"The first thing we need to do when we leave this house is go find you more of that sexy underwear," Court said, hoping to lighten his own mood.

Skye chuckled. "I had no idea you would like it so much."

"I should've paid more attention when I opened that drawer of yours and tossed everything in a bag. I may have to go back."

She didn't laugh again as he had hoped. Instead, she let out a deep breath. "I'm really scared."

He lifted his head from her chest to look at her. "Don't be. I won't let anyone get you."

"Things happen." She smiled sadly, her dark eyes holding a frown. "Accidents happen."

"Not to you. Not with me."

She laid her palm on the side of his face. "I don't want to freak you out, and I probably shouldn't say this, but I care deeply about you."

"I feel the same." It was on the tip of his tongue to tell her he loved her, but not yet. The time would come soon.

"I'm glad," she said with a nod, dropping her hand. "I don't know what's going to happen tomorrow, but no matter what, I want you to know this night has meant the world to me."

Nothing was going to happen to her. Court refused to let her get hurt. She was his love, the woman he never expected to find.

"I read your article," he said.

Her eyes widened. "Really? I kept waiting for someone to say something."

"I knew you would send it in. It was good."

She glanced down. "I was trying to fix what I did. Not sure I succeeded."

"It's a start." He was proud that she had taken a step back from telling the world where the supernatural lived and what they looked like, to helping people understand the dangers of the unexplained around them. "What did Helen think about it?"

"She changed some of it to make it scarier," Skye said with a frown. "She wanted me to rewrite it, but I refused. I'm surprised she even ran the article."

Court propped his head up on an elbow. "You're talented. You'll find another job if you need to."

"I'm talented, huh?" she asked with a smile.

"Extremely."

Her smile faded as she became serious once more. "I hate that I wrote the article that got me in this mess, but it brought you to my door. That, I'm most thankful for."

"Not nearly as much as me. Whether you know it or not, Skye Parrish, you've changed me."

He took her mouth in another kiss as thunder rumbled around them, desire taking them once more.

CHAPTER

FIFTEEN

SKYE WOKE to the sound of rain. She was lying on Court's chest, his arm wrapped around her. She opened her eyes and shifted her head to look at him. A smile formed when she saw his other arm propped behind his head as he watched her.

"Was I snoring?" she asked.

He winked. "A little."

Skye laughed as she ducked her head. "Great."

"It was a cute little half-snore."

"There's no such thing."

"There is now."

He kissed the top of her head, and Skye didn't think a day could start any better. His arm tightened, drawing her closer.

"How did you sleep?" he asked.

"Like the dead. How about you?"

"Good."

She shifted to prop her head up on her hand to see him. "Liar. Did you sleep at all?"

"I dozed," he admitted. "It was nice to hold you. Even nicer to wake up with you."

Skye was going to die of pleasure. Court's words weren't false charm. She could see he meant them. "Can we stop time for a few hours?"

"If only I could," he said and fingered a lock of her hair.

She fell onto her back and looked at the ceiling. "It'll work. Minka's idea is solid."

"And puts you in danger again."

"There's no way around that," Skye said as she turned her head to him. "They want me."

Court sat up and leaned against the headboard. "I got you first."

His jest made her smile again. "Keep talking like that and I won't ever leave this room."

"Now you're speaking my language," he said as he leaned over her with a sexy half-smile.

She could feel his arousal against her leg. Skye reached down and wrapped her hand around him, slowly moving her hand up and down his length.

He moaned low in his throat, his eyes closing. It didn't matter how many times they had made love through the night, Skye wanted him again. He knew where to kiss, how to touch to send her spiraling.

Her body yearned for his touch, for him to fill her again. She loved his weight atop her. More than that, she loved him inside her, his rod sliding in and out, thrusting deep enough to touch her womb.

Skye never knew she was such a wanton. Then again, Court brought out many things in her she hadn't known. It was because he was with her that she had slept so soundly.

Suddenly, she found herself flipped onto her stomach. Court's large hands grabbed her hips and lifted her butt up into the air. Her hands fisted the covers as his fingers delved into her sex to make sure she was wet.

And then the blunt head of his arousal entered her. Skye closed her eyes in pleasure as he filled her, stretching her. Her body was pleasantly sore, but that didn't stop her from wanting more.

She rose up on her hands and looked over her shoulder at him. His chest rumbled with another groan as he leaned over her. One hand remained on her hips as he thrust while the other cupped her breast and tweaked her nipple.

Skye moaned and rocked her hips back against him. Her body was primed, ready for another orgasm, and when his fingers found her clit, she instantly climaxed.

The force of it took her breath away. He held her until her body stopped shaking. Then he held her hips and began to thrust. He went deeper, harder. Faster.

He held her so she couldn't move, so that she clamped

down on him every time he entered her. Soon she felt him shudder as he orgasmed.

They fell to the side, laughing as the rain hit the window harder. Court nuzzled the back of her neck while her sated body relaxed against him.

"Should we go down soon?" she asked.

Court shook his head. "They won't bother us, or think twice about us being up here the rest of the day."

"But your brothers will need you."

He sighed. "Probably."

"I also know how you want to be in the middle of the planning."

Court kissed her ear. "You know me well."

She was beginning to, but she knew there was much more of him to learn. And she couldn't wait to start.

"Why don't you get in the shower," he suggested.

Skye scooted out of his arms to the side of the bed. She looked back at him and smiled before disappearing into the bathroom.

Court waited until the door closed behind her before he fell back and put his arm over his head. He had run through Minka's plan over in his head all night. It was a solid plan. But there were still things that could go wrong. Every time he thought of one of them, his heart felt as if it were encased in ice.

He rose and wrapped a blanket around his waist as he walked from the room down the hall to Solomon's room. He didn't stop until he reached the master bath and shut the door. Then he took a quick shower, not bothering to shave.

In less than ten minutes, he was out and dressed in fresh clothes. He paused beside his room and listened to the shower running. Quietly, he walked inside and got his boots. Then he walked back out and down the stairs.

He was putting on his shoes on the bottom step when Kane walked from the back of the house into the foyer. Court nodded to his brother.

"I'm glad you took my advice," Kane said. "You look better."

Court finished with his boots and stood. He punched Kane in the shoulder with a grin. "Mind your own business."

A small smile began to form but didn't reach its full potential. "Minka's plan is in action. Griffin and a few of his men spread the rumor through the Quarter last night."

"There's no going back now," Court said, glancing back at his room.

Kane grunted. "This needs to be taken care of now."

"I know."

"Nothing will happen to her," Kane stated.

Court ran a hand through his still-wet hair. "Yeah."

He and Kane walked to the kitchen where Myles, Addison, and Riley were. Myles was stuffing the last of his breakfast in his mouth when they walked in. He kissed Addison and waved at them as he hurried out the back door.

"Morning," Riley said.

Court pulled out a chair and sat at the table. "Morning. Smells good, cuz."

Riley flashed him a bright smile. "That's because my cooking is awesome. I'm nearly as good as Beau."

Everyone knew that her brother was one of the best cooks around, hands down. Court watched Addison look worriedly out the back door.

A moment later, Solomon opened the door and walked in. He stopped at the entry and shook water from his hair and clothes. Riley threw him a towel, and he wiped as much off as he could.

As soon as he spotted Court, he walked to the table and took the chair opposite him. "Did Kane fill you in?"

"He did," Court said. "How do you feel about it?"

"We're all ready." Solomon stared at him intently. "And you? How do you feel?"

Like he was about to puke. "Good."

"I keep telling him he's not a good liar," Skye said from behind him.

Court turned and instantly held out his hand to her. Her lips turned upward in a grin as she came to him, their fingers sliding together. Court pulled out the chair next to him with his foot and she sat.

"He's worried," Kane said.

Skye lifted one shoulder in a shrug. "So am I. But it has to be done. None of us can continue like this."

"We could call in our cousins," Solomon offered.

Court looked at Riley to see her shoulders stiffen. Then she turned to them. "If we need them, then do it. Now."

"And give Delphine another go at them?" Court asked. "I don't think so. We've got the Moonstone clan helping. That should be enough."

Solomon ran a hand down his face, the weariness showing. "It better be. We're putting a lot of faith in the witch."

"Minka knows what she's doing," Addison said.

Kane nodded. "I agree. It'll work."

Court wasn't willing to bet Skye's life on it. Then again, if he didn't, her life was still in jeopardy. It was a no-win situation, and it sucked. Royally.

"Y'all didn't have to get up so early," Riley said with a wink to Court and Skye.

Skye laughed. "We were hungry."

"All you had to do was shout from the room," Addison said with a big smile. "We would've brought some food up."

Court looked around the kitchen. This was his family. It kept growing, and he was glad of it. It added more worry, but the more of them that joined together, the stronger they were.

He wondered if Kane would ever get past what had happened and be happy again. Until he could, he would never make room in his life for a woman.

Then there was Solomon. His eldest brother was beyond frustrating most days. Yet, Court held out hope with Minka.

The way the two of them rubbed each other raw could be because they both fought their desires.

Or it could mean they really hated each other.

Minka walked in at that moment. Solomon didn't even look at her as he poured himself some coffee. Minka smiled at everyone, but she also refrained from looking Solomon's way.

The back door opened and Griffin came inside. His attention was instantly on Minka.

"I could hear you, you know," she said to Solomon. "If you don't like my plan, then come up with another one."

Solomon kept his face averted. His lips peeled back in a sneer. "Do you think we weren't trying to come up with something?"

"With you, I don't know," Minka replied sarcastically.

Griffin smiled at Minka. "Solomon might not like your idea, but I think it's a good one. Anything else you need help with?"

"No, thank you," Minka said sweetly.

Court slid his gaze to Solomon to see a muscle twitch in his jaw. Riley put the bacon and eggs on the table, along with sausage and biscuits. Everyone had a seat except for Minka, who was pouring herself some coffee.

She turned around and saw the only open chair was next to Solomon, putting her between him and Griffin. Court shared a secret look with Skye, who also noticed the situation.

Skye leaned over. "Do you think she knows Griffin is into her?"

"Definitely," Court whispered.

Skye then asked in a low voice, "Does Solomon really not like her?"

Court moved aside her hair so his lips were by her ear. "I think the point is that he likes her. A lot."

"I don't understand," she said as she leaned back, frowning.

"His fiancée was killed years ago," Court whispered.

Skye's mouth formed a big O. Enough years had passed that Solomon could talk freely about it, but Court wasn't going to bring it up unless Solomon did.

There was small chitchat around the table as they ate. Despite the group, Court felt as if it were just him and Skye. He couldn't look at her without smiling, his love growing by the second.

"Ugh," Riley said with a roll of her eyes. "I can't sit at this table a minute longer and see the two of y'all making eyes at each other. The smiles and secret looks are driving me batty." She rose and looked pointedly at Court. "You do realize I'm single, right? Geesh. You two are worse than Addison and Myles."

"Amen," Kane said as he rose and gathered some dishes to bring to the sink.

Addison merely smiled. "I think it's cute."

Court's smile died when his gaze went to Solomon.

Because he knew his brother was remembering Misty.

And how he had lost her.

Suddenly, the food in Court's stomach turned sour. It was going to be a long damn day.

CHAPTER

SIXTEEN

SKYE DIDN'T THINK she had ever been so nervous in her entire life. Her hands shook, her palms were sweating, and at any moment, she expected to lose what little bit of food was in her stomach.

She leaned against the porch column watching as Court and his brothers left. The Moonstone pack had already made themselves scarce hours before. Now it was just Skye, Addison, Riley, and Minka in the house.

A house, which hours before had felt so comforting and safe, seemed ominous and...empty.

Skye put on a brave face for Court, even though she was trembling inside. He hadn't wanted to leave. In fact, it had taken all of them—especially her—to convince him that it would all work out.

Right before he stepped off the porch, he had pulled her

against him, nuzzling her neck. Then he had whispered, "I won't be far. I'll be near, ready to kill any vamp who comes for you."

He kissed her, hard. But it was full of passion and promise. Then he whispered something beneath his breath that had made Skye's heart skip a beat.

She wasn't completely certain, but it had sounded very much like 'I love you.'

Skye bit her tongue so she wouldn't call out to Court and beg him to remain. She touched her lips, her eyes filling with tears. She loved him. Desperately.

"I love you, Court LaRue," she whispered, hoping the wind carried her words to him.

When she could no longer see Court after he'd faded into the woods, Skye turned around and saw Minka standing at the screen door.

Minka blinked and looked at her as she pushed open the door. "We have a little over an hour until dusk."

"Right," Addison said and turned away from the porch railing to walk into the house.

Riley was next, a frown marring her forehead.

Skye grabbed the screen door. "What is there to do other than wait?"

"Lots," Minka said with a smile. "This house is protected, but I've been adding to them for the past few days."

Skye stepped into the house and let the screen door close

behind her. Then she shut the door. "Court said for us not to leave the house, so we should be fine."

"Oh, girl," Minka said as she linked her arm with Skye's. "You know the supernatural, but you don't really know them."

"What's that mean?"

"It means that they'll get you out of the house any way they can."

Skye tried to swallow, but her mouth was too dry. She had been pretty confident that Minka's idea would work. Now she was beginning to understand Solomon's reluctance and Court's nervousness.

"The boys won't be far," Minka hurried to say. "Court won't let anything happen. He cares deeply for you."

"And I for him. That does neither of us any good right now."

"You'd be surprised," Riley said from the doorway of the kitchen. She smiled and waved them toward her. "Love has a way of beating the odds sometimes."

Skye thought of her parents. "And others?"

"My parents were murdered by a vengeful woman who wanted my father for herself," Riley said. She shrugged as if it happened every day.

But Skye saw the pain in her gaze.

Addison was leaning against the kitchen counters. "Solomon's fiancée was killed right in front of his eyes. He couldn't reach her in time."

"I had no idea," Minka replied softly.

Skye walked to the fridge for a beer, but as she looked at the bottles, she knew she needed something stronger. She closed the refrigerator door and asked, "Where is the alcohol?"

It was Riley who walked out of the room and returned a few minutes later with a bottle of vodka and a bottle of bourbon. She held each up. Addison chose the vodka while Skye picked the bourbon.

"What happened to Solomon's woman?" Minka asked.

Riley poured herself some bourbon and sat at the table. "The specifics are never discussed. I know she was killed, and that Solomon blames himself."

"How long ago?" Skye asked.

Addison tossed back a shot of vodka. "Several years. It's why you never see him with anyone."

"He refuses to let another woman close," Riley said.

Skye sipped her bourbon. "I can understand that after such a tragedy."

"We're not going to end up like her," Addison said. She set down the glass and looked at each of them. "We know what's coming. We know what they want. And we have a witch on our side."

Minka's smile was slight. "I'm here to help in any way I can, but until we know who it is that's helping the vampires, we can only wait."

"Personally, I think you're damn brilliant," Riley said to Minka.

The witch shrugged, though she beamed from the praise. "I wanted to help."

"Still," Skye said, impressed herself. "I would never have thought to spread a rumor to have them show up."

Addison smiled. "I know, right? Most want to keep hidden. But not Minka. She puts it all out there."

"We were in the middle of it not that long ago," Minka said to Addison. "Running doesn't do any good."

Skye knew the truth of that. The past week had been both tiring and wonderful. Yet it was no way to live. For any of them. She owed each person there a debt she would most likely never be able to repay, but she was going to try.

"It feels weird not having the guys in the house," Skye said.

Riley's lips twisted. "I have to agree that I miss seeing those sexy Moonstone wolves. Especially Griffin. Can we say yum?"

"I've seen how some of them look at you," Addison said to Riley. "You won't be single long with that bunch."

"Now that's what I'm talking about." Riley held up her glass and tossed back the contents. "It's been awhile since I've been kissed. Between Addison and Myles, and now Court and Skye, I'm feeling the need for a man."

Addison was still smiling when she turned her gaze to

Minka. "I'm pretty sure if Minka gave Griffin even a hint that she was interested, she would have some company, as well."

Minka rolled her eyes. "I've got enough to occupy my time, thank you very much. A man just complicates things."

"Unless he's worth it," Skye added, thinking of Court.

Who was more than worth it.

"Can't argue with that," Riley said.

Minka cleared her throat. "Let's get down to business, girls. The house is warded, but none of you are. I'm going to change that. I've made these," she said and set three bracelets on the table.

Skye sat forward to peer at them closer. The bracelets were silver, each a different design. Minka handed Addison a bracelet with long links. Riley was given one with several small cords of silver that were braided.

Minka then handed the last bracelet to Skye. Skye accepted the piece of jewelry, running her fingers along the two bands of silver. They looked dainty, but they were hard and substantial. Anchoring the two bands on either side was an oval with a fleur-de-lis etched in it.

Skye slipped the bracelet on her wrist. The bangle felt right resting against her skin. She looked up at Minka and smiled.

"Will this keep the vampires away from us?" Riley asked.

Minka shoved her long curls over her shoulder. "Hopefully it'll keep everything away from you. Including Delphine," she said, looking pointedly at Riley.

Skye frowned. That name again. She was truly an enemy of both the Chiassons and the LaRues. And she sounded awful.

"She knows you're here," Minka continued. "She's already tried to kill your brothers. It's only a matter of time before she turns to you."

Riley put her bracelet in place and smiled. "Let the bitch try."

"The bracelets will stop some magic, but not all of it. No ward will stop all magic. If whoever is after you is smart enough and has enough time, they can figure a way to get to you."

"We'll keep that in mind," Skye said. She touched the bracelet with her left hand. "If I do leave the house, will the bracelet keep the vampires away from me?"

Minka nodded. "It should. Keep in mind we still don't know who is working with the vamps. I used wards that will protect y'all against anyone—human or supernatural—out to harm you. It covers a broad range but could leave a gap open where the bracelets won't work."

"Where is yours?" Addison asked.

Minka linked her fingers together on the table. "I have my own wards."

Skye glanced out the window. The sun was sinking rapidly. It wouldn't be too much longer before the vampires surrounded the LaRue house.

Who else would be with them? The Djinn? The witches? Delphine?

"You aren't in this alone," Riley said as she laid a hand on Skye's arm.

Skye swiveled her head to the pretty brunette. "I know, and I can't tell you how thankful I am for that. I don't think I could do this alone."

"Yes you could." Addison smiled when Skye shot her a surprised look. "We're all stronger than we think we are. You proved that already, Skye."

Skye choked on a laugh. "By running?"

"By standing against the vampires with a knife," Minka said.

"I only had the courage to do it because I knew Court was there and the rest of you were outside the club."

Riley snorted loudly. "Whatever the reason, you impressed the hell out of me. I hate vampires."

"Ditto," Addison said with a shiver. "I had my own run-in with one."

Skye was intrigued now. "What happened?"

Addison smiled widely. "Myles ripped his throat out with his teeth."

They all laughed. Though Skye's mind turned to Court and how he had shifted to a wolf at the vampire club. His teeth had been scary sharp, not to mention long. And he snapped his jaws with a force that meant anything in his way was going to be cut in half.

Court's family had suffered their own tragedies. It was a wonder they could continue on as they did, but it was because they had a mission to carry out.

"For the first time in a long time, I have something to live for," Skye said. She tucked her hair behind her ear. "I've been wandering for so long, angry at the supernatural around me. Yet it brought me to this city and put me in Court's path. I…I don't want to lose him."

Riley sat back in her chair with a grin. "Trust me, Court isn't going to let you go anywhere. He's a wolf, an alpha, and once they find their women, they don't let go."

"I can attest to that," Addison said with a wink.

"I love him." Skye laughed after she let the words pass her lips. "I do. I love him."

Minka's smile was a little sad. "I think we all figured that out already."

"We'll get through this night because we stand together, Skye," Riley said. "The LaRues have always been good for this city. They're good men, but more than that, they're feared and respected here."

"That's right," Minka added. "Unfortunately, that means that if the LaRues show an ounce of weakness, the rest of the factions will see it."

Skye took a deep breath. She looked from Addison to Riley, and then focused on Minka. The witch was the only one who didn't have a tie to the LaRues. "No matter what happens to me, don't let them show any weakness. Remind them what they stand for and what their presence means to the city."

"I will," Minka pledged.

Skye looked out the window to see the last rays of the sun disappear. The time had arrived.

CHAPTER
SEVENTEEN

COURT WAS RESTLESS, edgy. He didn't like leaving Skye behind. Despite him knowing it was the only way to end this thing the vampires had out for her once and for all.

The minutes ticked by as slow as centuries. He thought the sun would never set. Then as soon as it did, he wished it hadn't.

Myles and Kane had already shifted. They were on patrol on the back side of the house. Court flexed his hand as he felt his wolf urging him to give in and shift. But he waited. He was faster, stronger...deadlier in wolf form. Yet he felt the need to fight as a man, not a werewolf.

In the end, his wolf would win. Until then, he was in control.

"You're smarter than I was," Solomon whispered.

Court frowned and jerked his head to his brother. "What?"

"With your woman. I didn't think anything could touch mine." Solomon's smile was full of regret and guilt. "I assumed that the other factions would leave us alone."

Court had never heard Solomon talk of Misty or himself this way. It took him aback to the point that he didn't know what to say.

"You've always been cautious," Court said.

Solomon shook his head. "Not always. I learned my lesson the hard way. The same won't happen to you."

"Because we planned this out?"

"Because you're not as prideful as I was." Solomon looked at the ground. "All hell is liable to break loose this night. It doesn't matter who is working with the vampires because all the factions will be watching us."

Court understood what Solomon was saying. "We can't show any weakness."

"Not even a drop. If we lose our foothold of authority, we'll be descended upon by all the factions within days."

Their hold had always been precarious no matter what generation it was. It wasn't easy being a LaRue, but it was a position Court relished.

"I have your back, little brother," Solomon said.

Court watched Solomon shift into a wolf, his clothes shredding and falling to the ground before Solomon trotted off. A moment later, Court gave into the wolf within him and shifted, as well.

He took in a deep breath. Even a mile away from the house he could smell Skye. Her scent was distinctive, alluring. She meant everything to him. He hadn't had the balls to tell her when he'd left, but he wished he had. His whispered words had been for him.

His gaze lifted to the sky. The moon was climbing fast. By now his brothers would've taken their positions around the house. The Moonstone clan were behind them. Griffin's weres were always ready to fight, especially against vampires or Delphine.

Court never thought to see the Moonstone pack return to New Orleans, but he was immensely glad Griffin had brought them back to the city where they belonged. The werewolves were no longer a minority within the factions. Their numbers were increasing daily.

But right now, Court's attention was on the vampires after his woman. He crouched behind a clump of young pines and waited, hidden by their branches. His hiding spot was along the most direct route to the house from the city, but none of them expected his to be the only one used.

None of the weres were to attack any faction until the vampires attacked the house. Hopefully, they would also learn who was working with the bloodsuckers.

Court's paw dug into the ground, muddy from the recent rain. His ears turned backward as he heard movement. It was faint, almost as if it never was. But he wasn't fooled. The supernatural were gifted in all ways.

Then again, so was he.

The first vampire walked by him so close that he could have leaned over and snapped his teeth around his ankle. Instead, Court let him go.

"You don't really believe the LaRues left, do you?" a female vamp asked the man next to her as they walked toward the house.

The male chuckled softly. "I do. Stupid werewolves think they will find us all at the club to teach us a lesson. We'll be the ones to teach them."

Court's lip lifted in a snarl, but he held his growl back before any sound could be made. Fury sped through him. He might have been too young to get revenge for his parents' murder, but he was strong enough now to ensure his woman was well protected.

It took everything he had to let those vampires walk away. More and more vamps were coming, spreading out through the forest. Most didn't even look around for enemies. They had truly bought the rumor Markus had begun the day before that the LaRues were coming for the vampires at the Viper's Nest.

The sheer number of vampires worried Court. He was more than up for a fight, but his concern was for Skye. She feared the vamps. After what had happened to her both in California and in New Orleans, she had every right.

It tore at Court that he wasn't at her side to help her. His only consolation was the fact that Riley, Minka, and Addison were with Skye. Riley was more than proficient in hunting and killing the supernatural.

And Minka...well, the witch had skills. She'd saved Myles from certain death when he'd had silver in his system.

Addison wasn't a shrinking violet. She had been learning from both Myles and Riley how to fight and hunt. Soon, she would be more than capable of taking care of herself.

After Court saw Skye in the vampire club slashing at the vampires, he knew she wouldn't curl up in a ball and wait for death to find her. It still didn't make it any easier for him.

Another five minutes passed before Court could take it no longer. He leapt from his hiding spot and clamped his teeth around the neck of a vampire. They fell to the ground as Court twisted his head, snapping the vamp's neck and ripping out his throat at the same time.

He saw movement behind him as the Moonstone weres began to silently take out any vampire near them. Court turned back toward the house and saw a vampire watching them.

Court started running, the ground blurring beneath him. He had to reach the vampire before it alerted the others that it was a trap. Court leapt and landed on the vampire just as he shouted. His voice gurgled as Court removed his throat.

But it was too late. The damage had already been done.

All around him vampires turned in his direction, hissing

their fury. He growled, hunkering down and showing his fangs. They wanted a fight. And they were going to get one.

SKYE JERKED when the first thud hit the house. All four of them jumped up from the table and rushed to the front of the house.

"Well shit," Riley mumbled as she looked out the window.

Addison paled as she turned to Skye. "There are so many of them."

Minka ran to the back and returned a few minutes later. "They're surrounding the house."

Skye began to panic. Then she saw the bracelet and remembered that both she and the house were warded. It was going to be all right. It had to be.

"We only want Skye," came a male voice from outside. "Send her out, and the rest of you will be unharmed."

Riley motioned for them to hide. Then she opened the front door and glared at the vampires through the screen door. She crossed her arms over her chest. "Do everyone a favor and go away. You're not getting near Skye."

"You're alone, woman," the vampire said.

Riley snorted. "Do you honestly think I need a man to protect me?"

"You're not supernatural."

"Nope. That I'm not. What I am is a Chiasson."

Skye leaned to the side of the doorway and saw the vampires muttering among themselves. If Riley had been keeping who she was a secret, she'd just told the entire city.

Skye couldn't see much of the male, all she could tell was that he was tall. She wished she could see his face for future reference. It galled her that they all knew who she was, but she didn't know them.

"We only want Skye," the male vampire said again.

Riley dropped her arms. "Get it through your thick skull, vamp. You're not coming near her."

The vampire stepped away from the others. "You think you're untouchable because the house is warded? Think again, human."

"Please, try something. I've not been hunting in a week, and I'd like nothing better than to take your head."

Skye covered her mouth with her hand as she hid her laughter at Riley's arrogance. The smile vanished when a vampire rushed the house. As soon as he reached the porch, he was thrown backward.

Again and again the vampires charged the house. Riley calmly closed the door then stalked to the coat closet and pulled out a crossbow.

"Well, that certainly worked," Minka said as she walked into the foyer.

Riley rolled her eyes. "It was better than letting them think we were huddled in here scared."

"Everyone get a weapon," Addison said.

Riley rested the crossbow on her shoulder. "Done."

Minka held up her hands and wiggled her fingers. "I am the weapon."

"True," Addison said with a smile. She then began to load a revolver with silver bullets. "Skye?"

Skye touched her waist where the silver-bladed knife rested in its scabbard. "Got it. How long can the wards hold up?"

"Forever with idiots like these," Minka said.

No sooner had the words left her mouth than the house shook as if the ground had shifted beneath them. Skye reached out her arms, grabbing anything she could to keep standing. She jerked her gaze to Minka to find the witch's face lined with worry.

"That was bad," Riley said.

Minka nodded. "Very."

Addison grabbed the box of silver bullets. "How long do we have until they're past the wards?"

"Seconds."

Skye's ears rang from the loud boom around them so she didn't know who'd said it, but it didn't matter. The vampires were breaking through the wards.

"We need to get outside," Minka shouted.

Skye shook her head. "Court said to remain here."

Minka rushed to her. "Look, if we stay inside, they'll

break through the wards. The wards need to remain intact so that we have a place to come to."

"But won't they know how to break them later?"

Minka shook her head. "They're throwing every bit of magic they have at it."

"Who is?"

"The Djinn."

Skye's legs buckled. She grabbed the banister to keep her feet. "That's who teamed up with the vamps?"

"Looks that way," Riley said, her hand on the doorknob. "Everyone ready?"

Skye walked to the door. "Not in the least."

"Me either," Riley said with a wink.

Then Riley threw open the door.

CHAPTER

EIGHTEEN

HE WAS SO busy killing vampires that it took Court a moment to realize he wasn't the only one. He stood with his front paws on the chest of a dead vamp on the ground as his gaze fastened on none other than Scott.

His one-time friend had some gall being there taking advantage of the situation by killing supernatural beings. Scott was dead wrong if he thought he would be able to sneak up on Court and kill him.

Scott swung his axe, beheading the vampire he was fighting. His chest heaved and sweat ran down his face. The black tee he wore was splattered with blood, as were his arms, neck, and face.

He turned his head and looked at Court. His lips parted as if he were going to talk. Just then, Court spied a vampire stalking Scott. Court took off running, tackling the vampire and killing him quickly.

If anyone was going to kill Scott, it was going to be Court. He swiveled his head and growled at Scott.

"I know you don't want me here," Scott said. "But I wasn't going to sit by and not help."

Court turned away from him. He didn't want to hear anything Scott had to say because nothing could make up for the betrayal.

A howl sliced through the air. Court stilled, his heart thumping hard against his ribs. He recognized the howl as Kane's, alerting him that the women were out of the house.

Court looked around at the dead vampires littering the ground. There were many of them, but not nearly enough. It was time to close in on the trap.

He started toward the house when Scott stepped in front of him. Court bared his teeth and growled.

"Let me help," Scott said.

Court lunged and snapped his jaws.

A frown marred Scott's face. "What is with you? You're not the type to decline such an offer in this situation."

Court didn't have time for this. He rushed past Scott, his mind on Skye. Every vamp he closed in on as he ate up the ground, he killed. Then he reached the edge of the trees and saw the vampires surrounding the house. But that was nothing compared to seeing Skye standing in front of the house. It made his heart stop.

She was supposed to remain inside. If she and the others

hadn't, it was for good reason. Out of the corner of his eye, he saw movement.

The Moonstone pack was slowly closing in on the vampires. They were all crouched low to the ground, their gazes trained on the enemy.

Court was about to take out a vampire when he caught sight of a Djinn. So that's who was helping the vampires.

To Court's left was Gage, Griffin's brother. He saw the Djinn, as well. The Djinn normally kept to themselves, distrusting everyone. It would have to take something big to have them partner with the vampires, which meant it had to be more than Skye's article.

The Djinn's magic was fierce. They were never easy to take down, but the LaRues had had run-ins with them before. Court wasn't afraid to fight them. He was afraid of Skye being harmed in the process.

With a nod to Gage, Court leapt in the middle of the vampires and began sinking his teeth into them.

SKYE WAS SO AFRAID, that for a moment she couldn't move. The vampire numbers were impressive, but it was the Djinn standing in front of them that stole her breath.

"Silver works on the Djinn, as well," Riley said to her.

Skye pulled out her knife, wishing it were a bit longer. Something like a machete. Or a sword. A sword would be awesome in this instance. Really, anything that would keep the monsters from getting close.

Everyone stood staring at each other, the silence deafening. Not even the animals of the bayou dared to make a sound. It was as if the world held its breath waiting to see what would happen.

Suddenly, Skye saw a blur of tawny fur in the moonlight in front of her. Court. He attacked the vampires, and immediately after that, there were werewolves everywhere.

Some vampires tried to scatter to get away, but there were more weres waiting for them in the trees. Other vampires took the opportunity to try and kill the weres. They succeeded in taking out six werewolves, too.

The male vampire who'd spoken earlier, those closest to him, as well as the Djinn, focused on Skye, Riley, Addison, and Minka.

Riley fired the crossbow, landing an arrow in the forehead of a Djinn. Those around him paused and watched as he fell back, dead.

Riley smiled and quickly loaded another silver-tipped arrow. "Come on, you ugly douches. It's time to die."

That's all it took for the vampires and Djinn to rush them. Skye could do nothing more than keep slashing her blade, praying that neither of them could touch her. Because if they did, they could put her under the same spell as before.

COURT FINISHED off another kill and felt the slash of a vampire's nails in his fur. Blood ran down his flank as he whirled around, snapping his jaws.

Before he could attack, Gage locked his jaws around the vamp's throat. Court let Gage finish him off as he turned to look for Skye.

He saw the vampire leaders, including Jacques and Anton, surrounding her. The Djinn in the mix only made things more dangerous. Court spotted Skye doing her best to hold her own with Minka on one side of her and Riley on the other.

Minka was doing a fine job with her magic keeping the Djinn at bay, but the Djinn were quickly weakening her. Court attacked the Djinn closest to him. His jaws clamped on his arm, halting him long enough for Skye to plunge her dagger into his heart.

Between the vampires' claws and the Djinn's magic, there wasn't an inch on Court that didn't have a wound. A Djinn rushed Riley, knocking her to the ground so that the crossbow flew from her hands.

A second later, Gage was on the Djinn. Riley rolled over to get an arrow. She sat up and thrust it into the side of the Djinn's head.

Court stayed close to Skye. When he next looked up, Kane, Solomon, Myles, and Griffin were there, as well. Court felt as if the tide were turning in their favor. Right up until a

Djinn got too close to Skye while Court was fighting a vampire.

The Djinn touched her, and Skye screamed and flew backward to lay unmoving. Court rushed to her, standing over her with his teeth bared. His gaze was locked on the Djinn who had hurt his woman. The savage would die. Painfully.

Court ducked a flare of magic from the Djinn, but he wasn't quick enough. It slammed into him, the pain causing his limbs to freeze. When he was able to open his eyes, he was no longer a wolf.

He glanced at Skye and saw her knife inches from her hand. Court acted as if he was too weak to sit up and fell sideways. As soon as his hand closed around the hilt of the weapon, he slowly climbed to his feet.

"Are you ready to die?" the Djinn asked, his black tattoos covering his bald head so thickly that there was barely an inch of skin not marked.

Court pushed back the pain from his many injuries. "Are you?"

"I'm not the one weakened to such a state," the Djinn stated. His gaze was contemptuous as he looked Court up and down. "Look at you. A LaRue werewolf taken to protecting a human who would expose us."

"She's my woman."

The Djinn's smile was slow and evil. "In that case, I'll

make sure she suffers even more. Perhaps I won't kill you. I'll take you with us and make you watch what I do to her."

"Do you really think you can?"

"The LaRues are no longer as strong as they once were. Your time in the Quarter is finished."

Court tightened his grip on the knife. "Then come and get me."

The noise of the battle faded as Court focused on the Djinn. He knew exactly what the Djinn would do to Skye, and it was worse than the vampires turning her.

But that wasn't going to happen.

Court waited for the Djinn to get closer. He swung the dagger up into the Djinn's mouth through his chin the same instant a shot rang out and slammed into the Djinn's head.

He pulled the blade from the Djinn and turned to Skye. He gathered her in his arms and held her while gently stroking her face.

"It's over," Riley said as she came to stand beside him. "The remaining vampires and Djinn are leaving."

Court looked up to find his brothers surrounding him still in wolf form. The Moonstone wolves slowly made their way to them.

"Thank you all," Court said to everyone. "We couldn't have done this without you. The werewolves have been absent from New Orleans for too long. This is your home. Our home. We showed the factions that tonight."

Minka squatted down beside him and touched Skye's

head. "She was given a heavy dose of magic, but she'll wake up soon."

"Thank you," Court told her.

Minka smiled. "It's my pleasure."

"The others know you're not dead now."

She shrugged. "It was bound to happen eventually. I'll deal with it."

"We'll deal with it," he corrected her. "You're not alone in this."

Minka stood and moved away, but Court noticed that Solomon walked so that he was near her. Court gathered Skye in his arms and got to his feet. Addison, Riley, and Minka were careful to keep their gazes away from him since he was nude.

He was about to turn to go into the house when Kane issued a growl. Court watched as Scott rolled a vampire off him and got on his hands and knees before he stood. Scott looked around until he saw Court.

That's when Court saw the gun in Scott's hand. So that's who had shot the Djinn he'd been fighting. He should thank Scott for that, but then again, none of them would be here if Scott hadn't betrayed him.

"You should leave," Court told Scott. "You're not welcome here."

Scott holstered his gun and ran a hand through his hair. "All because I couldn't handle my best friend being a werewolf?"

Kane growled again, Myles joining in when Scott tried to walk near. Scott stopped, his hands up.

Court shook his head. "You betrayed us."

"Betrayed you?"

Was it Court's imagination, or was Scott genuinely confused? "You were the only one who knew we were going to use Skye as bait at the Viper's Nest."

"I didn't tell anyone," Scott stated in an angry tone. "Who would I tell? Those in the precinct who don't believe? Or the ones who do who would use it against you?"

"You were the only one who knew," Court repeated. "You nearly got Skye killed. I didn't realize your hatred of me went so deep."

Court turned and walked to the steps of the porch. He was walking through the front door when Scott yelled, "I didn't betray you!"

But Court knew it was a lie, even if he did want to believe him. It always hurt to lose a friend. Yet that was life. People came in and out of your life all the time. Scott was one that was on his way out for good.

CHAPTER
NINETEEN

Court laid Skye on the couch and was hit in the back with something that fell to the floor. He glanced behind him to see a pair of jeans.

He put on the jeans. As he was buttoning them, he said, "Y'all can come in now."

"Is it safe?" Riley asked. "Because I don't care to be blinded."

Court chuckled as he put a blanket over Skye. He had no idea how long she would sleep. The situation was over. Hopefully for good. But if he had to, he would fight the vampires and Djinn every day of his life to keep Skye safe.

"I think your brothers want you," Minka said from the doorway.

Court sighed as he stared down at Skye.

Minka came to stand behind him. "I'll stay with her."

"Thanks," he said and turned on his heel.

Court walked back outside to see his brothers standing naked around Scott, who was arguing with Kane. Court stalked to them.

"Enough!" Court yelled as he reached the group. He glared at Scott. "You had your chance to leave. That's gone now."

Scott returned his scowl with one of his own. "I chose not to leave."

"Then it's your funeral," Kane stated.

Scott shot him a dirty look before his gaze returned to Court. "I didn't betray you."

"You keep saying that, but that doesn't make it true. You're the only one who knew," Court said.

"You expect me to believe that everyone who works for you is to be trusted?"

"Damn straight," Solomon said.

Scott ran a hand down his face. His gaze was beseeching. "Court, man, I didn't do it. As soon as I heard what happened I've been staking out the Viper's Nest. It's how I knew what was going down here."

Court wanted to believe him, but the past was difficult to forget. "You turned your back on me."

"I know." Scott sighed loudly. "I didn't know what to think, and I was young and stupid. That doesn't make what I did right. So many times I wanted to drop by the bar."

Court frowned. "Then why didn't you?"

"Shame. Embarrassment. Worry you might hold a grudge. Take your pick."

Myles crossed his arms over his chest. "It was Scott who reached out to me about a year ago."

"The fact is, someone betrayed me," Court said.

"I think I know who it was."

Court whirled around as soon as he heard Skye's voice. He was so glad to see her awake that all he could do was smile. Until her words penetrated his mind. "Who?"

"Helen." Skye walked down the steps and came to stand before Court as she held out jeans for his brothers to take. "I told her what I was going to do."

Kane grunted loudly. "Well, hell."

"That's putting it mildly," Myles replied.

Skye shook her head. "I believe Scott. If he betrayed you, why would he risk his life by being here now?"

"I don't know." Court pulled her against him and held her tight. It felt so good to just hold her.

"You're wounded."

"They'll heal." His heart wouldn't if something had happened to her.

"They better."

He smiled down at her as he ran his hand down her silky length of black hair. Then she pulled away from him and turned them toward Scott.

"Thank you for your help tonight," Skye said. "If you don't mind, I'd like to ask for your help again."

Scott glanced at Court, then nodded. "Name it."

Court looked at Skye, wondering what she was up to. He didn't want to stand amid the dead vampires and Djinn or talk anymore. He wanted her up in his bed, naked, so he could make love to her all night.

"I want you to help me get Helen," Skye announced.

Court blinked. "Skye."

She shook her head and stepped out of his arms, holding up a hand. "Don't, Court. Remember that anger a moment ago when you felt that Scott had betrayed you? Well, that's what I'm feeling. Helen isn't a friend, but she is my boss and a mentor of sorts. She was the one who urged me to write those articles after I pitched them to her."

"So she put Skye in danger," Kane said.

Court hadn't looked at it that way until that moment. Now he wanted to get his hands on Helen. He reined in his fury—barely.

"How do you want to handle this?" he asked.

Skye smiled and looked around. "With this bunch, it should be easy enough."

"When?"

"No better time than the present."

Skye had woken to shouts. Despite Minka trying to keep her lying down, Skye had gone outside to listen. That's when she came to the conclusion that it was Helen who'd betrayed her.

It wasn't nervousness that filled Skye. How could there be any after she'd faced vampires and Djinn earlier? No, there was only anger and the need for some kind of revenge.

Skye had failed theater in high school, but this was different. This was her life. And she wanted it back. She had trusted the wrong person, and she'd nearly paid the ultimate price for it.

"Are you sure?" Court asked as they stood in the shadows of the building across the street from the paper's offices.

His concern warmed her heart. She leaned her cheek into the hand he held against her face. "Yes."

"I'd rather go in with you."

"If this is going to work, then you need to remain out here."

"It sucks," he grumbled.

She kissed his palm. "Now you know how I felt earlier. I'll be back soon."

As soon as she tried to turn away, he pulled her back. "Skye, I need to tell you something. I should've told you before the battle."

"What is it?" His anxiousness was worrying her. Was he wanting to end whatever was getting started between them? The mere thought made her clutch the bricks to remain on her feet. She loved him.

He shifted his feet, swallowing loudly. Then he spoke in a rush. "I love you. I know we haven't been together long, but I know what I feel. I don't expect you to return the feeling yet, but I hope you will in time."

Skye threw her arms around his neck. "I love you, too."

"What?" He grew still, his hands barely holding her.

"I love you, too."

There was a moment where he didn't move, didn't utter a sound. And then his arms were around her, holding her so tight she could barely breathe.

His face was buried in her neck. "You've made me the happiest man alive."

Skye laughed as he placed kisses all over her face. Then he suddenly drew back, a frown upon his face. "What is it?"

"Don't go in there," he urged. "Forget Helen."

Skye was shaking her head before he'd finished. "She could do this to someone else, Court. I couldn't live with myself if I allowed that."

"Then let me be with you when you confront her."

Skye was about to refuse him again when she had an idea. She pulled out her cell phone and dialed Helen. As soon as her editor picked up the phone Skye put her acting face on. "Oh, Helen, thank God you answered."

"Skye? What's wrong?" her editor asked with just the right amount of concern.

"I'm in trouble. The vampires are after me. I've managed to elude them so far, but I need a place to go."

"Come to the office."

Skye rolled her eyes as Court stood close enough to hear the conversation. "I'm nearly there. Can you take me out of the city?"

"Um…sure. I'll meet you at my car."

Skye ended the call. "I should've thought of that sooner. It's better this way, instead of confronting her in her office where there are cameras."

"Come on," Court said as he held out his hand. "Let's get the others and let them know things have changed."

It took only a few minutes to fill Scott and the LaRue brothers in on the new plan as they walked to the parking garage where Helen had her car.

"Are you sure she'll call the vampires?" Scott asked.

Skye shrugged. "We'll find out soon enough."

"I'll hide," Court said. He kissed Skye before he ducked behind a car.

Skye began to pace as if she were nervous and scared. It seemed to take forever for the sound of Helen's heels to be heard on the concrete.

"Skye?"

She came around the back of a tall SUV at the sound of Helen's voice. "Thank you," she said and wiped at her eyes as if she had been crying. "It's been a horrible night."

Helen dug in her purse for her keys. "What happened? Where have you been?"

"Hiding anywhere I could for the last week. That night I went to the Viper's Nest they were expecting me."

Helen's head jerked up. She pushed her graying head of blond hair away from her face. "How?"

"I don't know." Skye hoped she was convincing enough. It was hard being so close to Helen and not letting the anger take her.

"It's all right. I'll take you somewhere safe."

Skye walked with her, looking over her shoulder as she did. "I need out of New Orleans for awhile."

"Not a problem. I've got some friends that can help."

Skye stopped walking. "The same friends you called to tell I was going back to the club?"

Helen slowed, then stopped. She dropped her arms and turned to face Skye. "When did you figure it out?"

"Not soon enough. Why would you betray me?"

Helen barked in laughter. "Not everything is about you, Skye. You're so focused on what you wanted that you never stopped to think that others might be affected."

"You told me to write the articles!" she yelled.

"Of course. It was a good way to get rid of you."

Skye fisted her hands at her sides. "Why? Why not just tell me the articles wouldn't be of interest?"

"Because you weren't about to give up!" Helen shouted. "You would've gone to anyone who would've listened. Or worse, put them on the internet yourself. This way, I could regulate what you were saying and take care of you if you got too close."

"Which is what happened with the Djinn," Skye surmised.

Helen shrugged. "Shit happens. You stepped in the wrong pile. This is my city. These are my people."

"The humans or the supernatural?"

"Both," Helen said with a lift of her chin. "It has taken me years, but I've made connections in both worlds that keep me protected."

There was a sound of male laughter as Scott turned the corner near Helen's car. "That's quite a confession."

"Oh, please," Helen said. "The police will do nothing to me."

"You're probably right," Scott said.

Helen flicked her shoulder-length hair back. "Detective, you'd have been better served staying out of this. Now you'll die with Skye this night."

At that moment, three vampires came out of nowhere. Skye cut her gaze to Helen. "You won't get away with this."

"Of course, I will," Helen said with a laugh. She turned on her heel to go to her car, but drew up short when she caught sight of Court.

Skye smiled at her man. He was glorious in his fury. The three vampires were quickly dispatched by Myles, Solomon, and Kane.

Helen stumbled backward and turned to Skye, beseeching her. "Don't let him hurt me."

"So you know who he is?" Skye asked.

Helen nodded, glancing at Court. "He's a LaRue. They police the factions."

"What do you expect me to do?"

"Mercy," Helen begged as she dropped to her knees.

Skye wanted revenge, but seeing Helen on her knees changed her mind. She looked up at Court. He was waiting on her decision, letting her make the call.

"Leave," Skye said to Helen. "Leave the city and never return."

Helen's face went blank. "But...this is my home."

"You asked for mercy," Court stated in a deep voice. "That's the extent of it. Leave or face the consequences."

Helen nodded and got to her feet. "I'll start packing."

"You have two days," Court said.

Skye walked out of the parking garage with Court. Solomon, Kane, Myles, and Scott were behind them.

"Do you think she'll leave?" Skye asked.

Court shrugged. "I don't know."

"I hope to hell she does," Solomon said.

Myles sighed. "Me, too. I've no wish to carry out Court's threat."

It was the first time Skye had walked down the streets of the city in a week. She looked around, noticing the forms in the shadows that watched them.

"Who are they?" she asked in a low voice.

Kane came up beside her. "They're from the other four factions. You'll be left alone now."

"We showed our strength tonight," Myles said.

Court laced his fingers with hers. "It was long overdue."

They walked for another five minutes in silence before Court turned her down a street. Skye saw the others continue.

"Where are we going?" she asked.

Court smiled. "My place."

"Is that right?" She smiled, excitement rushing through her.

"It's where I intend to keep you for quite awhile without any interruptions."

"What about what I want?"

They reached the door to a building and he pushed her against it, crowding her so that their bodies were touching shoulder to hip. "What do you want?" he whispered as he let his mouth draw close to hers before pulling back.

"You. I want you."

His mouth descended on hers in a scorching kiss that had desire pooling in her belly. A moment later, the door opened and they walked inside, still kissing.

EPILOGUE

A month later...

"I CAN'T BELIEVE we're at the courthouse," Court said.

Skye stopped him, putting the bouquet of flowers between her arm and body so she could adjust his tie before smoothing her hands down the front of his suit. "It'll be over quickly."

"I only put on this suit for you."

She smiled. "You look very handsome in a suit."

"Come on then," he said and took her hand.

They went up the remainder of the steps and walked through the doors of the courthouse. They found Solomon, Riley, Kane, and Minka standing together.

"Well?" Court asked.

Solomon looked at his watch. "It's time. They're late."

"No, we're not," Myles said as he and Addison walked up.

Addison was beaming. Skye was thrilled that she and Myles had decided to forgo a long engagement. Neither wanted a big wedding, so they opted to be married by a judge.

Skye walked with the others into the room and awaited the judge. He arrived, and the ceremony was quickly underway. As Skye listened to Myles and Addison exchange vows, all she could think about was her and Court.

She was deliriously happy. After all her hating of the supernatural, she couldn't believe she was dating one. It was actually more than dating. She and Court were all but living together. They had yet to make it official, but they were rarely apart.

They stayed at his place for a few days and then went to hers. Her days were spent at the newspaper, but she was no longer writing articles about the supernatural. She had moved to the advice column.

"What are you thinking about?" Court leaned over and whispered.

She glanced up at him. "You."

"Ah. That's good since I was thinking of you."

"What about?"

"That I love you, and I want us to live together."

"Isn't that what we're doing?" she joked.

He held out his hand. Skye looked down and saw a key. She realized then it was a key to his apartment.

"Move in with me, Skye. Or I'll move in with you. I don't care, as long as we're together. I want you with me always."

Skye took the key and held it against her heart with a smile. "Yes, I'll move in with you."

"Be with me? Always?"

Skye waited for the judge to announce that Addison and Myles were husband and wife. Then she turned to Court. "Yes."

They sealed their vows with a kiss.

RILEY LEFT THE COURTHOUSE, intending to meet up with Minka. She was halfway to her truck when the hairs on the back of her neck stood on end.

It was the third time in as many days. Riley turned her head and saw the woman across the busy street. She was dressed in all white, which made her dark skin appear even darker. Her black eyes were trained on Riley as she smiled knowingly.

Delphine.

Riley had faced many monsters in her days of hunting, but nothing put fear in her like the Voodoo priestess. Delphine was letting Riley know she was marked. She would be coming for Riley soon.

With a wave, Delphine turned a corner and disappeared. Riley leaned against her truck as she bent over and tried to figure out what she was going to do about this new situation.

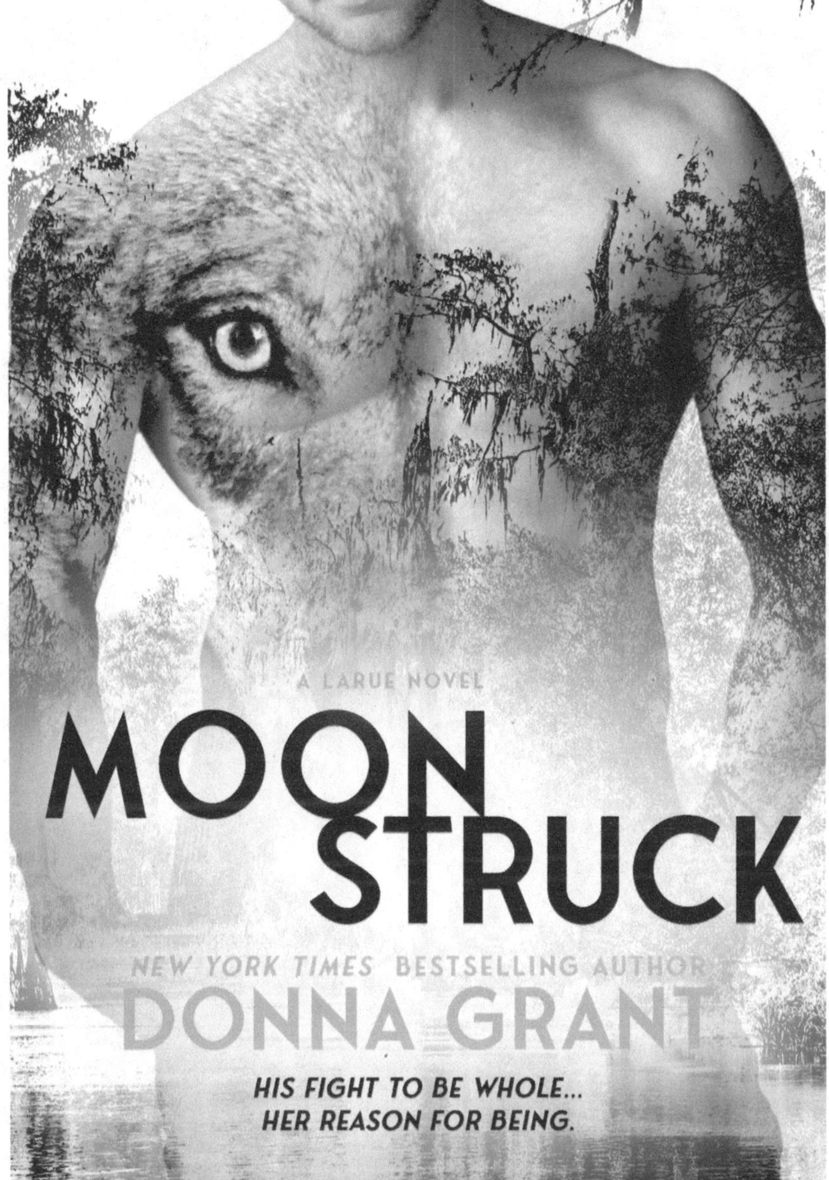

A LARUE NOVEL
MOON STRUCK
NEW YORK TIMES BESTSELLING AUTHOR
DONNA GRANT
HIS FIGHT TO BE WHOLE...
HER REASON FOR BEING.

CHAPTER
ONE

March

Outside of New Orleans

THERE WERE monsters in the dark. Minka had known of them since she was old enough to understand that there really might be something beneath her bed.

Of course, growing up in New Orleans, those monsters lived beside her. That didn't make them any less scary. In fact, it made them more so. To see them interacting with others as if they were normal human beings when they were anything but...

The same could be said of the witches. Only within the last year had she come into her power, but that hadn't made life easier. In fact, it had made it worse.

Minka had been lied to by her coven and then given to the most heinous monster of them all: Delphine. The Voodoo priestess was on a quest to gain as much power as she could, in whatever way possible.

It was only by the skills of the LaRues that Minka was alive. The werewolf pack policed New Orleans, keeping the supernatural world in balance.

After her escape from Delphine's clutches, Minka had taken refuge and found solace at her great-aunt's home in the bayou. It had been willed to her after her aunt died, and Minka had never thought to actually use it.

Had her aunt foreseen such events? Had she known it would be the only place for Minka?

She stood in the open doorway and looked out over the bayou. The moon was hidden by clouds, giving the land an ominous feel.

A soft splash to her left alerted her to an alligator. And in the distance was the soft howl of a wolf. The Moonstone pack had returned to the area, and their numbers were growing steadily.

The darkness was where evil liked to hide. It was why most people feared it. It was partly because they couldn't see, but there was another part that knew there were unspeakable horrors awaiting them in the shadows.

Whether that was from their ancestors' fears or encounters, she didn't know. It wasn't a learned trait. Instead, it was something people were born with.

One prime example was Delphine. On the streets of New Orleans, everyone shied away from the Voodoo priestess—locals and tourists alike. It was as if everyone could sense the malevolence within her.

Minka took a deep breath, enjoying the quiet of the evening. She wasn't sure how much more she'd get before Delphine came for her. But unlike the other monsters, Delphine wouldn't wait for the night to strike.

Once before, the priestess had attempted to kill Minka in an effort to take Minka's power. There had been a short period after her escape when no one but the LaRues knew where Minka was hiding out. All that had changed when she helped Court LaRue and Skye Parrish fight against the djinn and vampires.

Minka had shown herself to her enemies, but there hadn't been any other choice. Her friends would have died without her, and she couldn't allow that.

That had been six months ago. Every day that passed without Delphine coming for her only made Minka more nervous. Some might take that to mean Delphine wasn't interested.

But Minka had looked into the priestess's eyes. She knew that Delphine had marked her. That kind of stain didn't ever go away. Delphine could come for her in the next ten minutes, ten months, or ten years—but she *would* come.

Movement out of the corner of her eye drew Minka's attention. She walked to the screen covering the porch and looked down from the stilted height of the house to see an animal moving among the bushes.

She caught a glimpse of white fur, her heart kicking up a notch as she wondered if it was Solomon. Then the werewolf moved into the clearing, and she saw that it wasn't as silvery white as Solomon was. She waved when the werewolf looked up at her. The Moonstone pack had been good about watching over her, and they'd become her friends.

Minka didn't want to think about her disappointment at the wolf not being Solomon. It wasn't as if he checked in on her at all. As the eldest LaRue, his domain was New Orleans. He didn't have the time to think about her—nor would he. He didn't like her.

Which both rankled and hurt her because she liked him. A lot. She didn't want to. In fact, she'd tried to hate him, but that hadn't turned out well. All it had done was make her crave him more.

It was awful to be attracted to someone who couldn't stand your very presence. She didn't know why Solomon detested her, and it didn't matter.

So what if she'd warned Myles of his death.

So what if her magic had removed the silver from Myles's system and saved his life.

So what if her home had been used in the vampire/djinn war.

So what if, in an effort to save the LaRues, their women, and the Moonstone pack, she had shown herself.

The LaRues had rescued her from Delphine's clutches.

In her book, she'd never be able to repay them for that. And she didn't worry about the fact that they'd probably done it because Delphine had Addison, as well, and since Myles had fallen in love with Addison...nothing would come between a wolf and his mate.

It didn't matter why Minka had been saved, only that she had. She had come into her magic then, and she was a force to be reckoned with. Every day she pushed herself to her limits to train because every little bit would help when Delphine came for her.

Minka rubbed her tired eyes. She was only dozing a few minutes every hour. The last thing she wanted was to be caught sleeping when the priestess arrived.

The sound of her cell phone vibrating on the table had Minka turning and entering the house. She picked up the phone to see it was a text from Addison asking if she was all right.

Addison and Skye sent her texts daily to check in on her. Minka had made them promise to stay away until Delphine was taken care of.

Minka sent a quick response and replaced the phone on the table before crawling into bed. There were wards up all around the house. They wouldn't stop Delphine, but they would slow her. And that could be the difference between life and death.

She shut her eyes for a moment, intending only to rest.

Almost instantly, she was drifting in that space between sleep and wakefulness.

Suddenly, her mind screamed for her to wake, alerted that someone was in the room with her. Her eyes snapped open as she jerked upright to see a figure standing in the wide doorway leading out to the porch.

"Easy," said a male as he lifted his hands.

Minka blinked, recognizing the voice. She relaxed as Griffin, leader of the Moonstone pack, lowered his arms to his sides. "What are you doing here?"

"I've been knocking at your back door for ten minutes."

She glanced at the clock to see that she'd been asleep for two hours. "Is something wrong?" she asked as she rose from the bed.

"Not at all. I thought you might like some company."

It was then that she realized he was naked. Thank God the lights were out. Or perhaps, she should wish they were on to get a better look at his fine body.

Minka knew Griffin was interested in her. If only she returned his feelings. It would be so much easier than this thing she had with Solomon. Truthfully, it wasn't a thing. It was nothing.

"You've not left this house in six months," Griffin said.

She shoved back her wealth of curls from her face. "Not true. I walk along the bayou sometimes."

"You know what I mean."

"I do. I also know there are five witch covens out there, some of which helped my coven turn me over to Delphine. I've no desire to fight those witches when I need to save myself for Delphine."

"Who says you'll have to fight the covens?"

She shot him a look. "Seriously? Do you know anything about witches?"

"Very little, actually."

"Well, let me fill you in. They all hate me. That's insanely idiotic since they're the ones who turned on me, but they'll be gunning for me because Delphine has told them I have more power than they do."

He crossed his arms over his chest as he leaned a shoulder against the doorway. "Then why haven't they come for you?"

"Because they fear Delphine. They know she's marked me, so until I beat her, they'll keep their distance."

"Do you think you can best Delphine?"

She looked at Griffin's face, hidden by the shadows of the room, and shrugged. "I'm certainly going to try."

"What a woman you are."

As compliments went, that was a nice one. "Thanks."

"Come walk with me."

"You're naked."

A laugh rumbled from his chest. "I didn't take you for a prude."

"Oh, I'm not."

"You just don't want to see me naked."

"I didn't say that."

"You pretty much did."

She threw up her hands in defeat. "It's just…weird."

There was a beat of silence. Then Griffin said, "That's the first time I've ever had a woman say my nudity was weird. Most throw themselves at me."

"I'm not most women."

"And that's why I want you."

He'd let his interest show many times, but he'd never come out and been so blatant about it. And she was very flattered. There was something sexy about a man who wasn't afraid to go after what he wanted.

Griffin dropped his arms to his sides. "Say something."

"What does one say after something like that?"

"Anything."

She walked to stand beside him at the double doorway as she looked outside. "You say you want me, but I have to wonder how smart that is."

His head turned to her. "Why?"

"Delphine has your sister. She'll use Elin to get to me through you." Minka didn't add that she might already be doing exactly that. She wanted to think of Griffin as her friend, an ally—not an enemy.

He pushed away from the door and faced her. "My feelings have nothing to do with my sister or Delphine."

"It wouldn't be wise to test things. You're gathering your wolves again. The Moonstone pack was once one of the greatest in the area. Your wolves will expect you to find someone within your pack, not a witch."

"I don't give a shit what they want."

She smiled at the alpha coming out in him. "You're my friend, Griffin. One of the few I can count on. You and your pack have kept an eye on me, and for that, I'll be eternally grateful. And yes, I'll walk with you."

"But you won't be mine."

"I'm thinking of you with my decision. Your pack might accept me as your casual lover, but never more than that. And you know I'm right about Delphine. She'll find out. She always does. You returned to New Orleans for your sister. You'll do anything for her."

"Minka—"

"We never know what we'll do for family, and we both know what Delphine is capable of," she said over him.

He blew out a breath as he looked at the sky and the hidden moon. "That bitch needs to die."

"I agree."

His head swiveled back to her. He gently tugged on a curl and released it, watching it spring back into place. "I'm going to come for you every night for a walk. And every night, I'm going to ask you to be mine. I care about you, Minka. I have feelings for you."

She took his hand in hers and smiled. She didn't need the

light to know that his green eyes were alight with determination. It was in his words, his touch.

"Let's walk," she said.

It would distract her from her worries for a little while. And perhaps that's exactly what her mind needed.

CHAPTER
TWO

Gator Bait Bar
New Orleans

"Someone has to check on Minka."

Solomon was inspecting the food and handing it to the waitresses to serve while Addison and Skye were behind him, nagging. And they were fucking good at it.

"I don't have time for this now," he told them. "Come back after the lunch crowd."

Skye stepped in front of him, her dark eyes holding his. "We've been trying to talk to you about this."

Solomon looked around for his brothers to help, but the three of them were out in the bar, tending to customers.

He turned to grab the next plate to inspect, only to find

Addison in his way. She had her arms crossed and a blonde brow raised as she glared at him.

"It's been six months," she said.

Had it really been that long? The peace that had come after the battle with the vampires and djinn had been blissful. Everyone knew it wouldn't last, but Solomon loathed doing anything that would see it come to an end even quicker.

But he had to get to work.

"Fine," he relented. "I'll check on her."

With a smile, the girls sauntered off.

It wasn't until the lunch rush was over and Solomon walked into the front to see Addison, Myles, Skye, and Court sitting together waiting for him that it struck him—he'd been set up by the girls.

"So, they finally cornered you," Kane said as he came to stand beside him.

Solomon swung his gaze to his younger brother. "Shit."

Kane's lips twisted as he shrugged. His blue eyes—the same eyes all four of the LaRues had—pinned him. "I expected you to hold out longer."

"They were damn smart to come at me during the lunch hour when I was too busy to deal with things." Solomon ran a hand down his face, furious with himself for not seeing the girls' ploy.

"Is it really so bad?"

He frowned at Kane. "Is what so bad?"

"Going to see Minka? She's very pretty, and a powerful ally."

"Then why don't you go to her?"

"Who says I haven't?"

That set Solomon aback. "When did you go?"

"She risked her life for Skye. Not to mention Riley."

No sooner had Kane said her name than their cousin walked into the bar. She waved to the others and came to stand beside him and Kane.

"So," she said looking between them. "You're talking about me, huh?"

Solomon shook his head. "How could you possibly know that?"

"It's the looks on your faces," Riley stated. Then her gaze slid to Kane. "Have I told you how much I hate the DMV? I'd have renewed my driver's license online, but noooooo. I had to update my stupid picture. As if anyone ever takes a good picture there. They set you up to fail. With glee in their eyes, I tell you," she said and walked around them to the back.

Solomon watched as she sauntered away, still grumbling, and walked through the doorway into the kitchen. He hadn't exactly been thrilled when Riley had shown up. Partly because she'd run from her brothers and didn't bother to tell them she was in New Orleans.

Now that the Chiassons knew, things hadn't gotten easier. Mostly because they were so intent on hunting the paranormal in Lyon's Point that they'd forgotten their baby sister was a grown woman who could make her own decisions.

That's what she was doing now. Making her own decisions. And it was killing the Chiasson boys.

Solomon had never been so glad he didn't have a sister as he was at that moment. Riley was a true blessing, but he'd be a wreck if she were his sibling.

Yet, she'd done wonders for Kane. Solomon glanced at his brother. The messy, always late Kane was now quiet, withdrawn, ten minutes early for everything, and never had a hair out of place.

That's what happened when you pissed off a Voodoo priestess who then cursed you to hunt down someone. With their cousins' help, Solomon had prevented Kane from killing while in wolf form. Had Kane killed anyone, he would've remained a werewolf, never able to shift back into a human.

And he'd have gone mad.

Delphine's little experiment had changed Kane in ways none of them understood. Solomon saw the visible signs, but there were ones deep within Kane that he kept from everyone. Except for Riley. If he shared anything, it would be with her.

The two of them had gravitated to each other. She healed him, while allowing him to play protector. Their bond of friendship was strong.

Blood tied their two families together, but it was the

interaction that allowed such bonds to develop and strengthen the ties.

Friends and allies were the same. Addison and Skye were right. Someone should go see Minka. He briefly thought of sending Kane, but he'd told the girls he would go. So he would.

And the sooner he got out there, the quicker he could get back to the bar.

"I'm glad to see you've given in to the inevitable," Kane said.

"Yeah. I'm heading out there now. I'll be back in a couple of hours."

"Take your time," Kane said as he walked behind the bar and began to clean up.

Solomon nodded to Myles and Court before walking into the kitchen and then out the back door. He locked the wooden gate behind him and got into his truck.

On the drive through New Orleans, he looked for any signs of Delphine or her followers. They were easy to spot since they were usually in all white. There were times he saw them watching the bar.

It wouldn't surprise him to find one of them now. The fact that he saw nothing made him uneasy.

Six months. Six idyllic, heavenly months where the supernatural had been reminded of the strength of the LaRues—and obeyed the rules.

It wasn't easy policing the streets of New Orleans with all

the different supernatural beings that called the city home. But it was what his family had done for generations. And they were damn good at it.

Solomon wasn't sure who had it the worst. Was it he and his brothers monitoring and patrolling the city? Or was it his cousins who hunted and killed the supernatural that were drawn to Lyon's Point?

Once out of the city, Solomon turned up his music and tried to relax. But the closer he got to Minka's, the tighter his muscles became.

By the time he pulled up to the house, he was contemplating turning around. Before he could change his mind, he threw the truck into park and turned off the engine.

In his mind, he was running through hundreds of reasons anyone other than he should be there. Yet he found himself out of the truck, and his feet kept taking him toward the stairs regardless. When he reached the steps, he planted one foot on the bottom rung and hesitated.

Some might think the bayou was quiet compared to the city, but it was anything but. There was a cornucopia of animals who called the swamps home, and their sounds filled the air like a mystical symphony only those who appreciated it could hear.

It was a place that suited Minka. She was the embodiment of stillness, of calmness in the loud, frenzied city. Not that he would ever tell her such a thing.

He felt eyes on him and looked around until he spotted

the werewolves in the bushes. Somehow, he wasn't surprised that the Moonstones were still watching over Minka.

His gaze jerked to the house. Would he be interrupting her and Griffin? The thought brought a smile to his face as he headed up the stairs to the front door. Though he didn't allow himself to think about *why* intruding on the two of them made him happy.

But as he raised his hand to knock, the door swung open. Minka stood there in jeans and a cream sweater that accentuated her rich russet skin, the evidence of her Romanian Gypsy heritage.

For a long minute, they stared at each other.

Her long, curly, dark brown hair hung loosely about her shoulders. Eyes pale brown and ringed with black watched him without guile from beneath insanely long lashes. Her lips were wide, the bottom slightly fuller than the top.

She was a natural beauty with skin that was as smooth as silk. His gaze traveled down her slim neck to find a collarbone bared from her wide-necked sweater that hung seductively and alluringly off one shoulder. Faded, ripped jeans clung to her legs, but it was her bare feet with their dark-pink painted toenails that he found intriguing.

Then she stepped back and motioned for him to enter, which jerked him out of his thoughts.

He looked around the house, noting that she hadn't

changed much since the last time he was there. "How've you been?"

"I'm alive. I think that says it all," she replied.

"Yeah." He cleared his throat, not sure what else to say.

She closed the door and stood there, examining him. "I talk to Addison and Skye every day through text. You didn't have to come, especially since you obviously don't want to be here."

"I never said that."

She snorted loudly. "I hate to be the one to break this to you, but everything you feel or think is shown through your eyes. I don't know who made you come—"

"No one," he interjected.

"But you did. You came, you saw, and we spoke. Now you can leave with a clear conscience."

He pointed at her. "This. This right here is why I didn't want to come. You twist everything."

"Really? So you came on your own? No one told you to?"

Solomon opened his mouth, then shut it.

"That's what I thought," Minka said with a smug expression. "I'm not angry, if that's what you think. You did this for your family."

"And for you."

The words were out of his mouth before he had time to think about them.

Her brows rose, surprise in her eyes. "I admit, I'm surprised you'd say such a thing. I know how you detest me."

"I don't hate you."

She gave him a wry look. "Your actions and words say otherwise."

"I have a lot on my plate." It was a poor excuse, but it was the only one he had.

It wasn't as if he could tell her that she made him uncomfortable—and all too aware that it had been years since he'd tasted a woman's kiss or held a female in his arms.

"Are you really all right?" he asked.

Her gaze lowered to the ground, and he saw something flash in her eyes before she hid it. "Yes. Griffin and his pack get me whatever I might need."

"But?" Solomon pressed.

She took a deep breath and then slowly released it as she met his gaze. "It's the waiting that's killing me. I don't know why Delphine hasn't come for me."

"Don't think that way. Take this time she's given you."

"My power has grown," Minka said. "But I could train and practice for ten years and still not be ready. She's more powerful than I am."

Solomon took a step toward her. "Don't think like that either. You must stay positive. Believe you can win."

A smile turned up her lips. "You're right. I should, and I will."

Silence once more descended upon them. Solomon was trying to think of something else to say when the sound of footsteps coming up the stairs had Minka looking out the window.

There was a smile on her face when she opened the door to allow Griffin inside. He held several bags of groceries in his hands and he came to a halt when he spotted Solomon.

"I didn't know you were stopping by," Griffin said.

Solomon shrugged, glimpsing the flowers half-hidden in one of the bags. He was sure Minka hadn't asked for those. "Just wanted to check on things."

"It's only taken you six months."

Griffin's dig riled Solomon. Then again, two Alphas visiting the same woman had that effect. Solomon's suspicions were confirmed. Minka and Griffin were together.

Why then did he feel the need to fight Griffin?

Solomon ignored him and looked at Minka. "Let us know if you need anything."

He shouldered past Griffin only to have Minka put her hand on his arm. Solomon turned back to her.

"Thank you," she said softly.

He gave a nod, and then her hand was gone.

And damn if he didn't miss her touch.

CHAPTER

THREE

SOLOMON HAD BARELY REACHED the bottom of the steps before he heard Griffin shout Minka's name. Without a second's hesitation, Solomon turned and took the stairs three at a time.

When he reached the top, he found Minka's eyes had gone milky. "No!" he shouted when Griffin made to touch her. "She's having a vision."

"What do we do?" Griffin asked worriedly.

"Nothing."

Griffin ran a hand down his face. "I've never seen this."

Neither had Solomon, but Myles had explained what happened when Minka had had such a vision with him. Solomon couldn't look away from her eyes.

No longer could he see the pale brown irises. She made no sound or movement as the vision held her in its grip. He stayed near her in case she collapsed, yet all the while, he wondered what it was she saw.

Suddenly, her chest expanded as she dragged in a ragged breath. Her lids closed on a blink. As he watched, the milky color vanished as if it had never been.

Her eyes fastened on him a second before her knees buckled. Solomon grabbed her the same time Griffin did, and together, they walked her to the couch where they sat her.

Solomon reached for the glass of iced tea on the side table and handed it to her. She drank it down as if she hadn't tasted anything in weeks. He squatted beside the sofa, and when she finished, he took the empty glass to set it aside.

"What did you see?" Griffin asked.

Solomon shook his head at the werewolf. Now was not the time to ask such a question. Minka would tell them in her own time—if she told them at all.

She put her hand to her forehead and closed her eyes while laying her head back on the cushion. Solomon had never realized that having a vision took so much out of her. Then again, he'd never witnessed it before.

"Rest," he told her as he straightened and made for the door.

Solomon grabbed Griffin's arm as he passed, dragging him with him. Once outside, Solomon shut the door behind him and motioned with his chin for Griffin to head down off the porch. When he hesitated, Solomon raised a brow. Finally, Griffin relented and started down the stairs.

Solomon's thoughts were on Minka while he followed a few steps behind Griffin. It was because of that, that he didn't see Griffin's intention as he pivoted and slammed his hands into Solomon's chest.

Solomon stumbled back a few steps before a wooden pillar holding up the house stopped him. He glared at Griffin. "What the fuck is your problem?"

"You've got some nerve coming here."

Solomon smiled coldly and then pushed away from the stilt. "Worried I might be encroaching on your woman?"

"Leave."

"No."

Griffin's eyes flashed yellow, a sign that he was fighting to remain in human form. "She doesn't need you."

"That's not for you to decide."

"It's not yours either."

Solomon shrugged and circled him. "If you were secure with Minka, you wouldn't be worried about my arrival. Which means, the two of you aren't a couple."

"Yet."

"Be that as it may, you don't get to tell me to stay away. Minka is our friend. We watch over our friends."

Griffin's lips curled into a sneer. "Tell me, Solomon, why then did it take any of you six months to visit? Where have you been all these weeks as she remained hidden behind the walls of her home?"

"Keeping New Orleans in order. Or did you forget my family has an obligation? Just as yours did."

"You son of a bitch!" Griffin yelled as fury contorted his face. "You just had to bring that up."

They were circling each other now, each looking for a weakness to exploit.

Solomon shrugged. "I'm sorry if you don't like being reminded of the cowards your parents were. Perhaps if they'd done their job, a duty that had been bestowed upon your pack for generations, then my parents might still be alive."

"You don't know that."

"Permission for your return to this area has been granted by me. Remember that."

Griffin bared his teeth. "And remember, we can leave at any time."

"You're good at that, so it doesn't surprise me that you'd throw something like that in my face. You returned to New Orleans to take your rightful place, and you were doing a good job."

"You don't like being questioned," Griffin said with a taciturn smile.

Solomon saw members of the Moonstone pack watching them, but he didn't give a shit. "Your fur's all ruffled because I came to see Minka. If you want to make this about something else, I'll happily indulge you."

"You've still not answered why you're just now showing up."

He'd had enough. Solomon closed the distance between them until they were nose-to-nose. "Because Minka asked to be alone. She wanted the time to herself, and we gave that to her. In case you didn't know, we spoke with her every damn day. And I know Kane has been here."

Griffin's hands were fisted at his sides. "Kane runs with us, yes."

"Anything else you want to accuse me of?" Solomon demanded.

"A call or text isn't the same as visiting. We've watched over her, brought her what she needed, and offered her company. Whatever obligation you believed you had is long gone. Leave."

There was only one person who could tell him to go. Minka. Solomon made as if he were turning away, but instead, delivered a solid punch to Griffin's jaw.

The next instant, they were locked together, each trying to get an advantage over the other. Solomon blocked punches while connecting more hits. A blow to his mouth split his lip, blood filling his mouth.

He ignored it and elbowed Griffin in the nose. The sound of cartilage breaking filled the air. Solomon then found himself on his back after having his legs swiped from beneath him. He raised his arms in an X to block a downward kick to his face. Grabbing Griffin's foot, Solomon shoved him away, twisting the other man's leg so Griffin spun in the air.

Solomon kicked up to his feet and tried to ram his knee into Griffin's face, but Griffin blocked him. Instead, Solomon slammed his fist down between Griffin's shoulder blades.

Griffin bellowed in pain. His head jerked to Solomon, and without any warning, he shifted. Solomon stared at him, even as Griffin snapped his jaws toward him.

"You're a were by birth," Solomon said. "Your ancestors chose this life and passed the gene down to you. If you can't handle a situation in your true form without shifting, then you're not the werewolf Kane told me you were."

Griffin growled, his lips peeled back to reveal his large teeth. He crouched low, his muscles tense and ready to pounce.

But Solomon didn't move.

He wasn't afraid of Griffin. Not now. Not ever. New Orleans was his and his brothers' to protect by birth and by right—and that included any allies and friends.

"You want to sever the tenuous pact we have," Solomon said. "Then attack."

Griffin suddenly took a step back. Solomon turned his head and found Minka walking toward them.

She stopped between them, looking at each of them a long moment. "Enough of this."

"The sooner we get this done, the better," Solomon said.

A dark brow rose as her head turned to him. "Not here. I

need to think about my vision, and I can't do that with the two of you making all this racket. I need you to leave." Then she looked at Griffin. "Both of you."

Without another sound, Griffin loped away.

Solomon watched him, knowing that they would clash again. It was the way with two alpha males. It was one of the reasons Griffin's parents had failed Solomon's, because the elder LaRue hadn't addressed a similar issue.

Solomon wouldn't make the same mistake. Though once a great man, his father had grown lax at the end, believing the reputation of the LaRues would keep them safe. When Delphine had come for them, the Moonstone pack abandoned them.

Solomon didn't just have his three brothers and his cousin Riley to look out for anymore. He also had Addison and Skye. Six people were under his care, and that meant he couldn't fail.

Not as he'd done with Misty.

He swallowed. The thought of his dead fiancée always hit him hard. It didn't matter how many years passed, he would always carry the weight of her death with him.

Solomon wiped the blood away from his mouth and glanced at Minka. "I apologize."

"It's what two Alphas do, right?" she said with a small smile.

He nodded and turned his head to spit out blood. "You know we stayed away because you asked us to."

"I do."

"We shouldn't have."

She wrapped her arms about her middle. "It was my request, and you honored it."

"Promise you'll call one of us if you need something."

"I won't," she said with a shake of her head.

"Minka…" he began.

She took a step back, her gaze halting him. "Don't. You know why you can't be here. Delphine has already damaged Kane with her curse."

"That we got her to reverse."

"You're not a fool. You know as well as I do that she's not finished with your family. Especially Riley."

He didn't need to be reminded of the Voodoo bitch's attention on his cousin. Delphine had already tried to harm the Chiassons before, but no one knew why she was so focused on Riley now.

"The more distance you put between yourself and me, the better," Minka said.

"United we stand. Divided we fall."

She gave him a sad smile. "Then what I just witnessed with you and Griffin says it all, doesn't it?"

"I won't fail in this. I can't," he told her.

"Some things are out of our control."

He nodded slowly in agreement. "You're our friend. Not only did you save Myles, but you also helped us in the last battle. The LaRues don't forget things like that. I don't care who or what is coming for you, Minka Verdin. We look out for our friends."

"United, huh?"

"United."

She blew out a breath. "I'll contact you once I've pieced together what the vision has shown me."

"Come with me to the city." He wasn't sure why he offered, only that he wanted her with him.

"I can't."

"You can. When was the last time you had a meal you didn't cook? Or got any sleep. I didn't want to mention the dark circles under your eyes, but I will if it means you'll come with me and get a good meal and some sleep surrounded by those who can protect you."

She glanced at the ground. "I am protected."

Griffin. Right. How could he forget that? "I can't change your mind?"

"Not this time."

Even he had to admit defeat. This time. But he'd be back with reinforcements to help make a case for her to return with them, if just for a night.

"Be safe, then."

Minka flashed him a smile. "You, as well, Solomon."

He held her gaze for a long while before he turned on his heel and walked to his truck.

FOUR

Wᴀs it worse to want someone you couldn't have? Or to never know that kind of longing?

Minka wasn't sure which was more awful. She knew that no matter how much she hungered for Solomon's touch or craved his attention, that she would never be his. That kind of knowledge did strange things to a person.

Her heart had jumped in her throat to find him there. It had felt like forever since she'd seen his face and those brilliant blue eyes. All the LaRues and Chiassons had them, but Solomon's were brighter than the others'.

And his hair. The dark blond strands were laced with pale brown that made her want to sink her hands into the locks.

His face was all hard angles and ruggedness that she longed to touch and kiss. The shadow of dark whiskers on his jaw made her stomach flutter and her skin prickle with awareness.

Then there was that body of his. Could anyone wear jeans like Solomon? The denim clung to his trim waist and hips, curving over his fine ass before encasing his long legs. Though it was his ability to wear a plain white shirt over the impeccably hard sinew of his chest and wide shoulders that could make her heart miss a beat.

He was simply mouthwatering. The complete package... and utterly out of reach.

But there were other things she needed to put her mind to. Like deciphering exactly what she'd seen in her vision— and figuring out just what it meant for everyone.

She couldn't do that with Solomon there because every time she looked at him, she saw an image of Delphine standing among dozens of dead weres as she laughed.

Without looking in the direction Griffin had walked off, Minka turned and made her way up the stairs and into her house. She shut the doors and walked to the middle of the living room.

She sat in the center of the oval braided rug in shades of cream, brown, and orange, and with her legs crossed and her eyes closed, she concentrated on her breathing.

With each inhale and exhale, her body relaxed and her mind calmed. Only then did she call up the images of the vision. The first was of Griffin in wolf form. Solomon was next, the platinum fur of his beast unmistakable.

Next came more werewolves. There were so many images, flashing rapidly for what felt like years. So many that she couldn't distinguish one from the other. But the howls, yelps, and growls all pointed to one thing: fighting.

What she couldn't determine was who the werewolves were battling. Or even where.

That was important information. Without it, it was almost pointless for her to tell anyone what she'd seen in the vision. Because those snippets could mean absolutely anything. It could happen tomorrow or a year from now.

Minka took a deep breath and slowly released it as she came to the next images. Just thinking of Delphine caused her to tense, so seeing her in the vision sent Minka's heart rate skyward.

It took every ounce of her meditation skills to keep herself calm. Only with a tranquil heart and quiet mind would she be able to accurately determine what the images in the vision meant.

Once she was ready, she let the first image of Delphine fill her mind. The Voodoo priestess was in all white as usual, her long, black hair in dozens of tiny braids falling past her hips. She was standing tall, her gaze straight ahead—almost as if she were looking right at Minka.

Delphine's lips were moving, but Minka couldn't make out the words. The next scenes were of the streets of New Orleans, littered with dead werewolves. Everywhere Minka turned, there was one carcass after another.

Then she saw him. Solomon.

His silvery white fur covered in blood drew her. She studied the image closely, noting that he lay dead outside of Gator Bait with his three brothers around him.

If only that were the extent of the killings. She saw Skye lying within feet of Court. Here and there were humans who had gotten in the way during the battle.

But nowhere were there witches, djinn, or vampires.

Delphine entered the vision again, her laughter loud and boisterous as she walked among the dead werewolves, her white clothes splattered with blood. Her arms and face were coated with it, as if she'd smeared it over herself.

When Minka thought she'd looked at that image long enough, she moved on to the last one. The cemetery. She knew the place all too well since it was where Delphine had tried to kill her and Addison to enhance the priestess's power.

And in the vision, Delphine managed to do just that with Addison. There was a burned body next to Addison, and Minka could only guess that was her. But it was difficult to say without seeing anything to identify the body by.

One thing was for certain—everyone she knew and cared about was dead by Delphine's hand.

All Minka wanted to do was put the vision out of her mind and forget it, but her gifts had given her a glimpse into the future for a reason. Whether she liked it or not, she had to glean every last drop of information from it.

She went through each scene thrice more, filing away small things she hadn't noticed before. Only then did she finally stop at the image where Delphine was moving her lips.

Minka replayed that scene over and over, deciphering first one word, then two, and so on until she finally figured out what the priestess said. Minka's eyes flew open, a chill racing down her spine.

They were words she would never forget.

Look hard, Minka. This is all because of you. You're responsible for the slaughter of the weres. You're the one who got your friends killed. This is just a taste of what I have planned.

Minka put her hands behind her neck and leaned her head back, stretching the muscles. She was chilled to the bone by those words. There was no escaping them, however.

She got to her feet and looked outside to see that it was dark. A quick glance at the clock showed she'd been meditating for seven hours.

For months, she'd hidden away in the bayou, hoping that Delphine might forget her and move on. Minka had foolishly thought if she kept the LaRues away, that they might not suffer backlash from Delphine.

All of it had been for naught.

Minka couldn't keep what she knew to herself. Everyone needed to know so they could prepare. She picked up her cell phone and sent a text to the LaRue brothers, Addison, Skye,

Riley, and Griffin, telling them to get to her house immediately.

Then she walked out onto the porch and gazed out over the bayou. The tranquility she'd sought—and found—was gone. Perhaps it had all been in her mind anyway. She knew how far Delphine would go to get what she wanted.

"Minka."

She looked down to see Griffin staring up at her. She gave him a nod, and he hurried up the steps.

"What is it?" he asked.

She remained looking out over the water. "I only want to say it once. Let's wait until the others get here."

"It's nighttime. It's Gator Bait's busy time. It'll be hours before any of them are here," he said.

An owl hooted nearby while the frogs croaked loudly. She looked to find the bird of prey and spotted him as he flew from a tree, swooping down to catch his dinner.

"I don't care how long it takes the others to get here," she said. "We wait."

"Walk with me," he urged.

She glanced down at the hand he held out beside her. Her gaze lifted to his face as she forced a small smile. "Perhaps later."

Griffin let his hand drop to his side. He then walked away without another word.

She knew she'd hurt him. It wasn't her intention, but she didn't want to be with him. She wanted...it didn't matter what she wanted. She wouldn't be on this earth long enough to do anything about it anyway.

To her surprise, she heard the sound of a vehicle approaching. It wasn't long before the engine cut out and the vehicle door opened and closed. Then a second car could be heard.

Though Minka wanted to rush to the front of the house to see who had come, she remained where she was. The first ones to come into view were Riley, Skye, and Addison.

Her friends ran up the steps and threw their arms around her, all talking at once. There hadn't been another time when she'd felt so loved. She drank in the feel and sounds of her friends. It wasn't until they were there that she realized just how much she'd missed them. Talking on the phone or via text just wasn't the same.

She stepped back, her gaze drifting downward to land upon Solomon. Their eyes met, but Court soon took Solomon's attention.

"What happened earlier?" Addison asked in a whisper.

Minka frowned as she looked at her. "What do you mean?"

"When Solomon came," Skye said.

Minka shrugged. "Nothing much."

Riley flattened her lips and snorted. "Then where did he get the busted lip and bruised jaw?"

"He and Griffin...had words," Minka finally admitted.

All three looked at her with knowing grins on their faces.

She couldn't help but smile in return. They wanted her with Solomon, but she'd made sure they didn't know how much she would like that, as well.

She didn't like people interfering in her love life, and besides, if Solomon were interested, he'd have done something about it. The fact that he hadn't pretty much said it all in her mind.

Her small living room was soon filled with four men and three women besides her. She moved to the kitchen to get glasses for drinks. It wasn't until she turned to start handing them out that she found Griffin in the doorway, staring at her.

"We're all here," Myles said as he took his glass of sweet tea.

Minka wiped her hands on her jeans and stood, facing them. "Right. You are. I didn't expect you to get here so quickly."

"You said immediately," Kane replied from his position by the door with Griffin.

"Yes, but I know y'all have the bar to run."

Addison swallowed her sip of tea after sinking onto the sofa. "Solomon told us you had a vision. We've been waiting to hear from you."

"Gator Bait is tended to," Court said. He motioned for Skye to sit between Addison and Riley while he took the chair, and Solomon remained standing off to the side.

Now that everyone was there, Minka didn't want to tell

them anything. They were a family, a cohesive unit that loved deeply. Their smiles would be gone by the time she finished.

Riley lowered her drink to her leg. "I see you looking at us with an anxious expression. Whatever you have to say can't be worse than what we've already been through."

"That's true enough," Skye said.

They made it sound as if they were prepared for what she'd seen, when she knew they weren't. No one could be.

"It can if it's about Delphine," Griffin said.

Every head swung to him.

Minka shot him a frown. "How do you know that?"

"It's obvious," he said with a shrug.

A look around the room confirmed his statement. Minka licked her lips. "Fine. It is about Delphine."

"Go on," Addison urged.

Minka tried, but every time she looked at Addison, she saw her lying dead, her throat slit.

"Holding it in won't make it any better," Kane stated.

Minka closed her eyes and nodded. Then she took a deep breath. "My vision was about Delphine, but it was also about all of us. And every werewolf in the area."

You could've heard a pin drop it was so quiet after her statement. Minka opened her eyes, her gaze snagged by Solomon's. His intense blue eyes seemed to see right through her.

She wanted to shove aside the strand of dark blond hair

that had fallen onto his forehead. Wanted to stand next to him and feel his arms around her while he held her close. She hadn't experienced that kind of comfort in a very long time, and she ached for it.

Minka mentally shook herself. She had to continue talking. Yet the words were hard to get past her lips. "I saw the streets lined with dead werewolves. The LaRues were killed outside the bar along with Skye and Riley. Addison, she took you to the cemetery where she…finished what she began with us."

"And me?" Griffin asked.

Minka lowered her eyes to the floor. "I saw so many wolves…I can't say for sure."

"And you?" Solomon asked.

She blew out a breath and lifted her head. "I assume the burned body I saw beside Addison is me. As horrific as all of that is, it's the words Delphine delivered that are the worst."

"Words?" Court asked.

"In one of the images, I saw her lips moving. I figured out what she was saying."

Riley scooted to the edge of the cushion. "And that was?"

"Look hard, Minka. This is all because of you. You're responsible for the slaughter of the weres. You're the one who got your friends killed. This is just a taste of what I have planned."

CHAPTER

FIVE

THE BLOWS JUST KEPT COMING.

A bad feeling had plagued Solomon ever since leaving Minka's earlier. Now he knew he should've stayed in the area. Not that he could've helped her. Most likely she wouldn't want him anywhere near.

"Well," Kane said. "At least we know what's coming."

Minka's eyes bugged out. "That's all you have to say? I saw your deaths."

"You saw mine before, too," Myles added.

Solomon had to admit Myles had a point. Perhaps there was a way out of this, just as Minka had been able to draw the silver out of his brother to save his life.

"How many of the weres?" Court asked.

She shrugged. "Too many to count. They were everywhere. I've never seen so many."

Solomon looked to Griffin. "How many have joined your pack lately?"

"Fifty," he replied after a long hesitation.

Kane snorted loudly. "More like a hundred."

There was an advantage to Kane running with the Moonstones. Kane had insight none of the rest of them had. The fact that Griffin lied was something else Solomon would have to handle. The sooner, the better.

"Why would you lie?" Skye asked Griffin. "We have to work together."

"United," Solomon said and looked to Minka.

Her lips softened into a smile. Then in the next heartbeat, it was gone. "Unity is important here," Minka said.

"Is it?" Griffin crossed his arms over his chest. "From what I'm hearing, anyone associated with the LaRues will get killed. My charge is to protect my clan."

Kane faced the alpha. "Your *charge* is the LaRues. Didn't you swear to uphold the traditions set by our families before your parents allowed ours to die?"

Solomon felt Minka's gaze on him, but he didn't look at her. His attention was on Griffin. *Sooner* had become *right now*. "I told you earlier that if you couldn't uphold your responsibility, I'd revoke my forgiveness of your pack."

"We're over two hundred strong now," Griffin stated in a terse voice. "I don't think we need you."

Court and Myles slowly rose to their feet.

It was Court who said, "Don't be an idiot. The wolves

have joined you because Solomon granted your return. If he revokes that—if we all revoke it—the wolves will leave."

"Maybe," Griffin said.

Kane shoved him so hard that Griffin slammed back against the wall, rattling pictures. "What the fuck is your problem? I vouched for you to my family. I gave you access to return to your home and have your pack be the power it used to be."

Griffin held Kane's gaze for a long time before he shoved him away and walked out the door.

"Let him go," Solomon told Kane when he went to follow.

Myles's gaze slid to Solomon. "Are you insane? We need the weres."

"And we'll have them. I'll talk to Griffin later." Solomon glanced at Minka. "We'll stand united."

Riley crossed one leg over the other. "Well, this should be fun."

"What do we do now, then?" Skye asked.

Solomon said to Minka, "I really think you should come with us now. United, remember?"

"When was the last time you slept?" Addison asked her.

Skye nodded her dark head. "Yes. Come with us."

"It looks like I don't have a choice," Minka said.

Solomon knew her halfhearted attempt at refusing was for herself. She was a strong woman who felt she had to do everything on her own. He would show her she didn't have to.

He moved toward his brothers as the girls went to help Minka gather some clothes. While he stood with his siblings, his thoughts kept turning to Griffin and how to resolve their issue without them killing each other.

Court ran a hand through his butterscotch-blond hair. "I don't know whether to be pissed at Griffin or scared shitless at Minka's vision."

"A little of both," Kane said.

Myles grunted. "Yeah. Both. I understand what you're saying, Solomon, but if we stand any chance against Delphine, we need the Moonstone pack now."

"What about the other factions?" Court asked.

Solomon rubbed his jaw. "Minka didn't mention them, and she would have if she'd seen them. That could mean they didn't take sides."

"Or they did," Myles added.

Kane looked into the bedroom and lowered his voice to say, "I think maybe we need to call in our cousins."

"I've already thought about that," Solomon admitted. "The problem is that if we bring them here, we'll be delivering them right into Delphine's hands."

"True," Court said. "But they have a witch. Davena was strong enough to stand against Delphine. Her, along with Minka, might do the trick."

Solomon liked the idea, but he kept coming back to the vision. "Minka didn't see the Chiassons."

The discussion stopped when the four girls returned. After Minka had turned off all the lights and locked up the house, they walked together to the trucks.

Solomon climbed into the driver's seat of his crew cab as Kane took the passenger's seat. A moment later, Minka and Riley climbed into the back seat. He looked in the rearview mirror and found his gaze clashing with Minka's.

"Ready?" he asked her.

She nodded as she fastened her seatbelt. "Ready."

The drive back into the city was done in silence, each of them lost in their own thoughts. There would be more discussion, but Solomon wanted it to wait until everyone had had a chance to think things through. And he wanted Minka to get some rest.

He pulled up alongside the curb of the bar and shut off the engine. They climbed out and made their way behind the bar to enter at the back.

Right before he entered the building, he glanced up at the second floor. He used the studio as a place to sleep when he didn't want to drive out to the family house. In fact, in the last six months, he'd only spent two nights each month out there. It just made more sense to remain in the city.

His gaze lowered to Minka, who was having a hard time keeping her eyes open. It was lucky for her that he had a bed close where she could crash.

Solomon entered the kitchen and walked to the front to grab a glass behind the bar, filling it with bourbon. He returned to the back and found the others in the office. Minka kept blinking to keep her eyes open, but he knew she wouldn't give in to sleep easily.

He moved behind the desk and opened the bottom drawer where he got a pinch of the herbs his parents had used to make Court sleep when he was a toddler. Solomon had never gotten rid of them, and he was glad of that now.

After sprinkling them in the liquor and waiting for them to dissolve, he handed the glass to Minka.

She accepted it with a smile. Her exhaustion and all the conversation kept her occupied, so she didn't realize how quickly she drank it all. Solomon watched her closely. As soon as she began to sway, he took the glass from her.

She looked at it and then him with unfocused eyes. "What did you do?"

"Made sure you would rest."

"You...drugged me?" she asked in reproach, her words slurring.

He didn't get a chance to answer as she went limp against him. Solomon lifted her into his arms and looked down at her. Now that he was holding her, he wasn't so sure about putting her in his bed.

Mostly because the thought made his blood burn with hunger.

"Which of you is going to take her home?" he asked his brothers.

Myles shook his head. "I've got Addison, Court has Skye, and Riley is staying with Kane. Looks like you're the one with the room."

"You do have two places," Court added.

Damn. Solomon should've seen that one coming. He didn't try to argue with his brothers, mostly because, by the looks of everyone in the office, they wanted him to take the witch.

Kane walked ahead of him and opened the back door. As Solomon passed, Kane said, "If it's too much, I have room for her."

His words stopped Solomon in his tracks. Too much? No woman had been inside his home since his fiancée.

"Solomon?"

He turned his eyes to Kane and shook his head. "It's fine."

"Are you sure?"

"Yeah. I renovated the upstairs a few months before Misty was killed."

Kane's gaze held his before he gave a nod. "We'll take turns watching over Minka while she sleeps."

"All right."

Solomon turned to the right to a set of metal stairs leading up to the loft. When he and his brothers had bought the building, they'd intended to use the upstairs as storage.

Yet, the more Solomon had thought about it, the more he liked the idea of living there.

So with some work—and soundproof floors—he'd made it his. Being in the heart of the city they protected made things easier. It was why his brothers had also each chosen a place within New Orleans.

But he couldn't give up the family house.

Solomon reached his door and adjusted Minka so he could key in his entry. The door unlatched and swung open. He kicked it shut behind him where it automatically locked once more.

He walked to his leather couch and paused beside it, but he didn't set Minka down. Instead, he turned on his heel and made his way to the bed.

She didn't stir when he laid her down or when he removed her shoes. He then covered her and straightened. If he expected to feel something about another woman in his bed, he was wrong. There was only a twinge of pain at the thought of Misty's untimely death.

But it had been nearly seven years since that terrible night. A lot had changed since then—him most of all.

He smoothed a curl from Minka's face before he turned and walk to the kitchen area. Idleness wasn't something he enjoyed, but that left him little to do while he watched over Minka. So, he cleaned the kitchen from the mess he'd made at breakfast.

After that, he put in a load of laundry. Anything to keep

from staring at Minka sleeping in his bed and imagining her naked...and tangled in the sheets.

"I SUPPOSE YOU'VE HEARD."

Delphine watched a passing riverboat from the dock. She didn't look toward Tora. She was devoted to her followers, but Delphine knew better than to trust anyone. "You mean that Minka is in the city? Of course."

"Why don't we attack?" Tora asked.

"It isn't time."

"We've waited six months already."

Delphine turned to the younger woman and put her hand on her light-skinned cheek. With Creole heritage, Tora was a true believer in Voodoo. She was young and pretty, if a little headstrong.

"There is a reason for everything I do. Don't question me again."

Tora's dark eyes flashed with annoyance. "I know how much you need the witch to grow your power. She was alone and weak. Now she's with the LaRues."

"Do you fear the werewolves?"

"No."

Delphine smiled as she lowered her hand to her side. "Good. They are dirt beneath our shoes. They believe they control this city, and I've allowed them that fantasy. Just as I showed their parents who was really in charge, I will do the same to them."

"Why didn't you take over when you killed their parents?"

Delphine swept her arm wide to encompass the entire city. "Everyone fears me. They know me and what I'm capable of. I've allowed the weres to handle the little squabbles while I concentrated on the bigger picture."

Tora lifted her chin and smiled. "You're a force to be reckoned with. I can't wait until I stand beside you and show the werewolves and the rest of the factions what's in store. You will be their queen."

"Yes. And in so doing, I'll get my revenge on the Chiasson's, as well. But we wait. For now."

"Not too much longer, please."

Delphine turned back to the river. "I won't mess this up, but don't worry. You won't have to wait too long."

"Do you still want us to keep watch over the LaRues?"

"I want to know everywhere they go, as well as everyone they speak to. They're not stupid animals. They'll be preparing."

Tora laughed. "It doesn't matter what they do. They'll never be prepared for what you'll bring them."

Delphine smiled. "No. They won't."

CHAPTER
SIX

MINKA CAME AWAKE SLOWLY, her body relaxed and her mind calm. She stretched, yawning as she arched her back with her arms over her head. She opened her eyes and looked at the high ceiling.

That wasn't her ceiling.

She turned her head and saw a brick wall with a large picture of New Orleans at night.

That wasn't her picture or her wall.

She sat up and looked around in confusion. The loft was large with the windows letting in tons of light. A soft rain battered the glass before rivulets of water ran down to collect at the base of the window.

It took her a moment to hear the shower over the rain. She threw off the covers and noted that she was still in the clothes she'd worn when she came to New Orleans—with Solomon.

That's when it all came back to her. He'd drugged her.

Anger coiled within her like a snake ready to strike. Minka rose and strode to the sliding barn door to the bathroom that wasn't shut all the way. She pushed it open and continued into the room where she saw the white marble counter and white-and-gray-basketweave tile upon the floor.

She ignored it as she made her way to the glass shower where Solomon had his back to her as he washed. Despite her anger, she couldn't help but notice his impeccable body through the steam and water.

Wide shoulders tapered to a narrow waist and hips. His ass was...sublime. The fact that she noticed it only pissed her off more. And yet, she let her eyes travel lower to his long, muscular legs.

It was his hands running through his hair that jerked her gaze upward to watch the way the sinew in his back, shoulders, and arms moved sensuously. Damn him for being so gorgeous.

Minka threw open the glass door. "You've got some damn nerve."

Solomon whirled around, and for a moment, she forgot to breathe. If he'd been gorgeous from the back, from the front, he was magnificent. She fisted her hands by her sides to keep from reaching out and running her fingers along his thick chest and washboard stomach.

"Minka," he murmured, a small frown forming.

She kept her gaze upward, refusing to look down and see his cock. "You drugged me."

"You needed the rest."

He stood beneath the spray, seemingly unperturbed that he was naked and she was staring. Which only angered her even more. "You had no right."

"You'd have done the same thing had I looked the way you did. You were practically falling over you were so exhausted."

She crossed her arms over her chest. Her gaze lowered for just a moment to see his flaccid rod hanging between his legs. The length was impressive, and she was disappointed that he wasn't hard.

Then she was furious with herself for looking when she'd decided not to.

"You overstepped," she stated and pivoted.

She didn't get even one step away before a large hand wrapped around her arm, immediately soaking her shirt. The next heartbeat, she was yanked beneath the spray to stand in front of him.

"What the hell is wrong with you?" she cried.

Solomon loomed over her, his blue eyes flashing dangerously. "I was saving your damned life."

"I didn't ask that of you!"

"No, because you wouldn't stoop so low as to ask *me* for anything."

"What the hell does that mean?" she demanded.

His lip curled as he snorted. "As if you don't know."

"Oh, please," she said with a roll of her eyes. "I'm surprised you put me in your bed when I know you'd rather have dumped me in an alley somewhere."

"You don't know what the hell you're talking about."

Her eyes widened. "Oh! The gall! You know exactly what I'm referring to. All those condescending remarks, the not-so-subtle way you let it be known that you don't want me around. You hate that a witch is helping, don't you?"

"It has nothing to do with you being a witch," he stated coolly.

She shoved her wet hair out of her face and blinked through the water splashing on her cheek. "So you admit you have an issue with me."

A muscle ticked in his jaw. "I didn't say that."

"You didn't have to. It's in the way you talk to me."

"You don't know what you're saying."

She'd had enough. Not to mention, she was now getting wet. "Admit you hate me."

"I don't hate you!"

"Right," she said with a laugh. "Everybody sees it."

His eyes narrowed as he leaned closer. "You're wrong. They're wrong."

"Whatever."

"I try to do something nice for you, and you've got to throw it in my face."

She gawked at him before issuing a loud laugh. "Nice? You fucking *drugged* me!"

"For your own damn good, as I've said! Someone had to take care of you since you wouldn't do it yourself."

Her mouth fell open as his words registered. She was so shocked that her mind went blank for a second before a dozen replies filled her. She took a breath to give him a piece of her mind when she heard someone clear his or her throat.

Minka and Solomon turned their heads at the same time to find Myles standing in the bathroom. His blond brows were raised as he glared at both of them.

"Are you two finished? Because I've been standing here for some time trying to get your attention," Myles said.

Minka looked down at herself to see her clothes clinging to her. She'd been so furious, she hadn't even realized how wet she had gotten.

When she looked back at Solomon, his gaze was on her. No longer did those blue eyes of his pin her with arrogance and anger. Instead, there was remorse.

Myles pulled a towel from a hook and held it out to her. "Your bag is on the bed."

She moved to the entrance of the shower and took the towel. Then she waited until Myles had turned on his heel and left before she stepped on the rug.

Behind her, the shower cut off. She wiped her face and tried not to think about Solomon—naked—behind her.

"Stay," he said.

She stilled, unsure of what he meant.

He slid past her then. Her gaze dropped down to see his fine ass right before he wrapped a towel around his waist. Only then did he turn to face her.

"There's still plenty of hot water left," he said. "Take your time."

She watched him walk out of the room and slide the door closed behind him. For a long minute, she simply stood there. Then she dropped the towel and pulled the wet clothes from her body before tossing them into the sink to wring out later.

SOLOMON STOOD with his back against the bathroom door until he heard the water turn back on. Only then did he make his way to the armoire.

"That was some fight."

He paused in reaching for a pair of jeans at the sound of Myles's voice. "I thought you'd left."

"You should've looked around. You'd have seen I was sitting on a barstool."

Solomon blew out a breath and tossed the jeans and a

black tee onto the bed. He dried off before getting dressed and facing his brother. "What do you want?"

"Oh, I don't know," Myles said with a shrug. "Perhaps to talk about that fight I witnessed where you were standing naked in the shower, and Minka was with you. Fully dressed."

"Things got out of hand."

"Well, that's one way of putting it." Myles leaned an arm on the island. "We all knew she'd be pissed when she woke."

Solomon shrugged and walked to the coffee pot where he poured himself a large mug. "Yep."

"What now?"

"I think she'd be more comfortable staying with Riley and Kane."

Myles's lips curved into a smile. "That's what you think?"

"Yeah."

"You can be so stupid sometimes."

Solomon sipped his coffee, eyeing his brother. "Just sometimes?"

"Sometimes, you're actually smart, but this isn't one of those times."

"Gee. Thanks for the confidence."

Myles jerked his chin toward the bathroom. "You're a prime idiot when it comes to her."

"I have an idea. Why don't you tell me what you really think," he said as he set down his mug on the island and faced his brother.

"Fine. I will. You want Minka."

Solomon shook his head. "No. Yo—"

"You want her," Myles stated over him. "You try to treat her like shit in the hopes that no one—especially Minka—will realize it."

"Is that right?" It was the only response Solomon could come up with.

Myles nodded. "You know it is. You don't need to explain why, brother. I know the reason. You forget I was with you that night."

That night. No other words were needed to speak of Misty's brutal murder.

"Minka is different," Myles said. "She's strong and courageous. Not to mention, she's a witch."

Solomon ran a hand down his face. "And none of that removes the fact that Delphine is after her."

"Delphine wants us, as well."

Solomon splayed his hands on the granite of the island. "That's right. Delphine will come for us. I need to be focused on that."

"You can have some happiness," Myles said, a frown puckering his brow.

"I tried that. It didn't work out."

"You tried it with someone who didn't know who—and what—you were. Misty was a sweet soul, but she was weak, Solomon. She was delicate, vulnerable, and utterly defenseless."

Solomon knew Myles was only stating the truth. At one time, those words would've sent him into a rage. The fact that they didn't now was what angered him. "*I* was her defense."

"You didn't fail her." Myles rose to his feet and shot him a sad smile. "I know you think you did, but you didn't. It was a tragedy, plain and simple."

Solomon didn't bother to reply as Myles let himself out. For long minutes, he remained at the island, staring down at the mug of coffee.

No matter what anyone said, Solomon knew he was the cause of Misty's death. He hadn't been there when she needed him. Of everyone, he'd known how fragile she was. It was because of that that he should've been with her at all times to prevent such an outcome.

The thing was, he knew it was a blessing that Misty was no longer alive. She'd never have accepted his world. How many times had she laughed off the stories of vampires and other supernatural creatures? It was why he hadn't told her that he was a werewolf.

He hadn't shared the truth of himself with her because he'd feared she wouldn't be strong enough to deal with his paranormal world of danger and death.

The sad part was, it was because of him that she'd been singled out—and killed. Hiding the truth hadn't helped Misty. It had only made things worse.

The shower turned off, pulling his attention back to

Minka. She was the exact opposite of Misty in every way. Dark, strong, powerful, and a force to be reckoned with.

It was what had drawn him to her from the very beginning.

It was also why he couldn't allow himself to give in to the need pounding through him.

CHAPTER
SEVEN

Rest did wonders to reset the brain. Minka might not have wanted to admit how tired she was to Solomon, but it was obvious she'd needed the sleep.

Her stomach rumbled loudly. With the shower behind her, she wanted clothes and food. She walked out of the bathroom with the towel wrapped around her and found her bag on the bed. A quick search produced the clothes she was looking for.

Just before she released the towel, her head swung to the side at the smell of food. She spotted Solomon in the kitchen, cooking.

She ducked back into the bathroom and hurriedly changed. Then she hung up her towel and wrung out her wet clothes to dry before she made her way to him.

He glanced up at her when she climbed onto one of the stools. "That shower is amazing."

"That it is," he replied, without looking at her.

She licked her lips as she eyed the stack of pancakes. "Can I help with anything?"

Turning, he set down a bottle of syrup and the flapjacks. "The plates are in the cabinet."

She slid off the stool and grabbed two plates as well as forks before returning to the island. Solomon had already placed three pancakes on her plate by the time she sat down again.

Minka was too hungry to wait. She doused the pancakes with syrup and began eating. It wasn't until she'd polished off those and reached for more that she realized Solomon was watching her as he slowly ate.

"What?" she asked around a mouthful of food.

He shook his head, swallowing his food. "I'm impressed with your appetite."

"It feels like I've not eaten in weeks." When he didn't reply, she reached for the syrup and asked, "How long did I sleep?"

"Three days."

She couldn't believe she'd slept that long. Then again, she'd gone nearly six months without a solid night of sleep. She set aside the syrup. "Well, that explains why I'm so hungry."

"I shouldn't have drugged you."

She cut into her pancake and threw him a smile. "The herbs didn't keep me asleep. My body did. While I'm loath to admit it, things are clearer now that I've rested."

"That's good to hear."

"What happened while I slept?"

"Nothing."

She finished her bite. "Nothing? That's odd, isn't it?"

"It's been like that for a while now." Solomon set down his fork and pushed away his cleaned plate. "There will be days where there's no activity."

Minka finished off her last two pancakes. She then tucked her hair behind her ear and swiveled the stool so that she faced him. His blond hair was still damp on the ends, making her want to reach up and touch it. "Do you think it's Delphine?"

"Everything is about Delphine."

"So, what do we do?"

He tapped his index finger on the black granite counter. "We need to take her out."

"Can we? Everyone believes she's too powerful. Me included."

"And that power is continuing to grow. How much longer before she comes for you and Addison again?"

That thought was enough to make Minka's stomach clutch painfully. "I'm not strong enough to take her."

"Maybe not on your own."

"No." She shook her head and got to her feet, pacing

away from him. "You and your brothers have done enough. And I'm pretty sure the Chiassons would rather you not involve Riley in anything."

Solomon followed her toward the sofas. "Riley is a grown woman who will do whatever she wants. Much like you. I don't want to involve her, or my cousins. But the simple truth is that none of us can take on Delphine alone. We're stronger as a group."

"Delphine already wants each of us for some slight or another. Now you want to become a beacon for her to shine her attention on?"

He moved past her to the windows and looked down over New Orleans. "You're right. Delphine does want each of us. We can wait around and let her pick us off one by one, or we can band together." Solomon turned and faced her. "I fought against her when she cursed Kane. And I'll do it again."

"Why didn't you kill her when you had the chance?"

His gaze dropped to the floor. "I went after Kane in Lyon's Point to stop him from hurting Ava. Court and Myles were the ones who trapped Delphine here in New Orleans. It was Court who had his teeth around her throat until she released Kane from his curse—at least the changes she made to his curse. Court could've killed the priestess, but had he, the hex would've returned to Kane, and then would have come to each of us."

Minka slowly sank onto the sofa. "You didn't trap her. She allowed you to take her."

"Yes," he replied and looked at her. "We've kept that bit a secret. I was hoping I'd eventually work out the reason for Delphine's actions."

"She wanted something from you and your brothers, and since she released the curse from Kane, I'm betting she found it."

Solomon nodded. "She didn't ask a single question of my brothers while they held her."

"Where did they keep her?"

"A warehouse."

Minka picked at a chipped thumbnail. "It wasn't LaRue property?"

"No."

"Then what could she have wanted?"

He shrugged. "I've gone over everything Myles and Court told me about that night, and I can't figure out what it is Delphine wanted or got from my brothers."

"We may never know."

"That's not an option. She killed my parents. She terrorizes those in the factions as well as humans. It's time she was shut down."

Minka said, "I'm all for that. We're going to have to be careful."

"Does that mean you'll join us?"

As if she had a choice. It was suicide to face Delphine on

her own, and Solomon knew that. "I will, but I'd like to point out that anyone who Delphine hasn't already marked shouldn't be involved."

"I say we allow anyone who wants a piece of that Voodoo bitch to join in. We're going to need the help."

"And if we fail? Delphine will go after everyone who helped us."

Solomon lifted his shoulders in a shrug. "She'll go after them anyway."

"That's a lot of pressure we're putting on ourselves."

"I don't see any other choice."

She pushed herself to her feet. "You're right. We don't have one because she's backed all of us into a corner. I don't like being trapped."

"Neither does she."

"I'd like to be the one who corners her, so she has no escape."

One side of his lips lifted in a smile. "I'm sure that could be arranged."

Minka returned his smile, her gaze dropping to his mouth. It felt weird to not be bickering with him. Not that she was going to say anything to change it. But after so long of him constantly raising her hackles, she was seeing a different side of Solomon.

"What?" he asked with a slight frown.

She gave a shake of her head. "I don't think we've ever

had a civil conversation before yesterday. Or rather, when you came to the bayou."

"No, I don't suppose we have."

She didn't know what else to say. She glanced out the windows as the rain continued to beat upon the glass. "Thank you for breakfast and for letting me take over your bed these past few days."

"You say that as if you're leaving."

Her gaze shot to him. "I'm not leaving the city, if that's what you're worried about."

"I'd feel better if you stayed."

Her heart thudded in her chest. "Here?"

Alone, with him? Just the two of them? She wasn't certain that was a good idea. All she had to do was think of him naked in the shower to realize that.

"Here," he replied with a nod. "I'm usually always at the bar anyway, and the couch is comfortable when I do need to sleep."

Well. That's what she got for thinking—even for a split second—that he wanted her there because he liked her. It was just convenient.

"Um...all right," she relented.

"I won't bother you."

She forced a smile. "I should be the one saying that. This is your home."

"For now, it's yours, as well."

"Thank you."

He waved away her words. "You can remain up here, but you're welcome in the bar anytime. I'm sure the girls will want to chat with you."

"Let me help out somehow. I can stay in the back, but I've been idle for so long that I want something to do."

Rubbing a hand over his chin, Solomon eyed her. "How do you feel about filing?"

"It's busy work. Just what I'm looking for."

"Then come on. You're about to make Myles's day."

Minka followed Solomon to the door, a thread of eagerness running through her. "He doesn't like filing, huh?"

"It piles up until one of us finally has enough and does it for him," Solomon explained as they walked through the door.

She heard it lock behind her as they walked down the stairs to the bar below. As soon as they entered the back door into the kitchen, the vibe of the place filled her. Music could be heard coming from the front, while the cooks were shouting orders and replies to each other.

Unable to help herself, she watched them for a moment, mesmerized by how they moved like a well-oiled machine. Each had their own station and duties, but it was the way they relied on each other that kept things moving at a steady pace.

"Still hungry?" Solomon asked from behind her.

She glanced at him as she shook her head. "I find this fascinating."

"Don't let Marcus hear you say that. He'll have you in the kitchen with an apron on before you can blink."

Minka didn't think that would be such a bad thing. Reluctantly, she turned and followed Solomon inside the office. She spotted the two tall stacks of files and documents atop the cabinets.

"I did warn you," Solomon said.

Before she could reply, Myles walked in. "What's going on?"

"I wanted something to do. So, I'll be filing," she replied.

His face lit up. "I'd kiss you right now, but I'm already taken. Perhaps Solomon could do it for me."

Minka chuckled, all too aware that Solomon was glaring at his brother. "Where do I start?"

She listened as both Solomon and Myles explained their filing system. It was simple enough, and she immediately grabbed a handful of papers and opened a drawer.

She could feel Solomon's gaze on her as he and Myles spoke about a liquor order that was due in that afternoon. Their talk soon turned to teasing as they talked about a daily pool tournament and bets on if Solomon could beat Court again.

For just a moment, Minka was able to forget that she'd been in hiding, waiting for a psychotic Voodoo priestess to come for her. That small window of time gave Minka the normalcy she'd been missing since she left the Quarter after her coven betrayed her.

The LaRues were giving her an anchor she hadn't realized she missed—or needed. How could she ever repay them?

But the answer was clear as day. Delphine. Once that crazy bitch was gone, the city could return to normal. And the LaRues wouldn't be looking over their shoulders anymore.

CHAPTER

EIGHT

SOLOMON COULDN'T REMEMBER a day crawling by as slowly before. And he knew the reason. Minka.

When she'd offered to help out at the bar, he'd jumped at the chance to have her in sight of his brothers. Instead, Solomon sought her out with his eyes and ears any chance he got.

"Should I ask where your head's at? Because it surely isn't here."

He looked up at Marcus, the head cook, who was also aware of what the LaRues really were, thanks to Solomon saving him from a vampire years ago. "I'm fine."

"You usually lie better." Marcus handed him a basketful of fries, along with a crawfish po'boy. "Your mind is somewhere besides on the food. And I've an idea just where it's at."

Marcus glanced into the office where Minka was still filing. Solomon didn't bother to reply. Marcus wasn't just a good employee, he was also a friend. It was because of that friendship that Solomon kept his mouth shut instead of telling Marcus to mind his own business.

"She's staying with you, right?" Marcus asked.

Solomon nodded as he pulled a ticket from the line and checked each of the plates before calling for a server to deliver the food. Only then did he look at Marcus. "You can stop whatever thoughts you might be having. There's nothing going on between Minka and me."

"Perhaps there should be," Marcus said with raised brows. He nodded toward the office and winked.

Everyone wanted him to find a woman—preferably Minka. It wasn't that Solomon was against the idea…. That wasn't exactly true. He was violently opposed to the thought.

He'd already lost one woman he loved. He wasn't sure he could ever put himself in that position again. The loss had been devastating, crushing. He'd picked himself back up because he had no choice with his brothers counting on him, but he wasn't sure he could do it a second time.

And it was inevitable. All he had to do was look at his parents and his ancestors. The LaRues lived passionately, fought brutally, and died viciously.

He was prepared to do the same, but what he couldn't do —what he *wouldn't* do—was allow another woman into his heart only to have her ripped out of his grasp and killed. Even someone like Minka.

In some ways, it would be worse with her. She knew the secrets of the city because she was part of it. That meant she would be in the line of fire every time. It was simply a matter of the odds turning against her one time.

And with Delphine hot on Minka's trail, it was only a matter of time.

Though that could be said for any of them.

Solomon put Minka out of his mind and concentrated on his job. He refused to glance toward the office. And that's how he got through the next several hours.

It wasn't until mid-afternoon when things slowed that he was able to take a break. He had the night off, but now that Minka was in his place, he thought it might be better if he remained.

"I've got this," Court said as he walked up. "Your shift is over."

Solomon thought about arguing. Most likely, his brothers would think his staying was a ploy to keep away from Minka. And they'd be right. It was an argument he really didn't want to have. Ever.

With a nod, Solomon walked out the back. He stared at the stairs for a long time, trying to decide whether he wanted to go up or not. Everyone thought he didn't want to be around the witch. That wasn't his problem at all. It was because he *did* want to be with her that made him hesitate.

Movement out of the corner of his eye had Solomon jerking around to find Kane pushing away from the corner of the fenced area.

"I didn't know you were there," Solomon said.

Kane raised a blond brow. "That much is obvious. Did you not tell her the code to get in so she'd have to find you?"

Shit. Had he? Was that the reason he hadn't thought about giving her the code to get into the loft? Solomon wasn't sure. "I forgot."

"I let her in a few hours ago. I like Minka."

"Everyone does."

Kane's blue eyes held his. "Including you?"

"She's a friend, so, yes."

"That's not what I meant."

"I know." And Solomon wasn't going to say more.

Kane's gaze lifted to the door at the top of the stairs. "Be kind to her."

"I am."

"You haven't always been." Kane's look was dark when he returned his gaze to Solomon. "There were times you went out of your way to hurt her. But I know the real reason."

Solomon hoped that by not responding, Kane would drop it. He should've known better.

"You treat her with such disdain because you do like her," Kane continued. "In fact, it goes beyond like and straight to attraction."

"Leave it."

"Did you leave me to deal with Delphine's curse on my own? No. You risked your life to stop me. To save me. Well, brother, I'm going to be here pushing you to the very thing you're afraid of."

Solomon blew out a breath. "Why? What does it matter what I do or don't do with Minka?"

"Because you're a good man who had tragedy strike, and that shouldn't ruin the rest of your life."

He didn't know what to say to Kane. In fact, all Solomon could do was watch as his brother stalked back inside the bar. All these months, Solomon had believed Kane was locked within himself, dealing with his own demons. Meanwhile, Kane had been assessing everyone and everything.

Solomon raked a hand through his hair. He would have to keep an eye on Kane. Still waters ran deep, and Kane's were as still as glass.

He pivoted and made his way to the stairs. Every step that brought him closer to Minka tightened the knot of anxiety and anticipation within him. He honestly couldn't decide which emotion he felt more. And that made everything worse.

His hand hovered over the keypad before he punched in the code and heard the locks shift. He opened the door to the sound of jazz music. Slipping inside, he quietly shut the metal slab behind him.

A quick glance around the studio found Minka in the kitchen, moving with the beat of the music as she stirred something in a bowl. On the island behind her were a dozen cupcakes sitting out to cool.

She turned around and began to spread icing on the small treats. Solomon remained immobile as he watched her top each of the cupcakes before she stepped back with a smile and looked at them.

The *ding* of a timer had her spinning around to the oven where she took out another tray of cupcakes and set them to cool. He must have made some sound because her gaze jerked to him.

Minka reached over and turned down the volume on her phone then flashed him a smile. "Hi."

"Hi."

"I hope you don't mind. It's not easy to cook for just one, and after smelling all that delicious food today, I had the need to be in the kitchen."

He walked to the island and looked at the confections. "Of course, I don't mind. And you know these won't last very long."

"I, ah, thought I might cook you dinner."

He held her pale brown eyes and saw the nervousness she couldn't quite hide. Along with the spot of flour on her cheek. "You don't need to do that."

"I'd like to."

"Then I accept." Though he wasn't sure just what he'd

given in to. For some reason, it felt like much more than just food.

Her face lit up with a smile. "Great. I hope you like pasta."

"I love it."

She rocked back on her heels and glanced at the floor. "Good. That's good."

The silence that followed grew awkward. Solomon tried to think of something else to say, but he couldn't think of anything. Finally, he moved to go around Minka the same time she reached for an oven mitt on the island.

They bumped into each other. He instantly grabbed hold of her when she bounced off him so she didn't fall backward. A long, dark curl fell over one eye.

He reached up and smoothed it aside. Then he ran his thumb over the spot of flour, wiping it from her cheek. The contact of his skin against hers did strange, wonderful things to him.

It reminded him of having her close to him in the shower. What a fool he'd been to argue with her instead of drawing her close and tasting those full lips of hers. The water had soaked her clothes, but he'd been too incensed to pay attention as he should have.

That was his loss to be sure. One he wouldn't repeat—if he had the chance again.

"Flour," he murmured.

She blinked, nodding absently as their gazes remained locked. "It gets everywhere."

"Yes." He slowly brushed the tip of her nose and then her collarbone. "Everywhere."

The awkward silence shifted to one filled with sexual tension. As much as he wanted to kiss her, he couldn't. He needed to keep his mind focused on Delphine and the impending attack.

To give in to the need pounding through him, the hunger that threatened to bring him to his knees, would only cloud his thoughts. Instead of keeping Minka safe, he could be putting her in more danger if he didn't remain focused.

He dropped his arms to his sides and took a step back. It was one of the hardest things he'd ever done, but he was doing it for her. For if she died because of him, he wouldn't be able to live with the consequences.

"I think I'm going to take a shower and wash off the smell of the kitchen." He turned his lips up into a smile and walked around her.

He fought not to look back at her as he made his way into the bathroom and pulled the door closed. Standing in the middle of the room with his hands clenched at his sides and his eyes closed, Solomon tried to bring his body back under control. All he wanted to do was go back out there and pull her against him, to thread his fingers in her curls and hold her head steady as he ravaged her lips.

Blowing out a ragged breath, he opened his eyes and

turned on the shower. He stripped and tossed his clothes into the hamper.

When he opened the glass door of the enclosure, he pictured Minka standing there as she had earlier that morning. Her eyes had blazed with fury, making them sparkle. She'd been indignant, outraged.

And it had turned him on.

He stepped beneath the spray and quickly shut off the hot water. The frigid spray did little to cool his body. Not when Minka filled his home, mind, and his senses.

It had been easy to be around her while she slept. Now that she was awake, she was an enticement he couldn't ignore. A temptation he craved.

How in the hell was he going to survive the next few days? He snorted. Days? It could be weeks. There was no way he was strong enough to withstand her. Every minute she was near, it was becoming harder and harder for him to remember why he wanted to keep her at arm's length.

After all, Myles was right. Minka was strong. Physically, mentally, and magically. She was everything Misty hadn't been. That in and of itself gave Minka a fighting chance to survive whatever was coming their way.

Then an image of Misty lying dead in the street, her arm outstretched toward him, flashed in Solomon's mind. And just like that, all the yearning he'd felt for Minka vanished.

It was better that way.

For everyone.

CHAPTER
NINE

Laws of attraction had a way of putting things out of reach. Just when Minka thought there might be something between her and Solomon, she was reminded yet again of the gulf that divided them.

It didn't matter how attracted she was to him, because there was something that kept him from showing her the same. That meant it was in her best interest to leave things alone and forget about Solomon LaRue once and for all.

If only it were that easy.

She shook her head and set about washing the pans she'd dirtied while making the cupcakes. While wiping the island and counters clean, she heard the shower cut off.

Minka turned to dump the crumbs into the sink when everything faded. There was never any warning when the visions occurred, but more troubling was the fact that she was having another so soon after the previous one.

She tried to grab hold of something, anything, as she felt herself falling, but her body wouldn't listen. As the world around her wilted away to be replaced with another, the first thing she heard was the laughter.

There was no reason for her to look for the source. It was a voice she recognized. Delphine. That maniacal laughter sent chills of dread down her spine.

"It's all your fault, Minka."

Delphine's voice was all around her. Minka turned to discover she was in the middle of the street outside of Gator Bait. There were so many dead bodies—humans, djinn, vampires, witches, and werewolves—that she had to pick and choose where she stepped.

Yet there was no sign of Delphine.

But the crazy bitch was there. Minka could feel her.

"Look at what you've done," Delphine said. "Look!"

Minka gravitated toward the platinum fur of a werewolf. She knew it was Solomon, but the sight of his snowy fur tinged with red made her turn her head away.

"What do you want?" Minka shouted into the air, her head turning this way and that searching for Delphine.

Movement out of the corner of her eye had her spinning around. The sight of Delphine covered in blood made Minka take a step back.

Delphine continued toward her, walking on the bodies as

if they were steppingstones. She didn't stop until she stood before Minka. "You want to know what I want? It's you, witch. You're what I want."

"Why?"

"You can save the innocents. You can even save your friends," Delphine continued, her arm sweeping from left to right to encompass everyone.

Minka glanced down at Solomon's dead body. "What do I need to do?"

"Surrender to me."

"And if I don't?"

"What you see here is just the beginning if you fight me."

Minka swallowed hard. "This isn't a vision, is it?"

"Sort of." Delphine smiled. "You've had this vision before. I thought it fitting to use for me to talk to you."

"You could've called."

Delphine chuckled. "Oh, I do like your spirit, Minka. But you and I both know this is the only way."

Minka knew the priestess was powerful, but she hadn't realized Delphine was able to enter someone's visions. That was...troubling.

"You have twenty-four hours to come to me. Else, you've sealed everyone's fate," Delphine stated.

And just like that, the vision and talk with Delphine ended. Thankfully. Minka blinked and found herself looking up at Solomon, who was wearing a concerned frown. It was then she realized she was on the floor as he held her upper body, and she clung to his shirtless shoulders as if he were all that was keeping her alive.

His hand smoothed back her curls. "How bad was it?"

The impact of Delphine's words hit her like a wrecking ball. She kept seeing Solomon's dead body in her mind's eye.

"Breathe," he urged her.

She nodded, only then noticing that she was close to hyperventilating.

He didn't ask anything more, simply brought her against his chest and held her, rocking slowly back and forth. His hard muscles, warm skin, and secure hold were just what she needed. As the minutes ticked by, she found herself calming. Yet he continued to hold her, and it was the greatest feeling in the world.

"I'm scared," she admitted.

He rested his chin atop her head. "I'd be worried if you weren't."

"I think we've underestimated Delphine."

There was a pause before he asked, "How?"

"She caused this vision. It was a repeat of the one I had at my house. Except this time, she put herself there in order to talk to me." When Solomon didn't reply, Minka leaned back to look at him. "She said it was the only way she could tell me her offer."

Blue eyes narrowed as anger sparked. "What offer?"

"She said the slaughter I saw in my vision will happen if I fight her."

"No," Solomon stated with a shake of his head.

Unable to hold his gaze, she looked away. "Delphine said if I come to her in the next twenty-four hours, all of you will live."

"No," he said again, this time more firmly.

His finger on her chin turned her head toward him. Their gazes clashed, locked. Water dripped from the ends of his hair onto his chest before it made its way down his stomach.

She took a deep breath. "I could save all of you."

"It's a trap."

"What if it isn't?"

His face contorted with frustration and anger. "You can't really be taking her offer seriously."

"You didn't see what I did. I stood over your body, Solomon." Minka pushed out of his arms and climbed to her feet.

He was quick to stand. "If she can get into your head to talk to you, did it never occur to you to think that she could also *give* you that vision?"

"I...." She threw up her arms in defeat. "I don't know. It's a possibility, I suppose."

"Damn right, it is."

"What if it's not? What if my vision is real?"

His chest heaved as he pressed his lips together. "You can't go to her."

"I can't be responsible for those deaths. Your death."

His hands came up on either side of her face. "You won't be."

"I will!"

"I won't let it happen."

His words barely registered before his mouth was on hers. As soon as their lips touched, they both stilled. She leaned back and looked at him. The blatant desire she saw in his blue eyes sent her heart careening in her chest.

She wrapped her arms around his neck and kissed him. This time, he held her tightly and moved his lips over hers. As soon as she parted her mouth, his tongue slipped inside to dance with hers.

The moan that rumbled in his chest made her stomach quiver with desire. Then he tilted his head and deepened the kiss. She felt his arousal through the towel. It sent heat and need barreling through her.

She ripped off his towel and ran her hands over his hard, muscular physique. Scars littered his body, reminding her of how often he put his life on the line. He might be a werewolf, but he wasn't immortal.

Their passionate kisses paused only long enough for her to remove her shirt. The fire within her blazed hotly, the hunger consuming her.

He unclasped her bra as he walked her backward. Minka discarded the garment and went back to running her palms over his amazing body right up until her legs hit the back of the bed.

She toppled backward and rose up on her elbows to look at him. "Magnificent," she murmured.

"Yes, you are," he said as he leaned down and unbuttoned her jeans.

Then he grabbed the hems at her ankles and jerked them off with one yank. His blue eyes flashed yellow, a sign of the wolf within. Her breath locked in her throat—she was so turned on. He said not a word as he reached down and grabbed the waist of her lace panties before ripping them in half.

She lay back on the bed as he tossed aside the ruined garment. A smile curled her lips when he crawled over. Her hands found his hips before moving to his ass.

Skin to skin, body to body. Could anything be more decadent or intimate? He kissed her slowly, lazily, as if he had all the time in the world and wanted to savor every second.

It was erotic and stimulating. And she wanted more.

His mouth traveled down her neck before returning to her mouth for more of their fiery kisses. His hands were everywhere, softly caressing, pressing, and simply holding.

"God, I need you," he rasped in her ear.

She arched her back, offering herself. "I'm yours."

As if her words had unlocked whatever was holding him back, he groaned loudly and skimmed his hand up her side until he reached her breasts.

She held her breath, waiting for him to touch her. He

moved his hand gradually upward until he cupped her breast and gently massaged the orb.

Her breath rushed past her lips as her eyes slid shut. The feel of his large, calloused hand on her was heavenly. He knew just where to touch, just how to tease her to the point of pain.

He tweaked her nipple before skimming his palm over the aching tips. Then he rolled the nipple between his fingers, lightly pinching the peak.

Her breasts swelled from the attention. All the while, her hips bucked against him, wanting and needing the friction the movement caused.

"So damn beautiful," he murmured.

She gasped when his mouth locked onto a nipple and began to suckle while his fingers teased her other peak mercilessly. The assault on her breasts stole her breath and flooded her body with such desire that she shook with the force of it.

Her fingers dug into his arms as she moaned. He rocked forward, his arousal rubbing against her swollen clit. She sucked in a breath at the contact.

"I need you inside me," she told him as she opened her eyes. "I want to feel you."

He lifted his head and smiled. "Not yet."

She started to beg when his finger circled her clit. All thoughts vanished as her body shuddered and her legs fell open. Cool air hit her heated sex. The sight of him looking down at her exposed body brought another rush of warmth.

"I'm going to feast on this," he told her without looking up from her sex.

Minka couldn't take her eyes from him as he settled between her legs. He glanced up at her right before his mouth lowered to her core.

His tongue gently lapped at the juncture of her thighs. First one side, then the other. He softly blew against her heated flesh before he leaned down and circled her clit with his tongue.

The pleasure that jolted through her was intense and blinding. A cry left her lips when his tongue began to move back and forth over the tiny nub in quick strokes.

Just as he'd said he would, he feasted upon her sex. Each lick of his tongue sent her higher, her desire swelling until she was crazed with it.

Until she was crying out for him to give her the release she craved.

Then he slid a finger inside her.

CHAPTER
TEN

PERFECTION. That's what Solomon thought of Minka. From her rich russet-brown skin to her pale brown eyes to her curly hair.

He couldn't stop touching her silky flesh. Her body was soft and lithe, and so damn responsive. Her breasts fit in the palms of his hands while her dark nipples remained hard and ultra-sensitive.

Yet it was her hot, wet center that occupied his attention at the moment. Dark curls tried to hide her sex from him. He spread her woman's lips and licked her clit until she was a writhing, incoherent mess.

Only then did he thrust a finger into her tight body. He ran his free hand along her outer thigh. Her cries were music to his ears and pushed him to bring her higher. What a fool he'd been to try and resist the attraction, the overwhelming hunger to unite their bodies.

He added a second finger to the first as he thrust slowly and deeply. Her hips were lifting to meet his hand while her chest rose and fell rapidly.

Watching her reaction to his teasing of her body was mesmerizing. He could do it all day, and still never get enough. Not in a month. Not in a lifetime.

His cock jumped when he circled her clit with his thumb, and her back arched off the bed. He couldn't wait to be inside her, to feel the hot walls of her sex hold him, to move within her and feel her wet heat surrounding him.

He knew the moment her climax hit by the way her body stiffened and her breath hitched. His gaze was locked on her face as the pleasure stole over her features and softened her lips into an *O*.

There had never been a more beautiful sight than Minka in the throws of an orgasm. It was an image that would be with him until the day his heart stopped beating.

He withdrew his hand from her sex and spread his palm over her belly. Her eyes fluttered open with her lips curving into a seductive smile.

"I need you inside me," she said.

As if he could deny her now. In truth, there wasn't anything he would refuse her. He'd known Minka was extraordinary, that she would consume him—body and soul.

It was why he'd tried to be mean to her in order for her to hate him. Because he'd known he couldn't resist her forever.

He rose up over her, his hands on either side of her head. Pale brown eyes gazed up at him, sparking with a fiery passion that made his balls tighten.

Without a word, she rolled onto her stomach and looked back at him over her shoulder. Her sexy grin made him groan as he ran a hand down her spine to her round ass.

When she rose up on all fours and rocked back, grinding into his hard cock, he got on his knees and clasped his hands on her hips to hold her still. She fell forward onto her elbows, her head down, waiting. Then he guided himself into her entrance.

The moment he pushed inside her, she sucked in a breath. He slowly filled her inch by inch. The feel of her surrounding him like a glove brought him to the edge. It was only by sheer will alone that he held back his climax.

With one final push, he was fully seated within her. For several seconds, neither of them moved. He brushed aside her long curls and caressed a hand down her back.

He began to move, slowly at first to draw out their lovemaking. But the tempo soon quickened as passion wrapped around them tightly.

Minka came up on her hands, rocking back to meet each of his thrusts. He reached for her face, turning her head to the side to see her. His chest tightened when he saw that her lips were parted and her eyes were closed. But it was the pleasure he witnessed in every detail of her face that broke through the last shreds of his control.

He pounded into her as he lifted her upper body to his. There, he ran his hands over her breasts, tweaking her nipples as he brought them closer and closer to the bliss that waited.

She reached a hand back, wrapping it around his head as she twisted to put her lips on his. Their tongues danced in time with the movement of their bodies, tightening the bonds that were tethering them together.

He didn't even care. All that mattered was the yearning, the craving he had for the amazing woman in his arms.

"Solomon," she murmured between kisses.

Her hands were rubbing along his sides, down his thighs, and over his hands that caressed her body. Never had he experienced anything so sensual, so carnal.

She fell forward onto her hands again when he stroked her clit once more. With just a few swipes of his finger, she threw back her head and cried out as a second orgasm ripped through her.

He was so unprepared for the feeling of her body clamping around him that it tipped him over the edge. He welcomed the climax, embraced the rampant ecstasy that devoured him. It grabbed hold of him, consuming every fiber of his being until he felt his heart beating with Minka's.

Only then did he open his eyes as the last of the orgasm faded. And he realized he was a new man: a man who had tasted the pleasure of the woman who was his other half.

And he knew now that he would do absolutely anything to keep her safe and alive. Because she was his life, his very reason for breathing.

Solomon leaned over her and wrapped his arms around her as she struggled to get her breathing back to normal. He rolled to his side, taking her with him. He moved aside her hair and kissed her cheek.

"Why did we wait so long to do that?" she asked.

He put his lips against her neck and grinned. "Because I'm an idiot."

She laughed and turned her head to him, their eyes meeting. "I feel you inside me."

"It's where I always want to be."

"It's where I want you to be."

He skimmed his fingers down her face. "I don't know what just happened between us, but I've never felt anything like that before. It's almost as if...."

"It was destined," she finished.

"Yes."

She sighed and turned her head back to face front. Then she put her arms over his. "It's too bad we can't stay right here forever."

"What you said earlier about Delphine..." he began.

"Please, don't," she interrupted him. "I don't want to talk about her."

He pulled out of her and leaned up on an elbow to look down at her. "I do. Because I refuse to let you go to that nutjob as a sacrifice."

Her head turned to him. A sad smile pulled at her lips as she touched his face. "And I'll gladly do it to save you and the others. I can't have your blood on my hands."

"Who says you will?"

"My visions come true."

He twisted his lips. "Yes. And no. You saw Myles die, but you didn't see yourself pulling the silver from his body and saving his life."

She flattened her lips, refusing to reply.

"Admit it," he urged. "Your visions show you only part of a scenario."

"Of course, they do."

"And our decisions can change the course."

She shifted to face him, coming up on an elbow so they were face-to-face. "As long as I've had my visions, there's only been one who has changed what I've seen—Myles."

"Don't you want to try?"

"Yes," she insisted.

He took her hand in his. "Then stand with me, with us. Don't give Delphine what she wants."

"You're asking the impossible."

"No. I'm asking you to trust me."

Her face crumpled. "I do. I always have. But I saw you. Dead. Your ashy white fur covered in blood. That image haunts me. I can't have it happen."

He pulled her against him then. They clung to each other, each lost in their own thoughts. Solomon couldn't lose her. Not now. Not ever. He'd already suffered one unbearable loss, and he wasn't strong enough to endure another.

More than that, he knew in his gut that Delphine was tricking Minka. But how to convince her of that? She was sure her vision was real. Though he hated to admit it, he'd go to extremes to make sure his family and friends were spared a horrific death.

So, he couldn't fault Minka there. But that didn't mean he'd stand aside and let her go to Delphine. If she wouldn't fight for herself, then he'd do it for her.

No matter what the Voodoo priestess told Minka, eventually Delphine would come for all of them. She only spared someone if she thought she could give them more pain later on. It was how Delphine always worked.

Minka might have grown up in New Orleans, but her coven had kept its distance from Delphine. Solomon and his family hadn't had that luxury. They'd been front and center in numerous altercations with the priestess. Delphine was the cause of his parents' deaths, and she'd already made it clear she wanted Riley for something.

The LaRues and Chiassons readily gave their blood and their lives to protect the innocent. It was a family tradition, one that Solomon had never thought twice about.

Until now.

Minka made him long for a normal life. One where he worried about paying bills and his main concern was pleasing Minka. But longing for such a life didn't make it so.

He was a LaRue, a werewolf that policed the paranormal factions of New Orleans to keep everyone in line. Delphine's rise to power had been done with fear and murder. His parents had tried to stop her, and look where it had gotten them.

It was why he and his brothers had trodden carefully with the priestess. And what had led them to the current situation.

They should've taken Delphine down as soon as they could. The problem was, he wasn't certain she could be killed. Her power frightened him because it seemed far-reaching.

Everyone in the city feared her, whether they knew her or not. That kind of terror couldn't be erased easily. It had taken years to seep into everyone's subconscious, causing everyone to do exactly as Delphine wanted.

Well, Solomon wouldn't be one of those puppets anymore.

It might end up costing him his life, but it might end up

freeing others. He was ashamed that he'd taken so long to come to such a decision.

Yet, every time he thought of Delphine, it was the image of his parents lying dead in the street, their bloodied hands joined and Delphine looking on with a smile that he saw.

All these years, he'd thought he'd been handling the priestess carefully but with authority. When, in fact, she'd been the one handling him. It infuriated Solomon. That, combined with the fact that he'd been blind to it all, made him silently rage.

Delphine's time ruling New Orleans was over. If they didn't stop her now, she might very well be unstoppable. That would leave nothing but grief to any and all who came to the city.

He took one of Minka's curls and wrapped it around his finger. His heart ached for time with her. To learn what she loved and hated, to find her favorite food, to discover what flowers she liked.

He wanted to take her to the movies, to share a bottle of wine, and to sit silently as they watched a lightning storm over the river.

He wanted to grumble about her stuff cluttering his bathroom and go furniture shopping with her.

He yearned to hold her hand as they walked down the street, to pick out a Christmas tree with her, and to have her beside him at the table for Thanksgiving.

He craved to have her with him as they climbed into bed at night, and awake holding her each morning.

And he knew what all of that meant, what he'd known for months and wouldn't admit...he was in love with Minka Verdin.

CHAPTER

ELEVEN

MINKA HAD NEVER KNOWN such happiness. She licked the sauce from her fingers and stirred the mixture in the pan atop the stove. She looked over at Solomon, who was shredding fresh parmesan for her.

He met her gaze and grinned. "That shirt looks damn good on you."

She chuckled and looked down at his shirt that she'd put on. The denim button-down hit her upper thighs, and she'd had to roll up the sleeves in order to cook, but having his scent on her and wearing his shirt made her feel...like they were a couple.

Though she wasn't sure what they were exactly. Neither had spoken about it. And really, why? If she were going to Delphine, there was no need to go into a lengthy discussion on what they were or weren't.

No more had been said about Delphine or Minka's visions since Solomon had brought it up earlier, and Minka was just fine with that.

"That smells delicious," Solomon said as he came to stand behind her.

She leaned back against him when he put his hands on her waist. Stirring the creamy sauce, she added more cayenne pepper to the mix. "It's my grandmother's recipe."

"How much longer? My mouth is watering."

Laughing, she reached over and stirred the pot of boiling pasta. "Not long now."

"Good. How about some wine?"

"Yes, please."

Her gaze followed as Solomon moved away to the nice stock of wine he had. Everything seemed so normal at the moment, and she wanted to soak up every second of it. Her twenty-four hours was rapidly counting down.

While he opened the bottle of chardonnay, Minka added the shrimp to the sauce to cook the last few minutes before the pasta was finished.

Solomon turned on some background music. She smiled, wishing they had more time together. He was an amazing lover, both tender and demanding. With him, she felt special and beautiful, and she knew how unique something like that was. If there were a way for her to fight Delphine and keep Solomon and the others alive, she'd do it in a heartbeat.

But the vision had shown her exactly what would happen.

She drained the pasta and added it in with the shrimp and sauce, stirring it all together. Then she dumped in the parmesan and mixed it again. By the time she finished, Solomon had the two plates out, waiting.

He bent over and drew in a deep breath of the dish. "Damn. My mouth is watering. You'd better put some on my plate before I take the pot from you and eat it all."

She laughed and gave him a heaping portion before dishing some onto her plate. Then she joined him at the island where the wine was waiting for them.

Solomon lifted his wine glass. "Here's to the future."

"The future," she replied and clinked their glasses together.

She held his gaze as they both took a drink. The toast could be taken various ways, but she knew Solomon was thinking about her staying to fight against Delphine.

But she forgot all of that when he lifted his fork and brought a bite to his lips. His eyes closed and his face filled with delight as he chewed.

When he swallowed, he looked at her. "This needs to go on our menu. It's that good."

"I'm glad you like it." In fact, she was beaming inside.

The conversation remained light and flowed freely as they ate. They spoke of the bar, his brothers, and Court and Skye's wedding that everyone was expecting.

All too soon, their plates were cleaned, and the wine bottle was empty. She rose to take the dishes to the sink when Solomon took her hand.

"I'll do that later," he said. "Come with me."

She allowed him to pull her after him as he rose and walked to the sofa. With a click of a remote, the lights shut off, and she was able to look out the wall of windows to the Quarter.

"This is beautiful."

He pulled her down beside him and leaned back. "It's one of my favorite things about this place."

"It's magical. That's for sure."

Her eyes briefly closed when his fingers tugged on the ends of her hair. She turned to face him before crawling to straddle his waist.

"I wish I knew a spell to stop time," she said.

His hands came to rest on her hips before sliding beneath the hem of her shirt. "Maybe we can will it to happen if we both wish it hard enough."

"If only it were that simple."

"All these months, we could've been together." His forehead creased as he shook his head in agitation.

Minka ran her thumb over his bottom lip. "Don't look at the past. We only have the present. Let's make the most of it."

She slid her hands into his blond hair before leaning

down to kiss him. His hands flattened on her back and pressed her closer as he deepened the embrace.

Desire that had been banked blazed between them. Minka began unbuttoning her shirt before Solomon grew impatient and yanked it open, the buttons flying around them to ping softly on the wooden floor.

DELPHINE STARED at the darkened windows of Solomon LaRue's loft. She'd hoped to get Minka before the witch and the werewolf slept together, but she'd waited just a little too long.

That changed very little in her plan. She wasn't giving Minka any time to form a strong attachment to Solomon. In the end, Minka would come to her to save her friends.

The smell of bayou and werewolf assaulted her. Delphine turned her head to the shadows and motioned her visitor forward. "I don't like when you skulk, Griffin."

"I warned you about Solomon's attraction to her."

Delphine waved away his words with a flutter of her fingers. "Tell me, how long was she with Solomon before you came to me?"

"What does that matter? I told you where she was."

"Ah. So you did." She turned to face him, letting her gaze rake over his face.

His green eyes briefly met hers before looking back at Solomon's windows.

"When did Minka arrive in the city, Griffin?"

"A few days ago," he said with a shrug.

Anger flashed through her. With merely a thought, she had him pinned against the building. She curled her fingers into a fist. That gesture was enough to squeeze his throat, choking him.

He clawed at the invisible fingers at his neck, his eyes bulging.

"If you'd come to me as soon as they brought her to the city, I could've prevented her and Solomon's union," she told Griffin.

She wanted to end Griffin's life right then, but unfortunately, she needed him for the next part of her plan. With a roll of her eyes, she released him. He bent over at the waist, gulping in huge mouthfuls of air.

"You care about Minka," Delphine said. "But who do you want to save? The witch? Or your sister?"

Griffin's eyes flashed yellow in his anger as he straightened. "I'm doing all of this for Elin. You promised to release her in exchange for my knowledge."

"So I did. That directive didn't mean for you to wait days before sharing information with me. It makes me think you're regretting our partnership."

He gave a loud snort. "A partnership implies we have the

same goal. You want Minka and the LaRues. I just want my sister."

"How is the rest of your pack going to feel when they learn you helped to wipe out the LaRues?" she asked with a smile.

Griffin glanced away. "They won't know."

She took a step toward him. "And why not? Nothing in our agreement said I couldn't tell anyone I wanted that you're helping me bring down the LaRues." She tsked. "After all that work you did to get Kane to trust you and bring you into the fold with his brothers... That gave you the opportunity to call back all the Moonstone weres, who had scattered to the wind after your parents betrayed Solomon's. I suppose the apple really doesn't fall too far from the tree."

"You have my sister!" Griffin shouted.

Delphine raised a brow and narrowed her gaze. "Keep your voice down, wolf, or I'll take it from you."

He took a few steps away, running a hand down his face before he walked back to her. "All I want is my sister back."

"That's not true. You want your pack to be allowed to remain in New Orleans."

The frown that formed on his face nearly made her laugh. How easy it was to manipulate all the pathetic creatures—human and paranormal alike.

"You said we could remain, unharmed by you," Griffin replied in a low, angry voice.

"What I said was that you and your sister would be

allowed to stay. Everyone else in your pack I'm going to hunt and kill, slowly," she said with a smile.

He shook his head and gave her a disgruntled look. "Why? I've done everything you wanted."

"And you'll continue to be a good watchdog, or I'll kill Elin." She laughed when he looked confused and frustrated. "Did you really think you could try and make a deal with me? As soon as I took your sister, I knew you'd do whatever I wanted, whenever I wanted."

Griffin's chest heaved in fury as he glared at her. "You're a cold bitch, Delphine."

"I want power, and I know what to do to get it."

"Yeah." Griffin turned on his heel and stalked into the night.

Delphine watched him go before she looked to one of her disciples who always followed. She gave a jerk of her chin that sent the man following Griffin.

Holding Elin should keep the alpha in line, but just in case it didn't, she was going to have him followed. It would be just like the whimpering werewolf to have a conscience and go see Solomon. Or worse, Minka.

One time, before the weres had risen up against her, she'd squashed that rebellion easily enough by threatening Griffin's life. That's all it had taken to get his parents to do exactly what she wanted.

For years, the only werewolves she'd had to worry about were the LaRues. Neither the LaRues nor the Moonstone pack was aware of how close they'd come to killing her when they attacked her to free Minka and Addison.

It was why she was going to rid New Orleans of every werewolf and ensure that none ever ventured near the city again. To help her cause, she would put a bounty on any werewolf. Whoever killed one and brought her the carcass would get payment—either in money or erasure of debt.

Because everyone was indebted to her in one form or another.

She'd spent her life getting to this point, and she wasn't going to have it fall apart because one witch decided to stand up against her.

Yet it wasn't just Minka refusing to come to her. Delphine had seen it all in her own vision. If Minka stood with Solomon and the LaRues, it would unite the entire Moonstone pack. That would then be the end of her.

It was why she'd taken Elin years ago. Insurance. And Elin would be the sole reason Delphine got Minka's power, the LaRues would be wiped out, and the Moonstone pack would be hunted to extinction.

TWELVE

MINKA STOOD in the middle of Solomon's loft and looked around. They'd made love on every surface, in every way, throughout the night.

She was tired, but her body had never been so pleasured. And never would be again.

Her gaze went to the bed. It was a blessing that she'd woken to find him gone. It gave her the time she needed to get dressed and gather her few belongings without him attempting to convince her to stay.

She didn't know what Delphine had planned for her. Most likely, it was death, but that was preferable to having her friends die in her stead.

Minka grabbed her bag and walked to the door. As she stepped outside, she looked within one last time. She'd been amazingly happy there for the short time she'd had.

Closing the door behind her, she started down the steps, only to come to a halt when she spotted Solomon standing at the bottom as he leaned a shoulder against the building.

"I thought you were gone," she said.

"I've been waiting for you."

She frowned as she slowly descended the steps. "And you couldn't do that in your place?"

"Not when I needed backup."

"Backup?"

He nodded and took her bag when she reached him. Then he put his hand on her back and guided her through the kitchen door into Gator Bait. There, everyone stood—even Griffin.

She looked around at all the faces before she turned to Solomon. "What is this?"

"An intervention," Riley said.

Minka shot Solomon a stern look before she faced the others. "Thank you for this, but it isn't going to work. None of you saw my vision. You don't know what it's like to see all of you dead. I can stop that from happening."

"By going to that bitch?" Kane asked with a snort. "You're smarter than that, Minka."

And this was why she hadn't wanted to tell anyone her plan. "I'm trying to save all of you."

Solomon came up beside her and took her hand. "It won't work. Even if you go to her, Delphine will come for all of us. She sees us as a threat."

"She promised to leave each of you alone," Minka insisted.

Myles said, "She lies to get what she wants. Look at the extremes she went to in order to capture you and Addison."

"He's right," Addison interjected. "Delphine can't be trusted."

Skye's dark eyes were filled with anxiousness. "You helped save me not so long ago. Let us help you now."

"We're rather good at it," Court added.

Everyone had spoken except for Griffin. Minka thought that odd since he'd been so vocal while watching over her at the plantation. Why was he so silent now?

"I've got an idea," Solomon said, breaking into her thoughts. "Hear me out before you leave."

There was still time, but she knew every second she remained with Solomon, the harder it would be to leave him. Yet she couldn't walk away without listening to him.

His bright blue eyes held hers, silently waiting. She gave a nod and he rubbed his thumb along the back of her hand.

After he sat her bag down near the backdoor, they followed the others into the front of the bar. It was odd to see it so empty and quiet. Almost as if the place were waiting to come to life with people and music again.

Minka took the chair Solomon pulled out for her and found herself sitting between him and Kane. Others dragged up chairs, except for Griffin, who half-sat on one of the tables.

"Please reconsider your decision," Addison implored, her hazel eyes pleading.

Riley crossed one long leg over the other and tossed her long, brunette locks over her shoulder. "In your place, I'd probably do exactly the same, Minka. But the thing is, it's the wrong choice."

"What are Delphine's plans for you?" Kane asked.

Minka hesitated before she shrugged. "I'm not sure. I assume she plans to finish what she began with Addison and me."

"Which means she'll come for Addison again," Myles stated in a harsh voice. "I didn't let Delphine kill Addison the first time, and I won't this time either."

Minka shifted in her chair. "Delphine hasn't said anything about wanting Addison. Our agreement was that she would leave all of you alone if I came to her in the allotted time."

"And you believe her?" Skye asked.

Minka shrugged. "No, but I don't have another choice."

"You do," Solomon said and reached over to take her hand. "Stand and fight with us. We've proven what we can do together."

"If I do that, all of you die."

Kane leaned his arms on the table. "You're a powerful witch. It stands to reason that Delphine would want you out of the way. If you really believe that all of us will be alive years from now because Delphine held up her end of the bargain, then I'll take you to her myself."

"I see the doubt in your eyes," Solomon told her. "You know as well as I that Delphine will come for us. We're a threat to her. She wants us out of the way."

Riley nodded slowly. "And the first step is you."

Minka didn't want to die. She also didn't want to hand over her magic in any form to anyone, much less Delphine. But she wanted to save her friends more than anything. Were they right? Was she just handing herself over to Delphine, which would clear the way for the priestess to kill the others?

That thought left her cold.

"What if all of you are wrong? What if my vision comes true?" she asked.

Solomon brought her hand to his lips and kissed her knuckles. "Then we'll have died fighting against evil as we were meant to do."

"What about you, Griffin?" Court asked.

All eyes swung to the Alpha of the Moonstone pack. He had one hand by his lips. He dropped his arm and shrugged. "It's always been the duty of my pack to protect the LaRues and to fight beside you."

Court's gaze narrowed on him. "That's true enough, but the past speaks for itself."

"I'm not my parents," Griffin declared.

Minka frowned as she watched Griffin. There was

something off about him. As if he were nervous and his mind was elsewhere, which was decidedly odd since this involved his pack.

"What?" Solomon leaned over and whispered.

She shrugged, unable to pinpoint the problem. But, obviously, she wasn't the only one. Court had seen something, as well. Why else was he directing such questions toward Griffin?

"You were adamant about protecting Minka in the bayou," Solomon said to Griffin. "In fact, we came to blows over it. I get the impression your thoughts have changed."

Griffin got to his feet. "I vowed to protect Minka."

"What of your sister? Delphine still holds Elin," Kane said.

The longer Minka watched Griffin, the more she was sure that he was somehow involved with Delphine. She didn't want to come out and accuse him of it in case she was wrong, and she also didn't want him to know anything more about her decision. In fact, she had a plan of her own.

"I'm going to Delphine," she declared.

There was a moment of silence, then Myles asked, "We can't change your mind?"

"No," she said and glanced at Griffin.

Solomon jumped to his feet and stood with his hands fisted at his sides while glaring at her. "I sure the hell can. I'll tie you to my bed if I have to."

She calmly stood and put her hand on his chest while she

held his gaze. After a moment, Solomon blew out a breath and stalked to the back of the bar.

While the others began talking at once, there were two who remained silent. Kane, who watched her with narrowed eyes, and Griffin, who kept looking out the windows.

That was all the answer she needed. Minka held up her hand for the others to quiet. Then she looked at each of them. "I'd like to take a few minutes with each of you to say goodbye."

"Minka—" Skye began, but Court quickly grabbed her hand to silence her.

Minka walked to Griffin and smiled up at him. "Thank you for watching over me these last months. You were a welcome diversion. I treasured the time I had to get to know you."

A muscle jumped in Griffin's jaw as he frowned. She squeezed his hands and then stepped back. Without a word, he pivoted and walked out the back door.

As soon as the door had closed behind him, Minka blew out a breath. Her gaze landed on Solomon, who stood at the doorway to the kitchen, staring at her. He made his way to her, cupping her face in his hands and giving her a soft kiss.

"What was that about?" he asked.

Court propped a foot on a chair. "She saw what I did. Griffin is working with Delphine."

"He wouldn't," Kane protested.

Myles ran a hand down his face. "I'm inclined to agree with the others, Kane. Something was off about him."

"Not to mention that Delphine has his sister," Riley pointed out.

Minka linked her hand with Solomon's and faced the group. "This isn't Griffin's fault. I'm sure Delphine is using Elin against him."

"To do what?" Skye asked.

Minka shrugged, her lips twisting. "Probably to report on me."

"Are you really going to Delphine?" Addison asked.

She shook her head and felt Solomon's grip on her tighten. "It was a ploy to get Griffin to leave so we could talk freely."

"The fight is on," Riley said and slammed her hands on the table with a bright smile. "I've been waiting for this."

Solomon held up a hand. "Hold on. Things just got more complicated. My plan relied on the Moonstone pack for help. Without them...well, I don't need to tell you that that puts us at a distinct disadvantage."

"Perhaps not totally," Kane said.

Myles lifted a shoulder. "All right. I'll bite. What does that mean?"

"It means that I might be able to bring the Moonstone pack here," Kane explained.

Riley's smile died and a frown formed. "If Griffin finds

out, he'll consider that a challenge. Y'all will fight to the death."

"I know."

Minka looked at Solomon, who was staring at Kane silently. She moved closer to Solomon. "We're going to need all the help we can get besides the werewolves. The djinn and vampires won't ever unite to stand against Delphine, but there are witches who will."

"I'll come with you," Addison said.

"Whoa. Hold up," Solomon said. "Minka isn't leaving the building. As soon as Delphine realizes she has lied, the priestess will be coming for Minka and all of us."

Kane got to his feet. "Which means we have no time to lose."

"Wait," Minka said, stopping everyone. "Delphine has this place watched. If any of us leave, we'll be tracked. She'll know what we're doing before we can do any of it."

Solomon gave a nod of agreement. "Then what do you propose?"

Minka found a smile pulling at her lips as she looked at each of them. They had gathered together to keep her with them, and to let her know how much she was loved.

Now it was time for her to once more make a stand. This time, she knew what was coming. This time, she'd be ready to take on Delphine.

"With magic, of course," she replied.

CHAPTER

THIRTEEN

NEVER HAD SO MUCH BEEN on the line. Solomon barely contained his fury over Griffin. It didn't help that Minka excused his behavior. Nor did the fact that Solomon would do the same thing if Delphine held one of his brothers.

He stood off to the side in the bar, his gaze locked on Minka. She'd cleared a section toward a back corner where she sat cross-legged on the floor with her eyes closed and candles surrounding her.

"So," Myles said as he came to stand beside him. "You took my advice."

Solomon slid his gaze to his brother and stared at him before putting his finger to his lips. Then he whispered, "I won't lose her."

"No, you won't," Kane said in a low voice as he came up on Solomon's other side. "I'm going to make sure of that."

Court joined them. "We all are," he mouthed.

Solomon had known his brothers would help, but the voicing of their conviction alleviated the knot of tension that pressed upon his sternum.

For the next hour, Minka remained in her spot, her lips softly moving. It was growing closer to the time for Gator Bait to open for lunch, and Solomon was getting nervous.

Every person he saw pass by Gator Bait's windows was a potential enemy. Part of him wanted to close the bar, but to do so would give Delphine a win. And right now, he was all about disrupting anything the priestess wanted.

Riley, Skye, and Addison were moving silently about the bar, getting things ready for the lunch crowd while casting furtive glances in Minka's direction.

Finally, Minka opened her eyes. Her head swiveled toward him, but he didn't release his breath until she gave him a smile. Solomon walked to her with his brothers close on his heels.

"Well?" Court asked her.

Solomon shot his brother a hard look. Then he helped Minka to her feet after she'd blown out the candles.

"I sent the messages," she told them. "All we can do now is wait. I have no way of knowing if anyone will come to help."

Myles crossed his arms over his chest. "And if they do, they could be working with Delphine."

"We're damned if we take their help, and we're damned if we don't," Solomon muttered.

Minka put her free hand on his arm. "We're going to have to trust them. Though, I do propose we keep a close watch on everyone."

Kane gave a loud snort. "That's going to be difficult since they'll outnumber us."

"That takes care of the witches, but what about the werewolves?" Court asked.

Solomon frowned when Minka's face wrinkled. "What is it?" he pushed.

"Well, I contacted Jaxon."

Kane's brows shot up his forehead. "Are you sure that was a good idea?"

"I only told him it was imperative that the LaRues speak to him privately, and that he not tell anyone where he was going," Minka explained.

Solomon smiled at her. "Smart. That leaves it up to us to convince Jaxon to go against Griffin."

"That's not going to be an easy task," Myles stated.

Court shot Myles a flat look. "When is anything ever? I'll head up to the roof and keep a lookout. By the way, when did you tell everyone to come?"

"Today," Minka said.

Solomon sighed and met Minka's gaze. "Then we'd better get ready."

They disbursed around the bar, each doing their part to

make sure everything was in order before opening. When the doors were unlocked, Solomon kept Minka in the back with Kane while he remained at the front with Myles and the girls, looking for any witches or werewolves—or any of Delphine's disciples.

The first few hours were busy with no sign of any enemies or allies. There were many hours until the end of the day, so Solomon wasn't really expecting anyone until the sun went down. Because of that, he was more than surprised when two young witches walked into the bar.

The way Riley greeted them with a smile meant that this wasn't their first time there. After getting their order, Riley walked to him and said, "They've come to say they're joining us."

"Who exactly?" he asked.

Riley looked over her shoulder at the girls. "Those two. I'll tell Minka."

Solomon wasn't going to turn anyone away. The more that joined them, the better. But he knew their real strength would lie with the werewolves. If only Griffin hadn't turned against them.

As the day wore on, more and more witches came into the bar, declaring their intentions to join. By sunset, the LaRues had over thirty witches willing to stand with them.

Solomon walked to the back to give Minka the latest update. He found her pacing in the office.

As soon as she saw him, she said, "I expected more. There

are five covens in New Orleans. Five! More than thirty should've been willing to stand with us."

"It's thirty more than we had this morning."

She stopped, her shoulders dropping. "You're right."

He looked at the time and realized that the twenty-four-hour timetable Delphine had given Minka was up. "It's going to be all right."

"It will be once Delphine is dead."

He opened his arms, and Minka walked to him, resting her head on his chest. Solomon held her tightly. "I'm not going to lose you. I can't."

She leaned back to look at him. "What happened?"

Solomon didn't need to ask what she was referring to. He knew she was asking about Misty. Releasing Minka, he walked to one of the chairs against the wall and sat on the edge, his forearms on his knees.

"You don't have to tell me. I shouldn't have asked," Minka said.

He was shaking his head before she'd finished talking. "Misty and I dated for over a year before I asked her to marry me. She was sweet, almost too kind. People took advantage of her all the time."

"Did she know about your family's curse?"

"She had no idea I was a werewolf. I kept that part of my life secret from her." He ran a hand down his face. "That was my first mistake."

Minka took the chair beside him. "Why didn't you tell her?"

"Because I knew she wouldn't believe me. I knew I'd have to show her, and I realized that might send her away."

"Ah. I see."

Solomon glanced at her. "We'd gone to the movies that night. I dropped her off and returned here since it was my night to patrol. I saw that she'd left her purse in my truck, and I called her house to let her know I would bring it by the next morning. But she didn't answer. So I left her a message. I had no way of knowing that she was on her way here."

Minka reached over and put her hand atop his. That small gesture told him without words that she understood his pain.

"I saw five vampires on my patrol," he continued. "I fought two of them, while the other three took an elderly couple and drained them. It wasn't long before Kane and Myles joined me. We made quick work of the rest of the vampires. Except, I missed one.

"He slipped away when I first approached the group. In my haste to stop any violence, I miscounted. I didn't realize my mistake until we smelled the blood. Misty was at the corner, just twenty-five feet away, on the ground with her arm reaching out to me."

Minka squeezed his hand, her pale brown eyes filled with sorrow and compassion.

He cleared his throat that was clogged with emotion. "I

don't know if she actually saw us. She was dead by the time I reached her. The vampire had ripped out her throat. There was blood everywhere. When I tracked him down I...did the same to him."

Without a word, Minka slid from her chair and went to her knees in front of him as she wrapped her arms around him. He buried his face in her neck and simply held her.

It had been so long since he'd spoken of Misty. He would forever carry the guilt of her death, but no longer did it weigh so heavily upon his heart.

Minka's fingers slid through his hair to lightly scratch his scalp. "Even if you had told her, it might not have changed anything."

"I know that now."

"I know your secret. I know the truth of you. I've seen into your heart, Solomon LaRue, and I've seen nothing but decency and integrity. You're a good man."

He leaned back and cupped her face in his hands. "I wasn't to you. I wanted you to hate me. I needed it because I knew I wasn't strong enough to resist the pull I felt toward you."

"I figured that part out."

"I've been such a fool."

She shook her head. "Shhh. Don't go down that road. Remember, we're in the present. We need to focus on that."

He wanted to think about the future, to plan one with

her. But Solomon knew it wouldn't be wise. Not as long as Delphine still breathed.

Myles came to the door of the office. "Ah, you two might want to come and see this."

Solomon followed Minka and Myles into the front and came to a stunned halt when he saw the leaders of the five witch covens sitting at a table.

He and Minka made their way to the table. "Ladies," he said when he reached them. "I'm surprised to find you here."

"So are we," said the youngest of the group. She looked at her counterparts and then at Minka. "But it's the right thing to do."

Solomon glanced at Minka to find her staring at the woman who led the coven Minka had once been a part of. The same woman who had betrayed her to Delphine.

"I'm sorry," Susan said to Minka. "I shouldn't have turned you over to Delphine."

Another of the leaders put her hands on the table. "Delphine has a way of making you feel as if you have no other choice but to do as she wants. We're tired of her control. We're ready for it to go back to how it was before she killed your parents, Solomon."

"All of us are ready for that," said another leader.

The last of the women nodded. "Every witch has agreed to stand with you. We just need to know when and where."

Solomon smiled as he took Minka's hand. "Delphine

ordered Minka to come to her today. Obviously, Minka didn't. I don't expect Delphine to wait to exact her revenge."

The women rose as one. It was the youngest who said, "Then we need to get our covens ready."

"Also, if Delphine kills us, it won't stop the others from joining you," Susan said.

Solomon watched the women walk from the bar. He couldn't contain his smile as he turned to Minka, but her frown made him pause. "What is it? I thought you'd be overjoyed that all the covens want to join us."

"Susan isn't herself," Minka said as she watched the women.

"Shit." Solomon ran a hand through his hair. "And the others?"

"As far as I know, they are. Despite being our leader, Susan could be weak. Delphine must have figured out how to get to her."

"That means everything we tell them, Delphine will know."

Minka slid her gaze to him. "Exactly. There's nothing we can do that will come as a surprise."

Solomon looked at the bar where his brothers and the girls waited. "That may not be entirely true."

CHAPTER
FOURTEEN

A NIGHT HAD NEVER SEEMED SO TERRIFYING before. Minka looked at the clock to see it just shy of two in the morning. The boys had shut Gator Bait down before midnight. That's when Kane had snuck away to talk to the Moonstone pack.

Minka twisted her hands as she stared into the night sky. New Orleans never slept. It was a city that partied constantly, and yet the streets around the bar were deserted.

She walked to the window and looked out to where she'd seen Solomon dead in her vision. All she could do was pray that she'd made the right decision. If he died because of her... well, she wasn't sure what she'd do.

A presence came up behind her. With a swipe of his large hand, he gently moved her hair to one side, exposing her neck. Solomon then pressed his forehead against the back of her head while his hands gripped her arms.

"Promise me you'll be smart and use your magic to remain safe," he said.

She turned in his arms and smiled up at him as she put her palms on his chest. Then she slowly moved her hands upward until they were laced around his neck. "I will if you promise not to do anything crazy. I need you to be safe, as well."

"I think we're asking too much of each other. We will be battling Delphine, after all." His hands came around her back to press her against him.

As she gazed into his beautiful, blue eyes, Minka realized that this might be her last conversation with Solomon. She wanted—no, she *needed*—to tell him how she felt.

She licked her lips and glanced down at his throat. "There's something I need to say now before I don't get the chance. I don't expect you to say anything, but I want you to know that I—"

"Solomon!" Myles shouted from the back.

"Hang on," he called over his shoulder.

Myles quickly said, "It can't wait."

Minka looked around Solomon to the kitchen before her gaze returned to him. She didn't want to just blurt out the words, but she couldn't let the moment pass.

"Give me a sec," Solomon said before he walked away.

She sighed and turned back to the windows, crossing her arms over her chest. There had been plenty of opportunities throughout the day to tell him of her love, but she'd chickened out each time.

Her attraction to Solomon had gone on for months. As soon as she was in his arms and felt his desire, she'd known what had been hidden in her heart the entire time. Love.

Now, she'd have to wait some more. But as soon as he returned to her, she was going to tell him. Who knew how much longer they had before Delphine showed up.

Because she would. There was no doubt in Minka's mind that Delphine would want to lash out at her for refusing to come in the allotted time. The priestess would be swift and violent in her revenge.

Minka looked from one end of the street to the other. She jerked when she saw the lone figure in white standing in the middle of the road.

"Solomon," she called over her shoulder.

Delphine lifted her arm and motioned for Minka to come.

"Solomon!"

Out of the corner of her eye, Minka saw something on the opposite end of the street. A flash of white fur that sped past and disappeared into the night.

Her heart plummeted to her feet. So the battle had begun. There must have been something very important for Solomon to leave without any word to her.

She glanced over her shoulder into the kitchen. "Myles? Riley? Anyone?"

The silence that greeted her made her blood run like ice. They were supposed to face Delphine as a group. Minka turned her head to Delphine.

Perhaps it was better if she faced the priestess alone.

SOLOMON HATED LEAVING MINKA, but he knew she was safe within the confines of the bar. Right now, he had to get to Kane. Solomon ran faster than ever before. As soon as he saw Jaxon, Griffin, and six other weres at the edge of town, circling his brother with their teeth bared, Solomon growled and slammed into Griffin.

That gave Kane the chance to take out a few of the weaker wolves before attacking Jaxon.

Solomon had the advantage of size and strength as a werewolf, but he couldn't talk. He needed to shift in order to speak, but the rift between him and Griffin was now at the point where only one of them would be walking away alive.

And it was going to be Solomon.

"Enough!"

The bellow that came from Kane surprised Solomon. He growled low at Griffin and swung his head around to see Kane standing over a defeated Jaxon.

Kane was glaring at Griffin, his rage palpable. "You promised me that you were going to take your rightful place as alpha and lead your pack to do as they have always done —help us. I believed you."

Griffin remained in wolf form. He snapped at Solomon, which had the two of them circling each other. Solomon was ready and willing to get the fight with Griffin over with.

"What does he mean?"

Solomon glanced over to find that Jaxon had returned to human form. He was sitting back on his knees, his hands braced on his thighs as he looked at Griffin.

"Griffin," Jaxon demanded. "What is Kane saying?"

Solomon began the change that would return him to his human form. He pushed to his feet and stood naked among the others. "Tell him, Griffin. Or I will."

Several tense minutes passed before Griffin shifted. He straightened and shot Solomon and Kane a fierce glare. Then he looked at Jaxon. "You know Delphine has Elin. I made a deal with the priestess that I wouldn't join the LaRues if she turned over my sister."

"But it isn't that simple, is it?" Kane asked.

Griffin gave a reluctant shake of his head. "I was reporting on Minka's movements, as well. Delphine said if I helped Minka or the LaRues in any way, she would kill my sister."

"How long has Delphine had Elin?" Solomon asked.

Griffin shrugged. "She took her a few months before I returned to New Orleans."

"She's the reason you came back." Kane clenched his

teeth together and walked to Griffin, who he shoved in the chest. "You lied from the beginning."

Griffin pushed Kane away. "She's my sister!"

"And you should've come to us," Solomon said.

Kane turned to Solomon. "He's how that bitch knew where Minka was."

"I know." Solomon looked to Jaxon and the other weres standing behind him. "Kane met with you to give you an offer to remain in New Orleans."

Kane released a long breath. "Stand with us against Delphine. She wants Minka's power, which will only make Delphine stronger. We have other allies who will be fighting alongside us. As Moonstones, you pledged your loyalty to your alpha. Every Moonstone Alpha since the pact has vowed to help the LaRues when called upon. Today, I'm asking you to make that decision for yourselves."

"Do it," Griffin told his weres. "Delphine wants all wolves gone from New Orleans. I can't help the LaRues, or I lose my sister. But you can."

Jaxon frowned as he stepped forward. "Griffin. Do you know what you're saying? You're our alpha. We follow you."

"Not tonight," Griffin said as he looked from Solomon to Kane. "Tonight, each wolf in our pack gets to make his or her own decision. I'd be standing right alongside the LaRues if I could."

Jaxon blew out a breath. "That's all I needed to hear." He

turned to Kane. "I'm in. The wolves behind me will spread the word to the others."

Solomon turned to Griffin. "We'll get your sister free."

A howl split the air. Dread filled Solomon as he recognized Court's voice.

"Go," Kane urged him. "I'm right behind you."

Solomon didn't need to be told twice. He took off running, shifting as he did. All he could think about was getting to Minka. He shouldn't have left her.

It felt like an eternity before the bar came into sight. The silence was what slowed his gait to a walk. Pausing at the corner, he looked up at the roof of the bar and spotted Court. Solomon was about to continue when he heard Minka's voice.

No. She wouldn't have left the bar. Not without him. Solomon peeked around the corner and spotted Minka facing off against Delphine.

"Was that howl from Court supposed to call your friends?" Delphine asked Minka.

Solomon looked behind him to find Kane leading several wolves toward him. Once the group reached him, Solomon looked up at Court to find his brother motioning with his hands to where some of Delphine's disciples were hiding.

It only took a look to Kane for his brother to lope off along with some of the Moonstone wolves to take care of the followers. As Solomon's gaze scanned the area, he found more and more wolves quietly approaching.

Solomon gave a nod to Court and Jaxon before he walked around the corner and came to stand beside Minka. Her head turned to him, a slight smile pulling at the corners of her lips. But it was her fingers tightening in his fur that gave him the most joy.

He bumped against her side as a way to tell her he was ready for whatever came.

Delphine lifted her chin as she looked at Solomon and then Minka with disdain. "I suppose my warning wasn't enough, witch."

"Oh, it nearly worked," Minka said. "Until I realized that you're a liar. Once you had me, you would've gone after my friends."

Solomon bared his teeth when Delphine laughed. He'd been charged with protecting the city from evil, and yet the greatest evil that had ever walked the streets stood before him.

Though he hated to admit it, Delphine was good. She'd traumatized four young boys by killing their parents and leaving them orphans. She'd crept around the Quarter, gaining power little by little so no one really knew what she was about.

Solomon realized he'd failed as a LaRue. He should've paid more attention to the priestess. He should've disregarded the fact that she'd killed his parents. He shouldn't have held such fear of her.

But most of all, he should've seen what she was about.

How many people had died because he'd hesitated to go after Delphine? How many innocents had been crushed, their lives snuffed out because he'd feared the priestess's power?

Too damn many.

And he was ashamed.

His hearing, enhanced in wolf form, picked up on the sound of approaching werewolves. But that wasn't all. There were also human footsteps—dozens of them.

The sound of the bar door opening was punctuated a moment later by it being thrown closed. Solomon looked over and spotted Riley walking to them, stopping on Minka's other side.

"In case you're wondering," Riley told Delphine. "We're sick of seeing you slink around with your veiled threats. Not to mention all your disciples following us around."

Delphine crossed her arms over her chest. "And you think to end it all tonight?"

"To end *you*," Minka stated.

Delphine smiled before she gave a bark of laughter. "Oh, this is going to be better than I could've dreamed. I hope all of you are prepared. You're going to die tonight."

Solomon growled in warning. He was joined by his three brothers, who filed in beside both him and Riley. He crouched down, ready to attack and sink his fangs into Delphine's throat.

CHAPTER

FIFTEEN

MINKA WATCHED DELPHINE CAREFULLY. So the minute the priestess moved, she was ready. The first thing Minka did was deflect the magic the priestess sent their way.

The force of Delphine's power made Minka take a couple of steps back. As they locked in battle, there were shouts as Delphine's white-clothed followers rushed from alleys and other hiding spots.

Solomon stayed next to Minka, fighting any disciple who got too close while the others fanned out to do battle. After a few minutes, she spotted Skye and Addison joined in on the fighting. Riley then let loose a loud whistle, and all the witches poured into the street.

Minka smiled when she saw the concern flash over Delphine's face. Then she held up her hands and pushed her magic outward, slamming it into Delphine.

The priestess stumbled backward. The fear that filled Delphine's face for a fleeting second was all Minka needed to see to take a step forward and give another push of her magic.

Screams of the injured and dying filled the night, while snarls from Solomon and his brothers could also be heard. There was no clash of steel from swords and shields. Instead, this battle was fought with magic and the determination of those rising up against a being of infinite evil and destruction.

With every disciple that died, Minka grew bolder and more resolute. She wouldn't back down now.

"Your powers have grown," Delphine said.

Minka blocked a spell the priestess directed at Solomon, who had knocked a follower to the ground. "I feared you for too long. I'm done with that."

"So, you're ready to die?" Delphine asked with a laugh.

"I'm ready to live in a world without you."

Minka was readying to deliver another blow to Delphine when she felt herself flying backwards. She hit the concrete hard enough that it knocked the breath from her. Pain exploded in her head as well, leaving her dazed and struggling to pull air into her lungs.

Solomon rushed to stand over her. Minka could see Delphine getting closer. She tried to gather her magic, but her body was too intent on breathing to do anything else.

That's when Solomon released a short howl. Minka saw

him crouch down. She felt the strength of him a second before he launched himself at Delphine.

Minka rolled to the side as her lungs finally opened and she gulped in air. All the while, she watched as the impact of Solomon's attack knocked Delphine to the ground. But Minka's triumph was short-lived as Delphine tossed Solomon's huge werewolf body away with a wave of her hand.

The fact that it was so near to where Minka had seen Solomon dead in her vision pushed her to her hands and knees and sent icy fear pounding through her.

"No!" Minka cried and staggered to her feet.

She wasn't able to get near Solomon, though. Delphine's magic grabbed her from behind and began to squeeze. Minka started to struggle even as she heard the sound of werewolves descending upon the street.

But the more she fought, the tighter Delphine's magic became. Minka stopped thrashing and closed her eyes. The magic of the witches fighting against Delphine was thick in the air. It reminded Minka that she was strong, strong enough to break through whatever hold Delphine had on her.

Solomon was growling and snapping his jaws close to her, telling Minka that Delphine was right behind her. Spells Minka had never heard of before filled her mind. She used the one that called out to her loudest. It allowed her to turn and face Delphine. Minka fought back a smug smile when she saw shock fill the priestess's face.

Then, Minka broke free from Delphine's hold altogether. "Let's end this."

Minka could see the wolves circling Delphine as the witches also closed in now that all of the disciples had been killed or had run off.

The smile that suddenly filled Delphine's face caused a moment of panic for Minka until Solomon came to stand beside her once more.

"Yes," Delphine said. "Let's end this."

Minka spread her hands. "Look around you. You're defeated. You have no disciples to do your bidding. It's you against all of us."

"And you think you can kill me?"

"I can. More importantly, I will."

Delphine's smile was slow and so evil it sent a chill down Minka's spine. "You have much power, witch, but there is considerably more you've yet to learn."

"You mean how you took over Susan's body to find out what the witches were doing?" Minka lifted one shoulder in a shrug. "We knew and expected that."

At her words, the witches turned to Susan, who Delphine had been controlling, and began to exorcise the priestess out of the coven leader's body.

"It won't do any good," Delphine said. "Susan was weak. She died the moment I took over."

Minka sank her fingers into Solomon's fur. "Your time here is over."

"Far from it, actually."

No sooner had Delphine said those words than Solomon, Kane, and a dozen witches fell over. The witches clawed at their throats while Solomon and Kane whined and growled.

Minka rushed to Solomon as she hurriedly used her magic to release him. As soon as he was able, he shifted into human form. With a touch on his arm, she then moved to Kane. All the while, the other witches were trying to help those who had been struck with Delphine's magic.

It took several minutes before the chaos ended with everyone still alive. Minka whirled around, ready to tell Delphine just what she thought of such a trick, except the priestess was gone.

"She's gone," Skye said.

Kane stumbled to his feet as he returned to human form, unabashed in his nakedness. "Where's Riley."

"Oh, God," Minka said and turned her gaze to Solomon.

Without missing a beat, Solomon began barking orders for wolves to search for Delphine's and Riley's scents.

Minka then faced the witches. "Use your magic. Delphine is somewhere in the city, and she'll have Riley with her. We can find them."

Yet, an hour later, they still had nothing. It didn't matter that Minka had combined her magic with the others, forming the greatest gathering of witches in New Orleans history, or that she had tried on her own.

Not even the wolves had any luck.

It was like Delphine had disappeared without a trace—taking Riley with her.

One by one, the witches and werewolves returned to their homes after gathering their dead, leaving the LaRues, Minka, Addison, and Skye.

"What now?" Addison asked.

Solomon linked his fingers with Minka's. "We let our cousins know."

"I'll do that," Kane said as he disappeared into the night.

Court and Skye walked away, and then Myles and Addison followed. Minka was looking down the deserted street when Solomon called her name.

"There is the dead," she said.

"They won't be here long."

She frowned as she turned her head to him. "What does that mean?"

"Once a disciple of Delphine, always a disciple. Others will come to claim their bodies."

"We could follow them."

He stood naked in the night air. "Delphine is somewhere no one can find her. At least, not yet. Trust me, we've tried that tactic before."

Minka knew he was right, but she didn't like the idea of

giving up. Especially when they'd had Delphine cornered. But she'd turned Minka's attention to saving her friends, giving the priestess the time she needed to take Riley and vanish.

"Come," Solomon said as he tugged her after him inside the bar.

He locked the front door and faced her. He smoothed her hair back from her face and smiled down at her.

"Smiling?" she asked.

"You were magnificent tonight. My God, you make my pulse race."

She put her forehead on his chest, and despite the dire circumstances, found herself grinning. "Magnificent, huh?"

"Hot as fuck, actually."

Her head lifted as she laughed. "I've never been called that before."

"I'll tell you every day."

The smile melted from her face. Every day wasn't a declaration, but it was damn close.

"You were going to tell me something earlier," Solomon said. "I'd like to hear it."

Despite standing in the dark bar with only the streetlights flooding the windows and drenching them in a yellow-orange glow, the brightness of his blue eyes was stunning.

The anxiety she'd felt earlier about telling him of her feelings was gone. Whether it was because she'd stood up to

Delphine or because she and Solomon had fought beside each other, she didn't know—or care.

"I love you."

He leaned down and gave her a long, slow kiss before he pulled back. "You've had my heart for many months. I used to think you bewitched me, but now I know I'd just fallen in love with you."

"I thought we'd be celebrating a victory tonight."

"We are. We will. We've got each other and our love. That in itself is a major win." He wound a curl around his index finger.

Minka turned her face into his palm and kissed it. "The war has just started."

"No, that bitch began it when she killed my parents. But we're the ones who are going to end it. She made a mistake in taking Riley. Once my cousins are here, we'll rain hell down upon New Orleans."

She grinned up at him. "Then we'd better prepare."

"First, we have a few more hours until dawn. I plan to make use of every minute."

Minka's blood heated at the flare of desire in his eyes. "Is that right?"

"Oh, yes."

She couldn't contain her laughter when he grabbed her hand, and they raced out the back, barely stopping to lock up before they were running up the stairs to his studio.

Once inside, he had her against the wall, kissing her as if there were no tomorrow.

Because there very well might not be one for them.

EPILOGUE

Four days later...

SOLOMON STOOD on the porch of his family home as the two trucks pulled up the drive. The past few days had been some of the best of his life now that Minka was in his life. But they had also been the worst because they'd found no trace of Riley or Delphine.

Or Griffin.

Minka walked out onto the porch beside him. She took his hand and gave it a squeeze. "It's going to be okay. Riley's family is here now."

"Darlin', you've never met my cousins. They're... protective of family."

"Just as you are."

Solomon had to admit she was right. He looked down at her. "Have I told you today that I love you?"

"A couple of times this morning."

"Then let me tell you that I'm a better man with you beside me."

She grinned, her pale brown eyes flashing with love. "A witch and a werewolf. Who would've thought?"

"I should be spoiling you with dinners and trips, not putting you in the middle of a war."

She raised a brow and glared at him. "Solomon LaRue, you say that one more time, and I'll turn you into a toad."

"I like her," said a deep voice.

Solomon looked up, his gaze meeting that of the eldest Chiasson, Vincent. There was no need for words. The two embraced as Myles, Kane, and Court filed out of the house.

After the Chiassons and LaRues had said their hellos, and the introduction of the women had passed, Solomon faced everyone. "It's past time our two families spent time together. I'm just sorry the reason you're here is because we lost Riley."

Lincoln, the second eldest, shook his head. "You didn't *lose* Riley. She's a fighter, a true Chiasson. Delphine took her because she's been after Riley for something."

"And we're going to find out what it is," Beau stated.

Christian rocked back on his heels. "I'm ready to kick some Voodoo ass. When can we get started?"

"Right now. Follow me," Minka said and led everyone inside.

Solomon brought up the rear of the group. Vincent came up beside him and said, "Hold onto her. She's a good one."

"I intend to," Solomon said as Minka looked back and smiled at him. "She's the love of my life."

Vin slapped him on the back. "Then we need to rid the city of a certain Voodoo priestess."

"Damn straight."

No one stood against the Chiassons and LaRues. Delphine was going to find out what it meant to fight the combined force of the families.

All Solomon could do was hope that Riley was alive.

RILEY SQUEEZED her eyes closed from the blinding light as she came awake on her side. She tried to sit up but was racked with pain all through her body.

What the hell had happened?

She finally managed to open her eyes to find herself on the floor of a room. There were boards placed over the windows, many of them smashed or rotting. The curtains that were left were barely hanging on, the fabric ripped and so filthy, the color was indiscernible. Dirt, debris, and broken furniture littered the floor.

Riley gritted her teeth and pushed up onto one hand. She

refused to allow the fear that threatened to swallow her grow. Because she knew who had her. Delphine.

If the priestess thought she could make her cower, Delphine was in for a rude awakening. Riley was a Chiasson, a hunter of the supernatural who was ready and willing to fight anything. Delphine was just another evil monster that had to be taken down.

"Bring your worst!" Riley shouted. She then climbed to her feet and dusted off her hands, her gaze scanning the room. Then she whispered, "I'll be ready for you."

A LARUE NOVEL
MOON BOUND
NEW YORK TIMES BESTSELLING AUTHOR
DONNA GRANT
HIS CURSE TO BEAR...
HER WILL TO SURVIVE.

PROLOGUE

Flames licked at his fur, singeing it. The scent of burning flesh filled his nostrils as he circled his foe. Kane snarled, showing the entity inhabiting the human form that he longed to rip his throat out.

George, for his part, didn't appear to acknowledge Kane's threat. Instead, the man watched Delphine. The Voodoo priestess who'd murdered Kane's parents and wreaked havoc on New Orleans was surrounded by flames.

It wasn't how Kane wanted to kill her, but it would be enough for the bitch to finally die. This wasn't the only battle being waged, though. There was another on the streets, with his brothers and cousins facing Delphine's followers. At least Riley made it safely outside with Marshall.

Kane paused, his ears pricking when he heard Riley shout his name. Being in werewolf form had its advantages.

He wouldn't have heard her otherwise. The fear in her voice made him glance around for other enemies. Kane released a howl to let his brothers know he was alive.

He spotted the cracking floor of the building even as Delphine rushed George. They all wanted each other dead, but Kane was no fool. He took his chance when he heard the groans of the building as it began to buckle.

The floor beneath his paws sank. Kane leapt into the air toward George, who was being bombarded by Delphine's magic. Kane locked his jaws around George's neck and yanked.

He heard the sound of bone snapping right before the floor collapsed.

CHAPTER
ONE

July

THERE WAS nothing more enjoyable than a thunderstorm. Elise leaned a shoulder against the doorway and looked past the screen to the water falling from the eaves of the house.

It wasn't a soft summer rain, but a storm brought on by the intense heat. The floodgates had been opened, and the ground greedily drank its fill. The clouds were churlish, dark against the bleak, gray sky. Lightning flashed all around, and thunder boomed loudly.

Elise looked out over her back yard to the bayou beyond. The rain fell so hard and fast upon the water that it appeared as if the bayou were alive. The roar of the rain was comforting, the storm exhilarating.

A decidedly nice change from her quiet life.

She looked over her shoulder at the Siamese cat curled up on the back of the sofa, his blue eyes gazing with disdain at the weather. As soon as the cat rushed into the house earlier, Elise had known a storm was headed her way.

While Mr. Darcy liked to spend time outside, he preferred the comfort of being inside at night and anytime there was a storm. The scars on his face and ears proved that he was quite the scrapper—even against the animals of the swamp.

But at least the cat was smart enough to stay far away from the gators.

Elise chuckled and turned her gaze back out to the rain when Mr. Darcy yawned and put a paw over his eyes to sleep. She found her eyes scanning the area for signs of the black dog she'd spotted over the last few weeks. It was huge. At first, she'd thought it a wolf, but there were no wolves in Louisiana.

She'd left a bowl of food out for it, but so far, only the raccoons had enjoyed the meal. The last time she'd seen the dog, he was limping. It had been dusk, so she hadn't been able to see his wound, but it needed to be cleaned before it got infected—and the beautiful dog became a meal for something else.

While she enjoyed the storm, it was messing with her routine. All her life, she'd been a bit obsessed with keeping things in order. And once she made her daily schedule, she hated when things interfered or prevented her from keeping to it.

After three years in the bayou, she should've been used to her perfectly planned days going to shit, but she couldn't quite manage it. At least she no longer fretted about it—as much.

"One day changed both of our lives, Mr. Darcy," she said, though the cat wasn't listening.

Elise had gotten into the habit of talking to the cat, and sometimes, Mr. Darcy would stare at her as if he knew exactly what she said.

It wasn't often that Elise thought of the day that had altered her life so drastically, but when she did, it was hard to shake off the memories. Or the horror of it all.

Her gaze lowered to the scars on her arms that she kept hidden with long sleeves. They were a constant reminder of how close to death she'd come.

But they couldn't compare to the scars inside her.

She ran her hand down her arm, feeling the raised remnants through the linen of her shirt. It was silly to keep them hidden. Many in the small community had seen them already. Because they were the ones who'd saved her.

Elise swallowed as she recalled waking up delirious from a fever to find herself in a place that would've sent her running if she'd been able.

Thankfully, her injuries, as well as several pairs of hands, kept her on the table. Elise had drifted in and out of consciousness. One time, she'd opened her eyes to see an old Creole woman tending to one of the many cuts on her body.

"Be easy, child," she'd told Elise in a calm, assertive voice.

Elise had looked into the woman's black eyes and saw kindness and wisdom. The next time she woke, Elise found herself staring up at dried herbs, bones strung together and clacking with the wind, as well as the jawbones of several various-sized alligators.

Miss Babette used her skills and knowledge of herbal medicine that had been passed down through generations of her family to tend to Elise's injuries.

It took weeks of convalescing in Babette's house for Elise to heal. She'd learned to shell peas, often woke to the smell of freshly baked bread, and discovered that the slow pace and quiet of the bayou suited her.

Elise never returned to New Orleans after that. She bought a small house and continued her veterinarian practice in the bayou. Instead of the nice sums of money she used to make, she accepted food and other goods in exchange for her services.

And she found contentment.

It wasn't the grand life she'd imagined for herself, but it was a good one. She had true friends who cared about her. Instead of having neighbors she rarely saw and never spoke with in a city, those around her visited often, and there was no going to the store without running into someone and sharing a thirty-minute conversation.

It wasn't just time that moved differently here, the people

did, as well. They preferred companionship and waving to each other as you drove down the road to the hustle and bustle of the city, where everyone was chained to their electronics.

Her clientele included cats and dogs but had also expanded to include cattle, horses, goats, chickens, sheep, and pigs, among other animals. Every day was an adventure, but she was safe. And that's what counted.

Her phone rang, drawing her attention from the storm. She walked to the old rotary phone that hung on the kitchen wall and answered it.

Elise smiled as soon as she heard Ed Perkins' aged voice on the other end of the line. "It's best for you not to venture out for our appointment. I don't like the idea of you driving in this weather."

"It's just a little storm."

"Don't make an old man worry," he replied tersely. "I'll call tomorrow to reschedule."

"Yes, sir."

There was a pause before he asked, "Do you need anything, girl?"

She grinned. "I'm good, thanks."

"Remember, now. Stay indoors. Don't you go out after some animal until the rain stops. It's gonna be a bad one. Heed my words."

"I will, Mr. Perkins."

She hung up the phone and shook her head. Despite

giving her cell phone number out, many of the older folks preferred to call the house.

Mr. Perkins had lost his daughter to a head-on collision fifteen years before, and he often called to check on Elise. His fatherly attention was sweet. Especially since her own father was dead.

Elise walked to the fridge and took out the fresh beans Mrs. Baker had given her and began setting out the ingredients for red beans and rice. It was the perfect meal to cook all day in the Crock-Pot for dinner.

When she finished getting everything ready and into the slow cooker, she turned it on and headed to the corner of her small living room where she'd set up a desk.

After checking her planner, she began making calls to her clients to confirm scheduled appointments. Not a single person wanted to keep theirs. For the next thirty minutes, Elise rescheduled everyone.

It was rare for her to have a day to herself during the week. Well, even on the weekend, if she were honest. The lifestyle everyone led here didn't go by the usual times in the city. Few made appointments. Most just called or showed up with whatever animal was in need.

But Elise was going to take advantage of the storm. She set her pencil down, closed her laptop, and pushed back from the desk. She grabbed the top book on the stack that kept growing—weekly—and curled up on the sofa with Mr. Darcy lifting his head to see what she was doing.

As soon as she got comfortable, the cat jumped down from his perch and walked in a circle on her stomach three times before he finally laid down with a loud sigh.

Elise opened the book, but before she could read the first word, her gaze was drawn out the screen door again. The lightning flashed, her eyes following the zigzags as her door outlined it.

Mesmerized, she watched the storm until her eyes grew heavy and she began to drift off to sleep. Elise shifted lower onto the couch so her head was on a pillow.

Mr. Darcy butted her hand with his head. She yawned as she scratched the cat, his loud purring making her smile. This was the life. She didn't need—nor want—anything else.

She was doing what she loved, surrounded by those she cared about and who cared about her. She was no longer trapped in a materialistic society, working long hours while trying to maintain a social life. She no longer went to the gym and worried about her weight or if her stomach was flat enough. She ate what she wanted, when she wanted.

In many ways, she was richer now than she'd ever been in the city.

But it had come at a price.

CHAPTER
TWO

THE RAIN WASHED everything new again. Usually, Kane loved a good downpour, but not this time. It messed with his ability to smell. And he'd gotten so close to his quarry.

He blew out a breath and sat beneath a tree. It'd been over two months since Delphine and George attacked Riley, and Kane was no closer to finding the Voodoo priestess.

Kane spent many of his days in werewolf form. His senses were more acute, and they allowed him to track Delphine. Except every time he got close, she disappeared.

He stood and shook out his fur. The loudness of the rain made him antsy since anyone—or anything—could sneak up on him. Kane kept his head on a swivel.

Damn, but he was tired. The injury he'd gotten from a bobcat the other night wasn't getting any better. Not to mention the drunk idiots with their lights off who'd grazed his back leg with their car before he could get out of the way when he was distracted chasing Delphine's scent.

So many times, he thought of returning to his brothers. No doubt they were at the family bar, Gator Bait. He longed to walk into the establishment and gorge himself on crawfish étouffée and fresh bread while downing as many beers as he could.

His mouth watered just thinking about it. And he'd do it while being surrounded by his brothers and their women.

Family. It meant everything to Kane. It's why he was out in the swamp instead of with his brothers. Especially since he was the major catalyst in this catastrophe.

Kane lay down and rested his head on his front paws. He shut his eyes for a moment. The burden of protecting New Orleans and the surrounding area was a heavy one, but it was one his family, the LaRues, had accepted when one of his ancestors married a Chiasson.

The Chiassons had traveled to Louisiana by way of Nova Scotia and France, all to hunt the supernatural. They'd found a small town that seemed to be like a beacon for the paranormal. The Chiassons made Lyons Point their home and protected the residents from the evil that continually threatened to take them.

Sometimes, the Chiassons lost. Most times, they won.

While the LaRues didn't hunt like their cousins, their job could be considered even more dangerous. Because they'd been cursed to be werewolves. The LaRues kept New Orleans stable. All five factions—witches, weres, djinn, vampires, and Voodoo—had to answer to the LaRues.

At one time, one of the nation's largest wolf packs, the Moonstone clan, had made the city their home and helped the LaRues. That all changed when a Voodoo priestess named Delphine decided she wanted to run the show.

She convinced the Moonstone Pack to betray Kane's parents when they were out one night. Kane had known the instant he heard the explosion that it was the restaurant his parents were dining in.

The death of his parents left him and his three brothers vulnerable, and things went from bad to worse when the Moonstone Pack vanished. That's when he, Solomon, Myles, and Court realized if they were going to survive, they had to get smart...and quick.

They grew up overnight. Kane went from being a kid to an adult in a blink. The factions made him and his brothers prove themselves time and again. Hell, they were still proving themselves.

A few months ago, everything had been coming together. Kane met with Griffin, the Alpha of the Moonstone Pack, and convinced him to call the other weres home to take their rightful places with the LaRues. Except Delphine proved that alliances could still be broken and made sure that Griffin couldn't refuse her.

It'd nearly worked, but Delphine wasn't able to keep her

hold on Kane's cousin, Riley. So, in Kane's eyes, that was a big win.

Kane wondered how Riley and Marshall were doing. No doubt the two lovebirds were looking to their future. At least he prayed they were. He sincerely hoped they weren't focused on finding him.

His eyes snapped open. Though he hadn't heard anything, his instincts warned that something was near. He didn't rise, though he did concentrate his hearing on picking up more than the sound of the rain hitting the leaves above him.

While he didn't see where Delphine went when the building collapsed, he knew she had gotten out since the only body found in the rubble was George's.

Kane was going to track Delphine down and kill her, as he should've done years ago. No matter how long it took. She'd caused enough heartache and chaos to last twenty lifetimes.

Out of the corner of his eye, he saw a black mass that moved through the trees. It had no shape, moving this way and that as if trying to find itself. The edges of the form were wispy like smoke.

But there was no denying the feeling of evil that surrounded it. Whatever it was, it needed to be destroyed before it hurt someone.

The shape stopped suddenly. Kane remained still. He

didn't know if the thing could see or hear, but something had alerted it. Otherwise, why would it halt?

Kane stared at the mass, waiting for it to do something. He even drew in a deep breath, hoping to catch its scent, but the rain prevented it. Finally, it moved on, disappearing into the thick trees.

In all his years of policing the supernatural of New Orleans, he'd never seen such a thing. Was it something new? Something they just didn't know about? Did Delphine have something to do with it?

That seemed the most likely answer. Delphine did anything she could to grow her powers in order to claim the city as her domain.

Kane waited thirty seconds before he quietly rose and followed the being. He grew more concerned the closer it got to the few houses along the bayou.

Suddenly, it took a hard left and drifted out over the water toward a small section of land. Kane went to follow when he spotted dark shapes just beneath the water.

Gators. One step into the bayou, and he might not make it out again.

He walked to another section of land but found more gators. Everywhere he went to cross the water onto the atoll, he found alligators.

As if the dark mass had called them for protection.

Kane snorted to himself. He was giving Delphine—or whatever the thing was—too much credit.

Or was he?

He decided to give up on crossing the water for the moment. Instead, he headed back to the last place he'd picked up Delphine's scent. While he might not know what she was doing in this isolated place, he knew it was only a matter of time before he discovered what Delphine was up to. All he could do was pray that he stopped her before she harmed anyone.

Kane was nearly to his destination when he saw the house. He'd spotted a woman once, but he usually kept clear of residences since he didn't want to get shot at.

But to go around the bayou would take time. If he cut across the back yard, it would be quicker. As before, he studied the house to make sure no one was about before he trotted into the open.

He was almost to the opposite side and the trees that would hide him when he heard a sound behind him. Kane whirled around to find two weres running straight for him. There was no denying that they were after him, he just didn't know why.

So far, his hunt for Delphine had kept him out of Moonstone territory, but even if it didn't, he knew none of the weres would attack without provocation.

Except he was definitely under attack now.

Kane planted his front paws and bared his teeth, issuing a low growl. It slowed the two wolves, but it didn't stop them. After a moment, they renewed their efforts.

He decided to go for the biggest first. Kane waited until they were nearly upon him before he moved. He ducked his head and avoided the teeth aimed at his neck. Then he spun, slamming his hindquarters against the smaller, gray wolf.

Kane then latched on to the larger, red wolf's neck and flipped him onto his side. With his teeth sinking into skin, he eyed the gray were, who picked itself off the ground and paced before him.

Kane growled and bit down harder, causing the red wolf to whimper in pain. Kane didn't want to kill a fellow were, but he wouldn't allow himself to be beaten either.

It was the subtle shift of the gray that warned Kane more wolves were coming up behind him. He ended the werewolf's life with a snap of his teeth.

When he lifted his head, the gray wolf was gone. He turned for the next attack just as three wolves slammed into him.

Despite the fact that Kane was larger than any of them, the weres were determined to take him down. Jaws snapped, growls and snarls sounded, and the scent of blood filled the air.

Through it all, he could've sworn he heard Delphine laughing.

That in itself kept Kane going, in spite of the many injuries. He hurt everywhere, but there would be time enough later to see to all the wounds. Right now, he had to stay alive.

Despite each werewolf he defeated, another took its place like a never-ending battle. His enemies came in fresh, while he struggled to stay on his feet.

The sound of a shotgun, loud and sharp near him, startled him. The other wolves ran off, but he only managed to collapse.

"Get out of here!" he heard a woman shout as she fired off another shot.

He could feel the blood pouring from his many wounds. He tried to get to his feet, but his limbs wouldn't hold him. There was no way he could get a message to his brothers to warn them that, somehow, Delphine had werewolves working for her. With the way the weres had attacked, Solomon, Myles, and Court would be singled out and killed.

Just as they had done to him. Or tried to.

He'd set out on his own to bring down Delphine. Instead, the priestess had won again. If only there was some way to get word to his brothers.

CHAPTER
THREE

Vicious growls yanked her from sleep. Elise sat up so fast, she knocked Mr. Darcy off her stomach. A look outside showed a pack of dogs attacking an animal.

She rushed to the door and banged her hands on the doorjamb to break up the fight, but none of the animals heard her over the commotion. Then she spotted black fur and realized the pack was attacking the black dog she'd seen before.

The danger didn't even enter her mind when she grabbed the shotgun from atop her fridge and rushed from the house into the rain. She yelled, but nothing seemed to get the dogs' attention. Then she fired off a shot into the ground, not to hit the animals, but to hopefully scare them off.

It worked. At least, it did at first. Then a few of the dogs returned to the black one.

"Get out of here!" she yelled and aimed the gun towards the pack, firing into the ground again.

She didn't want to kill any of the animals, but she would if they didn't give her a choice. Thankfully, after the second shot, they ran off into the woods.

Elise shook the water from her face but kept her gaze on the woods in case the pack returned. Out of the corner of her eye, she saw the black dog collapse. She'd known he was large, but up close, he was massive. By the look of him, he had some wolf in him.

Yet the longer she looked, the more wolf she saw in his features. But that couldn't be right. Wolves weren't native to the area. After her months spent at a wolf conservatory, she knew the animals, and she was looking at a damn wolf.

After several minutes of quiet, she glanced around for any sign of the others. The animal was unconscious, his breathing shallow, and wounds all over him.

She couldn't leave him out there since she needed to tend to his injuries, but getting a wolf into her house and the room she worked out of would be difficult. Not to mention that if he woke, she might not make it out of the situation alive.

Since she didn't know the extent of his wounds, she didn't want to give him a tranquilizer. Which left her few options.

Elise was about to go in and call someone for help when she happened to glance at the water. The rain had caused her to miss the slight ripples, but she spotted the eyes of a gator as it swam toward them. She glanced at the wolf and saw that his back legs were in the bayou.

"Well, shit," she said and set down her gun to grab hold of him beneath his shoulders to pull his body out of the water and safely onto land, far enough away that hopefully, the alligator wouldn't follow. She saw the blood pooling from wounds on his back leg that had filled the water with smells the gator couldn't resist.

She took a chance and continued backing up toward her porch, glancing over her shoulder to check on her progress every few seconds—not to mention keeping an eye on the wolf while praying he didn't wake and bite her.

When she finally reached the side door that she had put in to lead into the second bedroom that she'd converted for her work, she gently released the animal and leaned against the house for a second to catch her breath before rushing to get her gun.

She was soaked—with both rain and sweat. The wolf was incredibly heavy. She had no idea how she was going to get him up the steps and into the house without waking him.

After taking a few gulping breaths to calm her racing heart, she knew she had to do something before the wolf woke. Elise opened the side door and leaned her gun against the wall as she looked around for anything she could use to get him inside.

Her shoes slipped on the floor, causing her to bang into the stainless steel table. She winced and pushed the button on the side to lower it to the floor. Then she rushed back outside. It would be so much easier if someone were there to help her carry the animal inside.

She was reaching for the wolf when a howl split the air. Elise stood frozen, chills racing over her skin. A moment later, several more howls joined the first. By the sound of them, the pack had surrounded her house.

Swallowing, she lowered her gaze to the animal at her feet. This wasn't her first time working on wild creatures. She'd gone to Montana to help the local wolf sanctuary with the animals for several summers, also helping the ones roaming the wilderness.

But she was never alone.

After so many years working on farm animals and pets, Elise found her hands shaking. She fisted them and took a deep breath. She could do this, but she had to move quickly because when the animal woke, he would tear through everything.

She bent to grab the animal when the fur began to recede—replaced by skin. Before her eyes, the black wolf changed into a man.

Startled, Elise stepped backward. Her heel caught the edge of the steps, and she began to fall. She waved her arms to right herself, but the next thing she knew, she was on the ground with rain pounding her face.

She hurriedly rolled onto her side and looked at the wolf/man. Thankfully, he was still unconscious.

A howl, closer than any of the others, caused her to jerk in fear. She jumped up and hooked her arms beneath the man's arms and unceremoniously pulled him inside the house.

When his feet cleared the door, she lowered him and quickly slammed the door shut. Then locked it. Her head whipped around when she heard something on her back porch. She jumped over the man and rushed into the living room before softly closing that door and locking it, as well.

She peered out the window to see one of the wolves jump off her porch and lope into the woods. Elise pressed her forehead against the wall and closed her eyes.

After a second's rest, she returned to her work area. She frowned when she looked at her table meant for treating animals. It wasn't long enough for the man, which meant he'd remain on the floor for the time being. She rubbed her eyes to focus and reached for some rubber gloves before she began to see to his numerous wounds.

First and foremost, she needed to stop the bleeding. With so many injuries, she had to look at each one to figure out which ones were the most severe and then work from there.

She had to turn him on his sides, and even his stomach,

to reach everything. Elise didn't look at him as a man. If she did, she might call an ambulance instead.

Wads of gauze were all around her as she stitched one injury after another. She had no idea how long she worked. When she put the tape on the last wound, she sat on her haunches and stretched her back.

But her work wasn't finished. She gave him a shot of antibiotics before cleaning up the mess. Only then did she stand over him and see him not as a patient, but as a man. An incredibly gorgeous male.

She squatted down beside him and fingered a lock of long, golden hair before letting it fall. With him unconscious, she was able to look at her leisure, and she found herself in awe.

He had the kind of face that stopped you in your tracks. A strong jawline, and cheekbones for days. A wide mouth with thin lips.

Her gaze drifted lower. Her lips parted when she took in the broad shoulders and rippling sinew and corded muscles of his chest and abdomen.

Unable to help herself, her eyes followed the light dusting of hair from his navel down to his cock. It had been three years since she'd seen a man naked. She bit her lip as she thought about his manhood thickening with arousal. Embarrassed, she continued her perusal down his thickly muscled legs.

He was rugged, chiseled.

Utterly masculine.

Elise blinked as she realized she couldn't stare at him forever. She needed to get him off the floor and covered before a chill set in.

It was the smell of food that first tugged at his consciousness. Kane pulled in a deep breath, his stomach rumbling at the mouthwatering aroma.

Next, he became aware of the soft cushion at his back and the weight of the blanket atop him. No sooner did that realization go through his mind than pain exploded through him.

Everything hurt. Hell, even breathing was agony.

Kane kept his inhalations even and remained still to try and get the discomfort of his injuries to subside. His eyes remained shut as he attempted to figure out where he was.

He recalled the attack and how the weres had kept coming for him. Did he make it past the house? He feared not. Now he knew he should've gone around the long way. But he might be dead if he had.

What really concerned him was whether he shifted before or after he'd been brought into the house. He thought back to the attack, trying to remember the wolves that assaulted him. As he pulled up the memories, he recalled the sound of a shotgun. That's what broke up the fight.

Fuck. That meant he'd shifted after he was found.

He was surprised his rescuer hadn't put a bullet in him where he lay. Most who didn't understand the paranormal—or were afraid of it—refused to accept that it was around them.

Kane's thoughts halted when he heard humming. A woman. He'd never remained around any of the houses long, so he didn't know if she lived alone or not. He could possibly open his eyes and find a gun trained on him by another.

His main concern was getting as far from the house as he could. He didn't know why the weres came after him, but he knew they wouldn't let up until he was dead. And he didn't think his current situation would change their minds.

The longer he remained, the more danger he put others in. He needed to sneak out and get far, far away from this place and anywhere there were people. Then he'd determine who wanted him dead and why.

Kane opened his eyes and looked around. A lamp near him was on, but the only other light seemed to be coming from the kitchen. The storm still raged outside as drops pinged against the windows.

Then his eyes clashed with the blue gaze of a cat sitting on the back of the sofa near his head. The Siamese let out a hiss but didn't move.

"Mr. Darcy, be nice," the woman said. "Let our guest sleep."

There was a slight pause, and then the sound of a lid

being replaced on a pot before the clink of something being set on a counter.

"Unless he's awake."

The cat made some kind of gurgling noise. Kane didn't take his eyes off the feline. It reminded him of the cat he'd had as a boy. A big male that had dominated the area around his family home. No one messed with that cat without coming away with scars.

Out of the corner of his eye, Kane saw a shape at his feet. His gaze swung to the woman. Her chestnut curls brushed the tops of her shoulders, while an errant tendril fell over her left eye. She brushed it away carelessly.

Green eyes that reminded him of the trees after a rain shower were trained on him. They were the color of a churning ocean during a storm. The shade of a seedling as it pushed through the ground. In her depths, he saw strength, determination, and kindness. As well as a steely resolve.

He took in the soft curve of her jaw and her heart-shaped face. Her plump lips were compressed as she furrowed her brow. Something else that didn't escape his notice was the way she continued to tug on the wrist of her shirt as if she were afraid the sleeve might ride up.

"Are you in pain?" she asked.

"It's manageable. Did you patch me up?"

She nodded. "Some of your wounds were grave."

Yeah. He knew. He could feel them. At least the weres hadn't gotten his neck.

"Thank you for helping me," he said.

She swallowed and moved the same curl again before it resumed its position. "Is this where you explain to me what you are?"

"It's better if I don't. As a matter of fact, it'd be best if I leave immediately."

As soon as he started to sit up, she was beside him, pushing on his shoulder to halt him. Her gaze narrowed. "I didn't spend hours tending to you for you to leave now. Not to mention how long it took me to get you into the house. And on the couch. If you move, you'll bust the stitches. Trust me when I say, it was hell getting some of those injuries to stop bleeding."

He blew out a breath and sank back against the pillow. Once he did, she backed up and gave him a nod. He was weak, and that put him at a disadvantage. But he hated putting her at risk.

"They haven't come near the house since I brought you inside," she told him. She shrugged one shoulder. "I have seen them in the trees, though."

"I shouldn't have ventured so close to your house. I'm sorry."

She smiled. "You've been out for hours. Dinner is nearly done. How does red beans and rice sound?"

"Like Heaven."

"Good," she replied and returned to the kitchen.

Kane pushed up against the pillows to see over the back

of the sofa so he could watch her as she moved about. "What were you thinking running out there against all of those wolves?"

"Well, to be fair, I just thought they were large dogs," she said as she tasted the beans before adding in more seasoning. "If I'd known they were wolves, I wouldn't have gone." She looked over her shoulder at him. "I've treated wolves before. Though these are much bigger."

He didn't bother trying to lie to her. What would be the point? She'd seen him shift. "We're werewolves. There's a rather large pack in the area. The Moonstone wolves used to call New Orleans home. They returned recently."

She turned back to the meal. "Apparently, there's some bad blood between y'all."

"The Moonstone Pack is my ally. Regardless, I need to find out who these wolves are following and why they targeted me."

A few minutes later, she returned with a bowl filled with rice and a heaping spoonful of red beans and sausage. "I'm Elise, by the way."

"Kane," he replied.

She grinned, the smile lighting up her eyes. "Nice to meet you."

He was surprised how easily she accepted the news about werewolves. That either meant she had some prior supernatural experience or she had knowledge of things.

She curled up in a chair and closed her eyes for a moment

before beginning to eat. Their gazes met, and she jerked her chin to the cat. "Mr. Darcy was feral not that long ago. He was badly injured, but for some reason, he allowed me to mend him. From then on, I suppose you could say he claimed me as his."

"It sounds as if you make a habit of rescuing wounded animals," he said, glancing at the cat that had its eyes closed, though his ears moved toward Elise when she talked.

"That's because I'm a veterinarian."

Kane chuckled. "Then it's fortunate indeed that you found me."

CHAPTER
FOUR

"I'VE no doubt that if one of my neighbors had found you, they would've brought you to me. Or shot you after you changed," Elise replied.

"Shifted," he corrected.

"Of course. Shifted."

She couldn't stop staring into his vibrant blue eyes. She'd never seen anything so enthralling before. They snagged her and refused to loosen their hold.

And she was their willing captive.

He took a bite of food and groaned, pleasure covering his features. "This is delicious."

She smiled at the compliment. "There's plenty."

He nodded and shoveled another spoonful into his mouth.

"Do you live out here?" she asked, wondering when he'd eaten last.

Kane gave a shake of his head and swallowed before taking another bite.

"So you just wander the bayou?"

He paused with the spoon halfway to his mouth. He lowered it back to the bowl. "I was searching for someone. I've been tracking them for a while now."

"Surely you have people worried about you?"

Kane's gaze lowered to his meal. "I do."

She nodded and stirred her food to mix the rice, beans, and sausage. "Do they know what you are?"

"My immediate family is all werewolves."

"Oh," she said, unable to keep the shock from her voice. "Then why aren't they with you?"

"I have to do this on my own."

She stopped her questions, and they went back to eating. In just a few minutes, he finished the bowl. Elise fixed him another and brought him some water.

In the time it took her to finish her meal, Kane downed three helpings. It was odd to have someone in the house with her, and she wasn't sure she was entirely comfortable with it. But then she realized that whoever Kane was, he'd been hanging around the bayou for weeks. He could've hurt her at any time and hadn't.

She looked over to find his eyes closed, so she grabbed his

bowl and fork and headed to the kitchen. She washed their dishes and cleaned up before standing in front of the window to see if she could catch a glimpse of the other wolves.

"You don't fear me."

She turned her head to the side at the sound of his voice. "I thought you were asleep."

"Just resting with a full stomach."

His comment hung in the air. She turned to face him and shrugged. "I've always been better around animals. They understand me, and I them. It's my calling to help them, and I've risked my life many times to do so."

She swallowed before continuing. "When I realized you were a wolf, it didn't deter me from mending you. Then you shifted. I didn't know what to think. If the other wolves weren't howling, I might have left you out there, but I didn't."

"Thank you for that," he replied softly.

Elise glanced away, rubbing her hand along her sleeve. "I live alone. Always have, just not as isolated as I am now. I've spotted you a few times."

His gaze lowered to her arm where she kept rubbing. Elise halted the action and inwardly kicked herself for the nervous habit.

"Are you from here?" he asked.

"I'm from Alexandria, but I've lived all over the US, going to different places where I could study animals as well as heal them. I came to New Orleans about three years ago to help out a colleague at the zoo."

She heard the wobble in her voice and hated it. It had been years, yet the terror of that night never truly left her.

"Someone hurt you," Kane said.

She briefly met his intense gaze. "Yes. I don't know who it was. For all I know, it was someone who followed me out of the city. Or it could have been random. I never saw them. They drove without headlights and rear-ended me, causing my car to spin and slam against a tree."

"A man?"

Elise's gaze swung to him. "You ask that as if you expected me to say it was something else."

Kane raised a brow. "If you knew what I know, you'd ask the same."

"It was a man. Apparently, I hit my head in the crash and sustained a concussion. I couldn't focus my eyes, so I never got a good look at him as he dragged me from my car and into the woods."

Kane's head tilted at her words. "The crash was just to stop you."

She nodded slowly. "I must have blacked out because when I woke, he was cutting off my clothes with a huge knife. That's when I started fighting him and screaming."

"Good for you."

"One of the townspeople saw my car. When they pulled

over to investigate, they heard my screams. They called the police before rushing out to help me."

Kane held her gaze. "You were saved."

She glanced down at her arms. "He didn't rape me, no."

"But he did something else."

Elise moved to the chair and lowered herself onto the edge. She pulled at her fingers as she recalled the pain each time the blade sliced through her skin. "He was furious that I wouldn't stop screaming. He kept telling me to shut up, that it'd be over soon. But I wouldn't submit. He retaliated by cutting me from my thighs to my chest. He was about to slice my face when the sound of the sirens scared him off."

Kane let out a long breath. "Sometimes, I'm so deep in my world that I forget that humans can be monsters, too. Why did you stay in this place?"

"The locals took me to their healer. If I had been conscious, I might have insisted on a hospital, but there would've been news reports and my face plastered everywhere. The locals swear by Miss Babette, even the police. I remained with her for a few months as she healed my wounds and my spirit. That's when I realized that I liked it here and that I could return the kindness these people freely gave me. I bought this house and now use my skills to help their pets and livestock."

Kane shifted, wincing slightly. "And your attacker?"

"They caught him six weeks later after he forced an off-duty cop off the road. She was ready for him, and had him at gunpoint when he opened her door. He's serving jail time now."

Kane's lips softened and curved into a half smile. "I'm glad you seem to have found your place."

"It took a while, but yes, I have."

"With what happened to you, some would become fearful of everyone."

She sat back and snorted. "Oh, I was for a while. I slept with the shotgun and never opened the doors once it was dark outside. But I refused to let my attacker keep that kind of hold over me. So I forged a new path."

"And your family?"

"My father died when I was five, and my mother when I was seventeen. I have a brother. He's in the military and stationed all over the world, which makes it difficult to keep in touch with him. I can't keep track of him. I hear from him about once a year."

Kane leaned his head back and looked at the ceiling. "I've three brothers. Two older and one younger. We have a family business, so we're close."

"Yet you came out here on your own."

"To clean up a mess I helped create," he retorted.

Elise tucked her legs against her. "Wouldn't it get finished quicker if you had your brothers?"

"Definitely. But they have others they're responsible for."

"You don't?"

"No."

She put her elbow on the arm of the chair and propped her chin on her hand. "No doubt they believe the worst. You should at least call them."

"I'll return to them when I'm finished," he stated in a hard voice.

"You sound like Danny. My brother likes to do things on his own, as well. But have you considered that you might not finish for years? Or, what if you die? You nearly did today."

His lips flattened as he sighed. "My family has known much heartache and suffered greatly. We're cursed to be werewolves. My brothers have found happiness and some semblance of stability with the women they love. I can't pull them away from that."

"Is it really your choice to make?"

He shrugged, shaking his head. "Maybe not, but I made it. I'm the only one not attached. I'm the one who created half of this shit we're in. I've sat around for too long, hoping we'd come out the victors. Many of our friends have died. I almost lost my cousin because of it. Riley isn't just my only female cousin and someone who needs to be protected, she's my closest friend. And she was nearly killed."

"You've been out here for how long?"

"Two months," he replied.

Elise's brows rose. "Have you come close to locating your target?"

"A few times, but she's an elusive bitch."

She pushed up from the chair and walked into the

kitchen to cut a piece of cherry pie she'd made the day before. She carried it to the living room and handed him the largest slice along with a fork.

"Then it appears you're going to need your strength."

He grinned and took the plate before sinking his fork into the dessert. She laughed when he let out a loud moan of appreciation.

CHAPTER

FIVE

THE HOWLS WOKE KANE. Every night for the last three nights, a wolf howled, perhaps to remind him that they were waiting. As if he'd forget.

He'd remained on the couch, only rising to relieve himself and for Elise to change his bandages. But he could feel his strength returning. It was slow, though. Too damn slow.

How much longer would the wolves wait to attack? He hadn't been prepared when they charged him, and now, with him being so weak, he knew he didn't stand a chance against them alone. But with his brothers...

No. Kane couldn't bring them into this. Especially if it was a trap set by Delphine—and it was definitely something that bitch would do.

He looked down to find Mr. Darcy curled on the only part

of his chest that wasn't wounded. The cat was never far from him, and Kane had to admit that he quite liked the little rascal.

Kane softly petted the Siamese, waking him. Mr. Darcy blinked his blue eyes at him before rising and moving to the back of the couch. Kane then gritted his teeth and slowly sat up before getting to his feet. With the blanket wrapped around his waist and held with one hand, he made his way to the window. He braced his other palm against the windowsill and stared out into the night.

Shadows cloaked the ground, but the werewolves were out there. The silence of the other night creatures was proof of that.

He might be making a mistake believing that Delphine was the one who'd sent the wolves after him. There might be a new enemy in town. Then again, everything he knew about the priestess pointed to her.

She hated the LaRues. She had gone to great pains to remove his parents, as well as the Alphas of the Moonstone Pack. Against all odds, he and his brothers had survived. Only to continue to battle Delphine time and again.

When would the nightmare end? Kane would gladly give his life if it meant his brothers and their women could be free of such a nemesis. There would always be evil in New Orleans, there was no getting around that. But someone like Delphine was ten-times worse than any djinn or vampire.

"You're not thinking of going out there, are you?"

He turned his head to find Elise standing in the doorway of her bedroom with a floral robe wrapped around her. "Not yet. I'm not strong enough."

"But when you are, you intend to fight them yourself?" she asked as she walked to stand beside him.

He shrugged. "It's me they want."

"It might be prudent to let your brothers help."

"That's exactly what she wants me to do."

Elise tucked a curl behind her ear. "Who is this woman you're after?"

"Her name is Delphine, a powerful Voodoo priestess."

"I take that to mean the two of you have clashed before."

Kane briefly closed his eyes. "Many times."

"And you plan to end it all?"

"I do."

"How?" Elise asked.

He drew in a sharp breath and contemplated her words. "By any means necessary. She kills without hesitation or thought in order to gain more power. My family and I stand in her way, and she intends to get rid of us."

"Because you police the city?"

Kane glanced at her to see a small frown on her brow. "And because we've continually thwarted her attempts to gain more power. We've been lucky. I'm not sure how we won, and I can't help but feel that our time is running out."

"It sounds as though you and your brothers are stronger together."

He grinned as he realized what she was trying to do. "We are, but I can't pull them into this."

"And I won't stand by and watch you get killed."

Kane dropped his arm and faced her, all too aware that he stood naked except for a blanket. The times she'd tended to his injuries, her touch had been light, soothing—and damned alluring. She had no idea how sexy she was.

Or how he fought not to place his lips upon hers.

Elise stood in the soft glow of the moonlight, looking ethereal and too beautiful for words. In their days together, he'd come to see the type of woman she was.

Compassionate, giving, and tenderhearted. She'd stayed up for hours helping a sheep give birth, worked tirelessly to save a puppy who'd shattered a hip after being hit by a car, and greeted everyone who came to her with a warm smile.

While he'd kept out of sight of her clients, he'd heard them through the closed door. They absolutely adored Elise. And he was coming to, as well.

In the evenings, he listened as she spoke of the people and animals she visited and told him stories about the residents while she cooked. After the meal, they played chess or read. Though she had a television, Elise rarely turned it on. And with the hundreds of books on the bookshelf lining the far wall, he understood why.

Not once had she demanded to know his full name or poked into his past—even after she'd told him her story. She asked nothing of him.

But maybe it was time she understood just what she had unintentionally gotten herself into.

"Delphine came to power after murdering the priestess she was studying under," Kane began. "I remember hearing my parents discuss her at night in their bedroom when they thought we were asleep. They were worried. Very worried. I began paying attention after that and listening for Delphine's name.

"She garnered status within the Voodoo community seemingly overnight. And, with that, her powers grew. Other factions began to come to my parents, wanting them to do something about Delphine. But everyone waited too long."

Elise frowned. "Meaning?"

"My guess is that Delphine either learned that my parents were plotting to take her down, or she realized that removing Mom and Dad would make the others bow down to her." Kane lifted one shoulder in a shrug, immediately regretting it as it pulled several sets of stitches. "She blew up the restaurant my parents were eating at, but that didn't kill them. One of her followers put a knife in their hearts."

Elise's hand reached out and touched his that held the blanket. "You said they died, but you didn't say how."

"It doesn't really matter. Delphine was the cause of it. She stood there and watched them die. Then she caused the Alpha of the Moonstone Pack and his wife to go insane, making it necessary for the other weres in the pack to kill their Alphas. The pack disbanded and ran in fear after that.

My brothers and I were young, and though we knew our role, we hadn't really gotten involved yet. Solomon, my eldest brother, sat us down and told us everything. Court was so young, he doesn't remember much of it, and we sheltered him as best we could. But I remember every horrible minute of it."

Her hand squeezed his before falling away.

He missed her touch more than he expected. How could someone he knew so little about affect him so deeply? "Solomon and Myles went out to the leaders of the other factions while I stayed with Court. I believe it was that action that saved us. We intended to continue protecting the city. The others feared Delphine, but they didn't want her leading them."

"They joined you, then?" Elise asked.

"Not really. They alerted us to anything they discovered about Delphine, which helped us stay alive. We learned our place quickly and put measures in place to prevent Delphine—or any of the others—from entering our home. That safety allowed us to grow into who we are now."

"Werewolves."

He laughed softly. "With some pretty cool fighting skills."

She grinned at his words. "Obviously, all of you reached adulthood."

"That we did. We couldn't have done it alone. But that doesn't mean Delphine hasn't inflicted her share of horrors."

Elise took his hand and turned him to the sofa. "You shouldn't push yourself too hard."

"I have to. I can't stay here forever."

Her green eyes jerked to his. "I know, but if you want to get healthy, you need to let your body heal."

He allowed her to lead him to the couch since she was touching him again. Even when she was poking at his injuries, he found her soft hands soothing. Just her touch was enough to ease him.

Once on the couch, he lay back as she sat in the chair. She licked her lips and clasped her hands together. "Why do you think Delphine is here? I thought her place was in New Orleans."

"It was, and is. She has numerous followers there, along with a large section of the city. Delphine wasn't just after my family, she also targeted my cousins. For reasons we don't know yet, Delphine went after Riley, who was staying with me. In a battle several months ago where we teamed up with the witches and the Moonstone Pack, Delphine took Riley."

Elise's eyes bulged at the news. "Took her? Please tell me Riley didn't die."

"Delphine wiped her memories and made Riley believe Delphine was her friend. A friend of the Chiassons, who was once a detective in the city, helped locate Riley and get her memories back. But the fallout was another battle."

"The building that collapsed," Elise said as she sat back. "That was you?"

"It was, yes. Riley and Marshall got out in time. I knew Delphine would try something, so I followed her into the building. I intended to kill her, but things didn't quite go as planned. The building began to crumble. I got out, but I know she did, as well."

Elise tilted her head to the side as she pursed her lips. "Are you telling me you've been hunting her ever since and you've not told your family you're alive?"

He glanced at the floor. "Like I told you, it's better that I go after her alone."

"Obviously not, if she was the cause of your attack."

Kane frowned at her words. "Delphine isn't someone who works with others. She uses them. I can't imagine how she got the werewolves to work for her."

A terrible feeling churned his gut.

"What?" Elise asked as she scooted to the edge of the chair. "What are you thinking?"

Kane ran a hand down his chest. "Some months ago, I managed to piss Delphine off. While it was a Voodoo priestess who cursed my family long ago, Delphine decided to punish me by sending me after someone close to my cousins. I couldn't control myself. With Delphine's hex, if I killed, I'd remain in wolf form forever, forgetting who I was."

"But that didn't happen," she said with a grin.

"My cousins stopped me. Barely. And Myles and Court caught Delphine. They had their jaws at her throat and demanded she lift the curse. They should've killed her when they had the chance."

Elise shook her head, her curls swaying. "They wanted to save you."

"And look what that has done. She's targeted our friends, gone after those my brothers care about, and kidnapped Riley."

"Don't you think all of that has made you stronger? That it allowed you to see Delphine and her motives, her moves?"

Kane sighed loudly, the weariness of the hunt settling into his bones. "I feel as if she leads us on a merry chase while pulling our strings. All we can do is react to whatever she shoves at us."

"And if something happens to you? Will your brothers know? How will they find out that it was Delphine, or learn what you've discovered these last weeks?"

Elise had a point. A good one.

"If I hadn't caused Delphine to curse me, none of this would have happened."

Elise snorted and leaned back, her spine curving as she rested her arms across her stomach. "Seriously? You said that Delphine was after your family. What makes you think any of this would be different? You believe you're the cause, but did you ever think that perhaps she led you right into her trap so she could curse you?"

Damn. Kane had to admit that he hadn't given that line of thinking any consideration.

"That's what I thought," Elise said. She blew out a breath. "Obviously, I know nothing about your world, but I can tell that family is important to you—and your brothers. How would you feel if one of them did what you're doing?"

"I'd rip them a new one," he declared.

She grinned. "That's what I thought."

"It doesn't change my mind."

She pushed up from the chair and came to stand beside him. "You're healing well. I know it won't be long before you leave. I think what you're doing is admirable, but foolish. What you're putting your family through isn't right."

He held her gaze, wishing like hell that he'd met her under different circumstances. He liked her voice, her smile... everything about her. And the longer he was around her, the more the attraction grew.

If he didn't leave soon, he might do something really stupid like take her to bed. That'd be the worst thing he could do since it would send Delphine straight for Elise. And Elise had suffered enough.

Resigned, she said, "You're going to need some clothes. I'll see what I can do tomorrow."

He reached out a hand to stop her as she walked away, but he missed her—and she didn't see him.

CHAPTER

SIX

ELISE HAD COME to enjoy living alone. The first few days Kane was there left her...perplexed, unsure of how to deal with him. But things got easier.

Comfortable.

Elise stared at the ceiling of her bedroom, thinking over their conversation. She'd gotten bits and pieces of his past, but the picture he painted was crystal clear.

Kane and his brothers knew very little peace. They prepared for—and expected—strife because that was their daily life.

On several occasions, she'd found him staring off into space, his mind a million miles away. She wondered what he was thinking about. Or who. The one thing Kane hadn't alluded to was a lover. He'd mentioned his brothers' women several times, but had said he had no one.

But was there someone he longed for? Wished for?

Elise hadn't considered taking a lover, not since her accident. She wouldn't feel comfortable with anyone seeing her scars. Hell, she didn't like to see them.

But Kane made her think of tangled limbs, sweaty skin, and sighs of pleasure. He made her yearn for something she had forgotten—passion.

Despite her best intentions, Elise didn't sleep the rest of the night. She tossed and turned for hours until she finally rose at five. After a quick shower, she dressed. When she walked into the living room, she found Mr. Darcy once more curled up on Kane's chest as he slept.

She gave the cat a scratch behind the ears, but she didn't touch Kane. Funny how she had seen him naked to mend his wounds, but now she was hesitant to put her hands on him. Mostly because when she did touch his rock-hard body and looked her fill at him, she pictured him naked.

Elise turned on her heel and did some inventory work with her medications until the sun came up. Then she grabbed her purse and keys and walked to the 1990s truck she'd bought.

She drove into town to the thrift shop. Norma, as usual, was already there and gladly let Elise inside. After Elise had checked on Norma's six cats that kept the small shopping center free of rodents, she then searched for some clothes for Kane. She wasn't sure of his size, so she bought a couple of different jeans and shirts. With Norma's help, she found some boots that might fit him.

"Do you have a male companion?" Norma asked hopefully, her gray eyes filled with excitement.

Elise paid for her purchases and looped her fingers in the handles of the bags. "Helping out a friend, is all."

Norma's face fell. She ran her hand over her graying brown hair pulled back in a braid. "Though I never found me someone to marry, I did have relations. It's a good release for the soul."

"Norma," Elise said in mock surprise. "You've been holding back on me."

The woman grinned mischievously. "Oh, the stories I have, my dear."

"I'd love to hear them."

"You need to make stories of your own."

Elise wasn't comfortable talking about her sex life—or lack thereof. She decided to change the subject. "Have you seen anything weird the past couple of months?"

"Weird?" Norma asked with a frown. "How?"

Elise shrugged, searching for the right words. "Anything unusual? What about howls?"

"Like wolves?"

"Yes," she said eagerly. "Have you heard them?"

Norma shook her head and moved the medallion of St. Christopher back and forth on the chain about her neck. "I haven't, but come to think of it, Ted over near you said he's heard what sounded like howls. But that can't be. We don't have wolves here."

"We have coyotes, bobcats, and such. Why not wolves?"

Norma held her gaze for a long silent moment. "I take it you've heard the wolves?"

"I have." There was no use lying. And besides, Elise hated being deceitful with anyone—especially her friends.

Norma came from behind the counter. "Is your male friend staying with you?"

"For now. He'll be gone soon."

"Hmm. Maybe he'll remain a little longer?"

It was something in the way Norma spoke, but for a second, Elise thought the woman knew much more than she let on. "We'll see. Thanks for these," she said, holding up the bags before walking out.

Elise made one more stop at the local donut shop and picked up an assortment of pastries, as well as some kolaches before heading back.

At the house, she put the truck in park and grabbed the box and bags before getting out of the vehicle. She was halfway to the door when a snarl stopped her in her tracks. Elise looked up to find a wolf between her and the back porch.

Her heart slammed against her chest so hard, she could feel it. Her fingers went numb, and the packages and keys slipped from her grasp.

The wolf bared its teeth and crouched low. Time slowed

as Elise glanced about for a place she could get to before the animal pounced, but there was nothing that offered safety other than her truck. And she wouldn't reach it in time.

The fur on the wolf's back stood on end, and right before it launched itself at her, a black blur crossed her field of vision.

As soon as she saw the wolves fighting, she rushed to the porch and into the house, slamming the door behind her. She leaned against it, her limbs shaking at her close encounter.

But the longer she stood there and listened to the fighting, the more she realized that others might join in to attack Kane, and he wasn't ready for that.

Elise ran for her shotgun and opened the door to find herself staring into the yellow eyes of a wolf. She fired the gun at the animal. The wolf howled in protest, blood running from its shoulder before it scurried off.

Elise ran to the edge of the porch and fired her gun again to get the attention of the wolf fighting Kane. The two broke apart, and the attacker turned his gaze to glare at her before it too loped off. For long seconds, neither she nor Kane moved as they waited to see if any others would attack.

Finally, she lowered her gun and found herself looking into Kane's werewolf eyes. They were bright yellow as he watched her.

She shook her head at him. "You're bleeding again."

He turned away from her and picked up the packages

with his teeth before bringing them to her. She accepted them, grabbed the box with the pastries, and they returned to the house together.

Kane went straight into her vet area while she put away their breakfast. By the time she made her way to him, he'd shifted into his human form and had covered his lower half with a blanket as he sat on the table.

"I should've looked for them," she said as she stood before him.

He moved a curl out of her eyes and shook his head. "It wouldn't have mattered. I knew they'd try something sooner or later. I've been waiting for them since I heard you drive off."

"Thank you." She lifted the bags of clothes. "I got you a few things. Hopefully, something will fit. I'll take back whatever doesn't work. But first, let's get you cleaned up."

"I busted some stitches."

She walked around him and lifted the blanket to see his left leg. "You busted all of them."

"Great," he stated dryly.

She lifted a vial. "Something for the pain?"

Kane shook his head of golden hair she constantly had the urge to run her fingers through. "No."

Elise set about cleaning him up again. "Whatever healing your body did has been undone."

"I wasn't going to let them hurt you," he replied.

His voice was low, edged with...something. Anger,

maybe? The heat of his skin made her hyper-aware of his nakedness—and just how gorgeous his body was. "There were only two of them. If they had wanted to do anything to me, more would've come."

There was a slight pause before he said, "I know."

She stopped in the process of wiping the blood off on his chest to look up at him. "You know?"

His blue eyes met hers. "They wanted to see how badly I was injured."

"Oh." She hadn't even thought of that.

Kane's long fingers wrapped around her arms, and he straightened her. "I've not only shown them that I'm not on death's door, but that I will protect you. That means they'll try and use you to get to me."

"Not if I don't leave."

He smiled sadly. "If only it was that simple. They've been watching the house. They know you're a vet. They'll make sure you have no choice but to leave to see to an animal, and that's when they'll make their move."

"Can't you remind this pack that you're allies?"

"Again, if only it were that easy," he said and dropped his hands. "I've got a bad feeling that these weres aren't part of the pack. I think they're new werewolves, people that Delphine cursed—or rewarded."

Elise gaped as she realized his implication. "She turned some of her followers?"

"It makes sense."

"Dear God."

He snorted softly. "It's a mess, to be sure."

She wanted to urge him to seek out his brothers again, but she knew it'd be futile. He'd made up his mind on the matter, and there was no talking him out of it.

"Have you considered finding the Moonstone Pack?" she asked. She laid a hand on his chiseled abs and cleared away the broken stitches.

He winced slightly when she cleaned out the wound. "I've considered it, but they'll only go to my brothers."

"It's folly to do this on your own. You've no idea how many Delphine has turned."

"It doesn't matter if these are her followers or just people off the street, they're going to do Delphine's bidding. She knows I won't stop until I kill her, so she needs me out of the picture."

Elise glanced up at him. "And anyone you're associated with."

"Which is why I'm leaving tonight."

His words made her freeze. She slowly straightened to look at him. "Please don't."

"The longer I stay, the worse it'll be for you."

"My fate was sealed the moment I helped you, and you know it. You're not ready. Granted, your body has done some incredible healing in the past three days, but you've undone most of that. If you walk out of here tonight, you're effectively committing suicide. I didn't figure you for that."

His lips flattened as he stared at her with narrowed eyes. "Fine. I'll give it another day. But don't go anywhere without me."

"I don't plan on leaving this house."

"Good. Because they could get in while you're gone."

Elise looked out the doorway into the living room where Mr. Darcy was sitting on the back of the couch looking out the window. She just realized that the cat hadn't left the house since the storm—or since she'd brought Kane inside.

"He's not stupid," Kane said of the Siamese.

She turned her gaze back to him. "If they touch my cat, I'll skin them."

He suddenly grinned. "I do believe you would."

Elise became trapped by his hypnotic gaze. She was all too aware that she stood between his legs where the blanket was bunched. She swallowed and looked down at her left hand that rested atop his thigh, so very close to his—

"Something wrong?" he asked.

Elise shook her head and moved around to his back to work on those injuries before he realized just how much she wanted to touch his cock.

She'd thought being away from those mesmerizing blue eyes of his would give her some relief, but she was wrong. Each time she touched him and felt the warmth of his skin and the strength of his muscles, she craved more.

Hungered for it.

CHAPTER
SEVEN

HER TOUCH WAS agony because he wanted more than just her tending to his wounds. Kane yearned to turn and pull her against him, to cup her face and run his thumb along her lower lip. He craved to see her green eyes flare with unconcealed desire.

All before he put his lips to hers and discovered the taste of her kiss.

His cock hardened uncomfortably. Kane was glad the blanket hid him. Or maybe he should let it fall away and find out what Elise would do if she knew how badly he wanted her.

But the fact that she was again treating his injuries reminded him that things were going from bad to worse. And quickly.

While he hadn't been the one to intentionally put her in

harm's way, the fact of the matter was that Elise was being targeted because of him—because she had helped him. He should've left days ago, but he'd let her talk him into staying.

That wasn't entirely true. He'd wanted to remain, so her argument gave him what he needed to linger. He was an idiot. Just because he liked being near her and having her fuss over him, he had all but signed her death warrant.

The fear that had gone through him when he heard the wolf's growls when she returned from town made his blood run like ice through his veins. He hadn't thought twice about exiting through the door she used for the clinic. Or shifting.

He'd gotten there just in time, too, because the wolf had been about to pounce. The sight of a werewolf about to kill Elise made him see red. Kane had wanted to kill the were, to rip its throat out with his teeth and howl his fury to the sky.

The few wards he'd put up around the house while she was gone wouldn't be enough. He would need to add more. Much more.

"Kane."

He blinked and discovered Elise standing before him once more. "Yes?"

"I asked if you needed anything for the pain."

He shook his head. "I can't have anything that will dull my mind."

"At least there are no new injuries."

"It's going to be all right. I promise."

Her green eyes were filled with concern. "I don't want you to go after them. I've...well, I've come to care about you."

He tugged his favorite curl and smiled. "It's because of our friendship that I'm going to make sure they never harm you or anyone else."

"You can't take them on all by yourself. You don't even know how many there are," she argued.

There was a way to remedy that, but it wasn't time yet. Soon. "Did I smell donuts?"

"You're changing the subject."

He brushed his fingers over her puckered brow. "I'm used to my family's worry. I don't like yours."

"Tough. I can't stop it, nor do I want to."

"I'm not the type of person you should be friends with."

She raised a brow and shot him a flat stare. "Is that right? Someone who dedicates his life to protecting innocents? Someone who holds his family close? Someone who willingly puts his life in danger to save others? Sounds exactly like the type of friend I want."

Damn, but he wanted to kiss her. Did she have any idea how utterly irresistible she was?

"Elise," he murmured.

She shook her head, determination in the set of her jaw. "Don't try to change my mind."

He slid from the table and let the blanket drop as he took a step closer to her. She blinked, a moment of confusion evident until she glanced down and saw his arousal. When her green eyes met his again, there was excitement there.

The thought of anything other than kissing her fled his mind. Kane had never known such longing for another before. He cupped her nape, sliding his fingers into her curls as he dropped his gaze to her lips.

They were parted, the pulse at her throat rapid. Desire surged within him and pushed him onward. He lowered his head and was about to kiss her when he heard the sound of an approaching vehicle.

He halted and looked at her. She stared at him with wide, green eyes filled with the same desire that consumed him. With a grin, he brushed his thumb over her lips and gave her a nod.

She backed up a step before walking to the door when the engine cut off. Elise looked at him over her shoulder before she stepped outside. As soon as she did, Kane grabbed the blanket and bags of clothes and walked to the bathroom.

He was trying on a pair of jeans when he heard voices. Grabbing the first shirt he found, he yanked it over his head. He didn't bother with shoes as he opened the door to better hear what was being said.

"Elise, please tell me," a man said.

"Everything is fine, Mr. Perkins. I promise."

He gave a loud snort. "You fired your gun again, and it wasn't target practice. Norma told me you bought men's clothes today. If there's someone here who is trying to hurt you, I'll get rid of him."

Kane walked from the bathroom to the doorway of the clinic to find a man in his early sixties. He was tall and slim with a full head of salt-and-pepper hair.

"I can promise you, I'm not here to hurt her," Kane said.

The man turned, spearing Kane with gray eyes faded with age. He looked Kane up and down before hooking his thumb in the front pocket of his jeans. "I'd like to hear that from Elise."

"Kane is speaking the truth," she said.

"Kane LaRue," he said, holding out his hand.

There was a pause before the man grasped his hand and shook it. "Ed Perkins."

"A pleasure, Mr. Perkins."

Ed held his gaze for a long minute before releasing his hand. "LaRue, huh?"

Kane inwardly winced. Did the old man know of his family? Surely not. "That's right."

"I knew a Dwight LaRue."

"My father."

"I thought so," Ed said. "I'm sorry about your parents' deaths, son. They were taken too early."

Kane bowed his head in acknowledgement. "Thank you."

"Where are your brothers?"

He narrowed his gaze on the old man. For someone he

didn't know, Mr. Perkins seemed to know a lot about his family. "Busy."

"What brings you out here?"

"He's hunting," Elise quickly said.

Ed jerked his chin to the visible wounds on Kane's arms. "Looks like you ran into trouble. Is it the wolves Elise asked Norma about?"

Out of the corner of his eye, Kane saw Elise jerk her head to Ed. The more Ed talked, the more Kane thought the man might know more than he was letting on.

"There've been strange sightings around," Ed continued. "A black mass that disappears as quickly as it's seen."

That caught Kane's attention. "Where?"

"It's kept to the bayou."

Elise's forehead furrowed deeply. "Black mass?"

Ed swiped a hand over his jaw. "Hunting is sometimes better done in...packs."

Now Kane knew Ed was aware of his heritage. "How well did you know my father?"

"When I was sixteen, I snuck out of the house and took my dad's truck to go meet a girl I was sweet on. I happened upon your father out in the woods being chased by some men. They shot at him, and one of the bullets grazed him."

Kane was taken aback. "The wound on Dad's neck."

Ed grinned. "That's right. I found your father and saw both sides of him."

Elise let out a loud sigh. "You mean you saw him shift."

Ed cut his gaze to her. "So you know. I wasn't sure."

"I'm the one who saved Kane from some werewolves a few days ago," she stated.

Ed blew out a breath. "Being this close to New Orleans, we know some of the goings-on, but not everything. And not all of us. Those of us who do, will help as much as we can."

Kane shook his head. "It'd be better if you didn't."

"When I helped your father, we formed a bond of friendship that lasted until he died. I was at your parents' wedding, and each of the christenings for you and your brothers. I'm aware that your parents were murdered."

"Then you'll understand why I have to do this alone. I'm after Delphine."

Ed took a step back, his face pale. "She's here?"

"I believe she's the black form everyone is seeing," Kane said.

Elise wrapped her arms around her middle. "Is this something she's done before?"

Kane shook his head, thinking back to the last battle. "Remember I told you I was fighting Delphine and George? Neither was concerned about my being there. They went after each other, sending magic back and forth. George got off one last spell before I killed him and the building collapsed. That could be what turned Delphine into whatever she is now."

"And the weres?" Ed asked.

Kane ran a hand through his hair, shoving the blond

strands out of his face. "As I told Elise, I think they're her followers that she's turned."

"So she can still do magic," Elise murmured.

Kane and Ed exchanged looks.

"That's not good news," Ed said. "Maybe it's time to call your brothers."

Elise threw up her hands before letting them slap against her legs. "That's what I've been telling him."

Kane ignored her and said, "I tracked Delphine. I think I know where she's hiding. I just need to get to her."

"We can help," Ed said.

Kane quickly shook his head. "It won't take her long to realize you're helping. You need to think about your community and the peace that's here. As long as Delphine believes her only worry is me, she might not lash out at the rest of you."

"That's a big chance we're taking," Elise said.

Kane walked into the living room to her desk and grabbed a couple of sheets of printer paper and a pen. He then began to draw some of the basic wards of protection.

He handed the papers to Ed. "Have these carved, painted, or drawn on every building you can. They're for protection and will keep anything evil out."

"And Delphine?" Ed asked.

Kane drew in a breath and compressed his lips. "Stronger wards will need to be added by a witch. Those are basic ones and a few my family learned."

"You should add wards here," Ed said.

Kane glanced at Elise. "I've already begun."

The old man gave a nod and folded the papers before putting them into his pocket. "Norma and I will get this started immediately. Are you sure the two of you should stay here?"

"This is my home," Elise said. "I'm not going anywhere."

"I'll watch over her," Kane promised.

Ed said his goodbyes and hurried out the door before driving off. Kane never expected to meet anyone who knew of him in the area. It was a nice surprise, but also gave him worry since Delphine always seemed to find out things like that and used them against her enemies.

"Wow," Elise said. "That's a story Mr. Perkins never shared. And he's told me many."

But Kane didn't want to talk. He turned to Elise and cupped her face with his hands before he leaned down and placed his lips on hers.

Her mouth was soft, supple. He nibbled at her lips, kissing her gently until his need became too great. He wrapped his arms around her and slid his tongue against hers.

She moaned and leaned into him. That's all he needed to deepen the kiss and let the fire burning within him consume them both.

CHAPTER

EIGHT

OH, God, she'd forgotten how much she loved kissing. And Kane was a master. His lips moved over hers seductively, expertly.

And when he deepened the kiss...it was utter bliss.

Elise wrapped her arms around his neck and succumbed to the raging desire that surged through her with the force of a hurricane.

He held her firmly, passionately. In his powerful embrace, she felt secure and treasured, coveted even. After her abstinence, her senses were being overloaded with the heady sensations.

She slid her fingers into his golden mane when he effortlessly lifted her before turning them and sitting her on the table. Even through her jeans, she felt the coolness of the stainless steel—a direct contrast to the heat rolling off him.

The strength of him was in every movement. It radiated from him each time his muscles flexed beneath her palms and against her body, reminding her that he was much more than a simple man.

She didn't fully understand the paranormal world he came from, but that didn't matter. Nothing mattered except for how she felt in his arms.

Her head was filled with the sense of him, and the intoxicating passion that swept through her—right up until Kane's hand slipped under her shirt and touched her side... and a scar.

Then reality crashed down on her.

Elise tore her lips from his and turned her head away as she pushed his hand from beneath her shirt.

"What is it?" he asked, his voice husky with desire.

Tears blurred her vision, so she closed her eyes. How could she have forgotten her scars? The very things she couldn't bear to look at—or have anyone else see?

"Elise?"

She swallowed and opened her eyes, but she wouldn't look at him. "Now isn't the time for this."

"That's not what you were thinking a few seconds ago."

His soft, sexy voice was gone, replaced by frustration that edged his words. She shoved him away and stood. "I've work to do."

She walked to the cabinet that lined the back wall and

opened it while pretending to look for something. He stared at her for long minutes before he stalked out.

Elise closed her eyes and drew in a shaky breath. Her scars were a reminder that she had lived through a horrific experience that could have killed her.

But the puckered, raised marks that varied in length and depth from her knees to her chest were mutilations, pure and simple.

While her inner scars might have healed, the ones on her skin never would. The one time she had tried to continue her life as before, it had ended with a child screaming in fear at the sight of her arms.

Ever since, Elise kept herself covered.

She busied herself with patients until lunch. The door to the living room remained shut, as normal. Yet she found herself glancing at it often, wondering what Kane was doing.

After she'd ended their kiss, she hadn't seen or heard from him. Maybe that was for the best. It wasn't as if she wanted to explain why she'd stopped them from going further.

At noon, she hesitated to go into the kitchen to get food because she wasn't ready to face him. Thankfully, a client dropped in with a pet parakeet, and that gave her the excuse she needed to remain.

After that, her appointments kept her booked. She went outside to check on some new baby goats, and when she returned, there was a plate with a sandwich and chips on it on her desk, as well as a *Dr Pepper*.

Elise knew that Kane was responsible. She looked at the door and hurriedly devoured the sandwich before her next appointment arrived. She ate so fast, her stomach hurt, which caused her to go slower with the salt and vinegar chips.

She had enough time to take a long swig of her soda before the outside door opened and her next client walked in. By the time her last appointment left at 6:30 p.m., she was exhausted.

A quick clean-up of her lab only took fifteen minutes, and then she opened the door and walked into the living room. She glanced around but didn't find Kane.

She smelled something cooking and made her way into the kitchen to check the stove. She found pasta cooking in one pot, and sauce in another. A glance in the oven showed chicken.

When she straightened, she saw something out of the corner of her eye and turned to find Kane standing just inside the back door.

"It smells delicious," she said.

He stared at her a moment before he closed the screen behind him as he entered. "You've had a busy day."

"It was a normal day," she replied with a shrug. "Thanks for the sandwich."

"How many meals do you miss daily?"

She moved out of the way as he walked to the stove and stirred the pasta. "I've got beef jerky I keep near to snack on if I know I'm going to miss lunch."

"Which means often."

The kitchen was small, so she stayed far enough away to give him room, but it felt odd not cooking in her space. "People come on their lunch breaks if they can't get free any other time. That means I don't get one."

"Maybe you should hire someone to help you."

"I've thought of that."

When he drained the pasta, she got out the plates and utensils and set them on the table. He bade her sit as he dished out the portions for each of them before he joined her.

She took a bite and sighed at the taste. "This is amazing. It's been a long time since anyone cooked for me. Thank you."

"My pleasure. Your house is warded, by the way."

Elise basked in the tasty meal as he explained everything that he'd done to protect her. While Kane was pleasant, the warmth he'd had before was gone. Not that she blamed him. She'd shoved him away without an explanation.

Because she was embarrassed—both of her scars and the fact that she didn't want to show him her body. He'd looked at her with passion. The last thing she wanted was to see his disgust or pity once he saw just what that maniac had done to her.

Their dinner conversation was light, as both kept to safe topics. She spoke of her appointments for the coming days, and he talked about the next storm headed their way.

When the meal was finished, she tried to clean up, but he stopped her.

"I've got this," he said. "Go, relax. Take a hot bath."

Which actually sounded good. It took her a moment to relent, but she finally did. She walked to the bathroom and started the water while Kane turned on her stereo that had a Michael Bublé CD playing.

Elise dropped in one of the bath bombs she loved and let it dissolve as she took off her clothes and pinned up her hair. Then she climbed into the tub and lay back in the hot water.

Her eyes immediately closed as she realized just how tired she was. The lack of sleep the night before, coupled with her busy day, had sapped her of nearly all her strength. If she hadn't eaten the sandwich Kane had brought her, she would've been dragging by dinner.

With the steam rising up around her, she let her mind wander, and it was no surprise that it focused on Kane. Ever since she'd come upon him in werewolf form, he filled her head.

She'd gawked at his fine body that first day, and then became drawn to him once he woke and they talked. There was something enigmatic about Kane that inexplicably pulled her toward him.

Behind those stunning blue eyes of his was a past he

attempted to rectify, and a loneliness that he tried hard to ignore. When he spoke of his cousin, Riley, Elise grasped that he had found someone who understood him without placing any demands on him.

Kane's love for his family was evident in his every word and every action. He truly thought that what he was doing was for the best.

But it was the way he looked at her that truly touched Elise. He offered friendship without strings, protection without being asked. He didn't look at her like the victim she was—perhaps because he was a victim himself.

She blinked and realized that the CD was on its second play-through. As she opened her eyes and sat up, she sighed because the water was growing cold. Elise let the water drain before rising and grabbing the nearest towel.

As a habit, she put her back to the mirror and dried off. She didn't look at her body, her gaze instead locked on a spot on the wall as she completed the task.

She then grabbed her robe off the hook on the back of the door and slipped it on. After unpinning her hair, she exited the bathroom and once again found the living room empty.

Was Kane gone? Had he left without saying goodbye? She hurried to one of the living room windows and looked outside, hoping to find him, but she only spotted a squirrel darting to a nearby tree.

Dejected, Elise turned and walked to her bedroom. She stood in the center for a long time before she faced the mirror atop her dresser. When was the last time she'd looked at her scars? Really looked? She couldn't remember.

She untied her robe and let it fall open. She held her own gaze in the mirror, afraid to look down, afraid of what she would see. When she first gazed at her scars, they had been red and ugly.

Taking a deep breath, she let her eyes lower to the scar below her right collarbone. It was about three inches long and angled toward her breast. The wound was no longer red but now faded to nearly match her skin.

That gave her courage to look at the next scar and the next. She was examining her stomach when she sensed someone in the doorway. She looked over to find Kane. By his position, he couldn't see the mirror, only that she stood in her robe with it open.

Their gazes clashed. Her heart did a little flip at the knowledge that he hadn't left yet. Emotion welled within her when she grasped that he was giving her the option to send him away.

Or invite him in.

She looked back in the mirror at herself. Instead of inspecting each wound separately, she looked at herself as a whole. While she still didn't like seeing her body riddled with the scars, they would always be a part of her. Either she could learn to accept them as part of who she was and perhaps open herself up, or she couldn't.

Elise shifted her shoulders to let the robe drop to the

floor before she changed her mind. She was terrified that Kane wouldn't like what he saw, but it was the uncertainty that pushed her to take the chance.

A shadow moved behind her a second before Kane appeared in the mirror. They gazed at each other through the mirror. He reached up and tugged on the curl near her cheek that he favored.

Then he put his hands on her shoulders. "Is this the first time you've looked at yourself since the accident?"

"Yes," she whispered.

"You pushed me away because you didn't want me to see."

She nodded.

His hands shifted forward so that his fingers brushed the scar at her collarbone. Elise jerked and looked away. Slowly, tenderly, Kane turned her head back toward the mirror with his other hand.

It took a few tries, but she was finally able to meet his gaze again. Only then did his hands travel down to the scars on her forearms.

He caressed her body, moving over each wound before turning her to face him. The desire she saw reflected in his eyes made her stomach quiver with need.

This time, she was the one who pulled him close for a kiss.

And she didn't intend to push him away.

CHAPTER

NINE

HE'D NEVER HELD anything so beautiful, so precious. Kane's heart skipped a beat when she kissed him. He wanted to pull her close, grip her tightly, but he feared she would run off again.

He deepened the kiss, letting her decide how close she wanted to be to him. When she wrapped her arms around his neck, her lush body pressing against him, he couldn't hold back his satisfied moan.

The taste of her was sublime, exquisite. He could barely breathe, the need for her was so intense, commanding.

Compelling.

With one kiss, she stole his will, his very essence.

He didn't know what it was about Elise that lured him ever closer. Was it her beauty? Her kindness? Her pure soul?

Her smile? Or perhaps it was all of those things and more that he couldn't name.

Her fingers gripped his hair as their kisses grew heated. Their breaths were ragged, harsh, their need fueling the desire that burned ever brighter, ever hotter.

He cupped the back of her head and kissed across her jaw and down her neck. The moment his lips grazed the first scar near her collarbone, Elise stiffened slightly. To prove to her that he saw her, not the marks on her body, he continued moving his lips over her flushed skin until she relaxed once more.

The woman in his arms was mentally and spiritually stronger than anyone he'd ever met—or, he suspected, ever would meet. She was everything beautiful and perfect, untarnished by the evil that he lived with daily. How could he bring her into such a world when he was stained with blood?

How could he dare to even think he deserved such a woman?

But how could he ignore the pull she had on his heart, his very soul?

He lifted his head to look upon her face. Her lips were parted, her chest heaving. Her eyes fluttered open to show her pupils dilated with a passion so deep, so flagrant that his knees threatened to buckle.

Elise was a dream come true. It boggled his mind that he was with her and that she wanted him. He didn't understand why, but he wasn't going to question such a gift.

He turned them and maneuvered her backward until she came up against a wall. Her green eyes watched him with curiosity and eagerness. He shot her a grin before he ducked his head to continue kissing her body.

Her nails dug into his shoulders when he reached her breasts. Her rosy nipples were hard when his lips passed over them. She sucked in a sharp breath.

With his mouth hovering over a turgid peak, his hand cupped the other breast and massaged it before he closed his lips over her nipple to tease her.

Breathy moans that made his balls tighten filled the room. By the time he moved his mouth to her other breast, she was panting, soft cries of desire falling from her kiss-swollen lips.

Elise was caught in the snug, gorgeous arms of rapture. She burned with need, a yearning so fierce that she knew nothing could tear her away from Kane.

Her eyes opened when his lips left a hot, wet trail down her stomach. He dropped to his knees and glanced up at her, his blue eyes blazing with the promise of pleasure.

She drew in a shaky breath when he hooked an arm behind her knee and lifted it over his shoulder. Her gaze was directed across her room to the window, but she didn't see the curtains or the blinds Mr. Darcy had broken in his attempt to see outside.

Her eyes were open, but her concentration was on Kane and all the wondrous, incredible things he was doing to her.

When his hands gripped her hips, the feeling of his long fingers wrapping around her as if securing her made her stomach flutter in anticipation.

But it was his warm breath on her sex that made her begin to tremble in expectation. He didn't make her wait long. The first touch of his tongue against her core was electrifying. And hot.

She splayed her hands on the wall in an effort to stay upright as that amazing tongue of his found her clit and relentlessly brought her to the brink of orgasm in seconds.

She remained on the edge until he slid a finger inside her. The force of the climax made her leg buckle. He held her upright and continued to swirl his tongue around her swollen nub until she couldn't stand.

With her body still shuddering from the powerful orgasm, Kane carried her to the bed and gently laid her down. She rose up on her elbows when he pulled off his shirt.

She'd seen him naked several times now, but she'd never get tired of his magnificent body. The life he led was in every honed muscle, every movement. She'd never known anyone like him. Commanding, compelling, and evocative. And for some unknown reason, he was with her.

Elise shifted onto her knees and watched as he unfastened his jeans and shoved them down his legs. A seductive smile curved his lips as his gaze held hers. Then he put a knee on the bed beside her and seized her lips in a kiss that stole her breath—and her heart.

She'd tried hard not to acknowledge her growing feelings for Kane, but baring her body and soul to him had stripped away all her efforts. And she didn't even care.

Her arms wrapped around him as he laid them on the bed before rolling onto his back. She straddled his hips and sat up. It was then that she realized he was letting her take control. Kane was a dominant personality, but he was handing the reins to her.

Her eyes teared up as emotion choked her. Unaware of her turmoil, he ran his hands up her thighs to her hips. Elise bent and placed her lips on his. If she hadn't already fallen for him, she would have tipped stupidly, crazily in love with him at that moment.

She straightened and rose up on her knees before taking his impressive length in hand. She stroked him up and down, watching his gaze darken as need tightened his face.

"Elise," he ground out in warning.

When was the last time she'd had such control over a man's body? She honestly didn't think she had ever brought her lovers to such a state. Just one more difference in Kane versus all the others who could never measure up.

She brought him to her entrance and slowly lowered herself. The feeling of her body stretching to accommodate him was a sensation she would never forget.

HE WAS BURNING. The fire scorching him was exquisite, but it didn't compare to Elise. Her head was thrown back, her curls a beautiful riot around her face.

Her breasts were pushed outward as her back arched, and she began rocking her hips. He skimmed his hands up her back and hooked them on her shoulders as he sat up.

He locked his lips around a nipple and suckled in time with her movements. She let out a groan that he felt all the way to his cock.

He moaned as she scratched her nails down his back. She rocked her hips faster, bringing them ever closer to the pleasure that waited. He both yearned for it and wanted to hold off as long as possible.

Decisions had already been made, and he wasn't ready to think about the next day—or the battle he knew was coming. But he'd already spent enough days with Elise. Delphine wouldn't hesitate to kill Elise to make him suffer, and Kane wasn't going to allow that.

He shoved aside those thoughts and gave himself to

Elise. There was a chance they would only have this one night, and he was going to make the most of it.

After watching his brothers each find the women that completed them, Kane had accepted that he wasn't meant to follow that path. Then Elise came along. It made him wish that his path was a different one, but he couldn't change what was in his blood.

He lifted his head and gazed at her face. It was filled with such bliss that it made his heart trip over itself. She altered her movements so she was moving up and down his length.

Every time he slid into her tight, wet sheath, he had to fight back his climax. Then he could wait no longer. He flipped her onto her back and thrust deeply inside her.

Elise let out a loud cry and urged him on with her hands. He began pumping his hips, driving into her hard and fast. She screamed his name as her body stiffened and another orgasm took her.

He kept thrusting, prolonging her pleasure as long as he could.

"I love you."

His gaze jerked to her face at her whispered words, but her eyes were closed. He wasn't sure if he'd actually heard the words, or if they were a figment of his imagination—of the hope and wishful thinking that filled him.

He rose up on his hands and pumped his hips faster until his own climax approached. Stupidly, he hadn't thought about protection, but he wouldn't leave a child behind to be cursed as he was.

Kane pulled out and fell against her as his seed spilled upon Elise's stomach. He'd done many stupid things in his life. But this was one time he had done the right thing.

He didn't know how long he lay in Elise's arms with her hands stroking his hair and back. He rose and cleaned her off before doing the same to himself. Then she pulled him back onto the bed with her.

As if he would've denied her anything in that moment. She curled against him. This simple breath of time was one of the most special of his life.

In the times he'd taken a woman since Delphine cursed him, Kane hadn't allowed any kind of cuddling. He hadn't wanted that kind of connection with anyone. Yet now, he couldn't imagine not having it with Elise.

He heard her breathing even out as she fell asleep, but he couldn't do the same. His mind was on the following day and everything it would bring.

A part of him wanted to speak to his brothers, but he'd end up telling them what he was doing, and it would defeat his purpose. Instead, he'd leave them a letter. It wouldn't be the same, but it would be something.

They needed to know that he loved them beyond measure—including the women that were now a part of their family. And Kane would leave Riley a note, as well. His cousin wasn't just family, she had become his best friend.

The stories the two shared had healed them both of pains neither realized they had. Riley was a beautiful soul who wanted nothing more than the love and acceptance of her family. She had that now.

Kane's arm tightened around Elise. It would be easier to leave her a letter, as well, but he wouldn't do that to her. She didn't have to save him. But by doing it, she'd created a bond that was unexpected and mind-boggling. It was stunning and wonderful, and an experience Kane wasn't sure he deserved.

He knew the odds of him coming out alive after his attack on Delphine were slim. But if he took the priestess out so she couldn't hurt anyone else, then it would be worth it. Because he knew Delphine would go after Elise.

That alone propelled Kane to make his decision. He didn't want to leave Elise. He wanted nothing more than to remain with her forever, basking in her smile and the unconditional love she gave to others.

It was a good thing the asshole who hurt her had been caught. Otherwise, Kane would hunt him down and rip out his throat.

"I love you, too," he whispered before placing a kiss on her forehead.

CHAPTER

TEN

ELISE CAME AWAKE WITH A SMILE, nestled in Kane's arms. She'd lost count of how many times he woke her during the night to make love.

She sighed contentedly. Her body was lethargic after being loved so thoroughly. She wanted nothing more than to spend the day in bed with Kane. Unfortunately, she had clients coming in to see her.

"Hungry?" he asked as he kissed her temple.

She smiled up at him. "Starving."

"I'll start breakfast. How do waffles sound?"

"Amazing." She watched as he rose from the bed and walked naked to his clothes.

Damn, the man was a sight to behold. He easily put all the men sporting muscles and underwear on billboards to shame. Her gaze landed on his shapely ass as he tugged on his jeans. He didn't bother to button them or put on a shirt before he winked at her and walked from the room.

She stretched before she threw off the covers and got up. As she made her way to the bathroom, she caught sight of her reflection in the mirror. Pausing, Elise smiled at the woman staring back at her.

A woman who didn't care about the scars anymore. They were proof that she'd survived. Perhaps she should wear them like a badge instead of hiding them.

She hurried to her closet, shoving aside clothes as she searched for a short-sleeve shirt. She finally found one that was hidden in the very back. Elise smiled as she took it off the hanger and brought it and the rest of her clothes into the bathroom.

Her shower was quick in her haste to put on a piece of clothing she hadn't worn in three years. When she finally stared at herself in the mirror, she let her gaze rake over the scars on her arms that would now be visible to anyone. Yet, she wasn't afraid.

Being with Kane had done that for her. He had helped her to get past the fear that held her back. She didn't even want to think about her life without him. While they hadn't talked about the future, she was ready to try whatever it took, so long as they could be together. It was too early to tell him of her love, but she would hold it safely within her heart until the time came to share it.

She shook out her curls and walked from the bathroom

just as Kane was finishing the waffles. Elise planted a kiss on his cheek and got out the syrup before pouring two cups of coffee.

To think, she had been happy living alone, just her and Mr. Darcy. She turned and saw the cat rubbing around Kane's legs, meowing up at him every so often. Mr. Darcy had fallen in love with Kane just as she had.

She sat at the table, ready to dig in to the breakfast. It wasn't until Kane sat across from her and she looked into his blue eyes that she knew something was wrong.

He ran a hand through his blond hair, shoving it back from his face before he reached for the syrup. She took a drink of coffee and watched him. He couldn't quite meet her gaze. The happiness she'd felt since waking was shattering right before her eyes.

"I like the shirt," he said, glancing up at her before putting a large bite into his mouth.

Elise set aside the cup and folded her hands on the table. Her appetite was now gone. "Whatever you have to say, just say it."

Kane slowly set down his fork and looked at her. "I was going to do it after our meal."

"I'd rather you do it now."

He gave a quick nod. "I'm going after Delphine."

She didn't need to ask if he were going alone. She knew he was. There was no point in arguing with him. Kane had made up his mind, and his stubbornness refused to allow him to consider another alternative.

"I'm surprised you didn't leave last night so you wouldn't have to tell me."

His brow furrowed. "Is that what kind of man you think I am?"

"No." She took a deep breath and looked away. "I'm sorry. That was uncalled for. I just don't want you to go."

"I don't want to."

"Then don't," she said, jerking her gaze back to him. "Please."

He held out his hand, palm up. Elise put her hand in his, chills racing over her skin when his fingers curled around hers.

"If I don't do this, Delphine will remain out there, gathering strength. She may let us have a few years. Just enough where I'll think she's gone for good or moved on. Then she'll strike. She'll take you from me first. It'll be quick and vicious. And bloody. Someone else close to me will be next. She'll do it to remind me that she has the power to make me suffer. And to let me know that I walk this path alone. After that, she may or may not kill me. She likes to toy with people, and she's had plenty of opportunities to kill me and hasn't. It would be just like the mental bitch to keep me alive and remind me every chance she got about everything she took from me."

Elise's heart hurt for Kane. She might have tried to

dismiss his words if she hadn't listened to his exchange with Mr. Perkins. It seemed Delphine's reputation exceeded well past New Orleans.

"Do you think you can win?" she asked.

Kane shot her a lopsided grin. "I'm sure as shit going to try."

"And if you do?"

He shook his head. "That's a conversation for when this is finished."

In other words, *if* he came back. Elise smiled and nodded. "Then go do what you have to do."

"There are some letters on your desk. Will you see that they're mailed?"

She glanced at her desk, frowning. "Did you sleep at all last night? I never even knew you got out of bed."

"I wrote them in bed with you."

That made her feel a little better. "I'll mail them."

"Your waffle is getting cold," he said and released her hand as he went back to eating.

It was all she could do to get half of the waffle down. Every bite stuck in her throat, threatening to come back up. Somehow, she ate and held a conversation with Kane as he told her the precautions to take.

All too soon, she was standing at the door with Kane, fighting back tears and the need to beg him to stay. She kept her back straight and her chin up, even though she was dying inside.

"If I lose, she'll come straight for you. If I'm not back in a day, head into the city to a bar called Gator Bait. One of my future sisters-in-law is a witch. She can help protect you," he told her.

She nodded.

He cupped her face and gave her a kiss that made her toes curl and her sex throb with the desire to feel him deep inside her. He sighed as he ended the kiss and looked down at her. "Be safe. Don't leave the house unless you have to."

"Come back to me."

His gaze filled with emotion as he pressed his forehead to hers. His lips parted as if he were going to say something, but he changed his mind at the last minute and gave her a hard, quick kiss before he was out the door.

Elise watched him as the tears fell unheeded down her cheeks. Mr. Darcy let out a plaintive meow and jumped on the windowsill to stare after him.

She wiped at her cheeks and turned away once Kane had disappeared into the trees. Elise walked to her desk and saw four letters—to Solomon, Myles, Court, and Riley.

Kane's last words returned to her, and she hurried to open her laptop to look up Gator Bait. In no time, she had the bar's website pulled up and her phone in hand, but she hesitated to call. Would they even believe her? Not to mention that Kane would be pissed if they showed up.

But she didn't care as long as he survived. That's what mattered.

Elise punched in the number. Her heart thudded in her chest as the line connected and it rang. Someone finally answered on the sixth ring.

The male voice on the other end gave her pause. "Can I speak to one of the owners, please?"

"If this is a complaint, I'll be happy to listen."

She briefly closed her eyes and tried again. "I need to talk to one of the LaRues. This is about Kane."

There was a brief pause before the man said, "Hang on."

She was put on hold, music playing in the background. Elise stood and walked to the window to look at the last place she'd seen Kane. He had been so adamant about keeping his family out of his plan.

Listening to him describe the things Delphine had done to him and his family had been appalling. The woman was seriously deranged, and she needed to be stopped. It wasn't that Elise didn't believe Kane could do it, she just didn't want him battling the priestess alone. Elise wanted him back beside her.

Because she was protecting him.

Just as Kane was protecting his family.

Elise hung up the phone. As much as she believed Kane shouldn't face Delphine alone, she now understood why he had chosen such a role. He loved his family so much that he was willing to die for them if it meant that they could live free of such evil.

How could she stand in the way of that? She was

thankful that she had been put on hold for so long. Otherwise, she would've told them everything. Elise cleaned up the kitchen and opened the doors to the clinic just as her first appointment arrived.

$$\sim$$

"She said it was about Kane," Court stated.

Solomon stood with his arms crossed over his chest as he looked from the phone to Myles and Court. "Did you ask her anything?"

"I put her on hold so all of us could hear what she had to say," Court said.

Myles leaned back in the chair and tossed another pencil into the ceiling above him. "We all knew Kane was alive, and now we have proof. I just want to know why he hasn't come home."

But Solomon knew. "Delphine. He's probably been tracking her."

Court shook his blond head. "He can't be so stupid as to go up against her alone."

"That's exactly what Kane plans," Myles replied softly.

Court gave a loud grunt. "Look at the times we've faced her. We managed to win each time, and some by the skin of our teeth, but every fucking time has been with the help of our allies."

"We know that," Solomon said. "And Kane knows that."

Court leaned his hands on Myles's desk. "Does he have a death wish? Is that what's got this bug up his ass?"

"He's doing it because Delphine came after Addison, Skye, and Minka. He's doing it for us," Myles said.

Solomon dropped his arms, a great weight settling on his shoulders. "I'm not losing him. I can't."

"*We* can't," Court corrected.

Myles nodded and leaned his forearms on his desk. "I don't know why this woman called, but we need to find her."

"Before it's too late for us to help Kane." Solomon turned as the back door to the bar opened, and their women walked in.

Minka's brown gaze collided with him, and she immediately hurried into the office. "What is it? What happened?"

"Kane," Solomon said. "A woman called about him, but she hung up before we could talk to her."

Minka grinned. "And you want me to find her."

"Her number, her address, anything," Myles said.

"I'm on it," Minka said.

Solomon watched her as Skye moved to Court's side, and Addison went to Myles. The LaRue family had just been the brothers for years, but now, it included their women, friends, allies, and extended family.

Their cousins—especially Riley—had been waiting for another shot at Delphine. Maybe one last battle was in order to wipe the priestess out for good.

CHAPTER

ELEVEN

LEAVING Elise was the hardest thing Kane had ever been forced to do. With every step, he wanted to turn back to her, to run into her arms and hold onto her forever.

But how could he live with himself if he did? What right did he have to happiness while his family, friends, and innocents—and even him and Elise—would suffer from Delphine's continued rise to power.

So he would sacrifice whatever future happiness he might have had with Elise so others could live free of the priestess's wrath.

Kane didn't shift. Being in wolf form would give him an advantage with his heightened senses, but he had a plan. Even with Delphine's weres following at a distance, he chose not to shift.

Anger simmered through him. The weres weren't attacking him, because Delphine wanted him for herself. The show at Elise's house had been to get him outside. Well, he was there now, and Delphine would pay for everything she'd done to the LaRues, the Chiassons, and everyone else that had been hurt or killed by the priestess.

And the list was long.

Kane had grown up on the streets of New Orleans, but over the last couple of years, he had ventured far from the city into the bayous. While his cousins might know the bayous as well as they did, Kane was comfortable maneuvering the waterways, as well as avoiding the many dangerous animals that thrived in such a place.

He returned to the place he'd last seen the black mass. His gaze raked over the area where moss dangled from the limbs of the cypress trees. A fallen log was the resting place of a turtle on one side and an adolescent gator on the other.

The cloudless sky promised still air, and the temperatures, already in the upper nineties, guaranteed a sweltering afternoon. Just another typical day in Louisiana.

Kane's eyes moved slowly over the water. He counted four alligators floating beneath the surface, just their eyes visible. He saw another two on the bank. And all of them watched him.

The only way to the isle was through the water—a swamp infested with gators. There was no way he'd make it. And Delphine knew it.

A large, twelve-foot gator off to Kane's left hissed loudly, to warn Kane not to venture any closer. Gators were very territorial.

While Kane had no wish to tangle with the animals, he had to get to Delphine. Except she'd made sure to go to the one place he couldn't reach. She obviously wanted him out here, though, which meant she had some sort of plan.

"I'm waiting," he called toward the isle.

The sound of a woman's laughter—Delphine's cackle—floated on the air, causing icy fingers of foreboding to run down his spine.

ELISE HAD JUST FINISHED TYPING the notes about her last client when the door opened. "Be right with you," she said.

After she'd saved the notes, she turned to find the small room she used as her clinic filled with three tall men and three women. The men with their various shades of blond hair and the same blue eyes as Kane held her attention.

She didn't need to ask to know that these were his brothers.

"How did you find me?" she asked.

One of the men nodded instead of answering. "So, you know who we are?"

She lifted a shoulder in a shrug. "You have the same eyes as Kane."

"Where is he?" another of the men demanded.

The third sighed loudly and gave a shake of his head. "Please accept our apologies, Elise. We should've introduced ourselves first. I'm Myles, and the beauty beside me is Addison."

Elise nodded woodenly at the realization that these people didn't just know who she was, they had found her. All because she'd placed a call to Gator Bait.

Well, Kane did say one of the women is a witch.

She halted her thoughts and paid attention as Myles introduced Court and Skye, with her long, dark hair pulled into a ponytail, and then Solomon and Minka, whose dark curls lay over her shoulders.

"Hello," Elise said, unsure what to say next. "Kane isn't here."

Solomon's eyes looked to the door that led into her living room. "Why did you call?"

"Because I thought you should know what he's doing."

"Which is what?" Minka asked.

Elise leaned back against the counter and braced her hands on it as she looked into six different faces. This was Kane's family, the people who cared about him most.

Court's forehead frowned. "Elise?"

"Y'all better get comfortable," she said and motioned to the door. "I'll close the clinic so we won't be bothered."

While she flipped the *CLOSED* sign on the door, the

others made their way into her house and took their seats. She rubbed her hands along her thighs as she stood before them, the denim scraping her palms.

She noticed each of them glance at her arms, but no one said anything about her scars. For her first day wearing a short-sleeved shirt, she was getting a dose of how others reacted.

Mr. Darcy walked to each of the brothers and sniffed them before coming to sit at her feet. Oddly, that small gesture gave her courage.

Elise swallowed and licked her lips. "I found Kane about five days ago. He was being attacked by a pack of wolves right out there," she said, motioning with her hand to the back yard and the bayou beyond. "I took my gun and fired it to run the others off. I saw the extent of his injuries and knew he would need help."

"Wait," Solomon said. "Wolves?" He and his brothers exchanged worried looks before he asked, "Am I to understand that you faced down wolves alone? With a gun?"

She nodded. "Foolish, I know, but I'm not one to let an animal suffer."

"So Kane was in his other form?" Court asked.

Elise grinned as she glanced at the floor. "I thought he was a large dog at first. He was unconscious as I dragged him to the door of my clinic to treat him. That's when he shifted."

"And you still tended him?" Addison asked.

Elise tucked hair behind her ear. "I love animals, but I'm not callous. And even though I didn't know what was going on, I had the means to stop the bleeding. Otherwise, Kane would've died."

"Thank you," Solomon said.

She looked out the window. "It was hours before he woke. I convinced him to remain until his wounds were healed."

"You didn't know him," Skye said.

Elise glanced at her. "True, but I had glimpsed him in wolf form for weeks. He never harmed me. In fact, he stayed far away. And there was something in his eyes that told me I could trust him. While he was here, he told me who he was and explained what all of you do in the city."

"Kane doesn't share such things," Myles said.

She shrugged, wrinkling her nose. "Perhaps it was because I saw him shift."

"What made him leave?" Minka asked.

Elise bent and picked up the cat, holding the Siamese as he began to purr while she scratched his chin. "I left to get him some clothes. There were werewolves here when I returned. One nearly attacked me, but he stopped it in time. He said Delphine was the cause."

"I knew it," Solomon said and ran a hand down his face.

She rubbed her cheek against Mr. Darcy's head. "Kane put up wards around the house. Then, this morning, he told me he had to go after Delphine. I tried, unsuccessfully, to talk him into contacting all of you. He said each of you had someone, and since he was the cause of all of this, he would fix it."

"I'm going to kill him," Court said angrily, his worry over his brother filling his blue eyes.

Myles covered Addison's hand and squeezed it before he looked at Elise. "Obviously, you called to tell us what he was doing. Why did you hang up?"

Elise's gaze returned to the window as she remembered Kane walking into the bayou. "I wanted to help him, but my reasons were selfish. I want him back."

"Because you love him," Minka said.

Elise nodded. "While I was on hold, I thought about all the things Kane had told me about each of you and the battles you've fought with Delphine. This is his way of ensuring that none of you have to fight her again and can live happily together."

"Not without him," Solomon said.

Skye's head cocked to the side. "And he has you."

Elise gave Mr. Darcy one more rub before setting him down. "He's doing this for me, as well. He said the first thing Delphine would do was come after me."

"He's right," Court murmured.

Solomon got to his feet and moved to stand at one of the windows looking out. "I'd do the same thing if I were in Kane's shoes. But while I understand his thinking, I won't allow him to fight her on his own."

"Then we find him now," Myles said as he stood.

Court snorted loudly and rose. "As if you even need to ask my opinion."

"Wait," Elise said. "You should know that the weres who attacked Kane and me aren't from the Moonstone Pack. Kane believes they're Delphine's followers. People she turned."

Court rolled his eyes. "Damn, this bitch just doesn't know when to stop."

Minka jumped to her feet and hurried to Solomon, who turned to face her. "I'm coming with you."

"That might be wise," Elise said. "Kane mentioned that Delphine was now a black mass instead of a person."

Addison's brow puckered into a frown as she looked at the others. "Does that mean she's more powerful?"

Minka shrugged. "It's a possibility."

"It could be a trap," Skye said.

Elise nodded. "Kane thought the same thing, but he said it had to be done."

"It does," Myles stated.

Court raised his brows as he glanced at his brothers. "Without a doubt."

"So, now what?" Addison asked. "Surely, the three of you aren't going to go barging out there."

"Four," Minka interjected as she looked at Solomon.

Elise watched as the eldest LaRue and his witch stared at each other for a long time. Solomon blew out a breath, his silent agreement obviously done in protest.

Minka grinned before she faced Addison, Skye, and Elise. "Kane did a pretty good job warding the house. I'm going to add more, but the three of you should remain inside."

"I think you should, as well," Solomon said.

Minka shot him a look but didn't reply. Elise wrung her hands as the witch walked onto the porch and stood at the door with her hand on the wood for a moment before she moved out of sight.

"Minka's very good," Addison said.

Skye nodded. "You'll be safe long after we're gone."

As if Elise needed a reminder that Kane would no longer be in her life. She was about to reply when she caught Addison staring at her arms.

Elise moved them behind her and shifted so that it would be difficult for anyone to see them. She was used to people being in her clinic, but not her house. Her small house felt even tinier with the others inside. She wanted to rush out and look for Kane herself.

The time they'd had together was amazing and all too fleeting. She hadn't comprehended just how special those few days could be, but she was coming to realize it now. And she ached to have more.

"It's going to be all right."

Elise blinked to find Minka before her and the others out on the porch. The witch's brown eyes held a wealth of kindness as she smiled. "I know you don't know us, but trust us, please."

"I'll help however I can to find Kane," Elise said.

"I've no doubt."

Elise remained in the house as the six spoke, the lovers saying their goodbyes before Solomon, Minka, Myles, and Court followed the same path Kane had taken hours earlier.

CHAPTER

TWELVE

"Oh, Kane. I knew it would be you that came for me."

It felt as if Delphine's voice was all around him. The blue skies were blocked out, the entire area darkening as if a blanket had been pulled over it.

Kane fisted his hands as the urge to shift slammed into him. He knew that, somehow, Delphine was responsible.

"I could've killed you at any time these past months," she said. "I've been waiting for you to come to me."

He looked around, noting that the bayou had gone eerily silent. "Show yourself."

"Hm. I don't think so. I quite like this."

"What do you want, Delphine?"

It felt as if something caressed his face. "You."

He jerked back, revolted at the thought of her touching him. "I'm not in the mood for jokes."

"I'm not joking," came her terse reply.

Kane drew in a deep breath and attempted to figure out the priestess's angle.

More laughter floated around him. "I've got you wondering now."

"You kill."

"Yes, and I'm good at it," came the whisper close to his ear.

Kane hated the fact that she was seemingly all around him, and he could do nothing about it. Proving that she was right—she could kill him anytime.

"George put you in this form," he said.

She made a sound somewhere between a hiss and a growl. "Don't ever mention his name again. It took everything I had to hold back his magic, but it was you who dealt the final blow. We work well together."

"If he had gotten the upper hand on you, it would've been your neck I bit," Kane replied.

She chuckled. "It's true, he did something to me. I couldn't take solid form. That hindered me for a while. I couldn't control anything, not even my magic."

Kane could've kicked himself. If only he had found her then, it would've been so easy to kill her.

"But then I learned just how powerful I am in this form. I'm no longer limited as I was with a body. I move faster, and can make myself as big or small as I need."

Fucking wonderful. The lunatic was now a certified

psychopath. That's just what everyone needed. And if she were difficult to find, he imagined she'd be even harder to kill.

"You don't look happy," she said with a laugh.

"I came to kill you. My job is a little harder, but I'm up to the challenge."

Once again, something slid along his cheek—and then down his chest to his cock. "Well, you can certainly try. Tell me, Kane, do you know why I cursed you to go after Ava?"

The fact that Delphine was bringing up Ava, who was now engaged to his cousin, Lincoln, was disturbing. Even more upsetting was that Delphine wanted to discuss the very thing that had altered his life.

"Because I pissed you off," he stated and moved away from her.

"I let you believe that was the reason. In truth, I'd been watching you and your brothers for some time. I saw the potential in you."

He was repelled by the notion that she'd watched any of them that closely. "Potential for what?"

"Blood. Mayhem. Death...evil."

Kane wanted to gag, to hit her with all the rage that was currently built up in him.

Suddenly, her voice came from behind him, her mouth close to his ear once more. "Look what I turned you into. You're a killing machine, Kane. You're focused, determined. I gave that to you."

He whirled around to get away from her, even though he knew he couldn't. She was the one blocking out the sun, which meant she might very well be able to keep him right there forever. Had he fallen right into her trap?

"No!" he bellowed. "I nearly killed my cousins and the woman Linc fell in love with! I'm like this for one purpose only—to kill you!"

She laughed long and loud. "Believe what you want. Your actions speak louder than your pitiful words."

Kane had never felt such hate before. "And Riley? What was she?"

"Someone I needed. Or, at least, I believed I needed her. Turns out, I got what I wanted without her."

Was Delphine implying that she could take over New Orleans now? God, Kane hoped that wasn't the case. His brothers—hell, the entire *city*—weren't prepared for that.

No doubt everyone had gotten used to Delphine being absent from the city, putting everyone in a false state of peace. The fallout from her return would be epic. The all-out war between the factions would spill from New Orleans into neighboring towns.

And the death toll would gain national attention.

This had to be contained. Now. Any way possible. Which meant it was all up to Kane.

"Do my words upset you?"

He fought to control his anger. "You know they do."

"I know how much you love your family. They mean a lot to you, don't they?"

"They mean everything."

He heard the smile in her words as Delphine said, "That's exactly what I'm counting on."

He was fucked two ways from Sunday. There was no doubt about it now. And no matter how hard he looked, he couldn't find a way out of the situation.

Had Elise been right? Should he have brought his brothers along? Or was he justified in doing this alone so only he had to suffer whatever was coming?

As soon as he thought of Elise, that was the only thing on his mind. But he quickly shoved her aside. He had no idea how much Delphine's powers had grown, and he didn't wish to test anything yet.

"You speak as if you have a proposal," he said.

There was movement in the dimness, as if everything became a little darker. "You've proven your worth by working with me to kill George. It showed me that there is no one better to stand by my side as I rule New Orleans than you."

"No," he answered.

"You might want to hold up before you reply. You've not heard my full offer."

"I'll not work with you."

Something wound around his body. He looked down but could see nothing. "Oh, you will," she said.

He didn't like her confidence. There was only one thing that could make him do whatever she wanted—threatening those he cared about.

And the bitch knew it.

"Oh, I see you've figured it out," she said, a smirk in her voice. "I knew you were smart."

"Spell it out for me anyway," he demanded.

"Fine, but I don't like your tone. You best curb that attitude. Quickly."

She was about to get more than sarcasm. She would get the monster she thought she created.

"Join me, stand beside me as I take over New Orleans. The LaRues have kept everyone in line for years. Instead of your family, I'll take over. With you by my side, there will be no uprisings, no war, because they'll see that I have the approval of your family."

She was certified, batshit crazy. There was no denying it.

The darkness around him shifted into the form of Delphine. Kane blinked against the harsh light of the sun suddenly visible again. He stared into the priestess's black eyes. Her black hair hung to her waist in rows of small braids. She wore a white gauze dress that showed the outline of her body and was a stark contrast to her dark skin.

She smiled and held out her arms. "A little show of what my power can do. Why not join me? If you swear to serve me, I give you my word that no one—including me—will ever harm your family again. Not your brothers, their women, or their children. Not your cousins or their families. I'll even throw in the veterinarian who patched you up. They'll live happily and be safe. All you have to do is join me."

There was a catch in there somewhere, Kane just couldn't see it yet. Asking her would be pointless, though. Delphine was willing to give him a lot to have him stand with her.

Her brow quirked, agitation making her lips thin. "You hesitate?"

"I'm wondering why you want me. If you need some lackey to stand at your side, you have dozens of followers. Hell, you even cursed some to be werewolves."

She cut her eyes to him. "They chose that option. And I want you, not just anyone."

"Right," he said with a nod. "Because I have the ability within me to do evil."

"Yes."

He laughed. "Everyone does. Just as everyone," he paused and wrinkled his nose at her, "well, almost everyone, can do good. There's another reason you want me. I won't give you an answer until you tell me what that is."

"I can kill everyone you ever cared about in an instant," she threatened.

"You've been doing that for years, so that doesn't pose the threat it might have, had you told me after murdering my parents."

Her black eyes narrowed on him. "You will be my enforcer."

"Of course," he said with a snort.

"That displeases you?"

He crossed his arms over his chest. "Your weres nearly killed me the other day."

"And they've been punished for it. They were only supposed to wound you, but their hatred was too great."

"You mean you lost control of them."

The way her nostrils flared told him he'd hit a nerve. Good. He wanted to hammer the shit out of it.

She tilted her head, her braids falling to the side. "They didn't do much damage to you the second time, did they?"

"They would have killed the vet."

Delphine smiled suddenly. "Nice try, making me believe you don't care about her by not saying her name. I'm not buying it for a second. I saw how quickly you came to her aid."

"What did you expect?"

She tsked loudly. "I thought you were smarter than that. By staying with the beautiful Elise, you gave me enough incentive to kill her. If you valued her life, you would've walked away from her immediately. Apparently, evil actually rules you."

Kane didn't want to believe that, but he knew that staying with Elise put her at risk—yet he had remained. What kind of fool was he? Had he done it on purpose like Delphine suggested? Had he known Elise could die because of it?

Delphine closed the distance between them. "You belong with me, Kane. I can show you power the likes of which you can't begin to fathom. No one will ever question you again. On top of that, your family will be safe. What more could you want?"

Elise. He wanted Elise, but it didn't matter because he knew that no matter what, he'd never have her. Delphine would see to that.

"The answer is on your face," Delphine said as she put her hand on his chest. "All you have to do is say the words."

He stared into her black eyes and thought of all the times he had tried to kill her, of all the times she had taken the life of one of his friends or allies.

"Say it," she urged, her smile growing tight.

His family had made a vow to protect New Orleans from evil. He would be going back on that if he agreed to Delphine's terms. But his brothers would have a life free of battle and death.

"Join me!" she shouted.

"Don't do it, Kane."

He whirled around and saw his brothers standing shoulder-to-shoulder, ready to fight. So much for him fighting Delphine alone.

CHAPTER

THIRTEEN

Elise lowered her cell phone to the desk. She marked her calendar after finishing the last of the calls to reschedule the rest of the day's appointments. Thankfully, they'd all just been check-ups—not to say that an emergency wouldn't show up.

She had been woken in the early-morning hours many nights to tend to injured animals. But that was just part of her job.

She looked over at Skye and Addison. Skye was flipping through a magazine, while Addison absently petted Mr. Darcy, who was curled up in her lap, as she stared at the floor.

"I feel so useless," Elise said.

The women looked at her. Addison smiled sadly. "It's something I struggle with constantly."

"It's easier for Minka," Skye said. "Being a witch allows her to get right into the mix of things."

The chair creaked as Elise leaned back. "I've never been in a situation like this. I'd like to think I would stand and fight, but to be honest, I'd probably run."

"We all want to run," Addison admitted.

Skye nodded, her lips twisted ruefully. "Delphine is terrifying. We've both faced her, and it's only because of the LaRues that we're still alive."

Addison jerked her chin to the degrees framed on her wall, as well as some of the pictures of the places she had worked. "You have impressive skills by the looks of it. Why remain out here? You could make a killing in New Orleans."

Elise placed her hand over a scar on her arm. She'd made the decision not to hide them, but she wasn't sure if she was ready to tell everyone her story. But this new her had to start with tiny steps. And this was a good one.

"I was attacked one night as I left New Orleans. Someone ran me off the road. My attacker wanted to rape me, and I fought back. It got me these when I protected my face," she said as she held up her arms. "The people here saved me. It was an old Creole woman who healed my wounds, and I never left. I've found a place in this community."

Skye grinned as she set aside the magazine. "I believe you're meant to be here. We can't thank you enough for helping Kane."

"I just want him to win against Delphine."

Addison sighed. "We all do. I pray every night for a future without her in it."

"I can't even imagine such a day, not after everything we've been through with her."

Elise listened to the two and understood fully why Kane had gone after the Voodoo priestess himself. She hated the thought of him facing her alone, but Kane was doing it out of love for his family. She only hoped he outwitted Delphine.

"I've got a bad feeling about all of this," Skye said as she rose and paced the living room.

Elise frowned because she'd had that same feeling since Kane left. "How so?"

"Delphine has a certain modus operandi," Addison said. "She doesn't wait around to kill those she wants out of the way."

Elise's hands were shaking as she placed them on her desk and rose to her feet. "There was ample time for Delphine to attack. Days, in fact."

"That's what I've been going over in my head," Skye said. "You told us how the weres attacked Kane. If she had wanted him dead, they would've killed Kane and you without a second's hesitation."

"But they didn't." Elise swallowed, her chest feeling tight. "Nor did they do anything on the second attack."

Addison's face was lined with concern. "She could have. I know that she's powerful enough to kill someone with just her mind."

"So why spare Kane and me?" Elise asked.

Skye crossed her arms over her chest. "That's a very good question. There can only be one reason."

"She wants him for something." The idea made Elise sick to her stomach.

Addison dropped her head back on the sofa. "Not again. After everything we went through to get Riley back."

"Delphine won't take Kane's memories," Skye said.

Elise frowned when Skye's dark gaze turned to her. "What?"

"She'll use you against him," Addison said. "She'll use all of us."

"And here I thought she'd left us alone because Kane warded the house." Elise pulled in a shaky breath. "Tell me there's more to do than sitting around waiting."

Skye snorted and looked away, which was answer enough.

Suddenly, Mr. Darcy jumped off Addison's lap to the arm of the sofa. He let out a hiss while staring out the window to the back yard and then growled low in his throat.

"I do believe we'd better prepare," Elise said.

Addison quickly stood. "Minka put spells on the house. No one can get in unless we let them inside."

"She's right," Skye told Elise. "We'll be fine."

Elise wished she could believe that. She'd feel better if Kane were with her, but she imagined he had his own problems to deal with.

"Come back to me, Kane," she whispered as the first werewolf stepped out of the trees.

"Holy fuck," Court mumbled.

Solomon silently agreed as they watched Delphine's form shift into something resembling black smoke before it wrapped around Kane, blocking him from their view.

"We've got to do something," Myles said.

Solomon was trying to think of the best way to attack when Delphine—and Kane—disappeared.

Court raked a hand through his hair in frustration. "What just happened? I mean, did y'all see that?"

"Of course, we did," Myles snapped.

With his brothers looking to him for answers, Solomon did his best to hide his growing fear and unease. "She wasn't surprised to see us."

"It was like she wanted us here," Myles said.

Court put his hands on his hips and shook his head. "If Delphine can change into that black smoke thing now, then we are screwed."

Minka walked out of the copse of trees behind them. "She's more powerful now."

Damn. That's not what Solomon wanted to hear. "Kane didn't fight her."

"She didn't give him a choice," Court said.

Myles blew out a breath. "Perhaps. But he wasn't happy to see us."

"Don't condemn Kane yet," Minka warned.

Solomon glanced at her before facing his brothers. "She's right. We don't know what Delphine told Kane. When we got here, they were talking."

"Yeah. Talking. Because that's what Delphine does." Court dropped his arms to his sides and turned away, cussing beneath his breath.

Solomon's gaze met Myles's. "What do you think?"

Myles slowly shook his head. "I know Kane well enough to know that he'll do whatever it takes to keep us out of another battle with Delphine. Even if that means sacrificing himself."

"I know." And that's what made Solomon so heartsick.

He should've seen this coming. He should've tried to talk to Kane about it instead of putting it all on Riley.

"We need to call Riley," he told them. "I want to know everything she and Kane talked about while they were living together."

Court immediately headed back toward Elise's house. Halfway there, they all came to a halt. Solomon grabbed Minka and pushed her behind him.

"What is it?" she whispered.

He turned his head to her. "Weres."

Court kicked off his boots as he pulled his shirt over his head. Minka turned away as Court removed his jeans and shifted before running off ahead of them toward the right. Myles gave Solomon a nod before he undressed and shifted and then disappeared to the left.

"Do it," Minka told him.

Solomon hesitated, but he knew just how powerful his witch was. He gave her a quick kiss and hastily removed his clothes before he called forth his wolf.

Once in were form, he looked up at Minka, who stood beside him, her hand sinking into the fur at his neck. Her gaze was directed straight ahead, in the direction of Elise's house. He didn't need to ask to know that magic was already building within his woman.

She took a step forward. He remained beside Minka, and with every step, words began to tumble from her lips as the spell she cast grew.

"Shit," Skye said when she saw the werewolf.

Almost immediately, two more joined the first. Elise went for her shotgun, but by the time she got it loaded, loud growls reached her.

"The boys are here," Skye shouted.

Elise hurried to the window and watched as two wolves attacked the three werewolves facing the house. She had no idea which one was which as they came at the others from opposite sides. The clash was fierce and brutal.

Both Skye and Addison were shouting and clapping. Elise stood with the shotgun in her hands, wondering what she should do. What were Court and Myles doing back at the house? Had they located Kane?

"Oh, hell," Addison murmured.

Elise's gaze jerked to the sight of Minka walking from the tree line with a huge white wolf by her side who was obviously Solomon. Minka's lips were moving, her gaze locked on the three interlopers.

Solomon crouched down, his lips peeled back to reveal his long fangs as he growled and jumped into the fray along with his brothers.

Minka remained, her arms now lifted out to her sides and her face turned to the sky. Elise looked up at the clouds to find them darkening and slowly swirling into a cone shape.

Suddenly, more werewolves surrounded them. Elise ran to the front of the house and saw them coming at them from all sides. She rushed back to Skye and Addison, her heart hammering in her chest.

"Minka needs to get inside. She's going to die out there," she said.

Skye shook her head of black hair. "The weres won't be able to get close to her. Watch."

Elise's gaze was drawn to the witch. Just as Skye predicted, every time a werewolf tried to attack Minka, they were struck down by lightning.

"Her powers continue to grow," Addison said, a smile in her voice.

Elise wasn't sure how to feel about any of it. She didn't fully understand what was going on, and it didn't help that this was her first time in such a battle—and meeting Kane's family. She was doing her best to keep her composure, but she couldn't stop thinking about Kane.

"*Elise!*"

Her head jerked to the side. That was Kane's voice. Hadn't the others heard it? She looked to Skye and Addison, but both were focused on their men.

"*Elise. I need you. Please.*"

"Did y'all hear that?" she asked, her eyes locked on the door to her clinic.

Skye clapped. "That's my man! Go, Court! Kick some ass, baby!"

Elise glanced at the women before she walked to the door and opened it. She peered inside, but there was no sign of Kane. Her hands were clammy as they gripped the gun.

"*Elise, Delphine has me trapped. I need help, but my brothers can't hear me.*"

"Kane? Where are you?" she asked as his voice grew fainter. "Kane!"

She looked over her shoulder again. There was no telling how long the battle in her backyard would last. But there was one thing she knew—Kane needed help.

"Skye! Addison!" she called, but neither heard her over their yells to their men.

She looked at the door leading outside. What was she going to do? She had no magic, no ability to shift. Perhaps she could use that to her advantage. Maybe she could surprise Delphine and get off a shot at the priestess's head.

Or she could be walking to her death.

CHAPTER
FOURTEEN

Kane briefly closed his eyes. He kept asking himself that same question. Delphine continued to push her proposal, and at first glance, it seemed perfect.

Too perfect.

Well, aside from the fact that he'd give her his support. It would almost be worth it if his family were free of such a person, but if she were in control of the city, would they really be safe?

Or would Delphine find some way to kill them?

Kane shoved aside the moss that hung from a low limb as he looked across the water to where his brothers had been. He'd tried to call out for them, but whatever Delphine did to block out the sun had also prevented his voice from reaching them. By the time the black mass left him, he found himself on the isle, and his brothers gone.

"I don't like to be kept waiting," Delphine snapped.

He turned his head to her and glared. "And I don't like being forcibly taken."

"We weren't finished with our conversation."

"What did you do to my brothers?" he demanded.

She rolled her eyes. "Really? We're in discussions, and you think I harmed them?"

"It sounds exactly like something you'd do."

Delphine grinned. "It does, doesn't it?" She shrugged, sighing loudly. "However, I promise that I did nothing to them. I kept you hidden until they were gone."

"Then where are they?"

Her lips curved into an evil smile. "I may have sent my wolves to keep watch on the house."

"If anything happens to my family or Elise, I'll never help you."

"I've done this long enough to know how far I can push things, Kane. My weres are merely there as a reminder of my power. They won't harm anyone, though they will protect themselves if assaulted."

He snorted and crossed his arms over his chest as he faced her. "No doubt your weres put themselves in just such a threatening position so they would be attacked."

"They have orders to do nothing but watch the house."

"Right. And I'm the Pope."

Delphine laughed as she eyed him. "Why not agree to my terms? I've given you everything you could want."

"Except my freedom. I'll be shackled to you."

A black brow rose. "Careful. My patience is running thin."

"It's the truth."

"What's wrong with siding with the most powerful being in New Orleans? Nothing. No one will dare go against you. I'll allow you to keep the silly rules your family instigated."

Kane laughed and dropped his arms. "You can't be serious? Those 'silly rules' as you call them, will stop you, as well."

"They'll apply to everyone but me and my followers."

"So my so-called power will be in name only." Figured.

She blew out a harsh breath. "Look at the big picture. New Orleans is just the first step. I've much larger plans. I'll take over the state, and eventually, the country."

"The country?" he repeated, shock reverberating through him.

Delphine gave him a knowing look. "You don't think I can do it?"

"I believe there are others out there who would fight you to keep you from doing exactly that."

"And they'll die. I've already got the djinn on my side. The vampires are waiting for you to side with me as I've promised them you would."

Kane was shocked to his very core. While he and his family had been trying to keep themselves alive and stop whatever scheme Delphine had going on, she'd been moving pieces behind their backs, altering the game altogether.

The mistake they had made was thinking she was only after the LaRues and Chiassons. It had never been just about them, and if they had stepped back and looked around, they might have seen it.

All these months, they'd thought they were winning against Delphine, when in fact, while they could claim the skirmishes, she would win the war.

"Why did you take Riley?" he demanded. "Was she just a diversion?"

Delphine shook her head. "Riley was meant for so much more. She was stronger than I realized. I should've kept a tighter rein on her."

"It was George who ruined it for you."

She cut her eyes to the side, anger in every feature. "He was obsessed with her. If he'd just waited, he could've had her and anyone else he wanted."

To hear Delphine talk so blithely about Riley made Kane's blood boil. Yet he kept it hidden. There was no way Delphine would get away with everything she had done.

The only thing stopping him from attacking her now was that she'd kill him without Kane being able to get any information to his brothers.

But the thought of siding with her, even as a sham, might be the end of him.

There were no other choices for him. If he refused her, Delphine would kill him then go after his family and Elise. They wouldn't survive. His cousins would be next. All the while, Delphine would continue her quest to rule the city, state, and country.

Who would be left to stop her? Who would dare rise up against her?

The only reason the witches had helped them in the past was because they worked as a team. Hell, even the Moonstone Pack was scarce. It was only the LaRues who held that tenuous pact together.

If the LaRues were killed, the witches would go into hiding. The Moonstone Pack would scatter like before. Even if he didn't side with Delphine, the vampires would eventually fall to her. It was simply a matter of time.

Then the way would be clear for Delphine to gain all she wanted.

"I need an answer," the priestess demanded.

Kane turned his head to the side and watched a crane snag a fish from the water before flapping its white wings and flying away.

"Let me talk to my brothers."

"No," she replied.

He swiveled his head toward her. "If I don't tell them

why I'm taking your offer, they'll attack you, and you'll kill them."

"I can stop them in other ways. Wiping their memories would be easy enough," she said flippantly.

Kane gawked at her. "Don't you dare."

She gave him a flat look. "If you're going to leave your family, wouldn't it be easier for them if they didn't remember you or anything they've been doing all these years? Let them believe the paranormal is something for movies and books."

"Will you do the same for me?"

"If you'd like."

Kane turned his back to her and braced a hand on a tree. No matter which way he looked at it, he couldn't find a way to best Delphine. Not now, at least. And if he didn't do it right away, and she gained more power, the harder it would become—until it eventually became impossible.

"Your answer, Kane," she demanded.

He was stuck between a rock and a hard place. No matter what, his life would be Hell. At least he could give his brothers and cousins some peace to live a normal life and raise their families.

"I want to talk to my brothers."

"Give me your answer first."

Shit. He was going to hate his life.

"Kane."

He frowned. What was Delphine's hurry all of a sudden?

She had been patient, coaxing even, but all that'd changed over the last few minutes.

Just as he was turning to ask Delphine, his gaze spied movement across the bayou. His heart fell to his feet when he saw Elise.

"What is the meaning of this?" he asked as he whirled to face Delphine.

Agitation lined her face. "I'd hoped you would agree without needing that final push. Seems I was wrong."

"I CAN DO THIS. I can do this," Elise told herself as she marched through the bayou to the place Kane's voice had led her.

She saw him across the water, standing with his hand on a tree. A beautiful woman with long, black hair and dark skin was behind him.

Delphine. So that's what the Voodoo priestess looked like.

Elise wanted to take aim with her gun, but Kane was too close to her, and at this distance, she might very well hit him instead of Delphine.

She walked closer, watching as Kane turned to Delphine, and they began arguing. Was that a good sign? Damn, she didn't know. Elise knew very little about what to expect. Maybe she shouldn't have followed the voice.

But she had been so sure it was Kane. Now, not so much.

"Elise, leave!" Kane bellowed.

His words halted her. It confirmed her worries. Kane hadn't led her here. Delphine had. That made Elise despise the woman more than ever—and she didn't even know the priestess.

Her blood ran like ice when she heard the low grumble of a growl behind her. Elise slowly looked over her shoulder to find a werewolf.

Kane walked to the edge of the small mound of earth in the middle of the water but drew to a stop when an alligator rose up from the water before him.

There was no going back for her. And she was fine with that. From the moment she'd saved Kane in his wolf form until now, she was where she belonged—with him.

Elise raised her shotgun to her shoulder. She took aim at Delphine, but before she could squeeze off a shot, the gun was knocked out of her grasp, and she found herself tossed unceremoniously to the ground.

When she looked up, she gazed into Delphine's black eyes. Even Elise could feel the power that flowed through the priestess. No wonder so many feared her.

Delphine grasped her jaw with fingers that bit into Elise's cheeks. "You stupid fool. I can't believe you fell for my trick. Since when has Kane ever projected his voice like that?"

Elise tried to tug Delphine's hand away, but she couldn't budge her even an inch. "You knew I would come for Kane."

"Because you love him," Delphine stated with disdain.

Elise grinned through the pain. "And I knew you'd come over here for me. Who's the fool now?"

CHAPTER

FIFTEEN

"Elise!" Kane bellowed when Delphine tackled her to the ground.

He had to get to Elise, to save her from certain death. Kane stepped into the water, only to jump back before a gator lunged for his foot.

"Fuck," he grumbled, his gaze jerking back up to Elise.

Kane quickly scanned the area, looking for a place to cross that didn't have alligators waiting to take a bite out of him. He moved from one side of the tiny isle to the other, but it was as difficult to get off, as it had been to get on.

No wonder Delphine had chosen it.

Frustration and fear pounded through him, slamming his heart against his ribs. He'd been about to agree to Delphine's proposal, to take her at her word that she would make sure his family and Elise were safe and unharmed.

How stupid was he to believe anything that came out of Delphine's mouth? She manipulated and lied her way to whatever she wanted. If anything, Kane should've known he couldn't trust her.

"Elise!" he shouted again.

He'd be shattered if she were killed—and nothing would ever put him back together. How could he bring her into this unwinnable war? How could he have dared to think about his own pleasure for even an instant?

A howl he knew well sounded to his left. Kane's head snapped in that direction as a silvery white wolf came into view with Minka by his side.

"Solomon," he whispered.

Minka walked to the edge of the bayou and held her hands out. Kane stared in amazement at the ripples moving over the water as alligators swam away.

Kane didn't waste any time hurrying into the water. The edge dropped off quickly, and he swam to the opposite side where Minka and Solomon awaited him. Just as he was about to run to Elise, Minka grabbed his arm.

"Wait," she cautioned.

He glared at her. "Are you insane? Delphine is going to kill her."

Solomon growled in response.

Minka rubbed Solomon's head and told Kane, "Your Elise has a plan, and it's a good one."

"What?" he asked, unsure if he'd heard her correctly.

Minka gave him a quick smile. "Trust us. And be ready."

He gawked at Minka, who hurried out of sight. Kane's head swung back to Delphine and Elise before he looked at Solomon. Kane had no idea where Court or Myles were, but if his brothers liked the plan, then it had to be good.

Solomon trotted off, and Kane grudgingly followed. He glanced back at Elise one last time, praying she knew what she was doing.

"NICE TRY," Delphine said with a smile.

Elise continued to attempt to pull the priestess's hands away from her jaw to no avail. Delphine was frighteningly strong. Elise didn't know if it was magic or not, but it didn't matter. She just needed to get free.

"No one can mess with another's mind like I can," Delphine stated. "But I will give you props for the attempt."

Elise laughed, though the sound came out more like a bleating cow. "Attempt? I've done more than that."

Delphine's black eyes narrowed as she squeezed harder. Then she looked up. Even with dots beginning to edge Elise's vision from lack of oxygen, she still enjoyed seeing Delphine's smile vanish when she caught sight of Minka.

Elise dragged in a gulp of air as Delphine's grip suddenly disappeared. She could hear Minka and the priestess talking, but she couldn't make out their words. Elise was losing consciousness. She fought to remain awake, but it was becoming more difficult.

"Stay with me."

Elise rolled onto her side, frowning at the sound of Miss Babette's voice in her head.

"That's it, my girl. Stay with me," Babette said.

Elise felt as if she were floating between worlds. She opened her eyes, but she was no longer lying on the ground. She was in Babette's house, gazing down at her blood-soaked body as the old woman spoke calmly while she and another frantically tried to stop the bleeding.

She didn't understand what was going on. Elise recalled very little of the night she was attacked. It wasn't until days later when she woke up in Babette's house that they told her what had happened.

So, what was she seeing now?

Elise blinked, and the scene changed. Her many injuries had been stitched, and Babette sat on the side of the bed as she put salve on the wounds before wrapping them in bandages.

"You still have much to do, my girl," the woman said. "You're needed, though he won't realize how much until everything may be lost."

Elise shook her head. What the hell was going on? But even as the thought went through her mind, she concentrated on Babette.

The old woman sat back and sighed loudly. "I've seen

what's to come, Elise. You have great strength in you, though you haven't recognized it yet. He will show you it's there. But you're going to have to use it. You can't hear my words now, but when you need them the most, they will come to you."

Elise reached out to see if she could touch Babette, and in the next instant, found herself once more on the ground. She dug her fingers into the grass as the words reverberated in her head.

Without a doubt, she knew Babette had been speaking of Kane, and while the old woman hadn't said Delphine's name, this was the event she must have seen.

Elise rose up on her hands and knees and ignored her bruised jaw as she swallowed. Minka and Delphine were going head-to-head with their magic, and while Minka was holding her own, she was weakening.

After getting to her feet, Elise looked for Kane on the isle, but he wasn't there. She smiled. Another part of the plan had worked.

Elise had the feeling someone was watching her. She turned her head to the side and saw Babette standing about fifty yards away. All around her lay dead werewolves who would no longer be coming to Delphine's aid.

KANE WANTED to dive into the battle. He and his brothers waited, hidden, for the signal. Not that he knew what the signal was. As soon as he followed Solomon, he'd shifted and joined his siblings. But he didn't need words to know that this was their final stand.

They would either kill Delphine or die trying.

Kane snapped his jaws. The longer he waited for a piece of the priestess, the more annoyed he became.

Solomon issued a low growl of warning that someone approached from behind them. As one, the four of them turned and crouched down, ready to attack.

Kane was shocked to find Griffin, Alpha of the Moonstone Pack. Behind him were others of the pack. The last time they had seen Griffin, he'd been helping Delphine. Granted, the priestess had his sister, but still.

Griffin raised his hands. "We're here to watch and act as backup if necessary. We've taken out several of Delphine's weres. I know you might not believe me, Kane, but we've got your backs."

Solomon gave a nod and turned back to the fight. Myles and Court did the same. But Kane bared his teeth to Griffin. He'd been the one to befriend Griffin and convince him to return to New Orleans. Kane went out of his way to bring the Moonstone Pack back together, and he and his family had been betrayed.

It was something he didn't easily forgive—or forget.

An Alpha didn't show submission easily, but Griffin bowed his head to Kane. "I'm sorry. I've spent these last months earning my pack's trust again. I'll do whatever it takes to earn yours. I lost my sister, Kane. She was the only reason I helped Delphine. I can't change the past, but I can prove myself. My pack has surrounded the area. Delphine won't get past us."

They didn't know that the priestess could shift into nothing more than a bit of smoke, and Kane didn't have time to tell them now. He turned to Delphine and Minka when he heard a shriek of anger.

Kane's gaze sought out Elise. He was happy to see she was on her feet again. Her gaze was off to the side, and by her smile, she saw something or someone she recognized.

Solomon began to pace when it was evident that Minka was weakening against the onslaught of Delphine's magic. Something had to be done, and quickly.

Kane started forward, but Myles jumped in his way.

DELPHINE WAS GOING TO WIN. Again. Elise couldn't imagine a world where the priestess ruled all. Because Elise realized that this was the final battle, the conclusion of years of skirmishes between the LaRues and Delphine.

Elise took a step toward Minka when the witch dropped to her knees and struggled to keep her magic going. Elise looked around for Kane and his brothers. This was when they should join in. Why weren't they?

She spotted the reason a moment later when Babette

walked to stand beside Minka. The old Creole woman lifted her chin and glared at Delphine.

"I warned you never to return here," Babette said.

Delphine laughed as she dropped her hands, halting the magic she had directed at Minka. "Babette. I thought you'd be dead by now."

"You tried hard enough, but I don't die easily."

Elise looked back and forth between them, paying special attention to the tension between the two women.

Delphine raked her gaze over Babette. "You look...old, sister."

Elise's mouth dropped open. You could've knocked her down with a feather she was so surprised.

Babette slowly shook her head. "Reverting to barbs, just like when you were a kid because you didn't have the intelligence to argue."

"No, I had the kind of power that really mattered," Delphine retorted.

Babette smiled sadly. "You took the wrong path. I hope you enjoyed the power you had because you're about to lose it."

"Oh, I don't think so. No one can touch me now."

Babette raised a brow, a grin forming as Kane, Solomon, Myles, and Court moved in a semi-circle behind Delphine. "You were always looking ahead, Delphine, grasping for things that were out of reach, which made you miss what was right in front of you."

Elise frowned. She knew those words. She wasn't sure how, but she knew them, had lived them before...somehow. Her gaze slid to Kane to find him watching her. In his yellow eyes, she saw recognition of Babette's words, as well.

She turned her head to Babette and then Delphine. As she did, a vision of sorts formed. Elise saw Kane lunge at Delphine and sink his teeth into her throat.

"I'm done with this!" Delphine bellowed. "All of you will die this day."

A chill ran down Elise's spine as Babette cut her eyes to her. Elise knew Delphine had to be kept in her current form, but how? Minka was so weak she could barely lift her head, and Babette didn't seem to have any magic at all.

Babette gave a small, barely discernable nod, as if to tell Elise to continue her train of thought. Then time slid to a crawl as Babette turned her head to Delphine and held out her arms. In the next instant, Babette was encased in flames.

"No!" Elise screamed as Babette flailed about before collapsing.

Minka was able to use her magic to put out the flames, but it was already too late. Babette was dead.

Rage burned through Elise. She looked around for her shotgun as yelps of pain mixed with growls of warning came from the LaRues. Her head jerked to the werewolves to find that Delphine had Myles, Solomon, and Court pinned down with her magic as she glared at Kane.

Elise briefly met Kane's gaze. She forgot her shotgun and

rushed Delphine, but the Voodoo priestess spun around to face her before Elise could do anything.

"I'm going to make Kane watch as I kill his family, but I'm saving you for last," Delphine announced.

The priestess's body began to grow hazy, and Elise realized she was shifting into the black mass again. The image of Kane killing Delphine with his jaws around her throat replayed again.

"No," Elise stated. "You'll remain here. In your human form."

Delphine's laugh cut off in the middle as she became solid once again. Her gaze held a wealth of anger and retribution as she looked at Elise. "What did you do? You've no magic?"

Elise smiled coldly. "That's right. I don't have magic, but what I have is command over you."

Delphine took a step back. "That's not...possible."

"Babette once told me that I have control over what's on my land. It's why you never fought the LaRues at any place they owned. It was always someplace one of your followers retained or was owned by the city. But you made a mistake here," Elise said as she moved a step closer. "This is my land."

Fear reflected in Delphine's black eyes as the truth settled over her.

Elise grinned as she saw Kane crouch down and get

ready to attack. "You were right. You are done. And I know just the wolf to finish you."

Delphine turned, her scream cut off as Kane's powerful jaws locked around her throat. There was a snap as he broke her neck before dropping her lifeless body.

Elise's legs gave out, and she crumpled to the ground. She couldn't believe it was over. Kane walked to her and shifted. She winced when she heard his bones popping back into place.

His yellow wolf eyes faded to bright blue, and then she was in his arms. She closed her eyes and savored the feeling of being held by him.

"I thought I'd lost you," he said as he leaned back to look at her. "How did you do that?"

Elise looked to Babette's charred body as Court, Myles, Solomon, and Minka walked to them. "When Babette tended me after my attack, she told me about this day. Not in exact words, but enough. I didn't remember any of it until today when she appeared."

"She was Delphine's sister," Minka said. "I didn't think Delphine had family."

Kane shook his head. "Babette saved us."

Myles and Court suddenly took off running toward her house for Addison and Skye. Minka shot her and Kane a smile before walking away with Solomon. Elise took a deep breath as Kane linked his fingers with hers.

"You kicked ass," he said with a sexy grin.

"I didn't do anything other than what Babette showed me needed to happen."

Kane shrugged a shoulder. "I beg to differ. That took serious courage. You were magnificent."

She smiled, happiness flooding her. "Magnificent, huh?"

"Hell yeah. Is it any wonder I love you?"

Her heart stopped as she blinked at his confession.

He skimmed his knuckles down her cheek. "I think I've loved you since I woke up in your house. You...inspire me. I want to spend every day for the rest of my life showing you how much I love you."

She swallowed and rose up on her knees to cup her hands on either side of his face. "How do you always know just what to say?"

"With you, it's easy."

She grinned and pressed her lips to his for a soft kiss. "I love you."

His smile was blinding as he got to his feet and lifted her into his arms as he spun them around.

The evil that had ruled his life for so long was gone. Something else would take its place eventually because it was the way of the world. But for now, there was peace and happiness.

And love.

EPILOGUE

Two weeks later...

COMPLETE. That's how Kane felt now. He lifted the longneck beer to his mouth for a swig as he watched the women of his family surround Elise. She smiled at him, and he felt as if his heart would burst.

Solomon came up beside him. "You got a good one."

"I know," Kane said with a grin.

"I suppose we'll be seeing much more of her?"

Kane looked at his brother and nodded. "I believe so. Especially since I'm moving in with her."

"Hot damn," Court said as he came up, slapping a hand on Kane's shoulder. "I knew it."

Kane frowned as Myles walked up, followed by their

cousins Vincent, Lincoln, Beau, Christian, and Marshall, Riley's fiancé. "What are you talking about?"

"We made a bet," Beau said.

Christian nodded.

"When you and Elise were going to move in together and where," Lincoln said with a grin before he took a drink of his beer.

Vincent elbowed Linc as he shook his head. "Ignore them, Kane."

"Bullshit," Marshall said with a laugh. "You were the first to place a bet, Vin."

They all laughed. When the laughter died down, they each looked around, realizing how precious their time was together, and how easily Delphine could've won and destroyed it all.

"Laughing without me is a crime," Riley said as she walked up and put her arm around Marshall. "I am engaged to a sheriff, you know. So don't piss me off, or I'll have you arrested."

Beau rolled his eyes. "Oh, God. That again?"

"Ah, yeah," Riley replied sarcastically.

Marshall winked at Riley before pulling her close for a kiss.

The circle expanded as Olivia went to Vin, Ava to Linc, Davena to Beau, Ivy to Christian, Addison to Myles, Skye to Court, and Minka to Solomon.

Kane held out his hand for Elise as he pulled her against

him. This was their family now. Regardless of what was to come, they would stand together.

He held up his beer and looked around. "A toast to family. For as long as I can remember, it was just me, Court, Solomon, and Myles. Fate brought us back to our cousins, and both families have been blessed that each of us has found love. May these bonds that hold us together only strengthen with the years."

"Hear, hear," the others said in unison.

Everyone began talking at once, but Kane didn't hear them. He pulled Elise close for a kiss, his heart nearly bursting with happiness. His love for her grew every day. It seemed impossible that he could love her more, but he did.

"Okay, okay," Riley said loudly to gain everyone's attention. "I know we're just getting this party started, but we did close down Gator Bait for the night so we could all be together."

Ivy chuckled as Davena and Skye exchanged looks.

"Sweetheart, you're making everyone nervous," Marshall said.

Riley rolled her blue eyes. "No, I'm making the guys nervous. Well, too bad, because now that we're all here, we're going to schedule all the weddings."

Kane laughed as the women pulled out calendars they must have hidden in their shirts. Elise was so shocked, she spilled some of her beer on herself.

"I don't know why you're laughing," Christian said to

Kane. "Take notes, dude. Your time is coming, and Riley is a damn drill sergeant when it comes to this."

Kane felt Elise's gaze on him. He looked at her and wrapped an arm around her shoulders before rubbing his thumb along her cheek. He raised a brow in question.

She shrugged, grinning all the while.

"Too soon?" he whispered.

Elise glanced at the others flipping through their calendars. "It doesn't hurt to take notes."

"You mean, let them make the mistakes, and we have the perfect wedding?"

She laughed, nodding. "I like the sound of that."

He stared into her green eyes and turned to face her. "You make every day wonderful. I can't wait to see what the rest of our lives looks like."

"Ohhh," she said as she rose up on her tiptoes and pressed her lips to his. "You always know what to say."

He turned and dipped her for a steamy kiss as his family shouted encouragement behind him.

No matter what monsters or evil came at them, they would fight it as a family. And there was no greater bond than that. Together, the Chiassons and LaRues were unstoppable.

And it was time the supernatural world realized that.

AFTERWORD

Thank you for reading **LARUE SERIES**! I hope you loved these stories as much as I loved writing them. The Chiasson and LaRue series are intertwined. First in the Chiasson series is book one, WILD FEVER…

A WOMAN'S PASSION…
A HUNTER'S DESIRE.

BUY WILD FEVER today at
www.DonnaGrant.com

If you love the LaRue series, you'll love the fan favorite world of the Kindred series which starts with EVERSONG…

She is a hunter, trained from birth.
He is a man sworn to vengeance.
Nothing can stop them. Except each other.

BUY EVERSONG today at
www.DonnaGrant.com

To find out when new books release
SIGN UP FOR MY NEWSLETTER today at
http://www.tinyurl.com/DonnaGrantNews.

Join my Facebook group, Donna Grant Groupies, for
exclusive giveaways and sneak peeks of future books.

Keep reading for an excerpt from WILD FEVER and a special
sneak peek at EVERSONG...

EXCERPT OF WILD FEVER

CHIASSON SERIES, BOOK 1

A WOMAN'S PASSION

Olivia Breaux left the small Cajun town the day of her high school graduation and never looked back. Until an unfortunate event sends her home ten years later. Returning to her hometown brings back memories and long held desires for the impossibly gorgeous – and aloof – Vincent.

A HUNTER'S DESIRE

Handsome, resilient Vincent Chiasson takes his job as hunter to supernatural beings in the bayous seriously. When an unknown creature begins killing women the Chiasson family has contact with, Vincent knows this has something to do with his parents' deaths years earlier. To make matters worse, the one woman he's yearned to call his own has returned – and is targeted by the beast. He'll have to face his past – and confront his future – to save Olivia.

~

Chapter One

Southwest Louisiana
June

Vincent Chiasson closed his eyes and remained hunched down at the end of the dock. The air was heavy, the heat oppressive even at midnight.

He heard the telltale splash as a gator on the other side of the bayou entered the water. Off to his right was a hiss from a water moccasin, and all around him the sounds of the bayou filled the night.

But none of that was what he searched for. It was the creatures of the night, the beings people only thought lived in imaginations and movies that he hunted.

It was what the Chiasson's had done throughout the centuries. It began in France, continued in Nova Scotia, and followed them all the way to Louisiana.

A scream split the air. Vincent's eyes snapped open as he

jerked his head to the left. He stood and rushed back down the pier until he reached solid ground. He knew the land as well as he knew himself.

He knew every stump, every curve in the swamp. Vincent ran as fast as the wind to find the woman before the creature could attack again.

Another scream rent the air, this one full of fear...and death.

Vincent pumped his legs faster. He jumped over a log and slid to a stop next to the water's edge. Every instinct told him he had to hurry to the woman, but stealth was all that would get him close to the creature.

With his breathing ragged, Vincent silently stepped into the bayou. The water reached to his knees, but didn't so much as ripple as he entered it.

Off to his right, a gator eyed him. Vincent moved farther to the left, hoping to come around and behind the creature he hunted.

"Please!" a woman yelled. "Someone help!"

Vincent ground his teeth together and reached down to the outside of his right thigh where his machete was attached. He pulled out the blade and kept his gaze ahead. His three brothers would be closing in on the beast as well. It would end this night.

The woman and the creature were about fifty feet from him on a small outcropping. The full moon shed enough light that Vincent could make out the woman trying her best to climb to her feet. Her hands clawed at the earth, and she kept looking behind her.

Vincent was determined to kill the being that night. He crept to the left were a grove of cypress trees nestled. As soon as he climbed out of the bayou, Vincent was ready to kill.

He slunk closer, keeping his legs bent and his body in the shadows. When he was just twenty feet away he saw the creature. It was hulking with dark fur and unimaginable claws, and yet he couldn't get a look at its face.

It loomed over the woman, and Vincent knew it was now or never. He burst out of the trees, his machete raised as the woman's scream echoed through the bayou.

Vincent skidded to a halt when he came to the woman. The creature was gone, and blood coated everything. He knelt next to her and winced.

"Molly Guidry," Lincoln's voice said from behind him. "That makes three in a week."

Vincent stood and faced his brother. "I don't need a recount, Linc. I know exactly how many have been killed."

"Son of a bitch," Beau mumbled as he came out of the bayou.

Lincoln ran a hand down his face. "I thought we had it for sure this time."

"So did I." Vincent had set everything up perfectly. They should have had the creature.

Beau looked around. "Where's Christian?"

All three began to search for their brother. It was a whistle that had them looking to their right.

"There," Lincoln said.

While his two brothers went to Christian, Vincent remained with Molly. He had known her since the day she was born. Their parents had been close, and consequently they were often together. At one time Molly had been infatuated with Christian.

Vincent looked over at Christian. Did he know it was Molly? Damn, but this mess was getting out of control. All three victims they knew.

That wasn't too rare in the small Cajun town, but it didn't make things easier. Just like contacting Molly's parents and telling them what happened was going to be one of the hardest things he had ever done.

Lincoln walked back over and squatted beside him. "I told Christian it was Molly. Did you know they went out last week?"

"No." Vincent didn't like the unease that rippled through him. Was it coincidence that Molly had been killed? "I thought she had given up on Christian."

"We all did." Lincoln blew out a breath. "He's not taking this well."

Vincent stood and shook his head at the gruesome sight of Molly. "What did Christian find?"

"Claw marks."

"We're hunting a creature we haven't even identified. We're completely fucked."

Lincoln slapped him on the back. "We've always figured it out in the past. We will this time as well."

"I have my doubts. We were in perfect placement to find this bastard. How the hell did it get away without us seeing or hearing it?"

Vincent didn't wait for his brother to respond, because there was nothing to say. He bent and gently lifted Molly in his arms.

"Want me to go with you?" Lincoln asked.

Vincent shook his head. "You three see what else you can find. I'll meet you at the house."

"Mom and Pop always knew what to say to the families. You've got their gift as well."

He sincerely doubted it. Most in the parish knew what the Chiassons did, but that didn't always mean they were welcomed into houses. Chiassons were respected, but feared. It made for a lonely life.

It was a long walk through the bayou to the Guidry's. He heard crying before he even saw the house. When he moved out of the tree line and the edge of the light caught his shape, a man stepped forward.

Hank Guidry, Molly's father. Vincent drew in a deep breath and continued until he reached Hank. On the porch the crying grew louder, wracked with pain.

"I knew something was wrong when she didn't come

home from locking up the store," Hank said as he stared at his daughter. "She's never late."

Vincent looked at the ground. How he hated this part of the family business. No matter how many times he did it, it never got easier.

"Did you kill it?" Hank asked.

It was the viciousness in his voice that drew Vincent's gaze. The need for revenge, the yearning to hurt something as he had been hurt shone in Hank's eyes as clearly as the moon in the sky.

"We almost had it." Vincent knew it wouldn't be enough. It never was, and it was what made them hated throughout the parish.

"Almost!" Celine screamed from the screened porch. "You almost had it? Isn't that your job, Vincent Chiasson? Don't you hunt these evil things? How could you have let it get my baby? My only child?"

Each word was like a knife to his gut. Vincent moved past Hank and made his way to the porch. He shouldered open the screen door, walked past Celine, and then into the house.

Vincent carefully set Molly on the couch and turned to leave, only to have Hank block his way.

"This was never supposed to happen to my baby girl," Hank said as tears coursed down his face. He pulled off his glasses and shook his head. "I'll help in any way that I can to kill this creature you hunt, Vincent. I helped your father on occasion. I'll do the same for you."

Vincent rested his hand on Hank's shoulder. "Be here for your wife. Bury your daughter. If God's willing, we'll have killed this thing by then. If not...I'll give you a shout."

He walked to the doorway and paused. When he looked back, Hank and Celine had their arms around each other as they mourned their daughter.

By the time Vincent returned home, he was in a foul mood. He let the screen door slam behind him. Next to the door were three sets of boots, one for each of his brothers. The only thing missing was the smaller pink pair.

That was his doing though. To give Riley a chance at a normal life that didn't include hunting in the bayous in the middle of the night, Vincent had sent her off to college in Texas.

That had been three years ago. It felt more like three lifetimes, but it had been for the best.

Vincent began to remove his muddy boots when the door opened and Beau walked out on the back porch. He handed Vincent a bottle of beer and took one of the rocking chairs.

There were no words as they both took a long drink of their beers. Vincent sprawled out on the swing with one leg hanging down.

"Tough one. You should've let one of us go with you," Beau said.

"Did y'all find anything else?"

"Not a goddamn thing. I tell you, Vin, this thing knows us. It knows what we're looking for."

Vincent squeezed the bridge of his nose with his thumb and forefinger. "Let's hope to hell you're wrong."

"We've not even figured out what it is."

He wasn't saying anything Vincent didn't already know. "We need a new plan of attack. If we can find where this thing is hiding out, we can kill it before it hurts anyone else."

The door to the house was thrown open and Christian walked out, followed by Lincoln. They each took a chair, though Christian chose the one farthest from all of them.

Vincent didn't know how close his brother had been to Molly. It was rare that a Chiasson dated anyone from the parish because of the family name. It was even rarer when a Chiasson found a woman he wanted to ask out. But as their father had often said, they had to keep the line going so more creatures could be killed.

"Riley called," Christian said to break the silence.

Lincoln let out a string of curses while Beau just shook his head as he peeled off the label to his beer.

Vincent looked at Christian to find his brother's gaze on him. "What did she say?" Vincent finally asked.

"She was checking in."

"You didn't tell her about what was going on, did you?" Beau asked.

Christian gave him a droll look. "Do you think I'm that thick? I was in agreement about sending her off. Of course I didn't tell her anything."

Vincent scrubbed a hand down his face. He was the

eldest of them, the one who was supposed to keep everyone in line and focused. It had seemed like an easy job when he was younger.

And when their parents had still been alive.

"What's the plan?" Lincoln asked.

Vincent drained the rest of his beer and looked at the amber colored bottle. "We go back out at first light. We split up and search every inch of the bayou. That thing is somewhere out there. I won't rest until it's dead."

For the next hour, the four discussed which sections of the bayou they would take, as well as individuals they knew they could get to help.

Lincoln was the first to call it a night, and Beau soon followed. Vincent rose from the swing and stood at the edge of the porch, staring through the screen to the bayou beyond.

"I didn't know you had found someone, Christian. I'm sorry it ended the way it did."

Wood creaked as Christian rose from the chair and came to stand beside him. "I liked Molly. I'd probably have asked her out again, but I wasn't in love with her."

"It doesn't make it hurt any less. You knew her."

"Do you ever wish we had been born to a normal family? The kind that goes to the movies, bails kids out of jail for buying beer underage, and staying out past curfew on Friday nights?"

Vincent rested his forearm against a wood beam and

chuckled. "For most of my life. It's not easy being a Chiasson."

"Dad was married and had you and Lincoln by the time he was your age. How long until you marry, Vin? Do you think you ever will? Hell, will any of us?"

Vincent wished he had answers for him, but he didn't. "Let's focus on one thing at a time. We need to find this creature and see what it is so we can kill it. There is also Molly's funeral we'll need to attend, and then Deb's on Sunday after church for lunch."

"That's a lot to do in three days," Christian said with a hint of a smile. He raised his beer bottle to Vincent before he lifted it to his lips. "Do you really think we can catch this creature?"

"Yes."

"Always so sure of things. That must make sleeping easier for you. Me, I'm not so certain. This...thing...is quick. It attacks differently every time, and we've barely gotten a look at it."

Vincent ran his thumb around the mouth of his empty beer. "Everything can be killed. Remember that, little brother."

BUY WILD FEVER now at

www.DonnaGrant.com

SNEAK PEEK OF EVERSONG

KINDRED, BOOK 1

She is a hunter, trained from birth. He is a man sworn to vengeance.

Nothing can stop them. Except each other.

Leoma does not back down from a fight. She must bring down the Coven before they awaken the First Witch to unleash an unimaginable evil. And there is nothing standing in her way.

Except the sexy, infuriating man who keeps crossing her path.

Wracked with grief, Braith is not looking for love. Hell-bent on revenge, he can't rest until he finds the witch that murdered his heir.

He finds Leoma instead.

These two hunters are tracking the same prey. They could fight together.

But they have to trust each other first.

West Morland, England
September 1349

It was a good day for hunting witches. Then again, Leoma believed every day was a good day to hunt.

She kept the hood of her cloak pulled forward to conceal her face as she meandered through the crowd. The few days of fair weather they'd enjoyed, allowed the soggy ground a chance to dry so that mud no longer squished beneath her shoes. The market was filled with people, and while she detested the crush of bodies, it gave her cover.

Chickens squawked, men yelled, women haggled, and even a dog or two barked. The smell of freshly baked bread and raw fish, along with rank body odor, clung to everything. Leoma ignored all of it, including the children that ran through the market without a care or worry—picking pockets when they could.

With her pace unhurried, it was easy to blend in with the

crowd while her gaze was focused on her quarry—Brigitta. The witch was easy to pick out with her flagrant beauty that she happily showed off.

Leoma battled the rising hatred within her. Edra, her mentor, warned her about letting anger rule. But it was becoming more and more difficult to keep it at bay.

While Leoma had begun learning to battle witches the day Edra and Radnar found her starving on the streets, it hadn't been until Brigitta cruelly and viciously killed Leoma's closest friend that she truly understood vengeance.

"Ease your mind."

Leoma inhaled deeply as Edra's words came back to her. While releasing her breath, Leoma centered herself. It had been six weeks since she left the safe haven of the abbey ruins Edra and Radnar had made into a home.

All those years of training with various weapons and learning how to fight against witches were being put to the test. This wasn't the first time Leoma had gone hunting, but it *was* her first time alone.

For weeks, she had been steadily closing in on Brigitta. Two days ago, Leoma finally found her. It was obvious by the way the witch traveled with determination that she had a specific destination in mind.

It was really too bad she would never make it.

Leoma smiled, her hand on the hilt of her sword hidden beneath her black cloak. She couldn't wait to sink the blade into the witch's heart. Or better yet, slice off her head.

Meg's face popped into her mind. Leoma had to close her eyes against the assaulting image of her best friend's decapitated body.

If only Leoma hadn't insisted they split up in order to corner the witch. If only she'd realized that Meg was terrified. If only....

There were so many regrets that haunted her, and Leoma was sure they would remain until her dying day.

She touched the inside of her left forearm. Before she left her family, another tattoo had been added to her body. The Vegvisir.

The Icelandic word meant signpost, but the magical stave was much more than that. It helped the bearer find their way and never become lost. The Vegvisir would not only help Leoma track Brigitta, but it would also bring Leoma back to her family.

She dropped her arm and moved away from a cart to continue following the witch. It was only Brigitta's habit of remaining right in the mix of people that kept Leoma from attacking. Because Leoma wouldn't have the weight of any more innocent deaths on her conscience.

If she had to track the witch for a year in order to get her alone, then that's what Leoma would do.

Brigitta suddenly halted and looked over her shoulder. Leoma ducked behind a building. She peered around the corner, her gaze taking in Brigitta's stunning face with her long, black hair up in braids, and bright blue eyes that seemed to hold everyone entranced—everyone except Leoma.

A few moments later, the witch continued on. Crowds parted without Brigitta ever saying a word. It was as if others recognized the power within her without understanding what they felt.

While men stared after Brigitta in a lust-filled haze, none were brave enough to approach. It sickened Leoma that so many were so easily manipulated by a beautiful face. Couldn't they tell the witch could end them with a thought? Did they even care?

To Leoma's surprise, Brigitta stopped again and simply looked around as if searching for something.

Or someone.

Leoma remained hidden, wondering just what the witch was up to. Had it not been for Edra, Leoma would never know that there was magic in the world, or that there was a Coven who recruited the most powerful witches in order to grow.

For what exactly, no one knew. Yet.

But that knowledge was something Leoma hoped to bring back to the abbey.

The Coven once sought Edra. They had hunted her for seven years until Edra took a stand. With the love of her life, Radnar, by her side, Edra defeated the witches sent to either bring her into the fold or kill her. That's when Edra decided to create her own coven—a Hunter's Coven.

Leoma was the first of the homeless, abandoned, and starving children that Radnar and Edra found. Some trained like Leoma, and others, like Meg, found different duties at the abbey.

No one was forced to do anything they didn't want to do, but everyone pulled their weight. It allowed Radnar and Edra to supply a safe place for anyone who wanted or needed it.

Leoma couldn't imagine growing up any other way. While Radnar had been her first teacher, he hadn't been her only or her last. Other knights and warriors found their way to Radnar and helped train those wanting to be a part of the Hunter's Coven.

The sword Leoma carried had been designed by Radnar and created by Berlag, their master blacksmith. And then Edra had filled it with magic so Leoma could kill witches.

Because a witch could survive a normal blade. It took something special to make sure a sorceress remained dead. And Leoma would make damn sure Brigitta never hurt anyone again. It might very well cost Leoma her life, and she accepted that.

As soon as she saw the witch move, Leoma scanned the crowd, looking for anyone who could be meeting up with Brigitta. Leoma might get lucky and find a second witch. It wouldn't be the first time she fought multiples.

She had the scars—and the tattoos—to prove it.

Leoma counted to twenty before she slid from her hiding

spot to follow Brigitta. To her surprise, the witch walked into the Three Moons. Leoma flattened her lips as she eyed the tavern.

It wasn't that she minded going into such establishments, it was just that she spent most of her time fending off advances from drunken idiots who thought that anyone with breasts was fair game for a tumble into bed.

But she wasn't going to let that stop her from discovering all she could about Brigitta, just in case Leoma did survive the battle and made it back to the abbey. Any information—no matter how inconsequential—was needed.

She made her way around the building made up of small stones and wooden pillars to make sure the witch didn't sneak out the back. Then Leoma waited until she found a group of men walking into the pub. She snuck behind them and went unseen by most.

The tavern was packed. Loud, boisterous groups singing and laughing occupied several long tables. Those enjoying food and drink took other, smaller tables.

Leoma noted the hearth and roaring fire, as well as the shadowed parts of the interior. She quickly found a smaller table with an elderly couple who didn't bat an eye when she sat with them. Leoma gave the woman a nod and set a few coins on the table before sliding them toward her.

The woman took the money and didn't look at Leoma again. That allowed Leoma to let her gaze wander the tavern as she inhaled the delicious aroma of food, which was probably why the place was so popular.

With little effort, Leoma picked out the men she knew could be trouble. Danger filled the air around them like a dark cloud despite their laughter and noise—or perhaps *because* of it. They drank too much and made sure everyone could hear their boasting. But so far, the men were content to focus on imbibing instead of fighting.

Just before her gaze moved away, she spied someone she had somehow previously overlooked—twice. He sat motionless in a shadowed corner with a mug of ale before him and his gaze directed toward the stairs.

She eyed him, wondering how she could have missed him in her perusal of the occupants. She put his face to memory. Dark hair, thick with just a hint of wave, that fell loose to his shoulders. A lean, rugged face that had sharp cheekbones and a square jaw with a slight indent in his chin ensnared all her senses.

His lips were wide and sinfully full. Thick brows slashed over piercing eyes a deep color she couldn't quite discern from the distance.

Leoma couldn't remember ever encountering a man with such a striking face before, and the fact that she didn't want to look away disturbed her greatly.

But it wasn't just his features that captured her attention. There was an air about him that declared he and battle were well acquainted. If he were a knight, his plain brown cloak and leather jerkin beneath hid the chainmail. He reclined in the chair as if he didn't have a care in the world, and yet his expression told a different story. He was intent on something.

Perhaps he was hunting, as well.

She regretted that she wouldn't find out for sure because she was intrigued. And she almost felt sorry for whoever the man was after. He seemed the type who would not give up until he ran his target to ground.

Leoma pulled her gaze away and looked at the table. This would be the time when Meg told her to flirt. Meg had always pushed Leoma to do the things she watched others do. Her friend made her a part of the world instead of just someone observing it.

But Leoma was better at watching. The few times she tried to do as others did, it hadn't turned out well. It's why Leoma was so suited to witch hunting. It was a solitary business. And she was damn good at it.

She began to wonder how long she would have to wait for some sign of Brigitta when the witch walked down the stairs with a young woman. Their heads were close together as they whispered.

Leoma saw Brigitta pass a small bag to the woman before they reached the bottom step. The woman hugged Brigitta and hurried to the back of the tavern with a bright smile in place as silence fell over the occupants.

Brigitta's grin was coy and sly when she caught men

staring. She gave them a little wave before walking out. Leoma glanced at the back of the tavern. A part of her knew she needed to see what the witch had given the woman, but Leoma didn't want to lose Brigitta.

Yet, if Leoma found her once, she could again. Leoma waited until the conversation in the taproom resumed, and then she discreetly rose and made her way to the back.

"I got it," came a feminine voice.

Leoma leaned around the corner to find the woman showing the bag to a man.

"We can have a child now," the woman said excitedly.

The man eyed the bag. "I'm not sure about such methods."

Leoma knew the risks involved with using magic for such things. The couple would be indebted to Brigitta forever. And the witch wouldn't hesitate to take what she wanted from them—most likely their firstborn child. There was no way Leoma could allow that to happen.

She put a smile on her face and walked toward the couple. "My apologies. I don't mean to interrupt, but I think I'm lost."

The woman set the bag on a table near the hearth as she turned to Leoma. "It sometimes happens. Would you like something to eat?"

The tavern owner hurried out to the customers when someone shouted for more ale, leaving Leoma with his wife.

The first thing Leoma had learned in her training was to be swift of hand.

She walked closer while the woman spoke. "This is a wonderful place. I'm glad I stopped in."

"That pleases me greatly to hear," the woman beamed.

When the wife glanced out the doorway, Leoma swiped the bag. "Can you show me the way out, so I do not get lost again?"

The woman's smile grew tight, most likely irritated at being interrupted, but she replied, "Of course."

Just before Leoma followed the woman out, she tossed the bag into the fire.

Leoma began searching for Brigitta as soon as she was out of the tavern. She caught a glimpse of the witch heading west and made to follow when the same gorgeous man from the tavern snared her attention. She allowed herself a moment to stare while he saddled a horse. But it was the way his gaze kept returning to Brigitta that made her frown.

Leoma hoped the man wouldn't interfere. She'd hate to have to put him on his arse, but she'd do it in a heartbeat. The witch was her prize.

BUY EVERSONG now at
www.DonnaGrant.com

ABOUT THE AUTHOR

New York Times and *USA Today* bestselling author Donna Grant® has been praised for her "totally addictive" and "unique and sensual" stories.

She's written more than one hundred novels spanning multiple genres of romance including the bestselling Dragon Kings® series that features a thrilling combination of Druids, Fae, and immortal Highlanders who are dark, dangerous, and irresistible. She lives in Texas with her dog and a cat.

www.DonnaGrant.com

www.MotherofDragonsBooks.com

facebook.com/AuthorDonnaGrant

instagram.com/dgauthor

bookbub.com/authors/donna-grant

amazon.com/Donna-Grant/e/B00279DJGE

pinterest.com/donnagrant1